• **The Bomb That Could Lip-Read** •

• The Bomb That Could Lip-Read

DONALD SEAMAN •

STEIN AND DAY/*Publishers*/**New York**

First published in the United States of America
Copyright © 1974 by Donald Seaman
Library of Congress Catalog Card No. 73-92184
All rights reserved
Designed by Ed Kaplin
Printed in the United States of America
Stein and Day/*Publishers*
Scarborough House, Briarcliff Manor, N.Y. 10510
ISBN 0-8128-1687-0

This book is dedicated to the officers and men of "Felix," the British Army's bomb-disposal unit in Northern Ireland.

Many friends helped me put it together. Some I cannot name, but they know I am grateful. Among those I can are Cyril Aynsley, former chief reporter of the London *Daily Express,* and others on that newspaper including Andrew Fyall, Frank Robson, William Hunter, and the men of its Ulster bureau—Robert Brady, John Ley, and Bobby Renton—who have twice been bombed out of their Belfast office.

• The Bomb That Could Lip-Read

•

Prologue

Before dawn on a bitter March day a man crouched against a rock on the coast of Donegal, waiting for a joyful sound—the call of the first cuckoo of the season. Storm clouds scudded overhead, salt spray and seaweed scented the air, and a scattering of gulls began to fly inland, crying for food like beggars for alms.

The watcher on the rock was swathed from head to foot in wool, underclothes, stockings, long-tailed shirt, Aran jersey, and a scarf the length of a winding sheet. Over these layers he wore a coat of oilskin and rubber "waders" reaching to his groin.

A haversack containing a notebook and pencil, field glasses, thermos flask, a mountain of sandwiches, and a miniature of brandy lay within easy reach of his mittened hands. A camera and tape recorder sat next to a folded canvas field chair.

Leslie James was an Englishman, an amateur bird-watcher—or so he said. Back in the village he was thought a queer fellow even for an ornithologist, he had spent so much time plotting the arrival and behavior of every bird that called on these northernmost shores of the Irish Republic.

To those who showed interest as to why he had chosen Donegal as his field observatory, he would simply produce a bird-watcher's magazine that carried unconfirmed reports of several sightings of *Coccyzus Americanus Americanus,* or the yellow-billed cuckoo, south of the Bloody Foreland, a spit of land that projected out from the wild Donegal coastline.

There had only been two confirmed sightings of the yellow-bill during the past 150 years in the whole of Ireland, the Englishman told the curious villagers. He clearly considered it sufficient reason to linger on, as he had done for weeks, despite being advised such birds were unknown in the district, no matter what the magazine

9

said. In the treacherous atmosphere of the day, when the shadow of Ulster fell across all Donegal, he was bound to excite suspicion.

Leslie James was so cold! Sleet was falling now in light showers, and visibility grew poor. His fingers hurt, his bones ached, his enthusiasm was on the wane. Bored, weary of waiting, hugely uncomfortable, he began to look about him. A quarter of a mile, maybe more, to his left stood the shell of a ruined farmhouse where he parked his car most mornings. Away to his right, meadows fell sharply into swamp and marsh to end in the sands of the vast blue bay.

In front of his blind was a pond—not much more than a puddle really, no more than thirty feet across at its widest point and screened on one side by a fringe of yellow reeds that swayed and rattled in the wind. In days gone by he had known it filled with duck flighting in. Today only a handful of mallard bobbed on the icy water, motionless save for a brief preening of feathers.

All else was bare, utterly exposed, a landscape of wind-ruffled grass and ageless rock. In fine weather the Englishman could see the outline of the Foreland with the naked eye. Now all was blurred, and as he waited for the rare bird to materialize he could barely see beyond the countless white horses that galloped across his front to fall on the unyielding coastline.

Twice he heard the drone of a distant plane and searched the sky in vain for a glimpse of it.

He remembered the brandy. As he reached out for his bag and fumbled inside, he noticed an alien movement out to sea. At first he thought it must be a whale surfacing, or a huge shark, a freak visitor in the winter season. All he could make out at first was a vague shape, a rounded dark outline dowsed in sleet and spray. By the time numbed fingers had brought the field glasses to his eyes, it had gone, vanished into the heavy swell. He stared and strained, he willed it to come back, and kept his binoculars fixed on the spot.

Fifteen minutes later, still in poor light, a fishing smack rounded the headland and steamed into view. The bird-watcher paid it scant attention. Fishing boats were common as gulls in these waters. By chance, the smack stayed between him and the thing lurking in the deeps, and it was minutes more before he saw the dark shape again, a submarine! He focused his glasses and watched intently.

He saw a dinghy inflated on deck and launched to float alongside the submarine, manned by a figure dressed in a black

10

rubber wet suit. More men climbed onto the deck and began to push out packages bound in yellow oilskin to the man in the dinghy. After a while he set off with his cargo and made for the side of the fishing boat. The bird-watcher estimated it to be about seventy yards off.

A line was cast down, the dinghy hauled alongside, and each parcel quickly transferred. Occasionally, as the spray and sleet cleared, he could make out the whole length of the foredeck of the submarine. It carried strange markings that he could not identify.

He heard nothing of the feet that stepped cautiously through the grass behind his blind. He had no premonition of danger. In a month of mornings spent there, he had not once seen or spoken to another living soul.

Death was instantaneous as the .45 bullet, fired single-shot from a Thompson submachine gun, crashed into the back of his skull.

• 1 •

The assassin lay down his gun and stooped to search the contents of the Englishman's haversack and coat pockets. The camera was first. He exposed the roll of film and put this in his own pocket; then he carefully set a new roll in the camera and placed it back in its cover.

He took the notebook and sat by the corpse, pausing to light a cigarette before he read through it page by page. Its entries intrigued him. Some consisted of letters only, others were made up of numbers and abbreviations. The page for the morning of the murder was filled with a jumble of both—it could, perhaps, have been a coded entry. The killer smiled to himself as he pocketed the book. He believed he might have proof the Englishman was nothing more than a spy.

Next he tipped the contents out of the bag and checked each item at his leisure. He opened sandwiches and peered inside. He unscrewed the top of the thermos flask and emptied it. He took off one glove to riffle his fingers through strands of tobacco inside an oilskin pouch. He took out, sniffed, and drank off a small bottle of brandy. He screwed back the cap meticulously and placed the tiny bottle back in the bag.

He left the field glasses reluctantly, for he coveted their Zeiss perfection. Now he examined the grass behind the hollow, blade by frozen blade, until he found the spent cartridge case that could brand him a murderer, and flung it into the pond. He turned his nose in every direction, like a gun dog scenting game, but found nothing he had overlooked.

Finally he lifted the body, drew a parka hood over its shattered head and bloody helmet, and lay it down, as though asleep. The singing of the birds began again and followed him through the grass as he left. Jesus, he thought, those noisy bastards!

A hundred yards off the coast, the unloading from the submarine proceeded. Two-score packages had been taken from the black belly of the submarine and ferried to the smack.

They were dangerously behind schedule, operating now in daylight, and from the conning tower anxious watch was kept for patrolling aircraft.

At one-minute intervals a single light blinked from a derelict farmhouse on the coast to report the coastal road clear of traffic.

Suddenly, away to the west, a great hole appeared in the bank of cloud, showing patches of blue behind.

Through it roared a jet plane flying fast and low, and it was on the submarine and fishing smack before they had any chance to scatter. The Russian sailors jumped into the open hatch as the order was given to crash-dive and abandon the deflated dinghy.

When the jet banked and came in for its second run, all that could be seen was the smack going about its lawful business in search of cod, mackerel, and whiting, and the black saucer made by the dinghy as it sank slowly beneath tossing waves.

"You get that, Joe?" shouted the pilot over his intercom.

"Got it, Skipper," said the cameraman jubilantly. "Sub, fishing boat, dinghy—the lot. Caught with their pants right down."

The Russian submarine captain felt ill with fear as he turned the submarine back into the Atlantic at maximum speed. It was his first independent command and he had bungled it.

His sealed orders had been brief and explicit.

First, he was to land the KGB agent he had taken on board at a cove on the Dingle Peninsula in southwest Ireland.

The man was a senior operator known to foreign intelligence networks as the "Red Colonel," and formerly on loan to the Egyptian Army as chief instructor at the Cairo School of Explosives and Urban Warfare Tactics (CSEUWT).

Russian weapons and ammunition were already reaching the IRA in sufficient quantity to enable some infiltration of the underground army. The breakup of the IRA into splinter groups made the task of infiltration still easier, and the Colonel had been chosen to coordinate the drive.

Intelligence chiefs in Moscow had spent much time debating how best to get this key KGB agent into Ireland.

Since the need for security was paramount, and airports have too many eyes, they were unanimous in the choice of a submarine for transport. The second task given the submarine captain—the delivery of weapons to Donegal—fitted into their overall strategy. It was viewed as entirely complementary to the Red Colonel's role as arms salesman, and an operation that at the same time would cause the British government maximum embarrassment in her anti-terrorist campaign.

The first drop went perfectly but the second had been a disaster. The submarine had already been tracked for four days.

· 2 ·

The admirals sitting around the war games table in the operations room at the NATO Headquarters in Bergen, Norway, were made instantly aware of the Russian submarine's identity—her class, armament, range, speed above and below the surface, maximum submerged depth, endurance capability, even an estimate of the normal number of crew. She was utterly betrayed.

Four hours later, back in London, in that small skyscraper near Whitehall where the nation's intelligence services are housed in what appear to be ordinary offices, the photographs taken by the Nimrod jet plane of Coastal Command of the Russian intruder were about to be shown to a highly appreciative audience.

Five of the men were intelligence officers, the sixth a commander hastily summoned from the Admiralty.

A tall man gave a sign, and the show began.

The sub was shown, helpless as a butterfly pinned to a board. The naval officer began addressing the civilians.

"I must say," he told them with genuine pride, "what a magnificent shot. A collector's item, gentlemen!"

He gazed on his audience and became just a little patronizing, as servicemen will with those out of uniform.

"Let's take a look at her fin first of all." Pause. " 'Fin' is Navy for conning tower, by the way. And this fin is unique, something found nowhere else among the navies of the world."

"Do you see what appear to be windows, running all around the fin? I won't bore you with the technical details, gentlemen, for they are not what they seem. But these eight windows, four up and four down, identify her beyond doubt as a Soviet 'F' class submarine.

"These are coming more and more into service as replacements for their older 'E' class boats. This one, photographed only this

16

morning less than a quarter of a mile off the Irish coast, is positively, absolutely, a Russian."

The five civilians looked from the Navy man back to the screen and nodded. Two of them were from MI6, the Secret Service. Two were from MI5, which is counterspy, and is responsible for security inside Britain, including Northern Ireland.

The fifth man was unknown to the commander, but had been described to him as the coordinator, a man with direct access to the prime minister.

All five were clearly entranced. They sat in wretchedly uncomfortable chairs, silent, absorbed, watching the screen avidly. "She's not nuclear-powered, by the way. This submarine is driven by electrically powered engines. She would surface as needed to charge her batteries and give the crew some fresh air. On this run, that would always have been at night.

"According to the American 'voice bank,' she was identified twenty-six days ago on arrival in the Soviet submarine base near Hammamet, off the Tunisian coast. And it's not without interest that no one detected her en route to the Mediterranean.

"As you may be aware, gentlemen, Russian submarines are specifically forbidden by treaty to pass through the Bosporus unless surfaced and then only with permission of the Turks. The Russians stick to the terms of that treaty because it works both ways and they get advance warning of all intruders from our side into the Black Sea.

"But to keep us guessing about the size of their undersea fleet, they bring their submarines down from the Atlantic and slip them through the Strait of Gibraltar.

"Take a close look at this picutre. A long spell of heavy weather has eroded most of her numerals but you can just make out"—he crossed to the screen and tapped the giveaway fin with his pointer —"the number nine. It's not clear what comes next, but definitely a nine first. To naval intelligence that means she sailed originally from the Russian northern fleet, almost certainly in the Baltic. She's ideally built for this particular run, of course, from North Africa across to the Irish coast.

"It is interesting to reflect that while our Nimrods picked her up without any trouble in the approaches to Donegal, they never spotted her either entering or leaving the Gibraltar Strait.

"This seems to confirm our fears that foreign agents in Britain are still feeding secret details such as the strait's surveillance

17

tables—and God knows what else—to Moscow. We at the Admiralty earnestly hope your long efforts to locate and smash this spy ring will soon succeed. Such a penetration makes a considerable breach in overall NATO sea defenses. It's the hole in the bucket, so to speak."

The civilians watched him coolly as he sat down. The commander studied his notes and felt rather pleased with his performance, really. He had been told to have a little dig and remind MI5 and the others of their failure to break the naval spy ring that was known to be operating. He thought he'd done it very neatly.

"I think we all know where thanks are due for this considerable feat," said the coordinator pointedly enough.

"However, I suggest we leave the subject of our own shortcomings until another time. Let's have some thoughts on what could be the possible role of such a ship in Irish waters."

The commander fidgeted. All submarines are, oddly enough, "boats" but never "ships" in the language of the Royal Navy. But he let it pass. "Comment, please," said the coordinator again.

"Two possibilities," said one of the men from MI5. "To shadow the NATO exercise, which is standard procedure. But we have to look for more than that here. Why did this submarine make such a long and complicated journey to make landfall off the Irish coast?

"I think one answer is obvious, a delivery of arms, hence the fishing boat alongside her in this picture. But maybe something more than that."

He looked around the table. "Maybe men as well. I think we should consider the possibility of men being landed, very closely indeed."

"Good thinking," said the coordinator briskly. "Any more?"

"If that is so," demurred one of the men from MI6, "and accepting that we've caught the pair of them in flagrante delicto, as it were, the question springs to my mind—would such an assignment have been given to so clearly inexperienced a Russian captain?"

"I agree," said the coordinator, "such a boob would be out of character for the Russian planners. But it could happen. They can make mistakes like anyone else, a point we tend to forget at times. We know from Oleg"—he was referring to Oleg Lyalin, the Soviet double agent who defected to London in September 1971—"how hard they have been trying to infiltrate the IRA. Not directly, of course, but by employing English as well as Irish Communists."

He went on: "These terrorists are getting supplies of Com-

18

munist-manufactured weapons from somewhere, as we know to our cost. But why a submarine landing? Would they risk a major diplomatic row to do something any steamship on charter could do as well, if not better? No, there has to be a first-class reason for using a Russian warship. I'm inclined to think the first assumption is right, namely, that agents were being put ashore, too."

The second man from MI6, just back from a spell behind the Iron Curtain as counselor in an embassy, said: "I think, sir, that perhaps they were a little too ambitious here. Perhaps they were given an opportunity to send arms to Ireland—on request—couldn't resist it, and to meet a timetable took the first available means of transport.

"Pique and anger, a desire to hurt us where it hurts most—in Ireland—especially after our great triumph with Oleg, all that would certainly come into their planning.

"I think it was sheer bad luck they ran into a full-scale NATO exercise. If it was an arms shipment, as I believe it was, and nothing more, then clearly the timetable must have been fixed with contacts in Dublin months back. They couldn't change it. I doubt if they'd have had time even to warn the submarine commander. He just walked straight into it. To my mind it doesn't necessarily follow that because they used a warship we have to look for something else, some motive for the journey other than a landing of arms.

"But I'd like to know a lot more about these arms. They might be a bit special, something new, to cause maximum trouble for our soldiers."

All heads in the room nodded agreement.

"Very well," said the coordinator. "Assume there's something in both arguments. First of all, an arms shipment—on that we are all agreed. I think we can safely assume it must have been a considerable shipment, either in terms of weight and size, sheer bulk, or in terms of its field value to the terrorists. I therefore want immediate steps taken to find out what that shipment was and steps taken to neutralize its effect on the Ulster situation.

"Secondly, I think the point about a man or men being landed was sound. It's close enough to home to warrant everyone's interest. I want that looked into and a report on action suggested before the night's out, is that understood?"

The naval commander spoke up.

"May I make one suggestion, sir?" The coordinator nodded. "The Russian boat's gone. We can't touch her. But we can have a go at the fishing smack. We can actually identify it. Why not ask our Irish counterparts to round up the crew and persuade them to talk? Someone on board ought to be able to supply us with a few facts we want to know."

"No," said the coordinator. "Once we do that, we are telling the Russians in advance that we're on to them. That submarine captain of theirs has a long voyage ahead of him before he returns to Hammamet, or wherever he's going. My guess is that he will be in no hurry at all to tell his high command he might have boobed and had his picture taken in the process. He's more likely to be praying we missed him, or most of him, in the bad weather. Look at these seas. In that first shot they damn near cover the whole of the sub.

"While there's life there's hope, and I'm willing to bet our Russian captain will keep mum as long as he can. Let's help him. If he's as dumb as this, any promotion he gets can only be to our advantage!"

He looked down at his shoes, stuck his hands in his pockets, and frowned as he thought for a moment more.

"I think the first consideration is secrecy, for the reasons I have outlined. I will inform the prime minister at once. He may have other ideas but even so I shall attempt to dissuade him.

"An immediate alert, John, to your men in Dublin. Tell them to get their noses to the ground and their checkbooks out. If they play one IRA splinter group off against the other, they might come up with something.

"I want a further message, accompanied by suitable classification rating, to be sent at once to the General Officer Commanding in Northern Ireland telling him what we actually know, what we conjecture, and asking how he can help through interrogation."

The others weighed his words in thoughtful silence, and each one had plenty to think about.

Dublin officialdom was already bristling as case upon flagrant case of British espionage activity was exposed. One agent under arrest and charged with bribery of an Irish Special Branch man, a sadly bungled job; then the Littlejohn affair with ministerial involvement. Every man in Dublin Castle, the home of Eire's security services, would be acutely sensitive to any further probing, however necessary HM government might consider it to be. The penalty of any new failure might even outweigh the success won by obtaining proof of a Russian naval presence in Irish waters. They needed to tread warily.

The coordinator left the intelligence building and drove at once to Number 10, where he placed the facts and the theories before the prime minister. No creditor calling on a bankrupt ever received a less enthusiastic reception.

The prime minister and his cabinet had troubles enough as it was. The ship of state was in decidedly rough waters, facing financial crisis, industrial chaos, crippling price rises, huge unemployment, racial tension, allegations of a vice-ring scandal concerning certain ministers, and widespread condemnation that the country was work-shy and living far beyond its means. The situation in Ulster was as bad as could be, while the Republic itself was in the throes of a closely fought general election, with neither party able to risk the smear of wheeler-dealing with the British.

So the PM promptly ruled against publicity, against sending evidence of the Russian submarine's presence to Dublin, at least until the result of the election was known, and when he could reasonably expect to arrange talks with the new Irish premier.

The Russian submarine captain was a far luckier man than he deserved.

·3·

The transatlantic Boeing 707 pointed its nose down toward the bank of cloud and began its final descent into Shannon, in the Republic of Ireland.

As one man, the passengers aboard turned their heads to the cabin windows and peered out hopefully for their first glimpse of the Emerald Isle and the safety of land after a long journey over the sea. It remained obstinately hidden—the sun shone dazzlingly on a great white expanse of cotton wool that blotted out everything below. Most passengers nearing the end of a flight are disillusioned people. Matches flared to light "duty-free" cigarettes, stomachs rumbled and rebelled against a surfeit of bad food served five hours out of normal time schedule. Push buttons over a score of seats pinged and pit up as the exuberant, the thirsty, and the plain greedy called for a last one for the road.

The voice of their stewardess soothed them.

"Ladies and gentlemen, we shall be landing at Shannon Airport in twenty minutes' time. All cigarettes must be extinguished, seat belts securely fastened, with your seats in the upright position, please, once the warning lights come on.

"May I remind those passengers who are leaving us here that disembarkation forms must be completed for their passage through Customs and Immigration.

"Those passengers who are flying on to London may stay on board if they wish during refueling but they are reminded—no smoking until after takeoff. Those who wish to leave the aircraft may do so but must remain in the transit lounge.

"Our flight number will be called fifteen minutes before takeoff for London. Estimated stopover in Shannon will be one hour.

"A new crew will be taking over for the onward flight to London, so on behalf of Captain Sorensen and his crew may I take this opportunity of thanking you for flying with us.

"We look forward to having the pleasure of your company again in the future. Thank you and good-bye."

At least one passenger in the first-class cabin grimaced as he listened to this unvarying airborne routine of total insincerity. One day, he thought, someone will give it to us straight: With competition so fierce and too many empty seats our airline needs your money, so come again, suckers. Don't mind the lousy service, we have a safeguard called IATA rules that say every company must charge you the same artificially high price.

He was an unlovely man.

He unclasped his seat belt, hoisted himself awkwardly out of the chair that had cramped him for the last six hours, and made his way to the toilet. He looked himself over with indifference as he washed his hands in the Tom Thumb basin.

The mirror showed him to be a very big man, more than six feet tall, deep-chested, with the wide shoulders of a swimmer. He carried no surplus flesh and would have turned the scales at two hundred pounds.

His hair was blond, turning gray at the temples, and cropped short in a style that had gone out of fashion a decade before. His eyes were blue, very pale and deep-set, and edged at the corners by crow's-feet that gleamed as white as knife scars. He was clean-shaven. He might have been any age from a young fifty down to the well-worn midthirties. The one dominant impression he gave was of strength.

A prominent nose and thin lips combined to present a face that was ugly, brash, scraped bare of humor or sympathy. The stewardesses on the plane had christened him Crabapple. All of the man that showed, face, neck, hands, was of uniform parchment color, the yellowing tan that proclaims much time in the tropics.

He was casually dressed in a rough tweed suit, checkered shirt, and plain green tie. He was weary and gave his face a last rinse of cold water before heading back to his seat.

He clipped the belt tightly round his waist, braced wide shoulders obediently against the upright seat back, and as he waited for the green carpet of Shannon to show through the cloud, flicked through the contents of a black leather briefcase.

His passport was numbered 686072 and gave his name as Brian Kelly. Under "National status, nationality" it recorded: British subject, citizen of the United Kingdom and Colonies.

Then it continued: "Occupation, surveyor. Place of birth,

23

London. Date, May 25, 1932. Place of residence, Kinshasa, Zaire (formerly Congo). Color of eyes, blue. Color of hair, fair. Special peculiarities, none." A line was drawn through the separate entry section headed "Wife and children."

The most recent immigration stamps showed that holder Brian Kelly had left Kinshasa two months previously to land in America, that his original stay had been extended, and that he had left Los Angeles on the day prior to the transatlantic flight to Europe.

He particularly liked the words inside the cover, where "Her Britannic Majesty's Principal Secretary of State of Foreign Affairs requests and requires in the Name of Her Majesty all those whom it may concern to allow the bearer to pass freely without let or hindrance and to afford the bearer such assistance and protection as may be necessary."

I might hold him to that, he thought.

Kelly put his passport to one side and thumbed through a wad of traveler's checks. They were in dollars—starting from the back in hundred-dollar bills and working forward in groups of fifties, twenties, tens, and fives, a total of twenty-four hundred dollars in all. He put these back in the briefcase and leaned forward, straining against the seat belt to pull a flat folding wallet from his hip pocket. He checked its contents. Driver's license, good for one year, a handful of calling cards such as any businessman might carry, bearing names and telephone numbers in Zaire, South Africa, the Middle East, and America. Inside the driver's license was a folded slip of paper carrying a number without identifying code or name.

The roar of the jets was now very loud, straining, and he watched out of the starboard window as Ireland came up to meet him. He waited until the plane taxied to a halt and cut its engines. Then he stood up, yawned, stretched his arms to reach down a smart lightweight tan overcoat, and put it on. He had all the time in the world, this passenger. He gathered up his briefcase, tapped his pockets, took up his "duty-free" bottle of bourbon and carton of cigarettes, and walked down the steps into a cold easterly wind.

Formalities at Shannon, Europe's friendliest airport, were kept to a minimum, and smiling Irish eyes were much in evidence.

Kelly handed over his health certificates, so vital in Africa. They were handed back after the briefest, most contemptuous of glances. He was waved through and joined the queue at the Immigration counter. He lit a cigar and stood patiently in line until it was his turn to be processed.

There was silence as the man at the desk flicked casually through the pages of passport 686072.

"You have to be an Irishman," smiled the official, "with a name like Kelly, no matter what the passport tells me."

Kelly gave a mechanical smile with his carefully rehearsed answer. "My grandfather was born here," he replied, "and I like to visit from time to time, but I live so far away these days."

His passport was handed back, he nodded his thanks, and passed through the barrier to Customs and baggage. "Here for long, sir?" asked a jovial man in uniform.

"A few weeks' holiday," said Kelly. "Then on to London." No attempt was made to open his steel-framed gray suitcase or leather briefcase.

"That's all right, sir. Have a nice time."

Carrying both cases easily in one hand, Kelly walked into the big hall and went to the bank where he exchanged four hundred dollars for pound notes. Next, the Hertz car-hire desk.

"I want a self-drive," he said, "for a few days at least." He signed the forms, showed his international license, and paid a deposit in cash. It took him less than five minutes after leaving the Customs hall. A girl handed him a key ring, escorted him to the car park, and showed him a dark-blue Ford Cortina.

Kelly thanked her, climbed in, and drove off in the direction of Cork. He kept going for half an hour, glancing into the rearview mirror from time to time to make sure no one was following. When satisfied he pulled up outside a small country pub and carefully locked the car before going in. There were four customers in the bar, a tiny room past the sliced bacon, bootlaces, sweets, and tobacco piled on a counter by the main door. They paid no attention to the stranger.

"Whiskey," said Kelly. He looked at the strange labels on the shelf and added: "Powers. And I'll have some water with it. Tell me, have you a public telephone here?"

"We have that," the barman told him. "On the wall right behind you. Now, I'll give you plenty of change in case you're wanting to call long distance. You'll need the exact money."

Kelly sipped his drink, lit a cigarette, and strolled to the phone. He read his slip of paper, gave the operator a number in Cork, and put in the coins as he listened to the ringing tone. After a while a woman's voice answered.

"Hello," she said and gave the name of a company. "Can I help you?"

25

"Yes," Kelly answered. His words were unheard in the noise of the bar. "I'd like to speak to Liam, please."

"I'll just see if he's in," said the woman carefully. "Who shall I say is calling?"

"No need," said Kelly slowly. "Just say I was with his brother Sean yesterday and I was asked to give him a ring on arrival."

"He's expecting a call," the woman replied. "Hold on a moment."

There was a pause, and a man's voice came on the line.

"Hello there," he said breezily, "it's nice to hear from a friend of Sean's. I had a message you were on your way. There's a room booked for you. They gave you the name of the hotel?"

"They did," Kelly agreed. "I'm not familiar with the roads, but I estimate I should be there in two or three hours at the most."

"Good," said the voice. "I'm booked in as well. I'll join you early tomorrow morning, about nine o'clock. Have some old clothes handy. How was my brother, by the way?"

"Fine," Kelly told him. "Sends you his best wishes. See you tomorrow at nine, then. Good-bye."

He walked back to the bar, finished his drink, and nodded to the barman as he left. "Thanks," he said politely. Outside in the car, he unfolded a map and checked his route northwest to Donegal. He found the village he wanted, looked at the signposts lettered in Gaelic and English, and with a last glance in the mirror drove off in the gathering dusk.

Two hours later he drove up to the hotel chosen in America for his rendezvous with the man called Liam. Kelly got out of the car, took his suitcase and briefcase, and locked the doors, all without haste. He looked up and down the village street, saw a few roofs shining in the rain and lamplight, and shivered in the night air.

The street—it was the only one and stretched the length of the village—was overwide in the Irish style and hideously plain.

Down the side nearest the sea a row of terraced houses stretched into the darkness. By the hotel stood a tiny cluster of shops, butcher, news agent, grocer, fishing-tackle store, one or two bars. There was no sound or sight of people.

Kelly could smell the sea, clean and tangy from the wild, wide ocean he had just crossed by plane. A dog ran across the road. Rain gurgled in the gutters. His hotel held pride of place in the desolate High Street. The entrance was set back a good thirty feet from the road, and its two stories dwarfed the slate roofs roundabout.

He could see the flickering light of a fire shining through a

26

window to the left of the entrance. Chinks of light showed through two upper rooms where the curtains had been drawn. All the rest of the building was in darkness, silent and still like the street outside.

"Christ," said Kelly aloud, "what a dump." He headed for the door and went in. He pushed it open with his shoulder, for he had the bags one in each hand. It closed behind him with a crash. His footsteps echoed in the tiled hallway. The lights came on, and a pretty young woman wearing an apron and a smile came through from the kitchen.

"Good evening, sir," she said. "You must be the first of the two gentlemen we're expecting. Take your wet coat off now, and go straight in by the fire. You'd like a drink to warm you before I show you your room?"

"I sure would," Kelly replied as he spread his huge hands to the warmth of the sweet-smelling peat fire. "I'm frozen." He kept his coat on and stamped his feet on the carpet as he tried to thaw out.

The woman thought he looked very yellow and old in the firelight and clucked sympathetically as she handed him his drink.

"Thanks." He drank it straight down. "I'll have another." He was shaking with the damp cold.

She set down a tray, a half-filled bottle, and a jug of water. "Help yourself," she invited him. "It's a shame you've come to such awful weather for your holiday."

She watched him as he looked around the room. He's as big as a house, she thought.

"Is your friend coming tonight, then?" she asked.

"No," said Kelly. "I rang him a couple of hours ago. He will be here in the morning, about nine, to take me out on the river. I'm just a beginner, you know—he's the expert." He smiled as though he had cracked a secret joke.

"In that case, sir," she told him, "I'll serve your meal in here. You'll be warm by the fire. There's no one else in the hotel for the fishing. I'm afraid the Troubles are keeping most of our regular visitors away. You know these parts?"

"No," said Kelly slowly. "Not too well. I've been away for quite a few years." He offered no further explanation and hovered over the fire. The woman stood up.

"Let me show you your room," she said. "Then you can have a wash and come back to sit by the fire while I cook you a meal. How do you like your steak?"

"Big," said Kelly. "Rare. No vegetables. Salad on the side."

"That's just how it will be," she promised. "Now I'll show you your room."

She led him upstairs and down a landing that ran left of the staircase, into a room where only the bedding had been changed since the hotel had been built in mid-Victorian days.

The carpet was worn thin by a succession of sporting gentlemen who cared for nothing but the salmon coming home in midwinter after years of wandering at sea and whose own tastes were Spartan. The ceilings were lofty and darkening with age. Faded prints of long-gone sporting scenes graced dun-colored walls badly in need of repapering. There was no scent save mustiness. The bed was colossal; at its head stood a crucifix.

He had a private bathroom with vintage fittings—gray washbasin served by a chipped china jug, a toilet with heavy wooden seat and raised wooden footrests, linoleum on the floor below a starred shaving mirror, and a geyser-fed bath big enough to drown in, standing on four curved iron legs.

Bedroom and bathroom were graveyard-cold, and Kelly shivered at the prospect of a night there.

"I'll light a fire in here for you," the woman said, "and I'll warm the bed with a couple of bottles. You'll sleep sound, I promise."

He thanked her, waited until her footsteps died away, and unlocked his case to take out pajamas and dressing gown. He put his passport and traveler's checks inside, locked it, and heaved the case on top of a wardrobe. He checked around the room like a gun dog after game, opening drawers and cupboards, and even looked under the bed.

After he had washed, Kelly hurried downstairs and drew his chair close to the fire. There he sat, whiskey in hand, cigarette burning, daydreaming as he waiting for his meal.

• 4 •

Shortly before the man called Kelly flew to America, rush orders had reached the First Seventh Wessex Lancers, British Army of the Rhine, to strike camp and embark at the Hook for immediate service in Ulster.

They were, in the main, veteran troops who had known a decade or more of upheaval, travel, and action, and like all professional soldiers on to a good thing, went into paroxysms of rage when their new destination was made known. Life in Germany was not bad, not bad at all, even for men on rates of pay that made their former enemies blush for shame at their own prosperity. As military realists the troopers of the First Seventh knew that they had never had it so good. The grub was fine, the beer out of this world, the natives friendly, and the *Fräuleins*—the crumpet, the dollies—unbelievably buxom and willing. But Ireland!

When the news came through they had drawn Ulster, every man jack in the regiment cussed his blind luck as all soldiers have done over the years when ordered to step off the gravy train into unrewarding hardship and danger. Not that they were afraid, for they were young, but as they told each other a hundred times a day, why oh bloody why did it have to be the old First Seventh that always got the shitty end of the stick? Cyprus, Aden, you name it, they'd seen it. Anyone in the Lancers could tell you they had heard more shots fired in anger than most units had eaten hot dinners!

Wasn't it just like the bloody Army?

Here they were, dead cushy, thank you, feet right under the table at last, just beginning to enjoy themselves and get a little bit of nookey, and then along comes the brass and sticks the whole sodding shlemozzle on the beat to Belfast.

Sod the Army. Sod all the generals. And above all else sod those bleedin' Micks who kept on picking a fight they could never hope to win in a month of Sundays.

All the officers were gathered in the anteroom awaiting a final word from the CO. They were young and fit and cocky and they sincerely hoped the Old Man would not be too long-winded about it, because this was their last night and they intended to have an almighty, monumetnal thrash before bidding adieu to Düsseldorf and Deutschland.

The Old Man did not disappoint them, for he, too, had been young once, and as impatient. For days he and they had studied maps, intelligence reports, and classified information with infinite care, and now—knowing themselves to be better and braver and more experienced than any other regiment in the entire British Army—they believed themselves to be as well equipped for the campaign in Ulster as soldiers could ever hope or expect to be.

So tonight the colonel, sensing the mood, made it short and sweet.

"They tell us," he said, "we may be in for a rough time, that the IRA are stepping up the pace. So be it. The First Seventh kept the peace pretty damn well in the worst days in Cyprus and again in Aden."

He slapped his leg with the swagger stick he always carried.

"They weren't exactly picnics either, as all of you know. I believe the men are in good heart"—here his subalterns nudged each other and struggled to keep straight faces—"and I personally welcome the move as a challenge, an opportunity for the Runners to win fresh laurels. Our role in Ulster, as in Cyprus and Aden, is to keep the peace, but with this difference—to keep it among our own people and on our own soil.

"Never forget that. Never let the men forget that. They are professionals, and I know they will respond, as they always have, to good leadership. That is the one steadfast quality always enjoyed by soldiers in our regiment from the days of its formation. And it is precisely why I look forward to our tour in Northern Ireland with such confidence. Gentlemen, thank you. That's all."

The First Seventh Wessex Lancers took their nickname the "Runners" from a desperate forced march in the Peninsular War that turned the flanks of the French and led to a famous victory. Turner's painting, showing the ragged, starving squadrons of heroes who survived the snowy march over mountains to defeat Sault's vastly superior force, now went with the First Seventh wherever it served.

Tonight, as mess waiters in white jackets served drinks after the

30

address, the colonel stood below the magnificent canvas and held court with his officers. He raised his glass in salute to a fair-haired young major whose tunic showed the purple-and-blue ribbon of the Military Cross.

"All under control, Dickie? No problems?"

"Under control, sir," said the major, returning the smile. Dick Welbourne and the colonel were old comrades-in-arms and had served together for eleven years.

Welbourne was experienced, had a fine record, and was happy in his job. Thirty-four years old, he had won his MC—and a considerable reputation—on active service in the Aden Protectorate.

The colonel remembered an oven-hot afternoon in the filthy streets of Sheik Othman when he had taken some new American correspondents to watch Captain Welbourne, as he then was, deal with a screaming, rock-throwing mob of Arab demonstrators. Welbourne's men were dismounted, and he stood in front of a line of suntanned, weary Runners awaiting the next charge.

The Arabs bore down on the British troops. On Welbourne's word of command, the troopers waded into the rioters using fists, boots, and the butts of their rifles to sort out the ringleaders and threw them into waiting trucks to be carted off to the compound. Some were dragged by their hair, and the afternoon was hideous with shouts and screams.

"Jesus, Colonel," protested one American, "but your men are sure playing it rough."

The Old Man called Welbourne over and asked him to answer the complaint. He stood there minus his hat, hair awry, with blood trickling from a cut over his nose, and a great grin of pride spread across his boyish face.

"Dead right, sir," said Welbourne coolly, dabbing away sweat and blood as he turned to the reporter. "We've been thumping these buggers hard for the past hour." Three or four of his troopers sat slumped against a mud wall, bleeding and dazed from rocks that had split open their skulls. He pointed them out to the newly arrived American correspondent.

"I told those chaps, 'If you want a bit of peace and quiet, open up with a Bren.' The trouble is, I just can't persuade them to kill anyone."

The colonel had told and retold that story a dozen times since and still relished it. It was crystal clear in his mind now, as he and Welbourne walked to a window and gazed down on the darkened parade ground.

31

"Ireland is going to be worse than the last time out, I'm afraid, Dickie. I spoke to Jimmy Thomson of the Grays last night, and he said it's a sight hotter than Aden—and he wasn't referring to the weather, either. We are going to need cool heads and monumental patience this time as never before. The international press are thick on the ground, watching every incident. No need for me to stress how much I shall be relying on you to set an example. The pep talk tonight was strictly for the benefit of the few youngsters who haven't been blooded yet."

"That's what I thought, sir."

The major, who was married and had two sons he would have seen in two days' time, did not mention his wife's comments when he had told her that leave had been put back because of the move to Ulster. Instead he said to his commanding officer:

"I explained to the men you'd have the leave roster cracking just as soon as possible after settling in. It was the best news they'd had today. Listen to them now! I don't think we've got a thing to worry about as far as morale and discipline are concerned. Can you hear them, sir?"

The Runners were quartered in prewar Wehrmacht barracks built tall and compact around a vast asphalt parade ground. The night was cold and clear, the ceremonial square deserted, and as the two officers listened, the strains of "Bless 'Em All"—the British Tommy's derisive answer to all the slings and arrows of outrageous military fortune—could be heard from the canteen.

"While you were at brigade this afternoon," said Welbourne carefully, "I had a quiet word with the Regimental Sergeant Major and suggested a blind eye might be turned on any revelry down there tonight. Matter of fact, sir, the squadron commanders chipped in to send a few cases of beer across to help things along. I took the liberty of implying that a certain amount of license would meet with your approval, Colonel."

"Quite right," the colonel replied. "A very sound suggestion indeed. Thank you. In fact, it's one I shall act on myself—I'll leave you and the others to get on with your own party. Really, I've a lot to do. Good night, Dickie, enjoy yourself."

"Good night, sir." All the officers stood up, silent, as the Old Man left the room.

Richard Martin Welbourne had come into the Army as a matter of course after leaving school, and into the First Seventh as a result of family tradition. A cornet named Welbourne had been

32

killed in the Peninsular War after surviving the forced march that gave the regiment its proud nickname. There had been a Welbourne serving somewhere in its ranks ever since. None had risen to high command, or even great fame, but the family had given a son to the regiment in all succeeding generations, and they had fought in many wars. Their bones lay moldering beneath the ground from India and the Sudan to Spain and the Low Countries, and from Kimberley to Alamein.

As a family the Welbournes were neither rich nor well-connected; solid was the word. Welbourne had one brother who was a farmer, and another a schoolmaster. As the one son chosen for the Army he was well content with his lot.

He was a normal, healthy, and cheerful young man, well liked by his fellow officers and both trusted and admired by his men. Both had seen him under fire and both—had you asked—would have given their opinion that Dickie Welbourne was a man who was steady under pressure rather than brilliant in strategy, a realist rather than a Hotspur in the field.

The major had won his MC for rescuing a wounded man and bringing him safely in under accurate sniper fire from tribesmen rated among the world's finest marksmen, the hillmen from the Radfan. He personally reckoned it all part of the day's work.

As he said to his wife Sue: "I couldn't leave the poor devil stranded, darling, he was there on my orders," and it was precisely the man's outlook. Having come to a decision, having placed a man in danger, it seemed to him as natural as night follows day that he should be the one to put matters right, and to him it was a matter of genuine surprise that others should consider such behavior not only brave but exemplary.

His present colonel thought him a fine officer and attributed Richard Welbourne's evident coolness to outstanding courage. A previous commanding officer, who had watched him at close quarters in Cyprus, had also noted this air of calm confidence but—perhaps more shrewdly—felt it owed something at least to the young Lancer's somewhat limited horizon.

Tonight, once the CO had gone, Welbourne went back to the bar and picked his team for a High Cockalorum joust against Baker squadron. As he stood against the wall waiting for the onslaught, he found himself mildly puzzled by the Old Man's caution.

"Bloody hell," he said to himself, "if we can't beat the Micks, what chance would we stand in a real war?"

33

· 5 ·

The name Kelly was half true—it was his mother's. His passport was new and had been provided by strangers in America two weeks earlier.

Brian Kelly had been born Brian Werner, in London, in 1932. His father was German and a Roman Catholic who had gone to sea as a young man to escape from the poverty and depression that was rife in Germany at the time. On a trip to Liverpool in 1930 he met and married Mary Kelly, an Irish waitress working in one of the city's second-class hotels. He gave up the sea and moved with her to London to work as a chef, the trade he had learned afloat. Brian was their only child.

Before the war the family spent three holidays in Germany, where Werner Senior had kept in close touch with his own family and friends. Back in London, and in drink, he praised loudly and often the changes that had taken place in the Fatherland under Adolf Hitler, the new chancellor.

It was innocent enough, the impressions of a man who sees only the shop window. But when war broke out he was denounced by his neighbors in Hammersmith, questioned, rounded up, and finally interned under the 18b security regulations framed to defeat any possibility of a fifth column in Britain.

His wife and son suffered considerable hardship. In 1941 after the blitz on English cities, Mrs. Werner took her child and traveled to neutral Eire to stay with relatives and there, penniless and resentful, brooded her way through years of separation. There was never any money. There was many a night spent crying. From his youngest formative days Brian Werner grew up to hate the English. Above all he remembered the day in 1945, two months before the war in Europe ended, when a telegram reached his mother to say her husband had died.

He heard his mother give a great cry of anguish and ran to her

34

side. She crossed herself and stood swaying with her eyes shut tight in a face pale as marble as she spoke to the frightened, weeping boy.

"Ah, they've killed your father," she said, "the poor dear man who never hurt a living thing. May his soul rest in peace."

Werner had died, in internment, from a cancer. Mother and son blamed the English for both and vowed never to forget or forgive.

In 1948 when he was sixteen and bigger than many full-grown men, Brian followed his father's example and went to sea. He lost touch with his mother. The bewildered boy turned into a moody, violent giant of a man. Within five years, after a knife fight, he jumped ship in San Francisco and turned drifter, part of the human flotsam wandering the United States. After a while he lined up at a recruiting office and with a bit of lying managed to volunteer for Korea.

It was his first step on a long, hard road; in the end it had led him to his present status—mercenary, gun for hire. Once enlisted he found to his surprise that the prospect of fighting fired and excited him. He genuinely wanted to go to Korea as an infantry private, but the American Army decided otherwise. His officers discovered in Werner a "natural," a born genius in the study and handling of the weapons of war, a rookie who could not just outshoot his tutors at the practice range but also outshine them in the classroom; so they posted him as instructor to Fort Benning, Georgia.

Five years later when he received an honorable discharge, Sergeant Brian Werner enjoyed a considerable expert reputation as well as U.S. citizenship, and the Army was genuinely sad to see him go. He had disciplined his wildness, and his knowledge ranged far beyond the normal weapons handled by American infantrymen.

He made a close study of intelligence reports flowing in from the Korean battlefields, of captured Chinese and Russian arms and explosives, and then—as an expert in their use—was sent from camp to camp lecturing on a whole range of Communist small arms and their capabilities. With this increase in knowledge a vague discontent gnawed at Werner—just as odors from some distant kitchen will worry even the best-fed appetite—and he began to dream how to turn his acquired skills into money. Suddenly he realized the answer stared him in the face each day. Whichever newspaper he read, magazine or book he picked up, or radio station he turned to, he would read or hear about fighting in some far-off part of the world, one more of the murderous miniature "bushfire" wars in which all

35

great powers like to dabble while never becoming publicly involved.

In each and every one there was a demand for mercenaries. The very word beckoned Werner, tempted him, and the promise of loot sounded like music to his ears. He could not wait to get out of one army into another.

He got his first opportunity in 1960 when the Belgians panicked and gave independence to the Congo. Frenchmen, Germans, British, South Africans, Portuguese, Rhodesians—all scrambled on the bandwagon. Werner bought a one-way ticket to Brussels and two months later found himself a captain in the rag-tag army of bums and bigots who homed into Elisabethville, capital of mineral-rich Katanga—the secessionist Congo state—to fight under the flag of Moise Tshombé.

Werner was given an independent command. He took over a mobile column of some forty men, mostly Katangese gendarmerie who had been bad policemen in the days of Belgian rule and who, now that they were free, were even more lazy and corrupt and brutal.

He also had six whites as subalterns—four South Africans, a German, and a Belgian. When all were thrown together his was not a band to inspire much confidence. An English correspondent who went to their camp christened them the "Black and White Minstrel Show."

His orders were to head for the Kasai border, subdue groups of Baluba tribesmen in revolt, and also turn back any invading columns of Lumumba's Congolese troops they might meet. It was a grandiose assignment for such a motley crew.

Werner ran an eye over his Minstrels, not much liking what he saw, and asked the Belgian administrator who had handed him his orders:

"Let's get this straight. You expect me to fight the Congolese Army with only forty men?"

The Belgian laughed. "It will not be as difficult as it sounds, Captain. The ANC, or Armée Nationale Congolaise, is no more than an armed gang officered by drunks. They will be like rabbits for your gunners."

Werner bit off his next question: How then had such a rabble forced the Belgians to flee in panic? Instead he saluted and went to war.

In the hot and dusty barrack square he ordered all his men on parade. They grumbled and they loitered, but eventually they lined up with their Jeeps mounting Browning machine guns, their filthy open trucks, and a single eight-wheeled lorry covered by a tarpaulin. All the men wore a uniform of sorts. Some of the Katangese had GI helmets, most wore berets. Werner and his white officers sported Belgian Army khaki drill shirts and trousers. The gendarmes turned out in filthy green fatigues.

Everyone, black and white, wore French jungle issue canvas boots soled with rubber more than an inch thick. A powerful reek of unwashed bodies carried downwind. As his adjutant Werner selected the Belgian, a man called Mielen, for he alone could understand the bastard French used by the Kats. He and Werner reviewed the troops on this dusty, hot day.

Werner carried a .45 Colt revolver at his waist. He wore a Mills grenade clipped to each breast-high ammunition pouch, and a Thompson submachine gun lay on the hood of his Jeep. Most of his blacks were drunk. Their captain felt it was time to let them get to know him.

"You," he said, pointing an enormous finger. He ordered a Katangese forward and made him stand with his back to his captain, squinting into the sun.

Werner took a can of beans from his Jeep and stuck it on top of the man's woolly black hair. He walked away deliberately, gauging the distance until they were twenty paces apart. Then he pulled his Colt from its holster and aimed it. The Black and White Minstrels watched him pop-eyed.

Werner fired. The *bang!* sounded incredibly loud in the sleepy stillness of the afternoon. The tin whipped off the gendarme's head, holed dead-center, and bounced along the dusty parade ground leaking bean juice the color of blood. No one dared to move. The eyes of the gendarme rolled in terror as he grasped what had happened, and a stain darkened the leg of his fatigues as his bowels gave way.

"I've been put in command of this company," said Werner, speaking loud and slow so Mielen could translate each word, "and that was to show you all I mean it when I say I'll shoot any son of a bitch who disobeys one order of mine.

"I run the show. You do *exactly* as I say. Is that clear? Anyone who wants out—say so now."

He glared at them. Nobody spoke up. No one moved. The dusty square was silent.

"This officer"—he pointed at Wust, a pale German—"will issue all rations from now on. He is also your doctor. Be prepared for a few mistakes because he is no more a doctor than I am. But don't worry,

37

the government here tell me they will fly out anyone who gets badly hurt.

"You all know what's in store if the Baluba or Lumumba's men capture you." He laughed at the row of shining black faces. "So just follow orders and make sure you don't get caught. Another thing. I don't care what you look like, I don't care if you stink in your own dirt, but God help any man who neglects his gun or his vehicle from this moment on. We move out tonight. No more drinking. Clean your guns. Get those vehicles in good shape, you hear me? Okay, dismiss."

The story of Werner's cowboy act went around every club and bar in E'ville before the night was over. A wag christened him "Buffalo Bill," and the name stuck wherever he went in the Congo. Werner knew, and knew why, and was proud of the tag. But no one ever called his company a Minstrel Show again. When it hit the enemy it smote them hip and thigh and showed neither mercy nor restraint. Werner had no old-fashioned notions about chivalry or humane treatment of those who opposed him. He shot first and asked questions afterward, always.

Werner's first battle against the ANC was a military classic, and it took place less than three months after he first landed in the Congo.

One night he camped in a kraal a few miles from a small mining town abandoned by the Belgians in the stampede at independence. Werner had been burned brown by the sun and looked fit and hard as a rogue elephant. He swaggered around the compound belching up roast pig and whiskey, smoking a cigar. A Katangese corporal drove in to report a sizable force of ANC had crossed the river, apparently heading his way.

"How many?" asked Werner.

Mielen took up the questioning. "He's not sure," he told Werner. "The information comes from the River Baluba, and they're pretty unreliable. But they told the corporal a big force, complete with transport, crossed here"—and he pointed on the map to a bridge beyond the mining town. "The Baluba say it took all day for them to get across with their trucks. Must be several hundred of the buggers at least."

"Any sign of the blue berets?" All UN troops were blue berets to the Katangese, and Werner had orders to avoid them.

"Nothing. Just ANC."

"How long before they get here?"

"Who knows? They're Congolese," said Mielen contemptuously. "If I know them they'll be flat on their backs, pissed as wheels, and camped close enough to the river to beat a quick retreat at the first sign of opposition."

"Just what we want," Werner answered. "We'll hit them before they wake up. I'll go ahead with some of the Kats and cross the river lower down. We'll move up under cover of darkness and mine the bridge. Muller can blow it later. He will set up machine guns to hit anyone trying to swim across after I've come back to rejoin the rest of you. Let's move."

It was dusk when Werner led his section to the riverbank. The River Baluba ferried them across on Werner's promise they could have first pick of any arms recovered from the ANC. Before he climbed into the first pirogue Muller drew the captain aside, away from the Katangese.

"Watch out for the crocs," he said. "They're wicked bastards in these parts. Eat you as soon as look at you, man. My Kats are jittery as hell."

"No shooting," Werner ordered. "We'll have to take our chance with the crocs. If anyone panics and opens fire, those Congolese sentries will hear us. I'll go first with the explosives. You come last. Two or three trips should see us all across. Leave one man guarding the Jeeps."

It took far longer than Werner had reckoned to cross the river. Each pirogue carried two oarsmen wielding short, heavy-bladed paddles, and once they took on passengers with weapons and ammunition they had to sweat to stay on course in the tumbling black waters. From time to time enormous masses of weed rushed downstream and as they struck the canoes, weed and boats spun crazily in midriver. Water slopped over the sides of each vessel, while the crocs launched themselves from the banks every few seconds, closing in on the tiny armada.

Soon the din was indescribable. The Katangese were city dwellers and wild with fear of crocodiles and water snakes. Fear made them desperate and heedless of discipline. They shouted to each other and cursed the Baluba boatmen, who cursed and shouted back. Close to Werner the Katangese corporal who had brought him the first message lost his head and fired a single shot blindly into the water. Finally they were all across.

Werner ran up to the corporal and clubbed him senseless with his revolver.

Then, as the others watched, he picked the Katangese up like a sack of coal, walked to the bank, and threw him into the mud shallows, close to the waiting crocodiles.

There was enough moon to watch him die. As he bubbled for breath in the stinking mud two of the beasts, like throwbacks from prehistoric times, fought over his body with spike teeth and flailing armored tails. In the end they divided the spoils. White men and black watched in horror as the reptiles crunched into a leg apiece and dragged the whimpering, living thing out to drown so they could eat him later, at their leisure. Within minutes the water was still.

Muller was sick. The River Baluba rolled the whites of their eyes in terror. The Katangese backed away from Werner, clutching their rifles as he raged at them.

"You pigs," he shouted, "you bloody, stinking pigs! Didn't I tell you not to open fire? If those Congolese have heard us I'll shoot the whole bloodly lot of you myself! Now get that goddamned equipment together, get yourselves formed up into a fighting section—and MOVE!"

When they were still a long way from the bridge it was Muller who picked out the guards and their lorry—two men standing together, smoking and chattering, rifles slung carelessly on their shoulders. He and Werner waved the Katangese to halt, slipped off their packs, and crawled soundlessly through the shadows. Two brawny white arms came out of the night to choke two black throats, two knives plunged as one, and the sentries were dead before they were lowered to the ground.

"Get your men up here," hissed Werner. "Tell two of them to put these tin hats on and walk about like the sentries. The rest of us will set the explosives on the struts of the bridge. Don't waste time now."

At two in the morning, under a waning moon, all was ready. "I'm heading back to the column," said Werner. "Don't blow the bridge until the last possible moment. Get your Kats to lob hand grenades in the truck here at the same time—no prisoners. See you."

He made his way back to the river crossing at a jog trot, keeping well clear of the elephant grass. The River Baluba ferried him swiftly across. Mielen was waiting on the far bank.

"Everything ready, Captain."

"About the only bloody thing that has gone right so far. Move out." There was already a hint of light in the eastern sky. One by one the vehicles rumbled out and began to race across open country, staying closed up to Werner. They were less than a mile from the bridge when a huge red flash lit the skyline.

"That's the bridge gone," Werner shouted.

40

They heard the *crump! crump!* of exploding grenades, followed by staccato bursts from the Browning. The ANC thought they were under attack from Muller on the far side of the river, and now Werner was among them with the advantage of total surprise.

Mielen was already firing over his head as he leaped out of the Jeep and started running, pouring gasoline on the ground from a can. He flung the can down and aimed a Verey cartridge directly into it to set the grass ablaze. The other driver followed suit. Each can exploded with a roar, and the elephant grass started to crackle and burn. In minutes the whole bank was alight, an inferno of flame and smoke, shouts and screams, shots and explosions. A morning breeze fanned the fire and whipped it into one long, rolling, spluttering, roaring red line, six, seven hundred yards across, advancing into the Congolese encampment with a fearful drumfire of sound.

Scores of ANC soldiers began to run out, hands in the air, screaming surrender as their uniforms burned and blistered each brawny black back. Werner's men sat back in their Jeeps and hammered away with every weapon they had, rifles, revolvers, Browning machine guns, and tommy guns. Hand grenades rained into the flames to add to the carnage.

It was a massacre, the first and biggest of all the Congo war. When Werner finally ordered "Cease Fire," some eight hundred Congolese troops lay dead or wounded from bullets, shrapnel splinters, burns, suffocation, and drowning. A pall of smoke drifted hundreds of feet into the blood-red morning sky, while the wind carried the stench of roast flesh miles downstream. Kites and vultures flew around the edge, spiraling higher and higher, afraid to close in yet for the morsels they knew would be theirs once the earth cooled. Rats by the hundreds scurried from the inferno; snakes and crocodiles splashed into the river to escape the heat. The ground shook as the ANC trucks loaded down with gasoline and ammunition exploded.

All the wounded were shot, on Werner's orders.

The River Baluba paddled down to marvel at the sight, and when the ash had cooled a little, ran through it on hardened bare feet to loot what they could before the animal scavengers took over in the dark.

Brian Werner had made his mark as a mercenary.

·6·

Brian Werner served other masters well as the years rolled by. From Africa he went to Yemen, where he lived in the mountains like a felon on the run as he fought for the deposed Imam against a huge army of Egyptian invaders.

His career nearly ended on a blazing hot day when an Egyptian fighter flew out of the sun to pound his column with napalm and cannon fire. Werner was wounded by rock splinters and shrapnel and carried to safety in neighboring Saudi Arabia by surviving tribesmen. He paid his own way down to South Africa and a hospital. He dug deep in his savings to meet the surgeon's bills and the cost of a long convalescence. At the end of the year he could walk again and began the long fight back to health and strength that would enable him to serve as a mercenary once more.

In the winter of 1966—it was July, down in Mozambique—he was approached by some old cronies who dangled the bait of another command, and high pay, to help them stage a fresh coup in the Congo, this time against a new leader, M'butu. Werner liked none of it but saw in the plan an easy way to make money. He sucked them dry of detail, promised to think it over, and promptly betrayed his old comrades.

He flew to Léopoldville in secret, warned the authorities, and sat back to await his thirty pieces of silver. Once his friends were rounded up and executed he was given a grace-and-favor house in the capital, a bank account controlled through Léopoldville, and the pretense of a job as military adviser. After a couple of years it went sour, as did everything in the Congo of those days. Successive ministers first "forgot" to pay his monthly checks, then began to filch his salary openly, while in turn his complaints brought empty apologies, evasion, downright lies, and finally thinly veiled threats.

In his service as a mercenary malaria, dysentery, and wounds had all left their mark on Werner, but the theft of his money hurt most of all. He stayed, and stayed quiet, but he did so because he had to, because for the moment he had nowhere else to go. He brooded and schemed and dreamed in vain, searching for a way out.

Then the miracle happened.

One night two strangers called on him unannounced as he dined alone in his garden, served by a solitary and ragged houseboy.

They knew him by reputation, they knew he needed money, and they came with a deal. They were Irish-Americans and zealous missionaries for the Cause.

They quickly got down to brass tacks.

"Mr. Werner," said one with a smile, "my friend and I are really happy to meet you. We've got a business proposition. We happen to know quite a lot about you—let's say from mutual friends—so we'll tell you something about ourselves.

"We work for a man whose name we won't mention, but who happens to be exceedingly rich. Recently his only grandson died in Ireland. The boy had gone there with the idea of helping the IRA but was killed when a bomb he was making exploded prematurely."

"Amateur," laughed Werner. His callers looked shocked.

"Perhaps. But it made the old man very sad, Mr. Werner. He feels strongly about the situation in Ireland and is determined such a fine young life shall not be wasted. He is going to replace it. He has commissioned my friend and me to use part of our legitimate business time in finding an experienced man to take his grandson's place in the fighting line. More than one, if we can find the right type.

"Naturally, we will pay. You can be quite certain any promises we make will be fully honored. Do we interest you?"

Werner drew on his cigar and regarded his visitors.

They were sleek and well-fed. No fighting had ever come closer to them than in the columns of a newspaper. He despised them, but he smelled money.

"In some ways it might," he told them. "Not in others. From what I read in the papers that's a pretty one-sided war as far as firepower goes. Your pay had better be good."

"It is," said the second man, beaming.

"How good?" asked Werner.

"I'll level with you," said the first speaker. "We're not even considering a deal that gives you so much a week. We're offering payment by results. The better you do, the more you earn."

"I don't know," Werner replied. "It's a war that's been going on for a number of years now. Cash every week adds up. The way you put it, sounds a very loose arrangement."

"There are administration problems," explained the second man. "The Irishmen you'd be fighting with don't do it for pay. They take pride in that. And there's another thing. We figure your value to the Cause is doing a few spectacular things, not just being another fighter. The man we speak for has a vested interest in one small splinter group. He'd like to help them with your expert services—and pay you on results."

"The way our employer sees it," said the other businessman, "is to provide a special awards fund. He would make money available in a Swiss banking account to be paid to you as soon as the group leader lets us know what you've done. It would be generous, I assure you."

Werner thought for a minute.

"You're new to this business," he told them, "so pardon me if I put you straight on a couple of things.

"Payment on results, with money coming in from a generous millionaire, sounds great in theory. But think about it.

"Anyone who takes the job will find himself up against a professional army using modern weapons and backed by a highly trained police force. You're not talking about the Congo, or the Yemen, you're talking about Ulster. Chances are your man wouldn't live long enough to earn a down payment, never mind anything else."

"That's not what we have in mind for you," he was told. "That idea was thrown out long ago, for the very reasons you have explained. You have other qualifications. You're an expert in the handling of Communist-manufactured weapons, isn't that right?

"Well, we have a shipment of Russian arms on order, a big one. You ought to be able to organize something rewarding with that.

"And we're hoping that with your knowledge of explosives you can pull off something sensational, something to make the whole world sit up and take notice. For that you could earn really big money—the sky's the limit. We're buying experience. You use that to set up a revolutionary spectacular. We read about it, and your Irish friends tell us: 'Werner did that.' The old man calls for a

44

secretary, and the money flows straight into a Swiss banking account. Big money, Werner.

"And there's another thing. You said it's a loose contract. So it is. It won't pin you down to a set length of service. When you've had enough, and more important, when you think you've made enough, you just pull out. What do you say to a deal like that?"

"And just what do you mean by 'big money'?"

They gave him some figures, and he whistled in surprise; still he wouldn't commit himself.

"I'll need time," said Werner, "to think things over."

"Take all the time you need," replied the first man easily. "We're here on other business and we expect to be here quite a while. We're registered at the Memling. You have our names. Call us anytime."

They shook hands. The two visitors could not wait to get back to their air-conditioned hotel rooms. Their pink faces shone with sweat, their soft hands slapped on itching flesh as a cloud of mosquitoes dive-bombed them from the bright garden lights.

"Uh, one last word, Mr. Werner. Secrecy is absolutely vital. We would take it badly if news of our offer, uh, reached any unauthorized quarter."

"Likewise," Werner assured them. "I can't afford to have my own name bandied about. The American embassy carries a lot of weight around here."

"You can trust us. Good night."

Werner's mind was already made up. There was more in their offer than money, acceptable though that undoubtedly was. For the first time he had a chance to even the score with those English bastards, to take an eye for an eye, a tooth for a tooth, and he was surprised at the way the passing thought stoked a warm glow in his belly. Even so, he let his callers wait a full week before driving to the Memling Hotel and swearing his new allegiance.

One more time, he told himself, just one more time, long enough to hit the jackpot, maybe, and then—out, for good.

A few days later he was on his way to America. A smiling and prosperous man met him on his arrival in New York and took him to a hotel. Within forty-eight hours Brian Werner had become Brian Kelly. Unlike Werner, this man Kelly was someone, a man of means, a man much in demand, a man who traveled in style with all his bills paid while his own wallet stayed comfortably full. Each day he answered questions about himself and each day he

45

waited while the answers were digested and checked out and approved.

He never once met his new employer or heard him called by name.

"You are to meet Sean Casey today. You are to have lunch with Pat Rooney. This guy wants to ask you some questions. You are to go to Boston for a couple of days and meet some fellers there. When you register at the Statler Hilton in LA a man will contact you with the new passport."

His employer picked up the tabs, had Kelly's flight timetable arranged to fit in with other deliveries in Ireland, and when his henchmen handed over the airline ticket they gave Kelly a number to ring as soon as he landed in the old country.

The tune had been called, and he had made it to this godforsaken hotel to meet his Irish contact. It was now Kelly's turn to pay the piper. He yawned after his meal and looked down on the fire that had grown cold. I think you're going to earn every single dollar that rich bastard pays you, he said to himself, and shivered violently as he climbed the stairs to bed.

·7·

Next day he woke up at the first shuffling footstep outside his bedroom door.

"Mr. Kelly! Mr. Kelly!" called a woman's voice, "are ye decent?"

"Come in," he answered. As he spoke, his hand instinctively reached under the pillow, but he checked its movement—there was no gun there. He was safe, in Ireland, in a sleepy old hotel, and as far as the outside world was concerned he was there only to fish.

"Your tea, sir," said the old crone who was carrying a tray. "It's seven o'clock. Breakfast in one hour."

He drank thirstily and swung out of bed, shivering. Christ almighty, but it was cold, with the fire dead and the hot-water bottles chilled. He drew the curtains and looked out to see sleet gusting down the deserted street.

He shaved quickly, dipped a toe halfheartedly in the bath, and dressed in long johns, thick shirt, two woolen jerseys, and wool-lined waterproof trousers, all products of the sports section of a New York department store. This morning he sent up a silent prayer of thanks for the decision to buy them on a wet, warm day when the winter seemed gone. He poured a huge tot of whiskey into a cup, to aid and abet the warm clothing, and downed it in a gulp as he went down to breakfast.

At two minutes to nine he heard a car pull into the courtyard. He stood with his back to the fire, watching the door. He heard voices in the hall; then the door creaked open, and a stranger walked in.

"Brian Kelly?" he asked.

"You'll be Liam," he answered, looking at the caller in surprise. He saw a little man in his late fifties, but Liam's eyes were blue and steady, with their vigilance giving the lie to the wide smile on his face.

"If you'd be kind enough to order me some coffee," he said formally, "I'll take my bag upstairs and get changed." The watchful eyes approved Kelly's own dress.

"You've got the right idea," he told the big man. "Christ, it's cold, this isn't Donegal weather! Have you ever done any fishing at this time of the year?"

"Never fished, period," said Kelly dryly. "Maybe I will have beginner's luck." He was already bored with the fencing.

"We can all do with some of that," the little man agreed pleasantly enough, "whatever our occupation. Hold on by the fire while I get into something warmer."

Kelly rang for coffee. Liam came down minutes later, hidden in wool—a gnome in sheep's clothing.

"We look like we're off on a polar expedition," Kelly said. "Want a drink to go with the coffee?"

The Irishman looked shocked.

"Never touch it," he replied. "We find it's apt to make a man careless at times."

The steady eyes quizzed Kelly.

"Depends on the man," Kelly snorted. He was yellow with cold. "If ever you find me getting careless, just let me know."

He picked up his glass.

"It looks as if I'll need plenty to stay alive in this lousy climate."

His brother's letter had told Liam about Kelly: "A prickly bastard. No sense of humor." The two men carried food and hot drinks to his car. When they were on their way Liam said, "There are two rods in the back. I can fish well enough for us to get by without comment. Now, my friend, there's a lot to tell you, and this is the safest way to to it.

"If the season's right, a riverbank is the one place in Ireland you can roam without rousing suspicion in anyone's mind. I've never found out why, but people automatically assume that a sportsman must be a decent sort of man."

He chuckled at his little joke.

"Tell me," asked Kelly, "is there any danger of being bugged back in the hotel, then?"

"Lord, no," Liam assured him. "The only bugs you'd find in any hotel I picked would be the sort that bite!"

He laughed again.

"Seriously, I doubt if there is one man in the local police in this part of the world who would know how to use such sophisticated

48

equipment even if he wanted to—and that's not certain, to my mind. By and large I would say the majority of policemen here are basically sympathetic to us.

"No, the danger lies simply in being two complete strangers in a tiny village. That goes for any country. You stick out like a sore thumb, and everyone wants to know who you are. As fishermen we are accepted without a second glance."

"Okay," said Kelly. "We're safe. I'll buy that. Now, what do I have to do?"

Liam told him, "We have a special delivery of arms and ammunition due any day in this area. I can tell you this much, they're coming straight from Russia, which is why you are starting work here rather than in Belfast.

"A long time ago friends in America offered to send us new equipment and trained specialists to help in the war against the British. Some of us had an open mind about that, I don't mind admitting it—about the men, I mean, not the guns. But since they were sending us a lot of money we didn't wish to appear too ungrateful.

"You have come, and I quote from the letter sent to me by my brother Sean, as 'specially trained in the use of Communist-manufactured weapons.' Your first job will be to show us how these new weapons work. I am not too sure what you're supposed to do after that. My council will decide. At this moment my orders are to see that you get all the help we can provide."

"Sounds good," said Kelly noncommittally.

"I understand you are to be paid on results. Is that so?" Liam was itching to know.

"Something like that," Kelly agreed.

"The risk of you getting caught worries us," Liam admitted. "It would be bad for the image, us hiring mercenaries."

Kelly bridled.

"Why?" he said. "Is your image that good?"

"That's not the point," Liam told him. "Our cause is Irish unity. How do we stand if we are found hiring foreigners to do the fighting for us?"

"I shouldn't let it worry you," said Kelly. "A lot of tough things happen when you fight a war. And I didn't ask for this job. Your men came and found *me.*"

It was a poor start for comrades-in-arms. They spent the next fifteen minutes in uneasy silence. Kelly decided to change the subject.

"You a big outfit?" he asked. "I know about the IRA, but I'm not too clued up on the splinter groups. How did yours get started?"

"It's a long story," said Liam. "The two big groups are the Provos and the Official IRA, also known as the Stickies the Pins. You show your allegiance by the way you wear your lily to commemorate the Easter Rising. Then there's Saor Eire, or Free Eire—they're much smaller. And there's us, the Fenian Martyrs. We all left the old IRA for our own reasons. Our strength is growing the whole time."

Kelly wanted to know about the men he was going to fight with.

"What kind of fighting do you specialize in? Do you have ex-Army men, explosives experts, sharpshooters, radio technicians, that kind of thing?"

"We have a ruling council," Liam replied. "They work from headquarters in Cork. Then we have units here in Donegal, in Monaghan, County Cork of course, and Dublin, and front-line battalions in Belfast and 'Derry."

Kelly gave him a shrewd look but made no comment.

"I just never heard of you," he explained. "Now tell me about this arms shipment."

"It was organized," Liam told him, "by our backers in America. My brother played a leading part. The actual buying was done by middlemen working out of Rome and Middle East capitals. It took a hell of a long time to get the Russians to play along."

"What are we getting?" Kelly pressed him closely.

"I'm not a technical man, Mr. Kelly. All I'm told is they are weapons never seen in Ireland before. You'll know right enough in a day or two."

"Level with me," said Kelly. "What kind of weapons? Don't tell me I've come thousands of miles to fight in the dark. I don't have any kind of magic wand, Liam, these things have to be organized. We need a workshop to assemble them. We have to have a proper training ground. I have to know what kind of experience your men have in modern weapons."

"I wish I could tell you," Liam told him, "but I can't. No one can, yet. The trouble is, these damned Russians are so secretive. Our organizers have paid the money and set a delivery date. It expires this weekend. But we have no point of contact. We didn't know you were coming until two weeks ago and then only in a vague kind of message from my brother."

"Christ," said Kelly. "That sounds great! Meantime, you and

50

me, we just wander around with fishing rods in our hands? What kind of an outfit are you?"

"Just hold your horses, Mr. Kelly. At least we've made a start. The important thing is, you are on the spot, I'm your liaison man, arrangements have been made for a delivery of arms this weekend, and the men are ready to go as soon as the Russians arrive. Let's play it by ear for the moment."

"Tell me about your men." Kelly was adamant.

"We stand about forty strong here in Donegal. They have all had some experience in guerrilla warfare. They've got rifles, pistols, and some light machine guns and enough ammunition to lay siege to 'Derry. We've got helpers who will lead us over the Border and back. There's a pretty fair local intelligence network. The Garda don't get a message we don't hear about. We've got transport, too, trucks and vans and private cars. There's a good nucleus for you to work on, all right."

"As long as you don't expect miracles overnight," Kelly replied, "we might do something with all that. You're up against a bloody good army, so I hear. I sure hope those new weapons are as good as you think."

They came to a bridge, and Liam pulled to the side of the road.

"This is it," he said. "There will be quite a few locals wandering about, early though it is. Let's make a start on the fishing. You'll find it simple enough."

Kelly got out and began stamping his feet.

Liam set up two rods. At the end of each nylon line he tied a steel trace. Next, he opened a can and took out two tiny man-made fish. Each had a hook set in a ring at its mouth and behind the dorsal fin.

"Here," he said, handing one of the rods to the shivering giant. "The bait on the end is called a Devon minnow. All you have to do is chuck it in the river and wind in the reel."

"Is that all?" asked Kelly, genuinely surprised. "I thought fishing was bloody difficult."

"It can be." Liam grinned. "You try casting a fly in this wind. Then tell me if it's easy."

The water was soot-black. Every tree bowed to the wind off the bay. Flurries of sleet and hail whipped Kelly's face and brought tears to his eyes. The grass had turned white, like icing on a cake, and the only sounds came from gulls and the gale and the gurgling suck of the river.

Kelly tried to warm up by casting a minnow and ducked in alarm as the hooks came whistling back over his head.

"Walk along the bank," Liam told him. "Keep it up. I'll talk while you fish."

Kelly nodded. He could not trust himself to speak.

"We'll get the call soon," said Liam. "Tonight, maybe, from our local commander. He has been detailed to see to the delivery of the weapons. He is under orders not to come near us until they are safely cached."

He hesitated, groping for words a stranger might understand.

"That's not quite as simple as it sounds. It's not merely a question of hiding them from the Garda. There's always a chance they might be hijacked after they have been brought ashore."

Kelly looked baffled.

"Who's going to hijack them?" he asked. "The British Secret Service?"

"No," said Liam. "Other groups in the IRA. That's the big danger. We're lucky, we have a very rich backer in America, as you know. But the other groups are far bigger and can never get enough weapons by their own resources. The demand is always greater than the supply. We've all stolen from each other in the past, God help us."

Kelly said he had read something about it.

"Jesus, you can't imagine how it can be at times," Liam told him. "We raid each other, there's a feud, we start shooting at each other to get even—we've even been known to betray each other for revenge. We can never win, divided like that. We know it, and the English know it."

He paused and turning to Kelly said in a different tone, "There will be some who might be tempted to take the law into their own hands when they hear who you are. You'll need to watch your step wherever you walk."

"I'll do that," vowed Kelly, "don't you worry."

"Whatever else happens," said Liam, "you must have the help of the organization just to sleep safe at nights. You and I got off to a bad start. Maybe it was my fault. Don't make the same mistake with any more of the lads. Now, first things first. We'll need your help with the new weapons. We can get a strong unit together for training in the mountains over there—the Derryveaghs."

"Any danger from air surveillance?" asked Kelly.

"Enough," said Liam. "The English use their helicopters like wasps, buzzing up and down just inside the Border. The Irish Army uses fixed-wing spotter planes, Cessnas. Between them they give us a hard time. So we make the most of good ears and bad weather."

"What about ground patrols?"

"Now there," said Liam, "is a real tricky one. The English soldiers have been known to cross the Border 'by mistake,' so unless we're on business we don't stray too close.

"If we open fire on them from this side of the fence, our own Army roars up, well, a whole platoon anyway, and they're liable to arrest anyone around these days.

"Maybe we could deal with them, but we never try. That's an order. In this group we never offer resistance to Irish authority whatever uniform it happens to be wearing.

"This way we can rely on the support of the local people, even the uncommitted ones. It's plain common sense—without that support we couldn't last a week.

"As it is we can get guides to take us across without risk and we can 'borrow' ricks and barns to drop things off when the going gets too hot.

"Another thing, we have a pretty strict code of discipline in the Martyrs. We don't allow petty theft and we don't tolerate drunkenness. We don't allow sexual assault on women or children in our areas. If we hear of a man stepping out of line, we hold our own courts, we sentence and carry out punishment ourselves.

"Tarring and feathering for minor offenders. A severe beating up for second-timers. A bullet behind each kneecap for continual offenders. Death for treachery, cowardice, and willful disobedience of orders."

"Christ," said Kelly. "That's some discipline."

"The Provos are strictest of all," Liam told him. "We've borrowed a bit of our code from each of the others. Discipline like that also carries terrific propaganda value. It shows we're an army under orders and not an undisciplined rabble. In other words, a force to be reckoned with when your enemy is offering peace terms."

Kelly changed the subject.

"What's he like, this new local commander of yours?"

"Damned if I know," said Liam, "and that's a fact. O'Brien was our man here for ten years, but he got careless on a raid last month. The council in Cork decided to appoint one of their own men, on the basis that Donegal is such a key sector. He is a terrible tough man, so I hear. Name of Ryan. I shall meet him here for the first time, same as you."

They sat in the shelter of some trees to eat.

Kelly asked the older man, "You don't honestly think you can win this war, do you, Liam? Against a well-equipped modern army, I mean, and with your own security forces against you?"

Liam fed crumbs to a robin and told him:

"We can't win battles, that's for sure. But there are more ways of killing a cat than choking it with cream. The more cold-blooded we are, the more we terrorize people, the more we provoke anger and overreaction, that's when we start to win.

"In the first place, we get worldwide publicity, and often a platform to state our case. For every underground movement fighting an established and legal government, that is the first essential.

"We argue that our only weapon in the fight against a professional army is terrorism. And in the twentieth century such an argument is accepted without question by a world that has grown up with terrorism.

"You asked me if I think we can win. We are already winning the propaganda war, the one that finally matters.

"The longer we fight, the more likely it is the outside world will think, "There has to be a reason why the IRA keeps fighting on against such huge odds. Maybe it has got a case after all.

"If that's not winning, it's certainly not losing.

"Why do you think someone had the bright idea to call in a man like yourself to fight here?

"Do you think for one moment it's because you can shoot straighter, or fight braver, or fight cleaner, than any IRA man in Ireland?

"Don't kid yourself, Mr. Kelly.

"You know that isn't so. You are a professional. And you know professionals can be killed by a British Army bullet just like anyone else.

"So why are you here? I'll tell you. They're gambling you will come up with something new and spectacular, a killing that will set the whole world talking about us. And that, my dear Mr. Kelly, or whatever your real name may be, will be one more success in the war we *can* win—the propaganda war.

"Yes, Mr. Kelly. I do think we can win, not on the battlefield but in the mind. And that's where you come in."

In the gray of the afternoon they saw two men approaching.

"Come on," said Liam in an expressionless voice. "Your turn to fish."

Kelly flicked the minnow into the river. He had an oddly uncomfortable feeling, after listening to the little man, that whatever the fate of the salmon *he* was the one who was hooked.

54

·8·

Liam himself might have seemed an unlikely terrorist. He was no "hooligan" and certainly no "psychopath." He was a family man with a wife and five children whom he loved.

He would have laughed if you called him a fanatic. He had started, as did so many of the older hands in the IRA, to avenge his parents. His father had been shot dead during the Easter Rising in Sackville Street in Dublin, and his mother had been jailed for her patriotic beliefs. He served the Cause in many ways, but rarely had much to do with firing a gun or planting bombs.

Liam was a born organizer. He had courage and in his time had run many risks as an undercover man organizing resistance to the British in the North. He had prepared a hundred "safe" houses where men on the run could get food, money, and clothing and sleep the clock around in safety.

He knew a dozen "safe" ways to smuggle arms and ammunition—through sea- and airports, onto desolate beaches and remote airstrips north and south of the Border.

Curiously, he was not anti-British as such. Liam had discovered, over the years and to his considerable dismay, that he liked many of the British very much indeed. But he had inherited a hatred of "the British Imperial Presence" in the Six Counties, and those words sounded in no way pompous or ridiculous in his mind. But to fight for money seemed all wrong to Liam. Looking at Kelly as they ate by the fire in the hotel lounge, he wondered if this man wouldn't lead their small group to disaster.

After a day on the river Kelly's face was as red as the embers. His cropped blond hair gleamed in the firelight. The whiskey glass was lost from sight in his great paws. He seemed the personification of brute strength—like a gorilla dipped in peroxide.

The curtains lit up momentarily as a car pulled across the hotel

55

front, its headlights raking the lower windows. Then they heard voices in the hall. Minutes later the young woman tapped on the door of the lounge and came in.

"There's two from the village," she said, "called in for a drink." She hesitated, unwilling to intrude. "The house is empty, and we've no other fires. Would you gentlemen mind sharing the lounge, here?"

"Not at all," said Liam. "'Tell them to come in, and welcome."

The men trooped in, each with a glass in his hand, and muttered their apologies. Their coats were wet with snow. They drew up chairs and held out chapped hands to the blaze.

"Good evening," said one. "Jesus, but it's cold."

He was a big man, taller than Kelly. His hair was black as tar, and jowls that would always need shaving gave him a Gypsy's face, swarthy and secretive. His eyes were brown as chocolate drops, and they glittered from the cold.

"Will you gentlemen join me in a drink, now?"

"I will," said Kelly. "My friend never touches it."

"That's so," Liam confirmed, in no way put out by the jibe. "I've got coffee in the pot. But thank you."

"Will you do the honors, Michael?" said the dark man, handing his companion a pound note. "Three Paddies, then, is it?"

Kelly nodded agreement. Michael took the glasses and walked obediently out of the lounge. He was very young—twenty, maybe even less—and thin as a scarecrow. His coat was shabby, and his wrists poked down below each sleeve. He was ill at ease in the hotel, with its carpets and liqueur whiskies and bouquet of cigars, and showed none of the confidence of his friend.

As soon as the door closed, the dark man announced, "I'm Ryan. I had a call from Cork to say you were here."

The three men leaned out from their armchairs and briefly shook hands.

"I'll send the lad on his way presently," said Ryan. "After a decent interval. I've got news for you."

Liam dropped his avuncular pose. "It went all right?" he asked sharply.

The Gypsy face looked sullen. "There was a mixup this morning, Liam, a bloody mess. We could be in trouble unless we move fast, that's for sure!"

Liam sucked in his breath and turned to Kelly. "I'm an Irishman," he said, "and proud of it. But let me warn you. No one in the world—not even an Arab!—can mess things up like the Irish."

Michael came back with the drinks and felt the silence. He counted Ryan's change carefully before handing it over. "Slainte," he said, without looking at the others, and drank his whiskey straight down.

Before the boy could sit down, Ryan said casually, "Thank you kindly, Michael. Now I want you to get back home and wait until you hear from me. Not a word to your mother, mind."

"Sure." He could not bring himself to look Ryan in the eye. "I'll not say a word." He mumbled a goodnight and quickly walked out. They heard his footsteps in the yard.

"Now then, Mr. Ryan," said Liam. His voice was quiet and brimming with menace. "Tell me. All of it. What went wrong with the delivery?"

"You're not going to like it, Liam," said Ryan. All the bounce had gone out of him now. "And Eamonn even less."

"Tell me."

"Well," Ryan began, "the weather's been so bad we couldn't put out to meet the sub until this morning. The skipper didn't want to sail at all, but this was our last day, and so I persuaded him."

Ryan rubbed his knuckles reflectively. "After all that damned if we didn't have engine trouble! We were as late as hell, and there was a hell of a row between the Russki and our lot about how long we'd got to unload the stuff before he'd have to shove off. I shouted to him and I said, 'What's the point of bringing it all the way from Moscow just to take it back again?' and he jabbered away, but neither of us could hear the other in the gale.

"And, sweet Jesus, what do you think happened then? A bloody great airplane from the RAF flew over so low it nearly chopped the conning tower off the sub while we were hauling the stuff on board!"

"What could it have seen?" asked Liam. "Think hard, man." He explained to Kelly, "When the weather's bad the British planes sometimes overfly the coast here. They're looking for the NATO base at Londonderry. It's just possible this was coincidence."

"Horseshit," said Kelly.

"Not so much," said Ryan, anxious to please Liam. "It was blowing a gale, with snow and sleet coming down thick right across the bay. The plane was over and gone in a split second. Visibility was terrible, and the plane was in thick cloud most of the time."

Kelly spat into the fire.

"It shook everybody up," Ryan admitted. "We never saw the sub again."

"Did you get the cargo all right?"

"We did. All of it."

"What about the police? And the Army? Have they been nosing around?"

"Not a soul," said Ryan. "I've been checking with the lads tonight. There's been no message to the Garda—that's certain. No one has seen the Army for over a fortnight now. If the plane had spotted us the British would have been calling Dublin within the hour, I'm sure of it, Liam."

Liam looked much brighter. "I don't see how you were to blame either way," he told Ryan. "But that skipper, now, I might have to think about him."

Ryan still looked forlorn.

"Then there's the dead man," he said. He looked longingly into his glass but found no comfort there.

Kelly looked at him as though unable to believe his ears. Liam's face was like stone.

"What did you say?"

"I put a man up at the old farm, covering the road," Ryan told him. "He found a stranger there, an Englishman who's been here for several weeks, supposed to be a bird-watcher. Anyway, he was spying out the land through his binoculars and he must have seen the whole show, start to finish.

"What's more, he had a camera with him. If our man had recognized him it might have been different, I don't know. But he was all wrapped up against the cold, and our feller thought he was a spy and he shot him. Christ, what else was he to do?"

"Did you know the man yourself?" asked Liam.

"Sure. He's been staying at Connolly's bar, must be a month now. I went there to check him out and I had his room searched regularly. Never found a thing wrong. I was convinced he was what he said he was."

Ryan paused and felt in his pocket. "I don't know what to think now. They found this on him," and he handed over a small blue notebook.

"It's full of notes about birds, so it is. But look at this last page—written this morning, remember. The snow has made some of the ink run, but you can make out this bit, here, about 'positive identification' and then down here, where he says, 'must phone tonight.' Then there are a lot of figures I don't understand. But the last entry is just about right for the number of packages we landed. D'ye think maybe there was a leak, and he was sent to spy on us all the time?"

Liam spent a long time looking through the notebook.

"Could be," he said finally. "It's anybody's guess. What was in the camera?"

Ryan dropped his eyes again. "We'll never know," he replied. "The film was exposed and destroyed."

"Boy, you sure did a great job," said Kelly. "All bird-watchers carry binoculars and cameras and notebooks in the field."

"In other words, the perfect cover for a spy," said Liam, putting Kelly in his place.

Kelly shrugged his shoulders. "Maybe. What happened to the body?"

Ryan looked positively abject.

"I've been with the boat, unloading and hiding the supplies. I've just learned the bloody fool left it here, shot through the head. We can get rid of it, bury it so deep they'll never find it—but to leave it there all day, it's criminal! I've dealt with the man, don't you worry. But there's another thing. The feller's been staying at Connolly's, like I said. They're bound to report him missing when he doesn't turn up."

Liam was white-faced with rage.

"You great bungling clot," he hissed at Ryan, "I'm reporting you to the council. You may be new but it looks to me as if you couldn't run a tea shop, never mind a company of the Martyrs.

"We were ordered to avoid any fuss. This is a big operation, and if it gets screwed up by unnecessary murder and police intervention you're going to have a lot to answer for.

"But we haven't got time to waste on you now. We'd better decide what to do with the body, and fast."

Kelly broke in. "How do we know somebody hasn't found it already?"

"We'd know," said Liam. "Look, Ryan, delay the search for a bit until we think what to do."

"Sure," said Ryan. "I'll get some of the lads to call in the bar for a drink tonight. If Connolly or his missus says anything, and they will for sure, our men can 'volunteer' to go and look for the bird-watcher. They could come back late enough to delay a full-scale search at least until tomorrow."

"Get that organized right away," Liam ordered. "Then come back here for orders. I'll make certain you don't bugger up anything else in this operation, so help me I will."

Ryan stood up. "And don't go galloping out like a runaway horse," Liam added, "or you'll have the landlady wondering what's up."

The door closed quietly.

"Let me have the corpse," said Kelly. "Hide it in the open. It will keep in this weather. We'll take it with us when we start training, and I can show Mr. Ryan and company how to booby-trap a dead man."

"That's all very fine," Liam answered. "But we've still got the problem of a full-scale search tomorrow. People are bound to start asking where he's gone. Somebody might talk—the British pay very well for information."

"Once I've booby-trapped him," Kelly promised, "there'll be nothing left to tell tales. I give him the treatment and *zap!* he's just a smoke trail in the sky.

"But first, why not lay a false trail? Get Ryan and his men to scatter the bird-watcher's gear over a cliff. Make sure the police find his knapsack or some piece of his clothing caught in the rocks. Pick a really dangerous spot. Make it look as if he went over before it got light this morning, fell in the sea, and was drowned."

Liam looked at him with admiration. "That's good," he said. "But they'll keep searching for the body just the same."

"Let 'em," said Kelly as he rang the bell for another drink. He was completely calm. "It's a big, big ocean. It was dark when he climbed into his car to go bird-watching, and there'll be no witnesses. People vanish in the sea. It happens all the time."

"What if his family come over and start asking questions? What if he really was a spy, and someone else comes poking around?"

"I'd be surprised if *no one* came," Kelly told him. "Either way it doesn't matter. Whoever comes, give them every cooperation, take them to where the body was 'lost,' buy them a drink, make them welcome. They're going to believe he was drowned, just as the police are going to believe it—because it's a wholly acceptable idea. It's so convenient. It's much better than thinking he's just vanished."

Liam nodded agreement. He wondered where Kelly had learned so much about covering up a killing.

•9•

Ryan personally led the search party that went out with the Garda and spent hours combing fields and gullies, cliffs and beaches. What he found in midafternoon pointed unmistakably to a drowning after an unfortunate fall in the dark.

The police sergeant was inclined to believe it himself, but he was a wily old bird and had heard of the rumors that circulated about the lost bird-watcher, and he wondered.

"I want the truth, now," he told the search party. "Did any mischief befall that old man?"

He looked from face to face and waited. "All right," he said finally, "drowning it is."

That night an official report was handed in to the embassy in Dublin. It was short and to the point.

> Mr. Leslie James, aged sixty-one, a single man from Reigate, Surrey, who had been on holiday for several weeks in Donegal, was today reported missing by the local Garda.
>
> Mr. James, who had been in the habit of leaving his hotel accommodation each morning before dawn and driving alone to the coast to pursue his hobby of bird-watching, failed to return overnight.
>
> An immediate, voluntary search found no trace of him. Today an official search party found Mr. James's haversack and some belongings snagged in the rocks on the cliff face.
>
> What appeared to be footmarks were also found in frozen snow at the edge of the cliff.
>
> They reinforced the belief that he may have slipped and fallen into the sea during darkness and bad weather early yesterday morning.
>
> There is no evidence whatever to suggest foul play, and a search for his body is continuing. In view of the strong belief Mr. James must have fallen into the sea, coast guards and all fishing vessels have been asked to keep a lookout for his body.

The local Garda have taken charge of Mr. James's clothing and effects and have asked that his next of kin be traced and informed accordingly.

After the news had been officially reported to London a summary of it was given to the Press Association reporter in Dublin to use as he thought fit. He passed it back to his headquarters in Fleet Street—they lie directly opposite the *Daily Express* building—where it was subedited and put over the tapes to every national newspaper office within minutes.

This was on a night when the newspapers were coping with Princess Anne at a hunt ball with Lieutenant Mark Phillips, more Ugandan Asians flying in, inflation soaring, a new industrial crisis, a sensational sex-murder trail at the Old Bailey, an F.A. Cup semifinal replay, and another moon shot.

Its treatment by subeditors in the offices of all the great dailies was identical.

"Line of agency here about a bloody bird-watcher drowned in Donegal."

"So what? Anything in it?"

"Nothing. 'Foul play not suspected.' "

"Silly old sod. Must have been pissed. Spike it."

Two hands reached out, and the P.A. copy was neatly pierced by a spike, Fleet Street's time-honored way of giving the thumbs-down to a story not worthy of print.

So the passing of Leslie James, an innocent abroad who had walked right into the best story of the day, failed to earn a single line anywhere in the British press.

There was no one to blame.

Newspapers have yet to be furnished with crystal balls.

·10·

Militarily speaking, with its miles of winding green hills the Border that separates Donegal in the Republic of Ireland from Fermanagh, Tyrone, and Londonderry in the Six Counties leaks like a sieve.

Armed terrorists from the South can cross without too much trouble. They do it by night, with only the fox and the owl to see them slip through meadows and down dark lanes, getting around the roadblocks set up to halt the continual traffic.

Here they wage a hit-and-run war very different from the set-piece confrontation in the cities. Their aim is to pin troops down, to draw them away from the towns, to stretch young men already tired to the very limits of fatigue. Their main weapons are stealth and terror.

From time to time they will break into a lonely house, usually of an ex-soldier or local politician, shoot their selected victim in front of his shocked and screaming family, and double back across the Border before the police or Army can arrive on the scene. Since they are small in numbers and outgunned in all departments, they avoid pitched battle with the British soldiers at all costs.

Short of building a "Berlin wall," there is no sure way of stopping them.

At night, and without its helicopter eyes, the British Army is like a blind man trying to prevent a crime. Its main deterrent can only be the mobility and punch of its armored car regiments. Squadrons of Saladins, the British Army's most powerful armored car, form the mailed fist poised to strike intruders. They are lined up at the Border like greyhounds straining at the post, ready to slip between the terrorist and his line of retreat.

Weather is usually no handicap to them. In the northwest of Ireland it rains a great deal, maybe for 250 days of each year, but the winters are normally mild.

This year the winter was unusually severe. Conditions all along the Border were hard and getting worse. Instead of rain there was sleet, then snow, even blizzards. Now frost at night regularly turned every road into a ribbon of ice.

The regiment given the task of patrolling the snowbound roads and Border beyond was the First Seventh Wessex Lancers, the Runners, recently arrived from the Army of the Rhine. Their Saladins were intended to form a curtain of steel, with four squadrons stationed as close to the Border as they could winter. Two of them were barracked together in a small, sleepy town in Tyrone, under the command of Major Richard Welbourne.

Major Welbourne had been only two months in Ulster, but already, along with most of his men, he loathed everything about the province. It was not because of the danger. He regarded sniping and bombing as everyday risks of the soldier's trade. It was not the discomfort of poor messing and makeshift quarters—most young men will take perverse pleasure, even pride, in enduring such minor unpleasantries in the service of their country. It was not boredom or fatigue or even the weather that so depressed him.

What he found utterly hateful was the cruelty shown by Irish to fellow Irish.

Fighting, even civil war, he could understand. But the senseless maiming and slaughter of totally helpless civilians by both sides in the conflict appalled him. He was a kindly man himself and a father, a man who in happier days had spent holidays in the South of Ireland and grown to love the land and its people.

The attitude of the South was one puzzler. He could not comprehend the cynical attitude of a government in Dublin that permitted known terrorists to operate at large and only occasionally administered a reproof with a minimal imprisonment. He found the Six Counties comprising Ulster equally disturbing. The bigotry of the extremist Protestants made him ashamed of his fellow countrymen.

He liked to think of himself as a keeper of the peace, yet each day he found women who would spit upon him and had seen children far younger than his own hurling bricks and epithets at his men.

The rule of law, the creed he had accepted and observed without question all his life, was flouted here every day by civilians who would cheerfully murder him, given the slightest chance, for reasons that he totally failed to grasp. He had come to look upon the Irish as mad. He could not comprehend why men and women and children he was sincerely trying to protect from harm, without prejudice or distinction, should wish him dead.

He came to loathe the lush green counties where there was no way to tell friend from foe until the bullet struck, no alien tongue or style of dress or color of skin to distinguish assassin from ally, and where no provocation was needed for murder other than the physical presence of a British soldier in uniform or mufti.

He knew his own bewilderment and frustration were shared by his men. Every man in the First Seventh—in the whole Ulster garrison—would have cheerfully marched out of Ulster overnight and left the Irish to fight it out among themselves.

Major Welbourne was not a particularly religious man. Church parades on Sunday, carol service during Christmas leave with his children, these were the limits of his open declaration of faith. There was a time when he had been impressed by Irish piety, by the fire-and-brimstone fervor of Northern Protestants just as much as the devotion of Roman Catholics. Now, their religious division sickened him.

He hated service in Ireland as he hated nothing else in eleven years in the Army, and he hated the Ulster Defense Association almost as much as the IRA. But he was a soldier and at all times he knew he must keep his feelings to himself.

The colonel had underlined his faith in him by appointing him commander of the "Ghost Squad," the regiment's main strike force, which had earned its code name because of its stealth and speed of movement. Welbourne commanded both Able and Baker squadrons, and the two messed together in a school damaged at the start of the Troubles in 1969 by incendiary attack. It had been cleared of rubble, its windows bagged and barred, the roof reinforced with concrete and turned into an observation post. There were bunks in each classroom, and machine guns guarded the playground where a line of Saladins stood, ever ready. A troop of light antiaircraft gunners, temporarily soldiering as infantry, was attached to the force.

The officers' mess had once been the faculty common room. Fittings were Spartan—coconut matting on the floor, trestle tables, wooden chairs, an original Giles cartoon on the wall alongside public orders, and security warnings. A pile of newspapers stood on a card table in one corner. There was a permanent draft and an air, somehow, of poverty. The Runners had nicknamed it "Bleak House."

In this bitter March weather a coal fire burned day and night in the common room. In a smaller, adjoining room, once the headmaster's study, Welbourne's signals officer and two troopers maintained twenty-four-hour radio contact with all vehicles out on patrol.

It was evening, and drinks were being served by the mess sergeant. A handful of subalterns stood chatting around the fire, sipping their first Scotch of the day (they were permitted a maximum of two per man, on duty). The door to the signals room was open, as always, and the officers fell silent as they heard a voice come crackling through.

"Baker Two to X-Ray, over."

"X-Ray to Baker Two. Come in, over."

"Heavy automatic fire reported from Customs post at Red One," said the voice, giving a map reference which a sergeant promptly ringed in fire red on the huge wall map. Welbourne walked across to have a look.

Red One was an outpost, completely exposed and therefore manned each night by six men of the Royal Ulster Constabulary as well as the two resident Customs officers. It came under fire regularly. Its stone walls boasted an outer skin of sandbags that turned it into a small fortress. As it happened, it lay in an area the Ghost Squad had reconnoitered that afternoon, and for a specific reason.

To the west of the post ran a track that Welbourne had discovered just that morning. Sheltered for much of the way by high, sloping banks, it led past a stone bridge right down to the Border itself. Welbourne realized he had found a terrorist route. The Runners could use it just as effectively as the terrorists had. They could send in their Saladins to cut off any IRA groups who tried to storm the Customs post, for example.

The reconnaissance Welbourne had ordered that afternoon had been necessary to ensure that the route was not mined. It was as if he had had a premonition of tonight's attack.

"X-Ray to Baker One and Baker Two. Move up to Red One ready to give close support, await my orders, over and out," Welbourne ordered. Then he ran up to the roof of the school and watched the intermittent flashes from IRA gunfire through binoculars. An armed sentry stood close to him.

"Look, sir," said the sentry. "Fresh firing coming from over there. Looks as if there's another lot working its way behind the post." As he pointed, an orange-red trail of fire climbed and fell in the night sky with that deceptive slowness of tracer mixed with ball ammunition.

A few days earlier, unknown to his fellow officers, Welbourne had been called in to a top-secret conference. All senior officers and all commanders on detachment had been summoned to the briefing.

A full colonel, chief of staff to the Londonderry brigade, addressed them. "I'll make it as brief as possible, gentlemen," he began. "I know only too well how busy you all are. I want you to know I am here on direct orders of the GOC himself. He has instructed me to warn you on pain of court-martial that the information I am about to give you must on no account be made known outside this room. No gossip, no inside tips to friends, and above all no hint of any kind to the press.

"Recently we obtained photographic evidence of direct Russian intervention in the terrorist war. We hold pictures of a Soviet submarine at rendezvous with an Irish fishing smack close in to the Donegal coast.

"We imagine it was delivering arms of some sort, but we don't know for sure. The IRA has been getting guns from overseas in many ways for long enough, but not hitherto by direct delivery from a Russian warship. All of which makes the GOC very curious indeed about that sub.

"What cargo did she carry? What sort of weapons were they? Did she perchance land any Russian agents as well as guns and ammunition? We want to know and we intend to find out one way or another, but the point is—we don't want the other side to know that we're on to them. The whole thing is being kept dark at this time for political reasons.

"Now, this is where you come in, gentlemen. We want all units to keep an especially tight watch along the Border. If need be, your standing patrols will be doubled and trebled until we find out what we need to know. Whenever possible in the next few days try to bring in IRA suspects for special questioning. Don't attempt interrogation at unit level. Let our intelligence bods get their hands on them and use a little friendly persuasion.

"So, if without jeopardizing security you get the chance to tempt some flies into the spider's web rather than swatting them, seize it. We want 'em alive and kicking, remember. Give some to me, and it will constitute a very big feather in your regiment's cap—not to mention the brigadier's and the general's. Go to it. And good luck."

After the briefing was over, the commander of the Runners, Colonel Allen, took him aside for a few words.

"My God, Dickie," he said, "but you're a lucky blighter. You should have a splendid chance of nabbing a few odds and sods in your country areas, what?

"Those wide-open spaces behind Bleak House are made to measure for old-style cavalry action. Let 'em in, get behind 'em, and cut off their lines of retreat before mopping up. That's if they move out at all in this weather. God, it's unseasonable, this cold! The weather boys say it's the coldest March spell in Irish history. Still, do what you can, Dickie."

Welbourne could hear the colonel's clipped tones in his head, as he peered into the exploding night. Now the IRA *had* moved, and they were out in the "wide-open spaces." It was his chance. He ran down the stairs to his signals room, calling for his second in command, Captain James Gideon.

"Gather around, the rest of you," Welbourne said to the officers in the common room. He pointed to the wall map. "Now look at this. They are attacking in two columns it seems, here—and here."

He looked around at his officers.

"You don't need to be reminded of anything I said when we reconnoitered that area this afternoon. Using that track we can get behind anyone attacking the post. Here's our chance. Jim, take Able squadron down the track. I'll take the rest of Baker and pretend I'm backing up Baker One and Baker Two for a frontal assault.

"I want you down that hidden track like greased lightning, to cut the buggers off before they can fall back over the Border. Take the gunners with you and put 'em out like ferrets after rabbits as soon as you get clear of the track itself. Remember, everyone, I want live prisoners—not, repeat not, dead bodies. All right, Runners—move!"

Any junior officer who blindly follows orders laid down from above is taking a big risk. If all goes well, then it's his colonel who gets the pat on the back—or maybe a medal. But if it's a snafu, then it's the junior who carries the can. Welbourne knew this. But he felt supremely confident. The track had been reconnoitered just that afternoon and found to be clear of all mines and booby traps.

He also had absolute faith in his armor. He had nothing to fear from the rifles and machine guns firing on the Customs post. His men were razor sharp. All his planning was based on the premise that the IRA would never—did not dare—fight a pitched battle with professional soldiers in open country.

Even allowing for all these reasons, he might as well have been hypnotized, so faithfully and predictably and quickly did he follow the exact pattern worked out for him by Kelly only a few hours earlier.

· 11 ·

Kelly was very conscious of his limitations as a field commander facing British troops in Northern Ireland. The men he had to command could never hope to match regular soldiers in training, discipline, or fitness. Even with an advantage in weapons, which the Russian arms gave them, they could never have the confidence in each other that only seasoned troops enjoy and on which is decided the fate of so many battles. Whatever action he planned, using the new weapons, he and his men would be heavily out-numbered as well; in the pit of his stomach, during those days at the hotel with Liam, Kelly felt the fear of defeat.

Liam and Ryan introduced him to the Donegal brigade exactly a week after his arrival at Shannon. The brigade numbered forty men ranging in age from eighteen to the midforties. Liam was the oldest among them and Michael, the boy he had first seen with Ryan that night in the hotel, was the youngest. Many of them, like Liam, were family men, but to Kelly they were all just untrained yokels he was supposed to whip into some kind of fighting force in a matter of days.

"We need something from you pretty quick, Mr. Kelly," Liam had told him at the hotel. "There are quite a few members who don't like the thought of you at all, as it is. The sooner you prove to us you're worth your weight, the better for you and for us."

"What kind of money are you talking about?" Kelly had growled back. "When I hear a sum mentioned I get all kinds of ideas. Until then my mind's a blank."

"Let us worry about paying you. I promise you you won't be disappointed. Just see that we're not."

Despite himself, Kelly felt a cold chill listening to the small, mild-faced man. That very afternoon, after they'd come in from a long day's fishing, Kelly was sitting in the bar when he overheard

69

a pair of locals discussing the outpost the Runners called Red One.

"I used to court out there by the old Customs house near the Border," said one old codger to another slighter younger man with the beaten red face of a farmer. "But these days, nowhere's safe. I was walking around there today, recollecting, and a British Army officer sticks a gun in my back and asks me all kinds of questions. Seems they're using the place now as an outpost, to keep an eye on the Border. Bloody British bastards, a lot of good that'll do. They'll not stop our lads from crossing that Border in a thousand years!"

Kelly thought he had the beginnings of a plan, a plan that would surely cause both the British and his employers to sit up and take notice. That night he got from Liam more details about the outpost; he even learned about the hidden track, often used by the Martyrs and other IRA groups to cross the Border. It only took Kelly one visit to the site and a few hours spent in studying the movements of the British soldiers in and around the outpost to formulate the entire plan.

The next day he met with the brigade to start instruction in the use of the new weapons. Before they began their exercises on the cold and lonely mountain training ground, Kelly outlined what he had in mind.

"For the first time in this war you've got a chance against the British Army's armored car, the Saladin. These weapons we've got here are completely new to the British Army. If we can corner them we can do a lot of damage. An ambush is what we need, and an ambush is what I'll get for you. You all know the old post on the Border?"

There were nods all around, and a young man called out, "And the track that gets you past it."

Kelly's voice broke through the laughter like an ax chopping down a tree. "You got my meaning. But have you thought of this? The Army's bound to find it sooner or later. They probably already have. Knowing the way they think, they probably figure they can use it themselves to get behind anybody attacking the outpost, as I understand a few of you do now and then, for the exercise." There were roars of laughter and whistles at that dig. Despite Kelly's tough, impassive manner, he knew how to handle men, or at least men who wanted to believe they were soldiers.

"And that's where we and the new toys we've got here come into it."

Ryan, grinning like a Leprechaun, understood what Kelly was driving at and spelled it out for the rest.

70

"You mean we take our 'exercise' as you call it, and when the soldiers come charging around the back, thinking they're fox-smart, we're there waiting for them with our shiny new toys?"

"Ryan, you just look dumb," said Kelly. "Don't he now? Like all us Irishmen."

Kelly worked the men hard, explaining, demonstrating, yelling, for up to ten hours at a stretch. Whatever else his Irishmen lacked, it was not enthusiasm. They hung on every word and toiled with all their strength to master the weapons and the plan Kelly had conceived for them.

The cargo delivered by Captain Leonovitch had been in two parts—rocket launchers with their grenades and a consignment of mines.

The T-52 land mine is shaped like a compact and is roughly the same size. It measures 18 inches in diameter, is 4 to 5 inches deep at the center, and weighs 8.7 kilograms, or 20 pounds. It is armed by a simple device. Any guerrilla fighter can site one in seconds in almost any terrain.

The T-52 is quite something as mines go. It will explode instantaneously on pressure. It is also waterproof. Thus, a resolute man can lay one, say, in a tumbling stream, arm it by removing the pin, and confidently leave it to sit there for as long as his war will last.

There was one possible flaw, and in the days of training Kelly spoke about it at length to his yokel army.

"An ordinary vehicle, like a car, will just about disintegrate with the blast from one of these mines," he said. "But those Saladins are built to take punishment. They can lose two wheels and still move around, firing back at you on the four that are left.

"So we have to hit them with the rockets and hit them fast, as soon as those mines go off. And I want every other weapon to open up on them at the same time. To do that, you need light.

"I'll turn the whole bloody place into daylight for you!

"First, there will be the flash as the mine explodes. It won't affect the man firing the rocket launcher, because he has the gunsight protecting his eye. It will dazzle all the rest of you for a second, though. Be ready for that.

"Now, I want every rocketeer to fire, and I want every other son of a bitch not actually loading to bang away with rifles and machine guns. I will give you the light for that sustained fire by fixing an incendiary attachment to each mine.

"This is how I'll do it. I'll run a fuse from the mine out onto the bank—the side away from us, so that the men and vehicles in the lane will be silhouetted as the flares burn. They burn for five minutes, by the way, and they won't be affected by snow or even water. Each incendiary is fitted with a safety fuse, and the heat it generates keeps it alight.

"The track we're going to mine is about twelve feet wide. Those armored cars, I guess, are seven feet wide. That leaves two and a half, maybe three feet on either side we have to mine. I'll put three mines on each side of the lane, there. They will be connected with a fuse instantaneous to the flare—the spark travels so fast along it that it will set off the flare before the fuse is shattered by the cratering of the road caused by the mine. You get me?

"You'll be like an audience in a theater, chucking stuff at the actors onstage—with the lights turned full on! You can't miss!"

When he had first opened the cache Kelly had found it easy to overcome the newness and strangeness of the weapons. The Russians, accustomed to problems of supply in foreign lands, had sent printed instructions in English and diagrams with both rocket launchers (known as RPG-7's) and mines. Kelly found he could instruct and train the same morning.

Since they are rocket-powered, the RPG-7s are recoilless. The gunner kneels down, rests the three-foot-long barrel on his shoulder, and takes aim through a telescopic sight. As there is no recoil, no kickback, he just rests the gunsight against his forehead.

The rocket launcher has a genuine half-mile range and is capable of holing a tank, never mind a thin-skinned armored car.

Escaping gases flame out behind, through a blunderbuss-shaped exhaust. The grenade fits right through the barrel, with the fins closed and extending beyond the exhaust. The fins open after the grenade has been fired and passed through the barrel, to control the line of flight. It is an immensely accurate and lethal weapon.

Kelly reckoned they could hope for at most two rounds from each RPG-7 before the weight and accuracy of the returning fire overwhelmed them. He planned to take along six, keeping the rest for another day.

The Russians had thoughtfully included a number of practice grenades for training. Kelly blessed them for their foresight and used an old quarry for firing practice.

After five days of training he had a reasonably competent squad. Not up to Soviet Army standards, but competent enough.

But just when he could tell the men were getting confident, *too* confident, he told them, their training was still incomplete.

"Remember," he warned them, "you are going to be firing at night.

"You'll find everything is different in the dark. Your hands have got to know what to do without orders from the brain. Any man who cheats on training will make mistakes. One mistake against those British soldiers and you're dead. So get it right now. Remember it. You won't get a second chance.

"I will fire one practice round on every RPG-7 to zero in it for you. Then it's your turn. And listen to me good, you've got to know your misfire drill. We can't afford any panic stations over a misfire when the shit hits the fan.

"Misfire! Okay, what do you do?

"*One*, check that launcher. *Two*, gunner—take your bloody hand off the trigger and tell the other man it is clear! Now then, Number Two, take the grenade out and lay it down carefully. Careful, I said! Don't bang it down like a shillelagh, you goddamned prick. If it gets jarred now you've both had it! Take your time. Lay it down real slow. Now you're getting it. Okay. One more time, everybody. Misfire!"

He made each two-man team repeat the drill ten, twenty, thirty times until they swore in frustration and he was satisfied.

He explained a lot more things to the forty Irish freedom fighters. Where the loader should lie, for example.

"The flash of that exhaust can damn near blind a man at night. Lie too close and you won't be able to see a thing for the next five minutes. That's time enough to get yourself killed. So *stay clear.*"

He called them around him and told them how the RPG-7 works.

"When you press the trigger, the rocket zooms away with a bloody great *whooooosh!* trailing a long tail of flame behind it like a comet.

"When it hits the target it makes a tiny hole, so small you'd be surprised—about an inch in diameter, that's all. In the nose it carries a crush-sensitive fuse that sets off the main detonator below.

"As it hits, the head of the rocket turns into a molten slug that penetrates the armored skin of the Saladin. Then it chips off tiny fragments of steel that buzz around inside like angry hornets.

"The poor buggers who get in the way die the death of a thousand cuts.

"That's all there is to see from the outside afterward—two tiny

73

holes where the slug goes in and comes out. But inside, Jesus! It will be like a butcher's shop at Christmas time, I promise you.

"They haven't made an armored car yet that can stand up to these babies.

"One point to remember—don't be disappointed when you fire the practice rounds. They're just rockets to train with, a different thing altogether.

"With practice rounds there will be no explosion on impact. They travel at a much reduced speed—four hundred fifty feet a second. Don't let that worry you. Just use your eyes and your heads, take your time, and *zap!* You've got one. Watch me show you how."

He went from launcher to launcher lined up on the targets and let fly. Finally he was satisfied.

"Okay," he said. "Your turn!"

In the week since the bird-watcher had been shot, he had been kept outside, hidden close to the inn where Kelly and Liam were staying, and his body was stiff as a board. One day during their training in the mountains Kelly showed the Irishmen how to turn the old man's body into a booby trap.

Ryan was one of the men who preferred not to watch. He'd never fooled around much with dead bodies and he wasn't going to start now. Anyway, he figured he knew already how to wire up a stiff. Get some explosive hidden on him, hook it up to a detonator that'd go if anybody touched it, and *wham!* Ryan slammed one big fist into his palm. But he didn't stay around Kelly.

At the edge of their camp in the mountains he came across Liam, who was also passing up the mercenary's demonstration. He'd hated Liam when the old man had bawled him out in front of Kelly, for fouling up the arms pickup, but the days in the mountains had changed all that. The old man had pitched into every exercise with all the enthusiasms of a man twenty years younger. He had given this group of men the lift it needed. Much as Ryan and the rest of them respected Kelly's experience, they could never like a man who sold his skills to the highest bidder. In the long, hard days, despite Kelly's expertise in handling both arms and men, there might have been trouble—if it hadn't been for Liam. Some of the younger men in particular figured they knew as much as Kelly and felt badly that he was the leader of this Irish striking force. But Liam talked to them and made them see how invaluable Kelly was.

"Look at it this way, lads. Kelly's like what the Russians sent us, a new kind of weapon. If we're going to win, we've got to use him.

Remember, he may be the weapon, but we pull the trigger. He knows that, and you should, too. Learn everything you can from him, and we won't need him anymore. Until then, jump lively!"

"Not going soft are you, Liam?" said Ryan, his voice low and friendly.

"My official position is that there are some things only the younger men should know about," said the small man. He was smoking his pipe as he looked out over the rolling hills.

"That Kelly could use a few drops of the fountain of youth himself," said Ryan.

"A man like that has no age. When his luck runs out he dies—like an animal."

"You sound angry, Liam. Could you be regretting having Mr. Kelly along in the first place?"

"I could *not*. But when you live with a man every day for two weeks you learn some things, things you may wish you didn't know."

"What kind of things?"

But their conversation was interrupted by the group around Kelly breaking up, and Liam never answered Ryan's question.

· 12 ·

After the Donegal brigade had finished a full week of training, Kelly moved it out of the mountains and to a camp only an hour's walk from the site of the ambush, ready to go into action. A ruined farmhouse gave them some shelter, but they'd been living in Spartan conditions for ten days now, and tempers were getting frayed.

"Not too long now, lads," Liam told them. Kelly gave them time-consuming tasks like taking apart their weapons and putting them back together again, while he went out with a guide to scout the Customs house.

Kelly was waiting for the British troops to find the pass. Every day he lay on the wet ground watching the troop movements. Two days passed. On the third day, with rising excitement, he saw Welbourne's men discover the track, and in the afternoon of the same day, return to reconnoiter it for mines. Kelly found himself grinning from relief as much as anything else as he watched them through his binoculars.

He was still wearing the grin when he got back to the farmhouse.

"It's all set," he told Liam. The rest of them quickly gathered around.

"When do we leave?" said Ryan, catching Kelly's grin.

"In two hours."

Kelly looked around the forty faces. Young and old they were lit with that exhilaration close to hysteria that hits any man about to go into battle. To him, whatever their Cause, they were just soldiers, men he had to lead. In a few minutes he would take on total responsibility, not only for their lives, but for the mission's success.

76

"You've got excellent weapons now," he began in a monotone. "Any army in the world would be proud of them. The trick is not to give yourself away. Don't shoot until I give the order.

"You're up against professionals, remember that. Men who've spent years in training. Men who won't allow you a second chance.

"We've got better arms, sure, guns they've never seen before. But those seventy-eight-millimeter guns on their Saladins are deadly, too, and they outrange our guns by miles. Those armored cars are fast, too. They can reach forty-five miles an hour. If they get away from us and fan out, we've had it. You'll never see Dublin again.

"So, before you shoot, wait. Wait until I've stopped them for you with the land mines and lit them up with the flares. Then you're in business.

"But first we have to do two things—get them in the trap and slow them down."

"How many are they going to be?" asked Michael.

"One hundred men and six Saladins, I would guess. Let's just say enough to do us damage if they catch us in the open field.

"All right, Liam, you know pretty much what to do. But once you get your men in position above the Customs post, the trick is to know exactly when to pull out.

"Your two Bren guns situated below the post will open up at nine o'clock on the button. Keep up your firing in spurts, sighting on any chink of light you can see.

"Ten minutes later your other two guns will open up from above the post. As soon as you hear the land mines go off, which will be I would guess fifteen to twenty minutes later, all your men must pick up the guns and start running back across the Border.

"I'm figuring once the Army has spotted your gun positions it will try to wheel behind you, which will take a little time.

"I shall be on the other side of the track, here." He pointed out the spot on the map spread out before him. "I watched the troops sweep that track this afternoon. They came right through, from the front, and around toward the post, checking the ground with mine detectors. My guess is that they will assume that line of attack is clear tonight. They will not even consider that the track could be mined that fast. But that's of course exactly where our mines'll be.

"Here, where a stream crosses the track, about a hundred yards in, I will site three mines on each side fitted with incendiary devices. The first Saladin to hit one will light everything up.

"Because the track curves at that point, with luck, the cars

77

behind won't be certain what's happening and will keep coming, making a hell of a traffic jam. That's when we hit them with our rockets firing from above and from the side of the track, here and here.

"The track is so narrow that the cars can't turn around. We'll have time for two rounds from the rockets. Then we'll clear out, fast."

Liam looked doubtful, the only somber face in that delighted crew.

"What happens if the armored cars don't go into that lane? Supposing they head straight for us, or go around the other side of the post, and you don't get a chance to fire at all?"

Kelly's laugh set the rest of them off as well.

"In that case, Liam," he said, "you're in for a bloody long crosscountry run!"

It was almost dark now.

The brigade moved out in single file, each man's face darkened with mud. Kelly's squad was in the lead, followed by Liam and his men carrying their Bren guns. The mercenary moved lightly, shouldering his heavy pack with ease, peering into the darkness, occasionally whispering last-minute instructions to Liam or Ryan.

When they reached a point about a half mile before the Customs house, Kelly and Ryan, carrying the bird-watcher's corpse, left the men with the mines and rocket launchers and along with Liam and his squad headed east around the Customs post. Kelly and Ryan laid the corpse on a route they knew Welbourne's troops had to follow when they came to relieve the post. They then ran back to their men, who had been waiting in the growing cold, stamping their feet and trying not to lose courage.

"Pull yourselves together," Kelly whispered fiercely to the Irishmen. "Remember, the bastards won't know what hit 'em. One last thing—when you've fired your rockets don't drop the launchers. Get out fast, head to the place agreed upon. All right, let's go!"

Liam lay on his stomach on a ridge overlooking the Customs post, looking at the minute hand on his watch creep toward nine o'clock. For the first time since he'd joined the IRA twenty years before, he felt what he had always imagined his father and grandfather before him had felt when they were fighting the British face-to-face, army against army. He was about to go into battle, not against Protestants, but agasint the force that had ruled Ireland all these years, the British Army. A gentle man by nature, he was realizing tonight one of his strongest and longest-held passions. To deal a significant blow to the British Imperial Presence. And despite himself he couldn't help feeling, in those minutes before nine, grateful to the hatchet-faced mercenary who had made it possible.

· 13 ·

Major Welbourne halted the column from Baker squadron a hundred yards north of the road junction. The sergeant in the leading vehicle had reported a body in the snow. He ran forward with his orderly by his side, resenting every lost second.

When he came in sight of the body he motioned the orderly to stop. "Wait," he said. Cautiously, he approached the body, sure that snipers would have the body covered. But it was dark enough to take a chance. He could hear the drumming of the Bren guns a mile to his right.

"Cover me," he ordered. Bent double, pistol in hand, he inched up to the figure in the snow. The body wore an Army uniform and what appeared to be badges of rank on the epaulettes and was covered with a fine layer of snow. There were no marks, no sign of footprints in the snow, but Welbourne was an old hand—he could smell a booby trap a mile away. What baffled him was that still no hidden sniper had opened fire through his night sights.

The firing continued heavy from the post, and Welbourne knew if he wasted time he would lose his quarry. He and the orderly ran back to the waiting column. Welbourne climbed up on the leading Saladin and spoke to Captain Gideon, who was listening to the radio.

"Jim." Gideon took off his headphones. "Jim. There's a stiff on the road. One of ours by the look of it, but I'll lay a fiver it's booby-trapped. Can't waste time on it now—I'll radio a general warning to keep clear and take a closer look myself in the morning. Right now we have to go for the post.

"I estimate there must be two Brens, maybe three, with the main attacking force. They've got to be at least a mile inside Red One, and I want you to grab the bloody lot.

"Stick to the plan. I'll head for the post itself, not too fast and advertising my presence. That should give you all the time you need. You take that track to the left, through the stream, and get around behind them.

"Once you're in the open go hell for leather, and we'll net the lot between us. Remember, I want as many as possible all alive-oh! Good luck, chum." He jumped down from the car and ran back to his Land Rover.

The column split into two. Welbourne headed slowly for the Customs building, with his orders crackling over the radio. Captain James Gideon led his eight cars through the snow straight into the mouth of the track—a total of sixty-five tons of steel thrusting down on sixty-four vulnerable wheels and mountings.

"Keep closed up," Gideon ordered. "Don't break till we hit the open country. Gunners, dismount at will. You have your orders, don't shoot to kill—the major wants prisoners. Tallyho!"

Each Saladin carried a 76-millimeter heavy gun, with forty-two rounds to give it authority. In addition there were two 7.62 machine guns. The Saladin had a crew of three—commander (who also acted as loader for the big gun), gunner, and driver.

The Saladin is like an armored greyhound. It is powered by an 8-cylinder Rolls-Royce engine and races along on six huge wheels that can take plow, stubble, mud, or good macadam in their stride.

Sandwiched between the Saladins came Saracens—10-ton armored personnel carriers packed with gunners for the foray. Each one carried commander and driver, plus eight more soldiers armed with FN automatic rifles and weighted clubs and one man operating a .3 Browning light machine gun. All were secure from sniper fire inside the belly of their six-wheeled suit of armor.

It was a formidable force and rumbled down the track like a line of deadly beetles.

Kelly and his band had been lying in wait for them for almost an hour, soaked in mud and wet snow, shaking with cold and tension, and all too aware of what would happen if the ambush failed and the armored cars caught them with their machine guns in the open fields. But now he had them.

Gideon's armored car led the way into the track and set off a T-52 mine as soon as its front wheels splashed into the foot-deep stream. A brilliant white flash seared the sky and was followed by another deep-red glow that hissed and bubbled from beneath the melting snow.

The blast of the mine ripped one wheel off and damaged two more, slewing the Saladin around and hurling it onto its side. Gid-

81

eon himself was stunned. His gunner had his head gashed open and was momentarily blinded by the flash. The driver was killed outright. The whole track was blocked.

Two more armored cars, with a Saracen in between, were trapped behind the leading car, unable to turn, unable to back, exposed like strippers in a Soho club by the light of the incendiary touched off by Gideon's vehicle. A fourth Saladin managed to inch back down the track as its gunner sought the unseen enemy.

"Fire," Kelly screamed from his position at the side of the track, and a ragged, flaming broadside hit the armored column. Six rockets tore through the night, each trailing a gilttering red tail as they struck home.

Before the Fenians could reload, the British machine gunners began firing back. The noise was deafening.

"Fire," Kelly shouted again, but could not tell if his men heard him. One of the rocket teams had a misfire.

Kelly himself fired his second rocket. So did at least two more teams. Then they panicked, turned, and fled for their lives, shouting with terror as machine gun after machine gun hammered and flailed their position.

But it was going to be a night when everything went their way.

Just when they turned to run, with the gunners coming right behind, it started snowing thick and hard. The flaming incendiaries turned the flakes into a whirling, pink blizzard that blinded and hampered the pursuing troops.

Machine gunners in the armored cars were ordered to cease fire, in case they hit their own men as the gunners stumbled and slipped in the snow.

Kelly ran like a stag with the hounds after him. He could see nothing to guide him, he just ran. After a while he came on three of his men jogging Indian file ahead of him, gasping for breath. They were drunk with gunfire and fear.

"Shut up and keep running," he ordered them. "If those armored cars get up here among us now—" and left the rest unsaid. He forced them to keep on, slipping, sliding, cursing, close now to the guideline of a single white hedgerow.

There he found the others. They were doubled over, spent, and hopelessly ill-disciplined. He sensed they had left their wits way behind—on the ridge where they had gone into action. Kelly recognized the bull shape of Ryan and shook him hard.

"Which way?" he said. "Which way, man, to the trucks?"

Ryan shook his head, thought for a moment, and then pointed left. "There," he croaked. "Over the rise."

"All right," said Kelly. "On your feet, all of you. Follow Ryan and keep closed up—and for Christ's sake, move fast and quiet. I'll bring up the rear. If anyone drops out, too bad. They'll be on us in no time."

The Irish scarecrows got to their feet and ran. For the first time Kelly discovered his left hand had been clamped like a vise on the hot steel barrel of the rocket launcher. His fingers had no sensation of pain. He felt lightheaded and shook his head, forcing scrambled brains to work out the next move.

He followed the others across a road, through a stream, over more white fields. They came to a rise and heard Liam's voice, low and urgent, calling to them, counting them in one by one.

Liam seized Kelly's hand and pumped it. "All back," he said. "Thank God for that."

Kelly nodded. For some moments he had no breath to spare for words. Finally he answered.

"Liam," he ordered. "No hanging about. Put Ryan and the others into the big lorry and tell them to beat it for home, fast as they can make it. They can leave the weapons with us. Quick, now."

Liam ran along the line of exhausted men, clapping each one on the shoulder, passing on instructions.

"Well done, lads," he said. "Ah, you've done wonders this night, so you have! Split up when you get back, you all know what to do. Straight indoors and lie low. Every man back to work tomorrow as usual. No celebrating and no loose talking in the pubs. I'll be in touch as soon as I can."

He bolted the tailboard as the last man climbed in and watched the lorry drive away, lights dimmed, skidding in the wet snow.

He turned to Kelly, obviously aching to talk. The big man ignored him, reached for his knapsack in the cab of the small van, and pulled out a bottle of whiskey. He tipped it to his lips and swallowed a huge draft.

"Christ," he said, "but I needed that!"

The odds against a clean sweep were huge, but in the blizzard the Irishmen managed to make off without losing a single man wounded, dead, or captured. They did abandon two of the RPG-7s and some missiles. One of the rocket launchers lost was the one that had misfired.

Army losses were comparatively heavy.

Two Saladins wrecked—one, Captain Gideon's, by a land mine, another by a direct hit from a rocket. A Saracen packed with troops had received another direct hit from an RPG-7.

Five soldiers were killed outright and four others mortally wounded in the the ambushed column. Two more were killed in the pursuit by wild bursts of machine-gun fire laid down by Kelly's men to cover their retreat.

The booby-trapped body of Leslie James claimed one more dead. Thinking him a comrade shot in the ambush, a gunner who had lost his direction in the blizzard tried to drag it to safety.

There was a loud *bang,* and both bodies disintegrated.

Welbourne's own detachment escaped without loss. They searched every square foot of ground down to the post and right up to the Border and came back to the battleground without having caught one glimpse of the terrorists.

·14·

The snow lay thick and white in that desolate patch of country in Donegal close to the Irish Border where Liam had hidden the trucks. It had quickly covered up the tracks of the vehicles carrying the Donegal brigade back to home and family and now shrouded the two that were left, as they sat motionless and unspeaking, contemplating in their different ways the victory over the British Army that had just been accomplished.

Kelly drank most of the bottle of whiskey before he could manage to speak. The fear that had gripped his belly for the last week had finally disappeared with the success of the ambush. Objectively, he might have concluded that they had been lucky, very lucky, but at the moment, with the liquor racing to his head, he preferred not to think at all.

Liam on the other hand was making all kinds of plans. Excited and thrilled by this, his group's first major engagement, he imagined a series of successful raids on the British forces, with Kelly at their head and using the modern Russian weapons, which would turn the war right around, at least in this section of the Six Counties. Kelly's gruff voice interrupted his reverie.

"Better get this stuff out of the snow," Kelly said, and began to gather up the weapons and ammunition and put them in the back of the truck. Liam immediately stooped to help him. Liam was enough of a sentimentalist to imagine Kelly wasn't as tough as he seemed.

After they had heaped the weapons and the soaking uniforms on the floor of the van, they covered them with a tarpaulin, and slammed the doors shut. Kelly took out a flashlight and shielded its light as he checked the ground for anything they might have missed. All clear.

"Right," he said. "Let's get moving."

Liam drove and spoke first. "I'll head for the farm," he said. "You keep out of sight. The fewer people who see you the better. With luck we can be back at the hotel before daylight."

"Okay," Kelly told him, hunching down.

They traveled some miles in silence. Dogs barked as they drew into a farmyard. A window opened, and a man's head poked out. He saw the van and minutes later walked silently up to it.

"Is that you, Liam?"

"It is. We've got to work fast. You'll have the entire Irish Army nosing around soon. Make sure your family keeps their mouths shut, now."

"Ah, Liam, there's no need to talk like that. They'll get more from the cows themselves than any member of my family, and well you know it. Drive over to the barn."

They unloaded at top speed. The farmer's cache was simple but effective. Two loose boxes stood by the side of the barn, with a horse in each.

In each box a narrow feed trough ran the length of the wall.

The farmer went into the first box and knelt down to prise away a plank that ran below the trough, revealing a false bottom. He cleared the straw and lifted two more wide planks. They wrapped the uniforms around each RPG-7 and stowed them carefully away. Then the grenades and finally all the small arms. The tarpaulin was spread over all. The planks were replaced, the straw relaid, and the horse led back. The whole operation took less than twenty minutes.

"Pretty neat, eh, Liam?" grinned the old farmer. "She'll be foaling soon, and no Irish officer worth his salt will disturb her too much. They'll not find a thing."

They shook hands warmly and Liam walked back to the van and drove off at once. He and Kelly were completely exhausted.

"We'll get at least one hour in bed before daylight," he promised. "I'll call you, and we'll go straight out fishing before the village is properly awake. I think that's the safest way."

Kelly nodded.

Liam glanced at him and said, "You did well tonight, by God. I don't know what the damage was, but from where we were it looked like a volcano down there by the stream. And the shooting! I thought half our lads must have been killed. I couldn't believe it when we counted them all in."

"We had a lot of luck," said Kelly. "And so did you. They came right into our trap. If they'd come straight at you instead, and got those armored cars moving in open country, I doubt very much if you would be sitting here now.

"If I hadn't twisted Ryan's arm, the whole bloody lot would have sat there till the soldiers picked them up."

Kelly took another drink from the bottle.

"You and me, we'd better think of pulling out of here soon," he said. "The men know how to use those rockets now. Ryan can take over, or you can distribute them to other units, that's your affair. But I can't see the British even being caught like that again.

"I'm going to lie low and think up something new, an operation in a different part of the country. Keep moving around. We'll live longer that way. What do you say?"

"I'll have to take advice on that," said Liam cautiously. "But I agree on the dangers of hanging around too long. Let's fish for one more day at least."

It was still dark when they reached the hotel. They had not seen a single vehicle en route. They let themselves in and went quietly to bed.

Neither man could sleep in the hour left to them.

Kelly felt his old wounds ache and throb as he lay in the warm bed and thought back on the night. It had gone better than he had dared hope. The machine guns should have slaughtered them. His mind began to race—it was as though the soldiers had been trying not to fight back, but to encircle Liam's men, until it was too late.

He wondered why. Obvious—they wanted prisoners. Even more obvious to Kelly was the realization the submarine must have been seen and identified and the Army alerted, waiting for them to show their hand with whatever weapons had arrived.

There would be a tremendous rumpus now that the attempt to take prisoners had failed—and ended in defeat.

Along the corridor Liam, too, lay awake, but for different reasons. He was delighted that his old body had come through the night so well. He felt in his bones they had scored a considerable victory over superior forces and he was proud to have played a part.

He could not wait for the radio news in the morning, telling him what damage and casualties they had inflicted on the Imperial Presence.

He tossed and turned and yearned for daylight to come.

·15·

For discipline, restraint, and compassion shown daily under the most testing circumstances, the British Army in Ulster has no equal in the military world.

It finds itself in the craziest situations. Its men find themselves guarding IRA terrorist processions and UDA terrorist demonstrations. All year round, British soldiers hunt down snipers in both Protestant and Roman Catholic communities, and kill some. On Christmas Day they·play Santa Claus to orphaned kids of both denominations.

There is nothing special about this Army. Sometimes it acts cleverly, occasionally it makes mistakes—like everyone else. Its ranks contain the same mixture of brave and weak, sensible and foolish, clever and dull, honest and dishonest people you find in every community.

Its strength lies in something called tradition.

Once in a while, the Army in Ulster gets a pat on the back. Sometimes its behavior draws heavy criticism, even judicial inquiry, for example, if it should dare to fire real bullets instead of rubber ones. Often it is the victim of clever and inspired propaganda designed to spread doubt at home and hatred among those it is trying so doggedly to protect.

Only one thing is certain—its good deeds are quickly forgotten while its errors bring maximum, and lasting, publicity.

Major Welbourne had no doubt he would be whipping boy for the defeat in Tyrone. Mistakes had been made, and they would bring huge publicity. But being a soldier leaves no room for self-pity, at least not until later—everything must be done by the book, as much in the aftermath of defeat as in preparation for battle.

The book says the first thing every British soldier in Ulster must do when he finds a bomb, any weapon or cache of ammunition, any building or thing that might be booby-trapped, any suspiciously parked car, is—send for "Felix."

Felix is the code name for the unsung heroes of the 123rd EOD (Explosive Ordnance Disposal) unit of the Royal Army Ordnance Corps, a handful of men who spend their entire service in Northern Ireland a hairbreadth away from eternity.

They were christened "Felix" because a cat is said to have nine lives. In this unit the men need every one.

Only the very best, an elite, serve in Felix, a few officers, senior warrant officers, and NCOs, with some specialist drivers and technicians. Each wears a badge on his arm. It is a burning grenade (irreverently known in the trade as "The Flaming Arsehole") and constitutes a most coveted honor. They are the bomb doctors of Ulster, and of all the world's great heroes there are few who can compare with these for bravery of the coolest kind.

They are commanded by an amiable, unconventional brigadier and headquarters staff based in Britain. He and they travel the world to sniff out death set in a variety of ingenious snares in buildings, planes, and ships. The trophies they have won litter their headquarters offices. Rare trophies, these, a jumble of crates and boxes and once-deadly packages, and a growing collection of X-ray pictures showing wires, switches, detonators, nails, and batteries carefully hidden from the human eye.

Outside the brigadier's office a gallery of photographs lines one wall, honoring those men who have used up all their nine lives.

There is a strange air of reticence, shyness even, about this headquarters. It wears none of the old panache, the flamboyance that hung like a battle honor at every airfield manned by Battle of Britain pilots—including the American "Eagle" squadron—back in World War II.

These men have to remain anonymous. To allow public recognition would be to invite assassination—they are prime targets already because of their skills and achievement. In Ulster each one runs as much risk from the hidden sniper as from the bomb he must try to defuse in a race against the clock. They work for the same "firm" that recently dropped men by parachute into the Atlantic to search the *Queen Elizabeth II* for terrorist bombs. The world is their oyster; the pearls they seek are rare and deadly. Nowhere are they kept busier than in Ulster. Death follows them there like a shadow. Between 1969, the start of the present IRA campaign, and the summer of 1973 they had to deal with more then ten thousand explosive devices ranging from a trip-wire hand grenade to a four-hundred-pound homemade bomb.

The first thing Major Welbourne did when his men pointed out an abandoned, and loaded, RPG-7 rocket launcher in the snow was to run to his Land-Rover and summon Felix.

"Able One to X-Ray," he called, "send Felix," and gave a map reference. Only when that was done did he turn again to the casualties and start to issue fresh orders.

For him the ambush had been a personal tragedy as well as a military disaster. Most of the dead and wounded men were his friends and comrades over many years.

He and his wife knew the men, their wives, and children. Like all regular troops, they were like family to him and he grieved as a family man every bit as much as a professional soldier in defeat. He mourned his comrades as he made the tally and smelled the charred flesh and cloth and battlefield debris.

At the same time he was under no illusions about his own future. He could not be punished for defeat, for he knew there had been no dereliction of duty. On the other hand, it was good-bye to a career, to promotion and a regimental command of his own. From this night on he would be remembered as "Dickie Welbourne, you know—the chap who was licked by the IRA."

It was a much shaken major who finally stepped forward to face his colonel when the CO drove up in heavily guarded formation later that night.

Felix came, too, in the person of a twenty-five-year-old captain with his own driver and escort of four riflemen. They linked up with the main column at Omagh.

Felix set to work before much was said between colonel and major. The captain went across to Welbourne, saluted, and asked exactly why he had been called in. He knew about the destruction of the armored vehicles and he listened intently as they told him about an odd-looking rocket launcher left in the snow with an unexploded grenade still in the barrel.

"Hm," he said to no one in particular. "Fair old washup to do here, that's for sure."

Patrols were sent out and guards stationed nearby as he started work. Welbourne and the colonel looked on while he examined the holes in the steel shells of the Saladins and the Saracen; he looked inside each vehicle and wrinkled his nose at what he saw and smelled there.

He asked to be taken to the abandoned RPG-7. "Over here, sir," said one of the gunners. The sky had cleared, and a moon shone down, pinpointing the black shape in the snow.

The captain moved like a cat. He drew on his plastic gloves, so that no evidence of guilt should be accidentally destroyed in his examination. (Felix always has to work in conditions so dangerous that no ordinary detective can be present, but unexploded bombs and booby traps carry incriminating fingerprints, so Felix has to play CID man as well as bomb doctor. Plastic gloves, like those the surgeon wears, are part of his uniform.)

He approached the thing on the ground quietly and carefully, not knowing if it was booby-trapped. A sergeant offered him a flashlight, but Felix knocked it gently away.

"Don't switch that flashlight on, Sergeant. Rule number one, *never* shine a flashlight or ordinary lamp on any device you find at night. They can be exploded by light-sensitive cells! Now, stand right away, all of you."

He spent some time alone in the half light, examining the ground near the weapon, looking for telltale tracks in the snow. He was too late for that. Troops had dashed all over the battlefield in pursuit of the terrorists.

"No one touched this, did they?" he called. They told him no. Next he put down what looked like an ordinary lamp and walked away slowly away from it, running out line until he, too, was a safe distance from the rocket launcher. He made doubly sure everyone was clear and switched on the lamp by remote control. Its beam fell on the RPG-7. No explosion. So far, so good, he said to himself, it doesn't have a light-sensitive device built in.

Now he came back, still cat-careful, and examined it closely by the light of his lamp. He saw there were no wires leading from it, nothing concealed by the snow. He felt around it and under it, very gingerly. Only then was he satisfied.

"As I thought," he announced calmly. "Misfire. And a pretty interesting one at that, Colonel. I don't think any of us has come across a weapon like this in Ireland before."

He removed the grenade from the launcher as if it were a babe being taken from the breast, walked with it a safe distance from the others, and blew it up. He came back to the RPG-7, held it carefully at each end in his gloved fingers, and slid it into a plastic bag provided by his driver.

"Exhibit one," he said. "Lay it carefully in the van." He searched again in the area, and recovered one more rocket launcher and four rocket grenades, unfired and still in their canvas holders, which the IRA had abandoned in their flight. They were all examined with the same minute care and packed away in his Land Rover.

He questioned the soldiers and made certain none had touched or handled the abandoned weapons. Had they done so, he would have had to fingerprint every man to eliminate the "good" prints from the "bad" for eventual police work.

"I'll want a good look at those Saladins and Saracens tomorrow," he said briefly. "That all right with you, sir? I'll take the other exhibits back with me now for a more detailed examination. I'll put in my report as fast as I can."

"Of course," the colonel told him. "Thank you, Captain." He walked a little way off with Major Welbourne.

"It's a bad show, Dickie," the colonel said very quietly. "The worst! I'm afraid there will be one hell of an inquiry to explain this lot away. How in God's name did you let yourself get led up the garden path like this, man? Why didn't you go straight in to clobber those terrorists and arrest them as laid down in my orders?"

"I tried," said the unhappy major. "We'd swept the whole area only hours before, covered that lane top to bottom and found it clear. So I sent Gideon down it to bag every terrorist we could drive into him—like a grouse shoot, with my men as beaters."

"And exactly as the opposition had anticipated," said the colonel dryly. "Not very good thinking, Dickie. Well, at least we've got the answer to the brigadier's question about the submarine and its cargo. You found it, the hard way, tonight!

"Sweep and search the whole area again in daylight. Felix will send another crew down to help you, in case of more finds. I have a feeling there may be a lot more mines around. Don't take any chances tomorrow. Shoot to kill if you have to. We can't afford to lose any more men."

The colonel tapped his tailored leg with the swagger cane.

"I'll also want a full report from the gunner officer concerned about that last man killed—by the booby-trapped corpse. I shall ask for a copy of your own orders regarding the body and I will want to

92

know how the man came to disregard instructions you say were clearly given."

There was the slightest emphasis on the word *you*.

"You will let me have a preliminary report as soon as you get back to your headquarters. Take statements from the section commanders involved, and let me have it on my desk within twenty-four hours."

Welbourne saluted the colonel and went back to work.

A brief and guarded communiqué was issued within the hour by Army headquarters. An hour after that the roads down from Londonderry and Belfast were buzzing with press cars.

On security grounds—danger from unexploded mines—the ambush area was sealed from them. So they descended en masse at Welbourne's own headquarters and fired a barrage of questions that could not be ducked by tired and angry spokesmen.

Britain first learned of the ambush from the BBC, for details of the fighting were gleaned too late for the morning newspapers.

"Full details are still not known. Army spokesmen said early this morning that the terrorists had used powerful rocket launchers of a type not seen in Ulster before. A splinter group of the IRA calling itself the Fenian Martyrs has claimed responsibility for the attack. A military inquiry is expected to be held into all the circumstances surrounding the ambush."

Nearly every home in Britain switches on the radio to hear the first BBC news bulletins of the day, before the TV programs have begun. No listeners are more attentive than the wives and sweethearts and mothers of the soldiers stationed in Ulster. And this morning, as the familiar voice told of fresh casualties, it was the turn of the womenfolk of the First Seventh to catch their breath and send up a silent prayer, saying, "Please God, not my man."

Sue Welbourne was living at the time in a rented country cottage close to the regiment's home depot at Aldershot, which lies less than forty miles from London. Her eldest son was away at boarding school; the younger boy, Stephen, was at home with her. He had been fed and now he played with this toys, ignoring the words of the announcer.

Mrs. Welbourne was accustomed to separation from her soldier husband. She accepted it as a cross all Army wives have to bear, but for her, Ireland was special—she had never worried about him more than she did now as he fought his unknown enemies only an hour's plane journey away. There was something disturbing, something infinitely sad and cruel, about having him so close and yet in such danger. In this moment she found herself hating Ireland and the Irish as she had never once hated the Greek and Arab terrorists Richard Welbourne had fought in the past.

She knew that Richard was not a casualty in this ambush. He had called her the night before to assure her of his safety, but still she wanted to cover her ears against the voice from the radio. She wanted to switch the set off, to banish the voice from her house forever, but she could not get up. She wanted to pick up their child and comfort him, but he needed no comforting. For one moment of madness she thought of her own death and welcomed the thought, believing it to be preferable to the terrible uncertainty facing her now, day after day.

There was no makeup on her face. A single broad band held back the long, dark hair from her eyes, so that the tears of her agony could be clearly seen by the startled child.

She knew the worst fear of all, the one that stems from helplessness to protect a loved one.

"What's the matter, Mummy?" said Stephen.

Sue Welbourne donned the mask of parental calm and gave the boy a long, reassuring hug.

"Nothing, Stevie," she told him. "Mummy has a headache, that's all."

She walked over to the windowsill and switched off the radio. She stood looking at it for a long moment. Then she went back to the kitchen table and began writing her shopping list for the day.

Suddenly she screwed the paper into a ball and hurled it into the waste bin. She took a fresh sheet and in big, bold letters right across the top she wrote:

NO IRISH BUTTER

She knew it to be a futile gesture, even an unfair one. But like a few thousand other Army wives in Britain, Mrs. Welbourne had discovered one bullet to fire in the campaign herself and was determined not to waste it.

•16•

It was mid-April and a magical time to be in Dublin.

Tourists wandered hand in hand along O'Connell Street, past the Trinity, down Grafton Street, and into the sanctuary of St. Stephen's Green, seeking and finding the city's most prized quality—a rare gentleness in the air.

No one hurries in Dublin.

In the Pearl Bar tourists and locals alike relaxed over glasses of stout and peat-flavored whiskey and told the joke about the holy hour and the man who was told that he could have a drink to while away the time until they opened again. Many strange tongues could be heard—French and Italian, German and Japanese, Danish and Swedish, and English of course (but rarely Gaelic).

Dublin is a fine place to be alive in the spring.

For most, but not all. Not, for instance, for the man called Kelly.

Kelly had traveled there from Donegal after a brief spell in Cork with Liam. The two kept in touch with occasional and innocently worded telephone calls, while a settlement was worked out in cash for the victory in Tyrone. For too long now Kelly had had nothing to do, and he felt uneasy, bored, and morose.

He lost count of the times he had found himself walking past the Post Office on O'Connell Street that served Pearse and his followers as headquarters in the Easter Rising. Nothing rubbed off from its great stone pillars onto his own wide shoulders, no inspiration, no sound of distant guns, no breath of freedom—to him it was just another building.

When he stood in the shadow of the thousand-year-old castle, all he saw was the specter of the Irish Special Branch—how long

95

before they got on to him, began tapping his phone, following his car and his footsteps, even raiding his hotel bedroom?

All the city's gaiety and blarney and lazy charm were wasted on the mercenary. He used eyes that would not see, and chafed at every delay, each day of inactivity.

This morning a note had been delivered to him at the hotel by an unknown messenger. He was still dumbfounded by its total indiscretion, still aghast at some references that would have convicted him of murder in any court of law.

Despite his childhood in Ireland, Kelly could not see the funny side of an Irish "logic" that insisted on security-tight telephone calls yet permitted total indiscretion in writing.

From the note sent to the hotel he learned that as payment for the twelve men who died as a result of the ambush (four in the hospital), plus bonuses for damage to three armored vehicles, he had been awarded four thousand pounds (ten thousand dollars). This had been credited to his bank account in Geneva.

Kelly guessed what had happened and was not greatly pleased, for he had earned much more. The Irishmen had obviously played down his leadership while exaggerating their own role in the fighting—out of pride. He recognized a system of accountancy in which his chances of becoming rich were distinctly less than those of his becoming dead. Why had he agreed to this loose, payments-on-results deal? Fighting the British Army was a hard and dangerous business, and hatred for the British was no compensation for monies lost. What was it those Americans had promised, the sky's the limit? Maybe it was. But the Irishmen were not feeding him with money-spinning ideas, the bastards were too intent on fighting.

And Kelly was a man who liked to see his money grow. He was not entirely sure why he wanted it, even now. As of now, possession was more important to him than any single thing money could buy. Of one thing he was sure, money meant power, prestige, a place in the sun. It was a dream that haunted the man who had once been a hungry, fatherless boy.

Years ago, in Katanga, a newspaper reporter had tried to find out.

"You take money," said the reporter, "for killing people you don't know, with whom you have no quarrel, and in a country where you don't belong. Does that ever worry you?"

"Christ, no," Kelly answered, genuinely taken aback by the

question. "Why should it? You got to have money or people walk over you."

"That may well be true," the reporter agreed, "but what we're discussing is the *way* you earn it."

"Look," said Kelly. "Killing strangers is no problem, in fact it's easier, I guess. I never really thought about it. I don't need a quarrel to shoot somebody. I'm paid to do it and I do it very well, strictly in my own interests! If I could do something better than soldiering, hell, I'd do it. But I don't know anything else."

The reporter pressed him. "But what do you do with all your money when you get it?"

Kelly was astonished by the man's naiveté. "You trying to take the piss out of me?" he asked. "I told you. People look up to a rich man. Nobody tells *him* what to do. Money means power, money means no one can ever push you around, it makes you someone big wherever you go."

"But your friends here are different. They take their money, they go on leave, and they burn it up on women and booze and gambling. Don't you ever let your hair down?"

Kelly pitied his questioner.

"They're fools," he said. "Sure, I get horny after a month in the bush, who doesn't? So I've got a million jungle bunnies to choose from, and they cost maybe a pack of cigarettes each.

"You think that when I go on leave I throw money away on a whore just because she's a different color and talks nice? Not me, mister. All cats are gray in the dark, you ought to know that. You asked me about booze. Okay, we all get good and drunk once in a while. But I take very, very good care no one robs me. I'm never *that* drunk. Same thing applies when I play stud. I set a limit for losing and I stick to it. The same rules apply when I'm on leave as when I'm here in the field. It's what you come away with that counts."

Now, in Dublin, he wasn't sure he was going to get away with very much, not from Ireland anyway. Every day he read in the newspapers of fresh violence in the North. The "big two" IRA groups, the "Reds" and the "Greens," seemed to be holding the stage without any need of help from tiny splinter groups like the one he was working for. Each week saw them more daring, more deadly.

Kelly was worried, too, about the enormous publicity that the ambush in Tyrone brought in its wake. There was widespread talk in the British press of mercenaries, agents, guns for hire by the IRA. He hadn't forgotten Liam's warning that these two major groups might show their resentment of his presence by betrayal, or worse. He began to look over his shoulder.

There was nothing to like about the present setup, the tedious, empty days when he spoke to no one but a barman, his mounting bills, the insecurity of his whole position. He thought of quitting, of reneging on his contract, but he doubted if the Martyrs would let him go quite so easily. He could be dangerous. He could talk, name names, give telephone numbers, he could sell his information to British intelligence. They would never allow that, ever.

On top of it all, he hated the climate, the soft showers and shining pavements, the cold breeze, the pale yellow beams that passed for sunshine in these chill northern parts. It was a climate he had grown out of many years ago.

He yearned for the blistering heat and soaring peaks of the Yemen, or the clinging, Turkish-bath steam of a Congo afternoon. He longed to feel the African sun again on his back, to gaze out on a land that shimmered at noon. He would gladly have traded every oak and ash in Phoenix Park for the glimpse of one dusty, towering blue gum. Like most men, he only discovered when he had been happy, when he was not.

His days were unvarying. Between six and seven he was always back at his own hotel, in case there were any messages. The invariably negative reply would lead him to the hotel bar where he'd start drinking in earnest. By seven o'clock each evening the hotel bar was filled with men and women laughing and enjoying themselves. He might have joined in, talked to one or two of them, but the fear of entrapment, by a spy from either side, stopped him. Always when he stalked in, a savage of a man with the light gleaming in his cropped blond hair and showing the spread of his huge shoulders, he was noticed.

This evening there was a woman at the bar who thought him quite attractive. My God, but he's big, she thought.

By chance Kelly found a space and stood next to her, almost touching. He stole a glance while the barman brought his drink. The woman was in her midthirties, with long, well-shaped legs below a dark suit that spelled taste and money. Her hair was glossy black. As he put his drink down, she moved her own glass to make room, smiling at him briefly before retreating into the security of her corner seat. Kelly had no idea if she was waiting for someone,

98

if the smile had been one of politeness or invitation, and for a moment he just stood there, vividly aware of the woman's body close to his, the scent of her. He resolved to take a chance.

"You on your own, lady?" he asked abruptly. "If so, I'm offering you a drink. We must be the only two people in this bar with no one else to talk to."

She smiled, hesitating to commit herself. "I'm on my own," she said, "but not exactly waiting to be picked up. I'm staying in this hotel. Business trip."

"Great," Kelly told her. "So am I. What do you do?"

"I'm a buyer," she said. "The international fashion show opens tomorrow. You see, we had an awful job to get hotel rooms."

"We?"

"The firm sent three of us from London. The other two are men and they're sharing a room somewhere on the other side of town. They phoned to say they won't be here tonight. I expect they've found a couple of girl friends."

"I'm glad," he said.

He felt suddenly randy as a buck. Two more drinks he signaled to the barman.

"Thank you," she said. "What do you do for a living?" She looked him up and down and burst out laughing. "Sorry, I didn't mean to be rude. But I just couldn't see you going to any fashion show! You look more like a boxer to me."

"Not me," said Kelly, flattered. "I work for an American firm with interests in Ireland. They have money, I look around for the best way to spend it, investment and return, you might say." He held up his tumbler—he was a little drunk already. "Cheers. Glad you had such trouble in finding a room."

He looked at her carefully as he flared his lighter for her waiting cigarette. The black hair shone like spun glass. Staring brown eyes, upturned nose, a mouth full of hunger and lips red as wine, a face not too old nor too young but ripe, a face that had surely awakened in many a strange bedroom. Her teeth were white and wide-spaced. The only jewelry she wore was a silver brooch on her lapel shaped like a letter "O."

"That's a clue to your name?"

"Clever man! Yes. My name is Olivia. I hate it, naturally. Olivia Merry. And yours?"

"Kelly. Brian Kelly."

They had dinner together. As she watched Kelly wolf his steak she thought, God, it's an animal I've got myself here, and her eyes

99

were bright with fantasy for the night ahead. She reached out a hand under the snowy tablecloth, and stroked his leg.

"Mmmm," she said. "You're so *big.*"

Olivia Merry was a nymphomaniac—even so, Kelly performed a rare feat and raped her the moment her bedroom door was shut. He ripped the expensive clothes off her back and threw her on the floor, smothering her with his bulk as she struggled and cried. Then he dragged her by her shining black hair across to the bed and mounted her, roaring like a stag at the rut. It was *he* who proved insatiable—he forced her down with his enormous hands, he abused her and cuffed her and slapped her, he towered over her and terrified her until all her whimpering protests finally ceased.

She had known many men, but no one had treated her like this one. She would do anything voluntarily, but this man had compelled her to do everything against her will. In the end she was numb, in mind as well as body.

"Leave me alone," she begged. "Stop, please, stop."

Kelly heaved himself off the bed and looked at his watch. It was six in the morning. He dressed without a word as she looked at him with eyes full of loathing. He saw the torn clothes, and a little sanity returned. He fumbled in his wallet and threw down some money. "Here," he said. "Buy yourself a new dress."

She threw it at him. "Keep it! Don't you think you've made me feel enough like a whore already?" Kelly picked it up in silence and went back to his own room. He heard her bolt the door behind him.

· 17 ·

A little before seven Kelly was awakened by Liam telephoning from Cork.

"Did I wake you," he asked, "or were you getting ready for a day's fishing?"

Kelly groaned. "I was asleep. What do you want?"

"I heard of a bit of business going that might interest you," said Liam casually. "Could you drive over here today?"

"Sure," Kelly replied. "Be with you about midday. That all right?"

"I'll be in the Metropole," Liam told him. "Don't worry about a room. I know a place in the country where we can fish for something big."

Kelly felt wretched as he climbed out of bed a second time. His tongue was furred, his head ached, his stomach was fouled with acid, and he stood a long time under the shower trying to recover. As he dressed again, he wondered what Liam had in mind.

"Will there be any forwarding address, sir?" asked the clerk, as he handed in his key.

"No," said Kelly. "I don't know where I'm going. Just a long drive in the countryside, then I'll take pot luck." He paid his bill and drove fast down the Cork road, marveling as always at the absence of heavy traffic. Long before Liam arrived, Kelly was in the bar of their chosen hotel and drinking heavily.

Liam led him to a table and called for a waiter. Kelly held up his glass and ordered, "More whiskey." Liam made no comment.

"Coffee for me," he said politely, and waited until the man was out of earshot. "Hey, take it easy. We have an idea that holds distinct possibilities for you. A one-man job in execution, but you'll need all our help in setting it up. Take a look at this"—and he passed a sheet of notepaper across the table.

101

"It's taken from a report sent in by one of our people in Belfast," he said. "You can be quite sure it's reliable. The only thing we need to know is the date, and we'll have that before long."

Kelly began to read, once again amazed to see so much committed to paper.

> Two British cabinet ministers will be coming to Belfast at the end of this month, or early in May. (Date still to be confirmed.)
>
> They will be accompanied by Army chiefs of staff and intelligence officers and will hold a conference with the prime minister of Northern Ireland, the British Army commander, and senior staff.
>
> Purpose of the conference is not known.
>
> It will be held secretly at the Old Covenanter Hotel by Lough Neagh. It will last two or three days.
>
> It is felt here that security will be so tight there will be no chance of attack on the hotel by our ground forces.
>
> What is suggested is a device to be exploded inside the building during the conference.
>
> Starting date for the conference will be telephoned to Cork as soon as we have confirmation.

As soon as Kelly had finished reading, Liam leaned over and took the paper from him.

"Now," he said, bright as a salesman in a car showroom, "isn't that a beauty? Doesn't that make you happy? If you bring that off"—he lowered his voice—"there'll be no need for you ever to work again. Holy mother, you'd become a millionaire overnight."

"Millionaire?" Kelly sounded scornful.

"Rich enough," Liam confirmed, "to let you retire. That would bring enough from your sponsor to make your last wage packet look like a tip for the barman here."

Kelly nodded. "Sounds good. But I'll want to know how much before I do anything."

"You'll be told."

Liam paid the bill, and they left the hotel.

"We'll go in your car from here on," he said. "There's always a danger my own is becoming too well known. Just head out of town along the Bantry Road. I'll show you where to go."

When they were on their way he spoke about the ambush.

"There was a full-scale Army inquiry," he chuckled, "and I hear they gave the officer in charge that night a hell of a roasting. They flew the bodies home for a military funeral, with gun carriages and a slow march, bugles playing the Last Post, and a million flowers.

"There was quite a public outcry over there. Did you read about it? Well, then, you know what I'm talking about. They held an inquiry immediately afterward, and we found out the results by listening to the reporters as they phoned in their stories. The officer in charge was a feller called Welbourne. He got another rocket—from his own people this time—and was sent home in disgrace."

"He was unlucky, then," said Kelly. "I told you before what I thought about it. He knew about the submarine and he was working to a plan, trying to catch us with the Russian weapons. Your men did everything they could to try to help him. We were lucky to come out in one piece."

"Let's just hope," said Liam, "we have the same kind of luck with this next job. We're going to need it. It won't be easy."

"Where are you taking me?" asked Kelly, looking around him.

They were passing through open country in the unspoiled southwest of Ireland, where Cork runs into Kerry and apart from the road all is untouched by time. They drove below green hills ablaze with gorse, past rippling trout streams lined by wild flowers. Liam's heart ached as he watched the miles unfold.

"Two miles farther on we cross a humpbacked bridge," Liam said. "There's a turning soon after that we have to take. I'll tell you when we come to it."

Kelly glanced in the rearview mirror and made certain they were not being followed. Ten minutes later they neared a farmhouse set well back from the side road with smoke rising from a single chimney. The fields around were noisy with the bleat of newborn lambs. There was no one in sight.

"That's it," Liam told him. "Pull around to the back so we're well out of sight. Don't worry—it's just a normal precaution. This is local headquarters."

Two outbuildings lay behind the farmhouse, with their doors open. Liam gestured, and Kelly drove into one, under cover. He saw two other vehicles neatly parked by the side of of a van in the other.

"They're old cars," said Liam, "but you ought to see them move. Souped-up engines."

Kelly walked with Liam into the yard and without looking up saw a curtain move at the back of the house. He sensed the faces watching him as they strolled to the door.

"We're expected," Liam told him. "There'll be quite a reception committee.

"They're giving you the plum job of the year after all!"

The door was pulled open by the farmer, a grizzled, apple-cheeked ancient. Kelly could smell him a yard off.

"Hello, Liam," the farmer bawled, crushing the younger man's hand in a gnarled paw. "You're late! They've been here a good hour, waiting for you. Come in, come in, the two of you."

He shook Kelly's hand and looked him up and down with knowing eyes. "Hello, young feller." Then he led them into a kitchen filled with tobacco and peat smoke. It was a big room. A mantelpiece propped up a line of faded snapshots. In the fireplace a witch's pot bubbled and brewed over red embers suspended from the brickwork by a blackened chain. The room had a raw smell of poverty.

Four men sat around the farmhouse table, rising as one to greet Liam and the stranger. Kelly was given a curt, one-way introduction, just three words from Liam: "This is Kelly." No names were given immediately in answer. But the nameless four were worth looking at.

At the head of the table the leader stood, a man in his midthirties. Premature gray salt-and-peppered his hair and a purple scar disfigured him from throat to ear on the right side of his head, the legacy of an Ulster policeman's markmanship in the Border campaign ten years earlier. The left side was cleanshaven and handsome. His eyes devoured Kelly, and thin lips pursed in obvious disapproval as he smelled drink on the big man's breath. He looked gaunt and taut as a wound spring. In all the time Kelly listened to him that morning and afternoon he never once smiled or relaxed.

His eyes were cold as pebbles on the seashore. Kelly shook hands and thought: You miserable bastard.

The two men on the leader's right hand were twins. They looked alike, dressed alike, and moved in harmony. Each gave Kelly a good three inches in height, and that made them huge. Both had the indigo eyes and curly black hair you find in men and women all through the West, from Galway to Fastnet. Kelly remembered his mother saying years before that such people were descended from survivors of the Spanish Armada who made their way ashore after the great gale. He wondered if it were true.

Not only were they dark, they were like Esau—hairy men. Hair tumbled and twisted from nape to forehead, forced its way through each open collar, covered their bare arms and hands like fur, and sprouted from their ears and nostrils.

They had forearms of prodigious thickness, like logs, barrel chests and thighs that bulged inside tight trouser legs. They reminded Kelly of two black bears.

104

"Hello," he said with genuine respect.

The fourth man was pale with prison pallor—Kelly learned he had been freed from jail only weeks earlier. He guessed the man's age to be around forty. His eyes were bright and his smile was wild.

"Kelly," he said, "I'm pleased to meet you, so I am. We've been hearing a lot about you. That was a fine job you did in the Six Counties."

Kelly thanked him and sat down.

·18·

The meeting of the council of the Fenian Martyrs and the mercenary Brian Werner, alias Kelly, began with the old man pouring tea. He served steaming mugs around the table, beginning with the leader and ending, clockwise, with Liam.

Kelly noted the ritual abstinence with a sly grin. He had the feeling that the twins and the white-faced man would have made short work of a drop of the hard stuff if their leader had been absent.

However, they all seemed to smoke like chimneys, and he lit up to add to the kitchen fug.

The leader, whose name was Eamonn, spoke first.

"The ambush went well," he said. "I understand you have already been paid?"

Kelly immediately assumed Eamonn's aloof tone was a personal slight. You know bloody well I've been paid and exactly how much, he thought, and nodded curtly.

"I accept your suggestion it will no longer be necessary for us to use you again in similar operations—the RPG-7 is so simple a child can fire one."

Kelly glared at him. "Don't talk crap," he said. "Every weapon needs something more than just a finger on the trigger, and you know it as well as I do. But I take the point. You won't need me to hold anyone's hand next time."

There was a long silence. It was not the best of starts.

"Precisely. Now, about our new proposal. Whatever the date of the conference, you won't have a lot of time to make plans, but it can't be helped. You know we have plenty of volunteers for this job. On balance, we decided to give it to you because you are unknown to the security forces.

"Any help we can give you, a place to work in, materials, up-to-date information—you can bank on all that. I want Liam to remain with you at all times from now on. Whatever you want, pass on the request through him. Don't go buying things or asking questions on your own at any time."

Kelly did not enjoy being lectured to.

"Yes, *sir!*" he said, in a sarcastic tone.

"One point for you to bear in mind," the scar-faced man went on. "We don't use real names, not in writing or on the phone or even in conversation. When you refer to me I am simply 'Eamonn.' The twins are Kevin and Sean. This man's name is Raymond. In this country we can afford the luxury of calling you Kelly."

There was not a flicker of a smile on his face.

"Now, Raymond, tell Kelly what you know about the conference site."

"Willingly," said the pale man. "It's known as the Old Covenanter Hotel, but it's not a hotel in the true sense of the word, more of a government guest house these days.

"It's reserved for VIPs coming over from London, for ministers, Army brass, intelligence men—the sort of person who has to have round-the-clock security when he's off the streets as well as on them.

"The building itself is over two hundred years old. It was once a stately home for a feudal landlord, then the residence of a bishop who made it a center for Catholic oppression.

"It's had all kinds of alterations and patchwork repairs over the years. After the Rising in 1917 the British Army used it as a general's headquarters.

"Since these Troubles began it has been used exclusively as a government guest house—a 'safe' house, in reverse. I know! I found a job there as gardener and tried to blow some VIPs up myself and was lucky to get only two years for my pains. A friend who was shot dead got most of the blame.

"Security there is always hot, and ten times hotter when they have visitors. The grounds are spread over eighteen acres or so, landscaped parkland mostly with some fine gardens right below the house.

"The whole estate is walled off, from gate to gate. And it's some wall—built of stone, two feet thick, rising at least twenty feet in height, and topped with a mass of iron spikes, and barbed wire, and glass splinters. The wall runs to within half a mile of Lough Neagh at its nearest point.

"However, they've got patrol boats on the lake these days, manned by Marine Commandos.

"There's only one official way in. You come down a road without a scrap of cover on any side—to rule out snipers—and it is always sealed off by a roadblock when VIPs are staying there.

"Inside the walls they have a permanent staff of RUC policemen—who use dogs to patrol the grounds twenty-four hours a day.

"In the past the British Special Branch has taken over command of all security when the visitors have actually moved in. Then the whole place is crawling with soldiers and police."

"So how do you propose to plant a bomb?"

"There's only one way. The British always go for bullshit whenever VIPs arrive, and that's your chance.

"They'll call in a small army of workmen to dress the place up. When I was working there they were drawn from trusted Protestant firms, and most of them were known by sight, at least, to the local policemen. But things are probably a bit different now that the Ulster Defense Association is showing its teeth. Somehow I doubt that religion alone will be enough. We might be able to get a man of our own inside."

"Why not drop a bomb on the bloody place?" Kelly asked, jokingly.

"We considered the possibility," said Eamonn, deadpan. "All we could get was a light aircraft quite unsuited to the task. We want everyone dead, and you can't guarantee that by bombing from the air. So we dropped the idea."

"Mmmm," said Kelly, thoughtfully. He looked at Eamonn with grudging approval.

"What else do you need to know?"

"A date and a time and the plans for the building," said Kelly.

"We'll know exact dates shortly. The plans we'll get right away," said Eamonn. "All we do is telephone a bomb warning to the ministry building. After everybody's gotten out we loot the place. No one can afford to ignore a bomb warning."

"Okay. One more thing I'll need—a place to work in with a minimum journey to the hotel afterward."

"We've already found a place for you to work in," Eamonn said. "Liam will take you there after the meeting."

"I don't know about that," Kelly retorted. "What do I need Liam for—a bodyguard?" He laughed. " 'Course, it might already be too late."

"Too late for what?" demanded Eamonn.

"The Irish Special Branch. After those days hanging around in

Dublin they may already be on my tail. Specially if they happen to read my mail."

Eamonn went white, then red.

"Are you criticizing this organization, Mr. Kelly?" he said finally.

"Why would I criticize such a swell bunch of guys, who pay me so well for my work?" said Kelly, smiling.

"You will go with Liam directly to the place we have selected for you and wait for the materials needed to construct your bomb. And you will *not* question this council again!"

Kelly looked down at the table, his face darkening with rage.

"Right," Eamonn continued. "Anything else, Raymond? No? All right, let's have supper."

At a sign from Liam, the old man cleared away the tea mugs and spread a clean tablecloth. He placed a handful of knives, forks, and spoons in the center and said, "Help yourselves, lads, the food's all ready."

He dipped a ladle in the caldron and passed around great plates of steaming mutton, pearl barley, onions, carrots, and boiled potatoes. The food was excellent. Liam helped him serve and gave each man a chunk of brown bread. Finally the old man poured a glass of milk for everyone.

Kelly, still smarting from his rebuke, pushed the milk away with a snort.

"Milk," he said. "That's for babies, not grown men. Haven't we got anything stronger than bloody milk?"

Eamonn took up the challenge.

"I don't know if there's liquor in this house," he said. "It's not my concern.

"What does concern me is an order from the council which lays down no drinking in the field. That order covers this meeting every bit as much as a fighting operation. It's not a Puritan decree, Mr. Kelly, it's a question of discipline.

"A drunken man is a bad advertisement for the IRA and is no longer tolerated in its battalions. If no drink is allowed then no one can get drunk.

"I'm sorry if you don't like our Irish milk. The alternative at this table is water. Liam, get Mr. Kelly some water."

Kelly left the water untouched. The chill in the atmosphere increased. Conservation dwindled to a few desultory sentences.

Eamonn turned to Liam.

"I think," he said without looking at Kelly, "we have to assume fairly extensive inquiries will be under way in Donegal by the Irish Special Branch after the appearance of our rocket launchers on the scene. I don't think there's any cause for alarm, but there's no point in taking the slightest risk.

"We were wrong to leave Kelly on his own so long in Dublin. He's obviously left a trail that can be picked up after a few simple inquiries. From now on, he stays completely out of sight. We can think about the future after this operation is over. But for the time being keep him hidden."

"Oh, I see," said Kelly. "*I* left a trail?"

Eamonn appeared not to have heard.

"Now listen, all of you," Kelly said. "I don't like being cooped up at the best of times. I'm going to like it even less with your weird ideas about drink. You're asking me to take on a dangerous job. I'm the one who'll be risking his neck—not you lot. You think I'm going to live on milk for the next few weeks? Piss off! You'll ask me to go to Mass next."

"I'll tell you, and for the last time," said Eamonn very quietly. "You're under orders like any soldier. You'll do exactly as you are told."

Kelly was spoiling for a fight. "Is that so?"

"It is. You will stay where we say you will stay. You will obey whatever security precautions we think are necessary."

Kelly pushed his chair back and stood up. "Right, that's the limit. Get yourself another boy to do your fighting for you!"

Eamonn looked up at him, keeping himself under control with a visible effort. "You don't just walk out on *us,* Mr. Kelly. Not because you're irreplaceable, God knows. I've told you before you're not in Ireland at any request of ours! But quite simply because you know too much. You will stay and see this through and obey orders—*my* orders, do you understand? You don't have any choice. Now sit down and calm down."

"Don't push me," Kelly shouted. "I'm not one of your dim peasants playing at soldiers!"

Eamonn pushed back his chair, wild with rage, and slapped Kelly's face. It sounded like a gunshot. Kelly bunched a great fist and went to hit him back.

The twins threw themselves at him, one from each side.

Kevin took him first, wielding his melon-sized right hand like a hammer to smash it down on Kelly's neck. He stumbled with the force of the blow and while he was off balance Sean hit him karate-style—the heel of his palm moved sideways in a vicious, chopping blow that set bells ringing and lights flashing inside Kelly's skull. Somehow he stayed on his feet. Then the old man stole up and swung a wooden kitchen stool that broke square on Kelly's head. Now he went down, in slow motion, like a bull elephant smitten by a hunter's dart. As he toppled, Sean hit him with a right jab that only traveled eight inches before it exploded on Kelly's Adam's apple.

Kelly's six feet two of bone and muscle bounced like a ball on the stone floor into the corner of the kitchen and slammed into a dresser.

"That's enough," said Eamonn.

Kelly thought his neck must be broken. There was no air in his lungs, and he flapped on the tiles like a fish on the bank. Spittle ran from his mouth, and he made strange whistling sounds as he tried to breathe.

"Pick him up," Eamonn ordered. The twins dropped Kelly into a chair.

Eamonn leaned down and spoke to the mercenary. "If you were anyone else," he said, "I'd have had you shot for that. But you're a stranger, and I'll make allowances for that. Step out of line once more, and you will be killed. Now, then. For the last time, Mr. Kelly, you will obey our orders until this operation is finished one way or the other.

"If you want to quit then, I won't stop you. Nor will anyone else. Do you hear me?

"In the meantime, think on this, Mr. Kelly. If you ruin this for us, if you bungle it deliberately, if you double-cross us, we'll hunt you down and kill you if it takes us twenty years to do it. Is that clear?"

Kelly managed to nod his head.

"But if you do what I say, and do the job, you get a hundred thousand dollars free and clear."

Kelly stayed on the floor, glaring up at the council.

"A hundred thousand?" he said.

Eamonn knew when he had won. "Well, then. It's all settled. There'll be no word of this outside this room, do you hear me? It's over, finished. From now on, the bomb is the only thing that matters."

Eamonn led Liam to one side.

"Stick with him the whole time, Liam. I don't trust him further than I can spit after the beating he's had this morning. If he tries to make a run for it, shoot him if you can. If you can't stay out of his way and get word to us, the sooner the better."

"Sure," Liam replied. "Rely on me."

"I always do," said Eamonn, pressing his arm. "But don't fight him, don't antagonize the man. Encourage him to work at this and do it well, if only for the money. If he pulls it off, it will be a tremendous victory for us. I mean it when I say he can depart with the money. Make quite sure he understands that. Greed's the only thing holding him together."

He shook hands with Liam, then turned to the others.

"Come on," he said. "There's a lot to be done." The four men left the farmhouse, each pausing at the door to press the old man's hand in farewell. No one looked at Kelly.

Liam watched them drive away and then pointed silently at the mercenary. The old man nodded. He opened a cupboard and pulled out a bottle of potheen. It was oily and colorless and clung to the glass belly of the bottle like honey.

He set bottle and glass on the table in front of Kelly.

"Try it," said the old man, not unkindly. " 'Tis the Connemara mule itself."

Kelly poured a half tumbler and swallowed it at a gulp. He felt it burn his gizzard as it slid down.

"Christ," he said reverently. "That's some drink! Is this what you give to all your customers who step out of line, Liam?"

Liam looked at him somberly.

"Only the lucky ones," he said. "The rest end up dead. You better remember that, Kelly. You were a fool. You picked that fight with Eamonn just to try to make him feel small. Do you think any man in his right mind could allow you to get away with that, here on his own patch? You're stupid, Kelly, stupid. That act of showmanship could have cost you your life."

Kelly looked at him, his face set like stone. First he poured another drink. Then he said:

"I'll remember that beating, by Jesus I will. And so will Eamonn—I swear it."

"Don't be a fool," Liam warned.

He was elfin small and older than Kelly, but his voice carried all the menace of the organization, and Kelly knew it.

"You may not like us and our ways but you're in this thing just as much as we are. I spoke to Eamonn before he left, and if you pull this off, you can go—with a hundred thousand dollars intact. There'll be no recriminations from our side.

"Eamonn won't go back on his word. But don't chance your arm.

Don't go around making threats, or he'll kill you. And if he can't do it, someone else will, no matter how long it takes."

Kelly stood up, wincing.

"A hundred thousand dollars. That's not bad at all," he said. "That kind of money's worth a little pain. But don't expect me to love the bastard."

"You don't have to," Liam told him. "Just do what you're paid to do. I'll do whatever you want me to do to help you. But I've got my orders, too—to stay with you until the job's finished. So don't take it out on me. Don't make trouble for yourself. Don't go shooting off your mouth about Eamonn to any of the others, ever."

Kelly spat into the fire but said nothing.

"I need to think," he said later. "And unless I move around now, I'm going to be too stiff to get into a car tomorrow. I'm going to take a walk. You want to come along to make sure I don't run away?"

"Yes," said Liam. "I might as well." He said nothing about the gun in his pocket. Kelly guessed its presence and punished the little man by walking more than twenty miles through the hills.

Neither of them uttered a word throughout the journey.

·19·

Major Welbourne walked in to the adjutant's office and saluted.

"Good morning, John."

"Good morning, Dickie." He looked at the major sympathetically. "The colonel will be ready in a moment. Take the weight off your feet while I find out how long he will be."

The past weeks had been a nightmare for every officer in the regiment. At last the court of inquiry had made its report, and all that remained was for the CO to deal with the men who had been beaten in the field.

Although Welbourne had been cleared by an official statement saying that "after full consideration of the circumstances involved" he was not held to blame for the casualties and damage, he knew the pound of flesh had to be paid.

The whole line of questioning at the inquiry had shaken him.

"You say you were ordered by your commanding officer to try to capture terrorists, rather than drive them off in frontal attack?"

"Yes."

"Can you tell us how this order came to be given?"

"It arose from a briefing of senior officers which we both attended, at which certain intelligence information was disclosed. It was, and is, completely classified. Am I allowed to reveal what was said?"

"Proceed, Major. Members of the court of inquiry are hereby reminded the information is secret, and of the consequences of any breach of security."

Welbourne was a poor witness for his own case.

"Well, sir. We were briefed by the GSO 1 a few days before the ambush. He told us the authorities had photographs of a Russian submarine making landfall off the Donegal coast and it was vital to learn what cargo she might have carried. We were told the best way to do that was to round up IRA suspects wherever possible and hand them over for questioning."

"Did you have specific orders to that effect from your CO on the night of the ambush?"

"There was no need. I received reports that there was heavy fire on the Customs post. My assessment was the terrorists had not only crossed the Border in strength, but intended to mount an attack on the post from two sides. It seemed a golden opportunity for us to get behind them and take prisoners. So I sent Captain Gideon with his strike force to cut off their line of retreat, while I made a show of force to their front. I still consider that tactically sound. Gideon had the speed and firepower to complete the maneuver within ten minutes at most of leaving me at the road junction."

"You are not saying you sent those vehicles into an area where an ambush was laid without precautionary measures?"

"Of course not. The route I picked for Gideon had been swept, and found clean, during the last hours of daylight."

"It did not occur to you that your sweep in the afternoon might have been watched? So that a trap could be set later?"

"It did not."

"I see."

The note-taking ceased for a minute. All eyes were on Welbourne.

This was a military court of inquiry—but with political undertones. There was never any real possibility that its findings, when sent to GHQ, would result in the major's court-martial. Its whole purpose was to silence mounting public disquiet at both the political and military handling of the worsening Ulster situation.

Welbourne, of course, knew nothing of that.

The ambush itself might have been quickly forgotten by the public had it not been for the sensational appearance, for the first time in Northern Ireland, of Russian-made weapons. There had been enormous press speculation, not only about the arrival on the Irish scene of Soviet military equipment so new it was still not fully available to the Warsaw Pact countries, but also on the intriguing possibility of the presence of instructors, too.

This public hue and cry, besides discomfiting Welbourne and the First Seventh, had one effect which no one outside of Russian Intelligence knew anything about.

The Red Colonel, whose arrival a month before had gone entirely undetected, felt it had become too dangerous to continue meeting with elements of the IRA. Through a contact in the Admiralty, he was able to arrange a passage on a regularly scheduled ship departing from Dublin to Le Havre.

The sighting of the Russian submarine had still not been disclosed. But in London the wisdom of that decision was being challenged. Some members of the cabinet were afraid it would leak and be used as the platform for all-out political attack by the opposition.

Hence the inquiry. Bigger in scope than was normal, presided over by a senior officer, held in private but known to be in session —and with a scapegoat at hand if need be in the person of the hapless Major Welbourne.

"When you heard the firing of the mines and rockets, what did you do?"

"My first reaction was that Gideon must have opened up with his seventy-six-millimeter big guns. I had no idea rockets were being fired. How could I? None of us had ever seen weapons like this in Ireland."

"I don't dispute that. But what did you do?"

"Closed in at once on the Customs post."

"And did you find anything? Round up any terrorists?"

"No, sir. We found plenty of spent cartridge cases, but no men, no equipment. It was obvious they had turned and run on a prearranged signal. I immediately turned back to help Captain Gideon. When I arrived he was hurt and unconscious. There was so much confusion I ordered a cease-fire to avoid casualties among our own men."

"In fact, everything went wrong with your plans?"

"Well, yes. The heavy snow hampered us very badly."

"Now, Major, on the subject of casualties. You had already suffered four dead, four fatally wounded, and others less seriously hurt in the ambush of Gideon's column?"

"Yes, sir."

"Some of them caused by the Russian T-52 land mine?"

"That is correct."

"Yet you had swept that same area only hours beforehand?"

"Yes."

"But using mine detectors that would not pick up the plastic-covered T-52s?"

"Maybe not. But I am certain we would have found something. My men are very experienced."

116

"Precisely. So we come back to the likelihood that the terrorists watched you sweep that area, made their plans accordingly, and then came back at dusk to lay their ambush?"

"There seems no other possible explanation."

"Very well. I don't have to remind an officer of your rank and record that we are simply trying to establish facts which we can set down as a report and not to establish blame. To continue. When you reached the place where Gideon's column was under fire did you then manage to apprehend any suspects?"

"No, sir. But as I said, it was snowing heavily, and visibility was nil. I thought there was a greater danger of hitting my own men than the terrorists, so I ordered a cease-fire."

"Nonetheless, they still fired on you?"

"Yes."

"And inflicted even more casualties?"

"Yes."

"What was your next move?"

"I began immediate evacuation of the casualties. Informed my headquarters what had happened. Sent for Felix. Put out standing patrols, but warned everyone to watch out for more mines and booby traps."

"Your colonel has told me he strongly disapproved of your orders, and tactics, that night. He said, and I quote, 'The IRA must have been hampered by the blizzard and bad visibility just as much as my own soldiers. I can't think what Welbourne was up to. I feel there should have been far greater determination shown in pursuit'—pursuit at that time, he means, Major, after you had found Gideon shot up.

"What have you to say to that?"

The major shrugged his shoulders. "In my judgment the moment to close with the terrorists had gone. We were so close to the Border and the confusion was very great."

"But wasn't that the whole essence of your plan, to cut them off before they could cross over?"

"I felt then, and maintain now, we were too late. I had the casualties to think of. That is why I took the decision I have mentioned."

"You feel you were right to do what you did?"

"Certainly."

"And that the colonel was wrong?"

"I don't mean that, sir. But things were looking a lot different when he reached the scene. It had stopped snowing, and visibility was good. There was even a moon. When I gave my order to break off pursuit there was a blizzard raging."

"Ah, yes, of course. Thank you, major."

He saluted and left the inquiry.

He remained a week at Brigade, awaiting the verdict. All he could think about was the terrorist who had humiliated him. He read avidly all the speculation which appeared in the more sensationalist newspapers, trying to form a picture of him.

Finally the brigadier sent for him.

"Come in, Welbourne. Sit down, sit down, this is informal. I have good news for you. No further action is to be taken over the ambush, now or in future."

"Thank you, sir." And what about the "Russian," he wanted to ask but restrained himself.

"Yes. I'm afraid, however, there is a little more to it than that. I want you to listen carefully to what I am going to say, and try to understand why I am saying it. No need for me to tell you how it grieves me to see any officer, particularly one with your record, involved in an inquiry of this kind."

Welbourne waited for the ax to fall.

"I profoundly agree with the general's decision not to hold a court-martial. I do not consider there was any dereliction of duty on your part."

"Thank you, sir."

"However, Welbourne, this kind of thing carries a chain reaction. *I* gave orders to find out what lay behind the appearance of that submarine. *I* ordered your colonel to grab some suspects and bring 'em in for questioning for intelligence. So some people might consider his judgment, and mine, as well as your own, are to some extent involved here. Do you see what I'm driving at?

"That is why he said he looked for a more vigorous pursuit. So did I, as a matter of fact. And I can tell you this much—such a pursuit would probably have paid rich dividends, had you pushed on regardless. If we had found out what those Russians had been up to, as a direct result, then our casualties—regrettable though they always are—would have seemed more acceptable.

"But as it is we've gotten a hiding for nothing.

"Headquarters have drafted a statement for the press on the findings of the court of inquiry. It says no blame is attached to you, after full consideration of all the factors involved that night. Insofar as your career is concerned, that is officially the end of the matter.

118

"However, I don't think you should go back to your own unit, Welbourne. If you were unlucky enough ever again to turn into a similar ambush, and if, for any reason, things went badly for you, that would be the end of morale in the Runners.

"I am not going to risk that under any circumstances.

"I am not punishing you. I feel immensely sorry for you. But I have to make decisions as the man in charge, and my mind is made up.

"Your regiment is going to be here for a long time yet. Intelligence is quite certain the terrorists have many more rocket launchers and T-52 mines hidden, ready to use against us. Therefore I consider it wisest in the circumstances to move you, at least for the time being, and I have accordingly recommended a certain course of action to your colonel.

"He will tell you his decision soon, I have no doubt. In the meantime, don't be downhearted, Welbourne, you are a young officer with a fine past record and many years ahead of you. Regard this setback as the rub of the green, so to speak."

The brigadier was a two-handicap golfer.

"That's all, then. Good-bye, and good luck to you."

Was it only two days ago, that interview? Now Welbourne was sitting in his own adjutant's office, about to discover how the brigadier's recommendations had been translated.

"Dickie! The colonel will see you now."

Welbourne marched in, saluted, and stood rigidly at attention. He had known the colonel all the time he'd been in the Army. Their wives were friends. The two men had been under fire together, they had messed together, they had laughed and lived together for eleven years.

Now each saw the other through different eyes.

"You've seen the brigadier?"

"Yes, sir."

"Then you know all there is to know, officially. The inquiry returned a favorable report, and as far as the Army is concerned, that is the end of the matter.

"As far as I personally am concerned, it is far from ended.

"It goes without saying that I know you, of all men, would never run away from a fight. But brave men can make mistakes like anyone else, and in my opinion all your thinking on the night of the ambush was wrong.

"That I can excuse, or at least keep entirely between you and me.

119

As colonel, I take full responsibility for all decisions made in this regiment, good and bad. Always have, always will. However, when any officer's conduct is such that an inquiry is ordered, I do not expect to see any attempt made by one of my subordinates to challenge that responsibility.

"It was not for you, Major Welbourne, to suggest to the inquiry that my orders were wrong, nor to question my evaluation of the military situation.

"Do I make myself clear?

"The issue was not whether you were worsted in that engagement, but whether you did all that could conceivably have been done to carry out my orders.

"In my book, and I may say, in the brigadier's, too, that includes a vigorous, sustained, and hostile pursuit of the enemy.

"You did not give it. You did not even attempt it. And that is something I am not prepared to overlook. It is my opinion that we lost more than casualties on the night of that damned ambush, the regiment lost something by the way of reputation, too!

"The brigadier suggested posting you back to the depot, or to the Rhine Army. I think that would be grossly unfair. You will not want to remain at home, or in Germany, while your comrades are sent here.

"Equally, I feel you should be removed from field command here. If you should become involved in any new situation which could be exploited by the IRA—such as another "Bloody Sunday" shooting—you would be an immediate target for accusations of revenge.

"This is a political war, every bit as much as a street war, with the British Army under the microscope of world opinion every day.

"You are somewhat of a liability. I can't help it and I don't say it lightly. It is a situation that has been created by your own errors.

"On every ground that comes to mind, I feel that you should leave the regiment, and most certainly this area, as soon as possible."

Welbourne was ashen-faced.

"I would like to make it as easy as possible for you, for we have known each other many years. I have recommended you for staff duty, possibly at GHQ in Lisburn. Technically you will be on special service. Officially you will remain an officer of this regiment, with badges and privileges, and with the right to apply for a run to regimental duty at a later date, if you so choose.

"In this way you will still be soldiering in Ireland, as will your

120

comrades, although in a different capacity. You will leave here with no stigma. Is that clear?"

"Quite clear, Colonel."

"It may take time to arrange. I don't want you hanging about here. I am therefore sending you home on leave. Orders will reach you through the depot. That is all I have to say to you. Is there anything you wish to say to me?"

"Nothing, thank you, Colonel."

"Then you may go."

"Yes, sir."

Welbourne saluted and marched out of the office, a broken man. His orderly drove him directly to Aldergrove to catch the first plane to London. Welbourne prayed for an IRA ambush en route. Anything was better than a life cut off from his regiment, but it was a silent and uneventful journey. On a gray afternoon in April his orderly lifted his baggage from the Land Rover and said good-bye.

"It's a bloody shame, sir. All the lads want to be remembered to you, sir. Good luck."

"Thank you," he said, and shook the man by the hand before climbing aboard the Vanguard that would take him out of Ireland.

•20•

Major Welbourne arrived an hour later in bright sunlight at Heathrow, the airport just outside London. Still dazed by the break in routine, he was relieved when he immediately spotted his wife waiting for him. She had been overjoyed at the prospect of leave when he had telephoned her, and he pinned a smile on his face for her benefit.

"Dickie!" She ran to her husband and clung to him.

"Hello, darling. Ah, it's good to see you! Sorry I couldn't give you more warning. Where's Stephen?"

"Joyce had him for the night. I thought we could have one night on our own, in town, before we go home tomorrow. Have a long chat, just you and me. Yes?"

"Great idea," he said. "Anything special in mind?"

"I thought we could stay at that nice hotel where your father always bought dinner. Let's ring from here and book. Then we can dump our things, wander off for a drink and a meal in Soho, or just stay in the hotel if you're tired."

"You're the CO in this family," he laughed. "And as I have been strongly reminded of late, the CO's orders should be followed through with sustained effort. Let's go."

As she drove, he looked out on London. He thought how much it resembled a colossal ant's nest, with millions of scurrying figures emerging from one set of holes at a secret signal, and immediately joining queues to pour back into other deep holes in the ground. They seemed to have so little time for speech or laughter. They surged along ten abreast, a teeming maze of pushing, shoving, frantic, silent human insects, all hurrying along to eat a little and sit for hours in front of pale, flickering screens. Welbourne thought of his regiment and the purposeful, orderly life he had led until this morning, and sighed.

A porter took the car and hid it in the hotel's underground

garage. The major and his wife preceded their suitcases into the foyer and stood at the reception desk.

"You have a reservation? Ah, yes. By telephone. Thank you, sir. Boy! Mr. and Mrs. Welbourne, Room 325. Your key, sir."

He smiled them on their way to the lift.

The porter took an age to open their door and switch on each light, to check the curtains and the heating before he carried in their cases. He had worked in hotels all his life. He read lovers' impatience in the tightly linked hands and he knew to a second how to bait Welbourne into tipping too much to get rid of him.

At last they were alone. She slid her bare arms around her husband's neck and drew him down, kiss upon kiss. He was acutely aware of her trembling warmth, he breathed deeply her familiar perfume.

"Sue. Ah, Sue, darling Sue."

They made love for what seemed like hours then lay silent, still, content.

She stroked his hair and clung to him as he lay with his head buried deep in her shoulder.

"That stinking Army," she whispered. "God, how I hate it at times, always apart, always worrying. Why can't we be together like this all the time?"

He sensed that the tears were very close. He kissed her with infinite tenderness and drew slowly away, wanting to avoid tears at all costs.

"Shame on you," he told her with the false bright smile back on his lips. "Leading me on like that, an old married woman like you. But I love you."

She lay still and looked away. "I have to know," she said. "What are you going to do now?"

He got up and wrapped a towel around his waist, not knowing what to say to please her.

"Have a shower," he said brightly, too casually. "Get changed and take you out for a dinner and drinks. We can talk all you want over a meal. Not now, darling."

Still she did not move.

"I want to know."

He leaned down and kissed her. "A desk job," he said with forced brightness. "Office hours, just like you said, sweetheart. No

123

more nights in the cold, cold snow. As much Scotch as we can afford, no more of that two-singles-only-sir rubbish for me from now on. A warm bed every night. What more could a soldier ask?"

"You'll hate it," she said. "But at least I'll have the satisfaction of knowing you're safe."

"In which case," he said, playing along with the mood, "you are going to be a very satisfied woman. I have the certain feeling the colonel intends my departure to be permanent."

"I don't ever want to see him again," she replied. "The silly, stuffy, pompous little man. You are worth two of him."

Welbourne forgot his shower and went into the bathroom. He put on a dressing gown over the towel and rang down for drinks. In a few minutes they sat in the unlit room, glasses in hand, groping for words of comfort for each other.

"It'll turn out all right," he told her. "You'll see."

"It's such a thankless job over there," she answered. "The worst job the British Army ever had. Maybe you'll be better off, not so involved personally, I mean, if they give you a desk job."

"It's you I feel sorry for," he told her. "Poor old Sue, facing all those wives. Married to the man who boobed."

"I'm sick to death of hearing about Ireland," she cried. "And it's not just because I'm a soldier's wife, afraid to switch on the six-o'clock news! Everyone in England is saying the same thing—leave the Irish to fight it out among themselves and bring our own men home."

Welbourne managed a grin.

"You won't find the troops arguing with that one! Seriously, though, it's worse than Aden by a long shot. You can understand why Johnny Arab wanted us out, different color, religion, customs, language—a whole different world from our own. Ulstermen are supposed to be British, and the Irish our cousins. They're all 'agin' us' because we stop them from murdering each other. You know something, Sue? My men despise the Irish. They never felt that way about the Arabs."

Sue looked at him, her eyes brimming with tears.

"And you are one more victim of a lunatic situation, just as much as if they had shot you."

"I don't know so much about that," he said. "At least I'm still in the Army. I feel pretty damned angry. I'd like to get a chance to square the account."

"Why are men so stupid? The locals don't want you. The Army has taken everything you have to give and turned its back on you.

124

It's not as though it's even a well-paid job. Every worker in the country calls a strike to get a rise in pay at the drop of a hat. If soldiers want a pound a week more, there's a government debate. Why don't you get out while you can?"

"Sue, I've got a debt to pay. Eight of my own men are dead. I can't just run away and complain that *I've* had a raw deal."

He began to unpack.

"Come on, darling," he said. "No point in sitting up here and brooding."

She sat gazing at him, not answering.

"Come on, Sue. It isn't the end of the world."

"You go down." She looked in the mirror. "I'll fix my face and join you later."

The bar downstairs was crowded. He bought a whiskey and regarded his fellow citizens. The war in Ulster seemed very far away. The men wore well-cut, expensive suits and drank their way through rounds of drinks each costing more than he earned over there in a day's pay. They looked relaxed and prosperous—it was ludicrous to imagine them in the grip of a financial crisis. Their women looked fabulous. No one there could conceivably have been thinking, far less talking, about Ireland. It would have been too tiresome.

Come to think of it, being shot at, being ambushed, *was* tiresome. He gave them that much and grinned at the thought.

"Hello," said a voice. "Can I share the joke?"

Welbourne stood up to greet his wife. "I was just thinking," he told her, "how tough life is here in London, compared with the Army loafing away in Ulster! Now, what are you going to have?"

He thought she looked very beautiful. Straight black hair hung below her shoulders and gleamed in the soft light of the bar. She wore a crimson blouse over a black skirt that swept to the ground, and the single ruby on her hand was as red and warm as the glow of the fire.

"Mrs. Welbourne," he said gallantly, "you are beautiful enough to make a soldier forget his duty."

"Have you no shame? Mentioning such thoughts to a respectable married woman."

They raised glasses and drank a silent toast. She looked at her husband and thought how well he looked in civilian clothes. White silk shirt, knitted tie, and gray-flannel suit, with his fair hair worn just a little long for the military image. His face was square and strong. Richard Welbourne boasted the whitest teeth she had ever

125

known. In their courting days, she had called him Mack the Knife. He was smiling a lot tonight, the same rigid smile she had seen him clamp on at the airport.

She decided to play along with the false mood.

"How long a leave do you have, Dickie?"

"Haven't a clue. John thought it might stretch to ten days, perhaps less. It shouldn't take them long to pick out a nice desk in a dark back room."

"Ten days? Marvelous. I think I'll celebrate with another. Then we can go for a meal somewhere. Are you starving like me?"

"Not really. More dry than hungry. Drink up."

Later, over dinner, in a tense, strangulated voice she had never heard him use before, he told her everything that had happened on the night of the ambush.

"The weather was tailor-made for them. You don't get such snow normally in that part of the world, that's the odd part about it. We had several days and nights of bitter cold and then, on this one night and only when they opened up on us, it snowed in north pole style. Couldn't see a thing!

"When I first heard the bangs I thought Jim Gideon had gone off his rocker and was using his big guns. I couldn't imagine why. They must not be used in Ulster without high-level permission, you see. And when I reached him I really thought the biggest danger lay in the chaps shooting each other, so I blew the whistle. The colonel thought I should have pushed on regardless. The rest, you know."

"Were you right?"

"I thought I was. I'm not so sure now."

"The newspapers and the television made such a song and dance about it," she said. "As though it was the Charge of the Light Brigade—in reverse."

"It's such an incredible situation over there," Welbourne said slowly. "The reporters are right in the thick of it, looking over our shoulder all the time. Somehow, whatever the Army does—whatever the individual soldier does—is recorded and analyzed. Fairly, too, on the whole. But it means there is always a kind of public inquest to follow. Under that kind of pressure it is sometimes twice as hard to make a decision and give an order. It's unnerving in a way. No soldier in action should feel like a goldfish in a bowl. He's fighting for his life, after all."

"These men you fought that night," asked Sue, "were they especially clever or well armed?"

"They were well armed, all right," he admitted. "They had

rockets powerful enough to knock out a tank, never mind an armored car. I can't say if they were exceptionally clever. I got the impresssion this lot were pretty well clued up."

"But you have fought lots of terrorists before. Were these different from all the others?"

"Sue, 'terrorist' is just a name you give to the other side if you are regular Army. They call themselves freedom fighters. They are soldiers, too, but they play a different game with very different rules. Terror itself is their weapon. The whole structure of British-ruled Ulster is their target.

"The British Army is under wraps. It really does have to fight with one hand tied behind its back. As a result, we find ourselves too often on the receiving end."

She thought about that. "Are these people brave, Dickie? Or are they monsters? Some of the things they do sound inhuman."

"They do some unspeakable things," he said. "So did EOKA in Cyprus, the Jews in Palestine, the NLF in Aden, and so on. The IRA leaders openly admit they made a close study of other terrorist methods before starting this campaign. They get qutie a few hoodlums and psychopaths climbing on their bandwagon—it's inevitable, when you think about it—but there is no doubting the dedication of some of their leaders. And they regard themselves as Irish patriots. Are they brave? Some of them are. As individuals. But we think their war on helpless civilians is despicable and cowardly."

"If you caught up with the leader of the terrorists who ambushed you that night, how would you treat him?" she asked, struggling to understand the fury she felt behind his every word.

"If I'd caught him that night," he told her, "knowing who he was, I would have shot him without stopping to find out if he was brave, or patriotic, or anything at all but a gunman who had just murdered a lot of my own men.

"I really grieved for those men. I cannot tell you how I felt when I sat down and wrote to their wives. God knows what I am going to say to those women when I meet them on this leave, as I must.

"I can't say what I would do if I met that man now. Generals meet after wars, and their dead are one long line of wooden crosses in the ground. They swap copies of their books, and compliments, and say what a shame it all was they were on different sides."

"But this war is still on," she said. "This man is capable of killing more people, more of your friends."

Again his face went pale, and when he spoke it was with that peculiar tenseness.

She frowned into her wineglass.

"That man owes me something," he hissed at her. "He took something from me I can never get back. I don't like that. I certainly can't forget it!"

She reached out her hand and placed it on his.

"Ssh," she said. "Not so loud. Everyone is staring at us. I didn't mean to taunt you, darling. I just wanted you to talk about things and get it all off your chest before we meet the family and our friends, that's all."

"Sorry," he replied. "I'll try, I'll try not to blow my top. And stop worrying about me meeting Mr. X. What's he going to do? Walk up to my desk and confess?"—

"Subject closed," she smiled, "on the promise you will never shoot him."

"I don't follow you." He stared at her. "Why did you say that?"

"Because if you caught the man now and shot him, that would make you as wicked as any terrorist."

"Whose side are you on?" His voice had risen again.

"Calm down, Dickie. What I'm saying is, if you insist on soldiering on, then you musn't make it a revenge mission. That's the point I am trying to make. I love you too much for that."

"Promise," he said. "Cross my heart, hope to die. I will never shoot the Irishman who blighted my life."

They smiled at each other, and she tried to believe he'd meant what he'd said. When the bill was paid and the waiter had bowed them to the door, they walked slowly through the streets of London to their hotel, hand in hand. Like Kelly in Dublin, they found streets busy with tourists and heard the babel of a dozen tongues. They could just smell spring through the fumes. As in Dublin, everyone ignored the newspaper placards recording the latest death in Ulster.

They passed tarts and touts, pushers and pimps, dreamers and drifters, all part of the huge citizen army that nightly marches through the West End of London only to disappear, Cinderella-style, around the witching hour. They were already thinning out fast.

"Where do they all go? It's like seeing water pour down the sink," said Welbourne.

"Home," Sue told him. "The trains in the world's greatest capital city all stop running at midnight. It's known as progress," and she giggled.

"In that case," said Welbourne, "I'm all for progress. At least it gets everyone to bed in good time! And I happen to know one soldier who finds the thought of bed particularly entrancing tonight."

Sue squeezed his arm and smiled, saying nothing.

She stood back as he walked to the reception desk and asked for their key. But as she saw the clerk hand him a note, her heart sank. Only Joyce, their neighbor, had been told where they were staying. Had something happened to the child? She ran to his side.

"What is it? Has Stephen been hurt?"

"No." For a moment he looked puzzled by the question. "Sorry, dear, I should have realized how you would worry about a message. Nothing like that, darling, it's a summons from the Ministry of Defense. Someone there must have asked Joyce for our number. Man wants to see me tomorrow morning. What the hell can that be about?"

"Could be good news," she said. "Wouldn't it be marvelous if they offered you a desk job in Whitehall? Then we could go to bed together every night."

She blushed as she realized how close they stood to the young and handsome desk clerk.

"That's too much to hope for," Welbourne laughed. "Like winning the Pools on the day you get the sack. Somehow I don't think my luck is running that way."

They walked to the lift hand in hand. He pressed the floor button and as the doors shut slipped his arm around his wife's waist.

"To hell with the ministry," he told her. "You look scrumptious. Here we are together for one whole, marvelous, unexpected, stolen night of our lives. Let's investigate the soft bed we were talking about, shall we?"

Hours later, as he listend to his wife's steady breathing, Welbourne racked his brains to think what could lie behind the message.

Perhaps the colonel had relented and posted him to another squadron in the regiment—he knew this had been the brigadier's first suggestion. His heart leaped at the prospect until he reasoned—why would such a call come from the ministry?

There was a chance he was to be transferred to another regiment, perhaps one awaiting its turn to serve in Ireland. He thought about that. A new start, a new unit, an opportunity to win back his spurs and reputation, maybe even catch up with the man he had grown to loath. He sent up a prayer this might be the case.

Or might it be a desk job in Whitehall? The prospect daunted him, but not nearly so much as the thought of a desk in Belfast, so close to so many memories. And as Sue had pointed out, service in London had its undoubted attractions.

129

What could it be? Who could have searched for him so urgently that he had traced them to a London hotel after endless calls to friends and neighbors?

He tossed and turned until daylight. When at last he fell asleep he entered a nightmare in which he came face-to-face with the opponent he had sworn never to shoot.

There was no man in the nightmare, only a shape, huge and menacing, and the confrontation took place in the shadow of an enormous clock. Welbourne was bound and helpless, and in the dream the thing killed him, and the death was attended by frightful agony.

·21·

The office to which Major Welbourne reported next morning was not, as he had expected, situated in the main Ministry of Defense building in Whitehall. Instead, after many delays, he was directed to a side entrance in an annex.

After presenting his name and identity card to a uniformed security guard, signing a book, accepting a time-stamped pass, and awaiting the outcome of a half dozen telephone calls, he was ordered, "Follow me, sir," and taken by an elderly woman secretary through a rabbit warren of corridors.

Finally both were stopped by another uniformed guard who knew the woman well, it seemed, but still scrutinized pass and major very closely before he led him into a room marked PRIVATE. NO ENTRY!

"Just wait there, sir," he said. "Don't wander around on your own." The woman secretary vanished.

Welbourne looked around him in surprise. It was a big room with a high ceiling and distempered walls and much empty space—a room devoid of color, warmth, and welcome. There was a carpet on the floor, but so drab, so innocuous, so pale as to hide from notice. It reminded him, oddly, of a guardroom in an old barracks. Its main feature was a desk, deep and wide but swept bare of all tidbits such as paper, notebooks, diary, pencil, ashtrays, books, or indeed anything save two essentials—a lamp and a telephone.

In contrast there rested behind it a huge swivel chair, worn but comfortable, almost benign, a chair to relax in, a resting place on which much care had been lavished to help its occupant forget the poverty of the room and its furnishings.

Opposite the good chair was a bad one.

It was the seat reserved for visitors, and thought had been given to its selection. The upright creaked noticeably should the visitor lean back, and was clearly too weak to support a lounger. To sit in it meant to sit up in it, bolt upright, awkward and ill at ease.

Welbourne sat down with a curious feeling of guilt, though he could not say why. There was nothing to do but look straight ahead.

After a while another elderly woman looked in.

"Major Welbourne?" she sniffed. The major stood up and said yes, he was.

"You're late," she said severely.

"I started out in plenty of time," he retorted, trying not to be cowed by this Athena. "But my message said Ministry of Defense, and the taxi took me to the main building. I'm afraid I had an awful job finding you. Sorry."

"Mr. Sydenham will be along as soon as possible," she said. "He held on for twenty minutes but was called into conference. You're to wait here."

Welbourne thanked her—he could not imagine why—and remained standing until she had gone. He debated whether to light a cigarette, decided against it, and wandered around the room, frowning. He wondered what was missing and suddenly realized the cell was windowless. With a rush of claustrophobia he thought, I hope I don't get an office like this—it would kill me.

When at last the door opened, Welbourne turned to stare at a joke figure, Humpty Dumpty come alive.

Sydenham was like a balloon, round and roly-poly with a circular head that merged into a wobbling, quivering, shaking, shivering pear-drop of a body without apparent neck or shoulders.

He was hairless, gleaming, and polished, and pink from pate to jelly-wobble jowls. Where his eyebrows should have been was a variation in skin shade, a suggestion. His ears were minute and set flat to his head.

Sydenham looked jolly, like Humpty, rather than sinister, and for this blessing he owed all to his mouth, which was generous, full-lipped, and set in a permanent sunbeam smile.

His eyes joined in on the joke. They were small and blue, set deep in his skull, intelligent, and they twinkled like starlight on water.

He was dressed with meticulous care, as a fat man will to compensate for nature's joke, and he positively reeked of soap and water. His voice was deep, like crusted port wine.

"We seem doomed to keep each other waiting, Major," he boomed in greeting. "I *know* what kept you! You cannot imagine

132

the lunatic, imbecile, shilly-shallying pranks of political masters that have in turn delayed me! My apologies, dear sir! How are you?"

A hand shot out of his cuffs, pink and soft as a meringue. Welbourne took it carefully, as though afraid he might squash it.

"Good morning," he said, standing stiffly at attention in the face of such civilian obesity.

The twinkling eyes surveyed him and sent back a message of total sympathy. He guessed how the major must have suffered in the long minutes of waiting.

"I have a feeling," he said, "that our meeting will prove one of mutual benefit. It is also likely to be a long one. So I suggest we start as friends. No, then, perhaps you'd like to join a thirsty man in a glass of sherry, a very small one? Good. Splendid."

Little pink fingers fluttered down the desk, selected a bottom drawer, and came out with decanter and glasses. Sydenham poured two generous measures into the glasses and himself into the big chair in a single movement. He left the decanter handy. From an inside pocket he took a curved cigarette case, handed Welbourne a Turkish cigarette, and bowed his round head in acknowledgment as the major produced a lighter.

He looked long and hard at the handsome officer.

"Know anything about bird-watching, Major?"

Welbourne shook his head in astonishment. "No."

"A fascinating hobby, sir. One sees so many rare creatures. Ah, well. I will return to the subject later. First, thank you for coming to see me. I know how precious every moment of your leave must be. Incidentally, I must tell you that I know all about your own circumstances, how and why you are here in London. All I need to add is that the military code is of no concern to me, and that you have my sympathy."

Welbourne waited. He said nothing.

Mr. Sydenham continued. "My own job, sir, is in intelligence. You will not seek a closer definition than that, I feel sure. I am exceedingly curious about the ambush that led to your, ah, present plight and I will explain why.

"Now, sir. Shortly before the ambush, you attended a conference for senior officers and were told we had sighted a Russian submarine close inshore on the Donegal coast?"

Welbourne nodded. "I was."

"Then have a look at this, sir."

The fat hands dipped into a folder and came out with a

black-and-white print measuring sixteen inches by ten. They dropped it on the desk, facing Welbourne.

He studied the photograph carefully. He saw the Russian submarine, partially submerged, the rubber dinghy, the fishing smack. "Gunrunning," said the major. "Caught in the act."

"Precisely. We weren't certain what kind of guns until you got caught in the ambush later. Your men recovered two rocket launchers, and some mines and rocket-propelled grenades, a most valuable find. We know for a fact that this equipment still has not reached some of the Warsaw Pact countries and that only limited supplies have arrived so far in Egypt and Libya. That submarine has been identified, by the way, Major. We know it sailed from the Mediterranean to Ireland to make the delivery and we can assume the supplies either came from Libya or from the submarine's mother ship. Whatever the truth, they can only have been sent on Russian orders.

"Fascinating though that background is, I feel it is more a matter for the Army and the Navy than for my own department.

"What I want to know from you is this.

"Did you form the impression that the men who ambushed you were different in any way from other Irish terrorists you may have come across, differently led—professionally led, perhaps? You see what I am driving at. In your opinion, could that ambush have been directed by a professional soldier, a regular like yourself, for instance? A Russian officer even?"

"It's very hard to say."

Welbourne put down the photograph and looked up at Sydenham. "They took us to the cleaners that night, no doubt about that. And whatever was said at the inquiry, you have my word that my tactics were sound enough. But there were other factors that contributed to their success, apart from tactics and the firepower of those rockets.

"We hit freak weather, very heavy snow, which doesn't happen very often in those parts, and this wrecked any chance I had of pursuit. That was pure luck.

"But they were well organized and sited. The planning was exactly right against a superior force. I don't know who led them, but he was good. To answer your question, yes, I suppose it's possible."

Sydenham jotted down some notes. "They certainly weren't led by a farm yokel?"

"It didn't seem that way to us."

"I didn't mean to sound sarcastic, Major. There are always

134

reasons for my questions. You see, on the day this submarine was identified in Donegal waters, a British vacationer was reported missing in the same area. Now, he was no ordinary tourist. This man was an enthusiast, an old man who had recently taken up bird-watching. We would never have known that, incidentally, except that a routine check on all Irish newspaper clippings for the day showed this man vanished after setting out for a 'hide' on the coast and slap opposite the point where the sub was spotted a few hours later.

"He hasn't been seen since. At first it seemed like a routine accident, old man, rocks, bad weather—and the sea. But now we strongly suspect he may have been murdered for seeing too much.

"We were extremely worried. I sent a man into Donegal to browse around. In the village where the bird-watcher disappeared he found the nucleus of a very active guerrilla force."

"And you relate this to the arrival of that Russian submarine?" Welbourne could not believe it.

"Ah," said Sydenham, letting out air from pursed lips like a leaking balloon, "there you have me. It would be easy to say yes. The truth is, we don't know which came first, the chicken or the egg. Therefore it is of paramount importance that we discover, and quickly, what that submarine carried as cargo. There is one theory she may have had men on board, as well as rockets. I intend to find out if I have to use thumbscrews to get at the truth."

"Are you seriously suggesting," asked Welbourne, "that I might have been attacked that night by a band trained and led by a Russian commando?"

"Something on those lines," Sydenham replied.

"It's more than a guess, actually. I told you we had a chappie pottering around the village where the bird-watcher vanished. He has evidence that two men, one since identified by photographic record as a senior member of a militant terrorist group, the other a stranger—and significantly, quite definitely a foreigner of some kind—were staying together in a hotel there at the relevant time. I can't imagine it was by chance."

"What kind of foreigner?"

"We don't know. And I feel this is where you enter the picture, Major. When you go back to Ireland, I want you to try to help us trace this unknown man. A moment, Major, I beg of you! No one is asking you to play detective, far less spy. We have specialists in counterterrorist sections who are very effective.

"Nor do I ask you for selfish reasons, sir. This is for your country. I seek your help as a patriotic Englishman."

"With or without the knowledge of the Army?" asked Welbourne, suspiciously.

"Let's say I prefer to keep it between ourselves for the time being," said Mr. Sydenham delicately. "The GOC will know, but no one else."

The major thought about that. It was one source he could never check.

"You are going to be given a staff job at Lisburn," the fat man went on, "one with the chance to keep your eyes and ears open. When I have a better picture of this unknown foreigner—there may well be others—I'll get in touch with you. I want you to ensure my 'wanted' notice reaches a few specially selected people, nothing more. Men who have special ways of watching out for him and who will bring him in fast, for direct questioning by me. I shall ask nothing more of you than that, sir. Every communication from me will be quite open."

He left Welbourne to think it over and turned back to his files.

"Look at this. It's all we have so far. Intriguing, nonetheless."

Welbourne read:

NAME. Registered as Kelly, B. Address, Tuckahoe, New York State, N.Y., U.S.A.

DESCRIPTION. Height 6'2" or more. Hair blond, slightly graying, crewcut style. Weight not less than 200 pounds. Very powerful build. Cleanshaven. Scar or scars around each eye. Big, prominent nose, thin lips, strong jawline. Very heavy smoker and whiskey drinker. Age somewhere between forty and fifty. Sometimes speaks with noticeable American accent.

NATIONALITY. Unknown. Not Irish, apparently, and not typically American according to local Guarda. Stayed at hotel with man believed to be LIAM O'CONNELL but registered under the name O'CONNOR (see separate description).

MOVEMENT. Booked into hotel separately. KELLY arrived one night before submarine was sighted, and last occasion when bird-watcher JAMES was seen alive. O'CONNELL joined him next morning. Left together twenty-four hours after Tyrone ambush, for unknown destination.

"Now," said Sydenham, "that is most interesting, is it not?"

"Fascinating."

The fat man pushed an Identikit drawing across the desk. Welbourne felt the blood rush to his head at the sight of the terrorist. His tone, however, was cool.

"That's a tough-looking bastard, whoever he may be."

"Indeed. People remembered him, of course. Oddly enough, very few seemed to have noticed the gentleman called Liam."

"I should have thought your man would have a hard time asking questions there?"

"Not really," replied Sydenham. "He went as a grief-stricken relative, and the Irish are very devout. It was only natural he should seek to find anyone who had met the old bird-watcher."

"What makes you sure the death was no accident?"

"We know the very moment he left the pub where he was staying. We know the exact time the submarine was photographed. James must have been close enough to reach out and touch it, damn nearly! His belongings were recovered, but with one significant omission. His bird-watcher's notebook. They all carry one, it seems. Had he perhaps made some incriminating notes on sighting the submarine, a record of some kind? I think it highly likely.

"Also, he had a camera. We found that, certainly.

"There was a film inside, a whole roll, unused. I find that too much coincidence. Notebook gone, blank film, man missing. I don't like it.

"Curiosity alone would have prompted him to snap the submarine, assuming he saw it—and the odds are fifty to one that he did. When that camera was handed back to our man it was neatly buttoned down inside its leather case. Full of unused film. Remarkable!"

The smile never left Humpty's face, as though he were permanently enjoying a secret joke.

"Assuming the poor fellow was killed for the reasons I have stated, what became of his body? It could have been dumped in the sea, Major, and we are keeping an open mind on that possibility. Or it could have been disposed of elsewhere. Ireland is a big place. Donegal is close to the Border.

"Personally, I find the timing of each event fascinating. Leslie James, bird-watcher, falls into the sea and is conveniently drowned at the very moment a Russian submarine delivers a mystery cargo. Two strangers turn up for a spot of fishing, one now know to be a member of a fanatical terrorist splinter group, the other unidentified.

"Fishing keeps them out of the hotel, and out of sight, for many hours each day.

"Within a week of their arrival, your squadrons of trained professsional soldiers are lured into battle with a guerrilla band, who have almost *advertised* their intention of overwhelming an isolated Customs post.

"In the fighting, your professionals take a mauling from the brilliantly led enemy, who happen to be using brand-new and highly sophisticated Communist-manufactured weapons. *Russian*-made weapons.

"That, sir, is more than I can stomach as a chain of pure coincidence. It smells Red right the way through to me."

"An odds-on bet," Welbourne agreed. "I don't really see how I can help, though."

"A chance to strike back!" exclaimed Mr. Sydenham, agitated now and all a-wobble. "An opportunity to avenge your comrades! Apart from them no one suffered more than your good self on that night, sir, so you have a vested interest in bring these murderers to account.

"The only clue we have, Major, to the vital question—did any men come off that submarine, somewhere down the coast per-haps—lies in the sketchy description of two people somewhere at large in Ireland. We think these two will lead us to the others, if in fact there are any others. We have to find out.

"I can think of no one more dedicated, more willing than your good self, to help try to track them down. Will you help us do that? What I need is an Army officer ready, willing, and able to sit up half the night, poring over every single regimental intelligence report for the slightest clue. I must have a man who knows how big are the stakes, someone who will give that little extra to the hunt. I will see to it that you are ideally placed for such a task. You will not be given the messenger boy's job that you feared on your return to Ulster, Major.

"We are not without influence here and will see to it that you drop into a minor intelligence role as cover. You will be given certain jobs to do, none too arduous, which will leave you ample time for your undercover duties.

"You see, we must think along these lines—if there are Russian agents in Ireland, and I say 'if' because we have no proof, they are sure to strike again and again. You will be helping the Army, perhaps your own regiment, if you work with us to thwart them. Perhaps we can lead them into an ambush of our own making, next time out. That will be your revenge."

"Amen to that," said Welbourne.

Sydenham asked him: "You agree?"

"I do. I'm your man."

"Thank you," said Sydenham. He poured more sherry. "I'll drink to that."

Welbourne raised his glass in reply. He remembered his conversations with Sue overnight and felt a twinge of guilt. What *would* he do, if he had that man in his power?

"If such a man," he asked, "was handed over to you for questioning, what would happen to him?"

Sydenham rolled the delicious thought around his tongue.

"Who can say at this stage? I appreciate you have little love for this man, Major. But I will tell you the truth. We should interrogate him at very considerable length and try to break him. It would not be overpleasant.

"If he is a Russian, as I suspect, there is a chance he will turn, go 'double.' Some do, you know. Not many.

"If he wanted to get off the hook, but was unwilling to run the undoubted risk of going double, there is the chance he might blow the gaff on his Irish friends, in return for favors. If he betrayed the schedule for future arms deliveries, that sort of thing, an untraceable double cross, that would certainly do him a lot of good.

"You'd be amazed how people will bend to save their own skin. The old notion of tight-lipped heroes walking calmly to their death by firing squad went out of fashion a long time ago.

"It's only fair to tell you that your man may even profit by his treachery. He will certainly be given every opportunity. If that turns your stomach, think of the lives we might have saved in your own unit if we had bribed him early enough.

"We are assuming, of course, he is a Russian. I have to keep stressing that.

"Above all, your professional spy is a realist. He is aware that even if he refuses to cooperate in any way—however hard we press him—we should still lose by killing him. He still holds a trump card by virtue of his exchange value.

"Major, there is an international market in spies today. All of them are graded, like professional football players, with an appropriate transfer value. I say that as a measure of my confidence in you, even though it constitutes a kind of treachery even to admit such a thought.

"An agent gets senior officer's rank, good pay by home standards, unlimited perks in the sense that his government foots whatever bill he runs up on their behalf. And he has an unwritten guarantee that, if caught, he will eventually be returned under the exchange system.

"We can do nothing about it. It is almost as if, without the

139

consent of their governments, they have formed their own exclusive international trade union.

"A few nations refuse to play the game. An Israeli spy caught in Baghdad has no chance. His very best hope is for a speedy public hanging after torture. Those are very brave men. Russian agents working in the West are a very different kettle of fish.

"The idea of one's spies being returned on a transfer scheme is reasonably acceptable, although we are then faced with the task of ensuring they have not gone 'double.' "

The ash from his Turkish cigarette fell on the table. He puffed and huffed and blew it onto the carpet.

"I do hope I haven't disappointed you too much."

"The fact remains, he's still sure to get off scot free."

"If he turns out to be a Russian."

"Then there doesn't seem much point in my working hard to catch him."

"It will mean saving Army lives. And if he's not a Red, I can promise you he will rot in jail for a long, long time."

"Yes," Welbourne agreed, but his tone lacked conviction.

The telephone rang on Sydenham's desk. He picked it up and listened for a while. He looked a little embarrassed.

"Yes," he said at last, "we have reached an understanding. Unofficially, of course."

He listened again and looked at Welbourne. "So soon? Then I must not detain him. Thank you."

To the major he said, "Those were your marching orders, I am afraid. You are to return to Ulster as soon as possible, sir. Dare I ask you to restrict your leave to two or three days at the most? I regret that I am under considerable pressure at this moment in time."

"I really don't mind. Not now." Welbourne meant it.

"Be prepared for a long and disappointing task. You are not required to do anything except keep your eyes open and report anything you feel is of the slightest interest. Always call me on this number and on no account leave messages with anyone else. Say nothing of our conversation to anyone once you leave, most especially family and regimental friends.

"I won't keep you now. I am greatly indebted to you, Major. I have the feeling we shall do great things together. Au revoir. Oh, one more thing. Once our Mr. X is apprehended, your banishment from your regiment will come to an end, if you so wish. That I can promise."

"I'd like that," said the major. He put the card that the fat man

140

gave him into his wallet. "Meantime, I'll do what I can for you. I'd give my right arm to get my hooks into this mysterious Mr. X."

"If you do," replied Sydenham, "make sure he comes to us unharmed."

"It's the second time in twelve hours that's been put to me," Welbourne remarked, under his breath.

Sydenham rang for his secretary. She might have been listening outside the door, so quickly did she arrive. She took the major's pass, scribbled an exit time on it, got Sydenham to initial it, and ushered Welbourne out with amazing speed.

"He's very busy," she said severely to the major. "You've kept him a long time." She made it sound like a crime.

Welbourne took a taxi back to his hotel, all smiles.

"You've been drinking!" Sue accused him. "And I thought you were in for such an unpleasant morning. And such a change in the man! Tell me, have they posted you back to the regiment? Or to a lotus life in London?"

"No, darling," he said. "But I've had a lot of things explained to me, and I feel better now. If I have any luck, I shan't be long on that desk in Belfast—it's back to the regiment one day, for sure. Now I've got forty-eight hours—sorry, that's all—so let's get down to the kids. Tonight we really celebrate. Let's get out of here."

When he caught the plane to Belfast two days later he felt like a man saved from drowning.

•22•

Kelly and Liam had moved to the lakeside farm in Monaghan in the first week in May. The twins, Kevin and Sean, had gotten the place ready, and the facilities offered were in keeping with their tastes.

There were three bare bedrooms in the remote stone house, all on the second floor. Each contained a camp bed, a canvas chair, and a washstand. There was, of course, no central heating of any kind, and Kelly spent most of his time half dead with cold.

The graystone face of the farmhouse looked north, and the rise on which it sat took the brunt of every wind that blew and all the rain that fell in those lonely parts. Inside it was always cold, always damp. The big stone fireplace which burned peat made little impact; even Liam found it depressing.

The nearest village was six miles away. The "owner" regularly advertised in the best English papers offering it to let for fishing; farming had long since ceased in that area. When readers inquired if it was free, and many did, back would come a letter from County Cork where the "owner" lived, regretting that it was no longer available. It never was. It was let in advance, in and out of the trout season—a fact which aroused no comment anywhere—for this was one house never visited by priest, garda, tourist, or journeying shopkeeper. Whether any of the locals knew or guessed at the real identity of the fishermen who sometimes drove there, but had never once been known to put out a rod on the water, was a matter for conjecture. None had ever put curiosity to the test and knocked on the door.

It was a two-story building. The ground floor consisted of a tiny kitchen, about ten feet by eight, fitted with a peat-fed boiler and a single tin bath, and an ill-lit living room with the one inadequate fireplace. Down at the bottom of the garden was an outdoor privy.

142

There was no village electricity. Oil lamps or candles were used at night, and all cooking was done on a portable gas stove fed by butane containers. The gas supply was always renewed by incoming visitors.

Furniture in the living room was just as Spartan. A mat of coconut hair covered the floorboards in front of the fireplace; the rest was bare and unpolished. There was an old two-piece settee, one armchair, a wooden rocking chair that was reputed to date back to the days of the Potato Famine, and a single scarred oblong-shaped table which had seen a lot of eating and drinking and plotting. Men had sat at that table dreaming of an Ireland free from English rule since the first stone had been laid more than three centuries back.

The walls of the living room were a dull and uniform green. The walls flanking the stairs were gray. The master bedroom was decked out in fever yellow, well mottled with time, and the other two in khaki. In the kitchen and "bathroom" the owners of this desirable holiday cottage had given up the struggle and settled for walls clad in good, honest dirt.

The only decoration in the whole building was a single painting, framed and faded long ago, of a lake trout that weighed in at eleven pounds.

Twenty years before, an IRA man had bought the painting at a sale in Mayo, that home of giant trout, and carried it back to Monaghan to lend credibility to the fishing cottage "cover."

Kelly and Liam found a mountain of canned meats, powdered milk, soup, and beans. Visitors brought bread in bake-yourself, American-style packages, which Liam put in the butane-fired oven. Kelly, to Liam's surprise, insisted on doing all the cooking and made delicious meals out of the kitchen's very unpromising materials. "I've been in the Army all my life," joked Kelly. "Nothing kills time like cooking."

In his bedroom Kelly found a whole crate of Irish whiskey and cartons of American cigarettes. The twins visited the farmhouse from time to time, but apart from a civil enough greeting, avoided Kelly. They were under strictest orders not to lay a hand on him again, at least until the mission was completed. Copies of all English and Irish newspapers were delivered every third day. Not that there was any shortage of news—the farmhouse was rich in radios. Each bedroom had a transistor set, and a big battery-powered radio stood in the kitchen. Liam always had one set blaring.

From the farmhouse windows the view was breathtaking and

extensive. There was no accident in the provision of such enormous visibility. The original republicans who built the farm chose the hightest point for miles around and made sure they fitted windows with a clear field of fire on every approach.

On the house's western face, the master bedroom windows looked down the lake. Fringed with reeds, it was fed by a stream from the mountains and harbored swarms of trout and perch.

When it rained, which was often, the lake turned black as an undertaker's hat, but when the sun shone the water laughed back at the farmhouse, glittering and shimmering and rippling with the breeze. Uncut meadows ran down from its stone walls in a uniform coat of emerald green as far as the eye could see. There was only one approach, a road made of dirt centuries back and never improved, a road for snails rather than motorcars.

Kelly and Liam spent two peaceful days, speaking rarely to each other.

One night over supper Liam told Kelly about his early life in the IRA and the tragic history of Ireland which had set the rebels in motion once again.

"The 1922 agreement was the big betrayal," Liam told the big man as he ate. "We all thought it was a brilliant solution. The Six Counties were created, sure, but we figured it wouldn't take long for the Protestants to see the value of joing the Republic."

Kelly snorted, "Those Tory landlords joining a Catholic republic. You must have been daft."

"We were, a little," Liam admitted. "Anyway, things didn't work out. The Prots kept squeezing the Catholic population dry, kept them out of the local councils and the trade unions. Catholics in the Six Counties were treated like natives, and Westminster refused to do a bloody thing about it. Those of us in the South couldn't sit around and see our brothers brought to their knees."

The mercenary said nothing. Wherever he'd been, whomever he'd fought for, there had always been somebody like Liam who tried to get him involved, get him to understand why other men risked their lives. He risked his for money; he'd been doing it for fifteen years; he intended to keep on doing it. When he wasn't working, the whole world could take a flying leap into the ocean for all he cared. But he didn't tell Liam that. He just nodded and said nothing. Liam thought he was getting to him; they all did. In the end it didn't seem to make much difference. He did the job for them, he pocketed his fee, and everybody was happy. He liked to keep it

144

simple. The only thing different about this job was the extra pleasure he would get killing a few Englishmen.

The third evening after their arrival in the farmhouse Liam and Kelly were visited by the four members of the Fenian council. It had been a long, sunny day, and already the spring flowers were making their way up the hillsides. Kelly had taken a long walk and was in sight of the farmhouse when he saw the old black car come down the drive.

Eamonn made no reference to the last meeting. After they'd greeted each other with a few words and settled around the battered table in the main room of the farmhouse he got straight down to business.

"I want you," he told Kelly, "to let us know everything you will need to make your bomb. You have to be its architect and decide on shape and size and weight. I'll tell you first what information we have, and you can tell us how this helps you or otherwise. If you decide that you need to cross the Border and look at the site for yourself, we can arrange it, but we will need at least one day's notice. According to our latest reports, by the way, you have twelve days left before the conference begins.

"Now. In two days' time local workmen will start to move in under Army escort and will work under police supervision to paint and clean and tidy up for the English visitors.

"When they have finished, the Army will call in a bomb-disposal team to serach the building top to bottom.

"They start in the cellars, so I'm told, and work their way up to the roof. Then they check the outside walls and the roof itself. As soon as they pronounce it 'clean,' they seal off each room to be used by the VIPs. These seals are broken one hour before the conference starts, in the presence of the Army experts. Once the seals are broken, the only people allowed in before the delegates arrive are police and Army. And no exceptions are permitted. This is an unbreakable rule.

"We have acquired several photographs of the main conference room and the dining room and the main hallway. They may help you in some way. We have nothing else save general views.

"Unless you use the lake, and find a way through one of the sewers, you must cross part of the eighteen acres of parkland to enter the building. The grounds are patrolled day and night by RUC in pairs and using dogs.

"The Army intends to set up at least one roadblock on the direct road approach. This will be based on a hamlet which lies a mile or so from the hotel. It has thirty houses in all, a couple of shops, and a pub. We have friends there.

"As you requested, we have brought plans of the building and Ministry of Works drawings showing every alteration made in the last five years or so."

Kelly looked at him with a grin.

"And all I have to do," he said, "is find a way through that lot, place a bomb, and set it to explode when the conference gets under way, right?"

"Yes," said Eamonn. "That's what you have to do."

"Well, I better get started then. The big room upstairs will be my workshop. I'll take the photographs and your reports and I'll let you know my ideas when I've studied them closely. There is one thing I have to know right off. Do we have someone planted inside the hotel itself?"

"We have." Eamonn debated how much to tell him and finally decided he would have to know. "One of the official secretaries is working with us. She is the one who gave us all details of the conference and such security arrangements as are known. She also supplied those photographs you have there."

"No danger she might lead us into a trap?" asked Kelly.

"You can depend on her," said Eamonn. "Her family are as good as dead if that ever happened."

"I'm interested in this bird," Kelly told him. "How come she's so obliging?"

"A number of reasons," said Eamonn, still patient.

He went on, "I'll tell you a little about here, to put your mind at rest. Her name is Moira McCabe. Her marriage was never very happy. She blamed her husband for the death of their only child several years ago in a car accident. He was a leading unionist, a real fanatic. After the boy died she had a breakdown and in her deranged state she thought the best way to take her revenge was to help her husband's political enemies. That's how it all started. They hated each other and the more they quarreled the more she hit back at him in her own way.

"We were baffled when she first contacted us, and highly suspicious. She started by giving us little bits of information, nothing very important then, but when she was promoted to senior secretary in a government department there wasn't much she didn't pick up. Now she's invaluable. She takes fantastic risks at times and seems to get a kick out of it. I'd stake my own life on anything she passed on."

146

"Okay," said Kelly. "I just wanted to know. And you say she's going to be working inside the building during the conference?"

"Yes."

"Then that's the way we'll have to get in. Through her. Maybe I'd better go to Belfast and contact her.

"What do you say to that?"

"That's for you to work out," Eamonn replied. "You do it all your way from now on. Let us know whenever you need help, and we'll give it. If you go to Belfast remember this—if you're caught, you're on your own. If you talk, you're a dead man. Keep your mouth shut, and we will work day and night to get you free."

The oil lamps were alight now, smoking slightly, and the peat sang in the fireplace. Liam thought of his family and ached with loneliness for them and the peace that he felt when he was with them.

Kelly took the photographs and the heap of architect's drawings and ruffled through them as he picked his next words.

"I can't help thinking," he said, "that the easy way in lies through the woman. Let me sleep on it. I could make a device that the girl could take in, maybe, and set it herself, but I don't want to chance it. It's got to be me all the way through. That's the only sure way of knowing it will be done right."

Eamonn waited. Then he said. "True enough. We can't afford a mistake."

"Neither can I," Kelly said.

The four council members rose together and said their good-byes. "We'll be back at the same time tomorrow," Eamonn promised, and the council went out the door into the driving rain that had begun an hour after sunset.

Kelly asked Liam where they would be staying.

"If I know Eamonn," the little man replied, "he will be back across the Border speaking to the woman he mentioned and trying to get every scrap of information he can to help you. He's a worker, that Eamonn. You won't find him sitting around and wasting time. He badly wants this plan to work! It's a great chance. We all know that. It could turn the whole campaign around."

"Yeah, you might get the whole British Army breathing down your necks with no holds barred!" said Kelly.

"We'll have to take that chance. In Cyprus and Aden the rebels did, and the backlash gave them the victory. We'll be exerting a hell of a lot more pressure than ever EOKA or the NLF did, if the British crack down!

"We are counting on the British public getting tired of Ulster as surely as the American people did of Vietnam. As soon as that reaction begins to make itself felt, we've won. There will be a national outcry for the troops to be withdrawn. We won't have to fight once that happens, for Irish unity will follow as sure as the sun rises each morning."

"And what about the Protestants? They're not so bad at the terrorist game themselves."

"If it's just them against us, they don't stand a chance. They can't support themselves. Independence for Ulster is parrot talk. Give 'em a few years of big dole queues and short rations and the idea of a federal union will sound like heaven."

"And you'll keep bombing till that happens?"

"We will."

Kelly laughed. "Everybody's got a solution for Ireland," he said, "but in the end it always comes back to bullets and bombs. If you got your unity that way, do you think it would be any different for the government in Dublin? They'd have an IRA situation of their own, only this time it would be run by Protestant terrorists demanding union with Britian. It would go on for years—just like your own campaign—and it would serve you bloody well right."

Liam began to argue but Kelly pushed him aside.

"I don't want to hear any more about politics, Liam. I'm in this just for the money, remember? Hand me those photographs. I've got an idea, just the smell of one, and I'm hoping your woman friend can make it work."

· 23 ·

Rain tapped on every windowpane and the wind howled like a banshee as the Martyrs gathered at the farmhouse on the following night.

Kelly was huddled in overcoat and sweaters and he paced up and down the kitchen, stamping his feet with the cold. Liam crouched behind him, piling peat bricks on the fire. The room smelled of damp and age.

"After you'd gone last night," Kelly began, "I spent many hours studying those photographs taken inside the hotel and then reading and rereading the girl's notes on procedure at these conferences.

"The key to this whole operation lies in that British Army explosives expert. If we can find a way to get past him, we're home and dry. I've drawn up a plan to smuggle the bomb into the building, hide it in a place he won't dream of searching, and then move it into the conference room *after* the seal has been broken.

"I'll explain that in a moment. First of all, I'll tell you what sort of a bomb I intend to make and what method I will use to make it explode.

"Some of you may not know, but there are a great many ways of doing this. I can make you a light sensitive bomb, one that will go off as soon as they switch the lights on in the room. I can give you a time bomb if you like, or a bomb that will fire at a radio signal. I can fit one with a simple antihandling device, in the same way we rig a booby trap, or I can use a pyrotechnic technique —that means a bomb you explode with a lighted fuse. You are all familiar with the chemical-delay device, I think—the acid eats its way through various barriers one by one until *zap!* up she goes.

"There are so many varieties available, and each one has its attractions, depending on circumstances.

"I can make you a bomb to explode with the opening of a door, or at the slightest pressure. Such a device can be incredibly sensitive.

149

I could kill a man in bed, for instance, by making a bomb that would fire with the weight of his head on the pillow.

"I can fire one in a variety of ways—by switching on a TV set, or simply by ringing a telephone number.

"There's one snag with most of these. They're blind. They cannot select the victim. *Anyone* putting his head on the pillow gets it, some fool could get a wrong number and detonate the telephone bomb.

"What I must do in this case is design a bomb that will explode only when we know for certain our VIPs are in the room. Also, it must be powerful enough to kill them all outright. The best way to ensure that is to set one to explode at head height, close range.

"We mustn't leave anything to chance. Look how the Germans boobed with that bomb attempt on Hitler's life.

"Bearing in mind the tight security inside the building, I have settled on a 'radio bomb'—a bomb that in fact will 'talk' to me and tell me when everyone is present in that room and when to fire it. A bomb that I can talk to in turn and give orders to from a safe distance."

Raymond began to protest. Kelly cut him short with a raised hand. "Believe me, it can be done. I don't have to spell out its obvious advantages. It is controllable. There is no danger it will be wasted on the wrong target or by premature explosion."

Eamonn framed the question that was in everyone's mind.

"That all sounds fine," he commented. "A talking bomb now, is it? But you've still got to move it from its hiding place, and place it in the conference chamber under the noses of a small army of Special Branch men and security guards. How do you propose to do that? The girl can't do it. We can't afford to risk her."

"Easy!" said Kelly, looking around the room. "We'll get a policeman to carry it in for me!"

Eamonn looked unimpressed.

"You think I'm joking, don't you?" said Kelly. "Well, I'm not. I've got it all worked out. It just needs a little help from the woman. We make the bomb here. I smuggle it into the building by posing as a workman before the Army expert makes his search for explosives and I hide it inside *this.*"

He held up a soft piece of paper showing a rough drawing.

"That's what the policeman is going to be asked to carry in to the conference chamber, and he won't suspect a thing. You hear a lot of fancy talk these days about bombs, but in the end it all boils down to this—the closer it sits to the target, the greater will be the damage. So I've chosen something the victims won't suspect even

150

though it's right there in front of their eyes. Something so obvious it's laughable.

"Explosives experts have a routine for this kind of search. The first thing that gets a going over is always the table. They tap it for hidden recesses, look in the drawers if any, get dogs to sniff it—the smell will nearly always give the homemade bomb away—and even X-ray its legs. A long time ago one Belgian colonel I knew told me that ambassadors in the so-called revolutionary countries have their dining rooms searched every night before dinner as a routine precaution.

"So we won't waste our time putting a bomb under the table.

"Then there's the fireplace. This gets a lot of attention from the security boys because it's so attractive to the assassin. If you could suspend a bomb down the chimney, say, or position it in the hearth fractionally above floor level—ready to blast outward into the room—that would be curtains for all inside.

"You'll find the guards sniffing around the fireplace and the chimney like dogs around a bitch in heat. So we'll leave this one strictly alone."

Kelly paced up and down the kitchen, smacking his right fist into his left palm to emphasize each point.

"So, we leave the table alone, the fireplace alone, the chimney empty, no booby-trap devices on doors or chairs or light switches. We want the British to think that room is 'clean' because no one knows about their damned conference or because it's too well guarded."

He pointed a finger at Eamonn.

"So *you* make sure that none of your men is caught anywhere near the building and that there are no independent bomb attempts in the area. And I take care not to move the explosive device into the conference chamber until just before the talking begins. It can be done with careful timing. My sketches show you how."

He placed the hand-drawn diagrams in the center of the table, where everyone could see them. Then he sorted through the batch of photographs and took one out. This he passed around, from hand to hand.

"Now that picture," he said, "intrigues me. It was taken, so the caption says, a year ago. The room is crammed with top brass, led by the British home secretary of the day and the prime minister of Northern Ireland.

"Take a good look at it. I think we can assume the final scene will be much the same at this coming conference.

"The thing to bear in mind is that the room must have been

searched for explosives and sealed for at least a week before those men sat down at the table.

"Look on the table. What do you see? Ashtrays, note pads, water jugs, glasses—*and two tall vases*. Have a closer look at those vases. Both are filled with flowers of some sort. See what I'm getting at? Flowers—fresh-cut flowers—can't be kept in a sealed room for a week or more. They were put in at the last moment to tart the place up for those VIPs, most probably at the same time as the pencils and note pads and so on.

"If, as you say, no one but policemen and Special Branch detectives are allowed in that room after the seal has been broken and before the VIP arrive, then those flowers must have been carried in by a cop. There's no other way they could have gotten on that table.

"I accept that they might examine those flowers one by one before they go in the vases, but that's our way to place the bomb just the same.

"I asked Liam about those vases. He found out they are antiques, dating back to the early eighteenth century, which means they will be quite valuable and most certainly kept under lock and key when not in use as showpiece items.

"Liam," he said. "Tell your mates what you told me about those vases."

Liam read from some notes he had prepared.

"They are," he began, "historic pieces, all right. They were a gift to the first bishop from craftsmen in the Dutch town of Delft. According to my information, they are dated 1768, at a time when craftsmen there used a marking of their wares as a guarantee of its fineness and quality.

"A trademark, if you like.

"In their case, though, they made it part of the decoration, in the form of hayforks and billhooks, everyday things like that. They mean you can tell the genuine article at a glance.

"These two here bear the initials of the makers, a 'B' and a 'W,' followed by the letter 'D,' for the name of the town. I am told they are worth more than fifteen hundred pounds each. They are well-known pieces, so I'm told, and apparently it's common knowledge that the present prime minister of Northern Ireland is himself a collector. It's a million pounds to a pinch of snuff that these vases will be there on the table, stuffed with flowers, for the conference.

"Kelly here first of all thought of trying to get copies made. We both accept it can't be done, especially with an expert in the room. These two are blue and white, with the markings in darker blue.

The bomb has to go inside a vase that's there. If we try to fake it we're inviting trouble."

Kelly took up the talking again.

"Thanks to Liam," he said, "we got a complete rundown on these vases. Each one has a centerpiece pedestal that actually holds the flowers and is removed for cleaning. What I'm going to do is build my bomb around a pedestal of the right size and shape and carry it in with me. I'll put it inside the original vase and take the other one out with me.

"I'll make the bomb in such a way the girl can put the flowers in herself on the day without any risk. She can even get a policeman to fill it with water for her—water won't harm my bomb!—by which time it will be heavy enough for her to ask him to carry it and set it on the table without rousing suspicion.

"It's essential she understands there is no danger of premature explosion, because I will be monitoring the bomb from outside. It can't go off until I press the switch.

"She can then receive a convenient phone call, from her sick mother, say, to get her out of the building in plenty of time.

"I'll be the nearest one of us to that bomb when it goes off—and I'll be *one mile* away. Let me tell you how we can do that."

Kelly lit a cigarette and looked at his companions. Their eyes never left his. The only sound to be heard was the scrape of his match, followed by the patter of the rain outside.

"My part of the equipment—the control panel—contains a transmitter and receiver. So does the bomb. Whenever a man in the bomb's audio range starts to speak, or farts, or sneezes, or blows his nose, or slams a door, or makes any kind of noise at all, the bomb registers each decibel of sound and transmits a signal to me.

"That registers in my control room, one mile away, via a needle flickering on a dial. Now picture the conference room on the morning of the conference.

"First, the Army explosives expert will arrive and examine the seal. He will find it unbroken and declare the room safe for the VIPs to enter. That finishes his job in the conference room. Then the only people allowed to enter for any reason until the delegates turn up will be the policemen.

"The secretaries themselves will have to hand over pencils, paper, ashtrays, glasses, and so on for the RUC men to set around the table.

"The vases themselves, being very valuable, will be kept under guard until the last moment, when they are filled with flowers and taken into the room.

"These vases stand three feet in height. The outer shell is thin and light, beautiful workmanship. The pedestal inside the vases must be heavy to give them stability or they'd topple over with long-stemmed flowers in them. My bomb will be so constructed that when the vases are eventually carried in, they will both weigh exactly the same. Mrs. McCabe will not even have to switch the bomb on at a given time. Instead I shall build an automatic timing device to make the bomb 'live' from 9:30 A.M. to 1:30 P.M. each day.

"Those times are arguable. I can change them as required. Some of you may think such a conference would start earlier in the day. I don't agree. The top brass is coming from London and will not spend one more night in Ulster than absolutely necessary because of the risk. They'll fly in on the same morning as the conference. They have to allow for weather, ground mist, or even fog, they will be forced to allow some kind of leeway for any unforeseen IRA activity. Mrs. McCabe has told us the last such conference began as late as 10:30 in the morning and continued right through the day, with food and drink sent in and no break at lunchtime.

"There are other considerations when setting my timing device. I have to plant that bomb inside the building a week before the conference opens. We have been told there may be delays even after that. I have to spread the life of my main transistor batteries as much as possible. All considered, I reckon four hours a day the most we can allow and the times I have picked are the logical choice. You men agree with me or not?"

Raymond, Eamonn, and the twins nodded, their eyes shining.

"Okay, then let's imagine it's the morning of the conference. It's 9:30 and the Special Branch men are having a final look around, one last check, before letting their VIPs come in. There's a constant *flick!* *flick!* on the needle of my control panel as the cops speak to each other, telling me almost as much as if I was right in that room myself.

"I am counting on the invariable procedures that go on before an important conference like this. What's the word I'm looking for—protocol? The protocol never varies on big occasions like these.

"Everything has to be done by the book, everything has to conform to a pattern—the police, the secretaries. Remember the last conference didn't get off the ground until half-past ten in spite of every effort, and they'll be conditioned for delays this time. Meantime my bomb will be there to keep watch and listen, to lip-read for me!

"Say this final look around takes ten to fifteen minutes. That's acceptable given the need for security. Then the policemen leave the room. Total silence for a while, with my control needle lying quite still.

"In come the VIPs and start walking around, looking for their name tags on the table, some of them shaking hands, all of them talking at once, 'Hello, sir, how are you?' and 'Did you have a good flight, Minister?' and crap like that, while away goes my needle, *flick! flick! flick!*"

Kelly's audience was spellbound.

"At last they're all in their places. Someone will rap on the table for silence, the chairs will stop scraping, for a second my needle will drop back. A voice will announce, 'All right, gentlemen, settle down for the minister,' or something like that, and away will go the needle again, up and down, up and down.

"Silence for a second while the big man looks at his notes, with the needle still. As soon as he begins to address the others, its movement will become regular, constant, *flick! flick!*, just like *that*"—Kelly jerked his forefinger side to side above the kitchen table.

"There they'll be, like sitting ducks. I'll press the transmitter key and *wham!* up she goes."

Liam was watching the faces of the others. He'd heard all this while Kelly was working it out. But to the rest of the council it was like a fairy tale. They were afraid to even shift their chairs in case they broke the spell.

"Now, let me spell out for you the effect of my bomb on this particular room," said Kelly in the dreamy stillness of the farmhouse. "The blast will roll along the table top for a fraction of time and literally cut everyone there in half before spreading out to shatter walls, doors, ceiling. The two urns will disintegrate into ten thousand pieces of shrapnel. Murderous splinters from the woodwork, together with fragments of brick and stone and glass, will gouge and shred everything and everyone in their path. The conference room will turn into a charnel house. And there'll be nothing left except maybe rubble and burned flesh, because fire from severed gas and electricity mains will certainly follow the explosion."

Kelly sat down and looked at Eamonn. "How does that sound to you?"

Eamonn managed a nod and a small smile. "Magnificent."

Liam prompted the mercenary. "So what do you need from the council right now?"

"I'll give you a shopping list of parts I need for the bomb," said Kelly. "You will need to contact the girl first, or Liam's vase expert. I have to know the exact weight of the urns as they stand, with their

155

pedestals weighed separately. I will need scales to weigh each component part of the bomb. The two urns must weigh exactly the same to the ounce when the policeman carries them in. And I will need a plausible reason for entering that building as a workman.

"I need to be someone who would arrive with large cans, paint, polish, anything like that, as part of his normal working equipment. I need to be there as a man with a job to do inside the conference room long enough to look around and get to the vases without raising suspicions.

"Liam is going to spend every minute of the day sharpening my accent—I used to have a bit of one from when I was a boy. He's got to perfect a new background story and turn me into someone who can talk to an Irish cop without raising suspicion. We've already thought about that. I want you all to put your minds to it, and soon. Any idea will be welcome.

"There's one last thing, and it will be crucial to the success of the whole operation. Eamonn, you have already said you have 'friends' in the hamlet near the hotel. Liam says they run a pub, and we worked it out on the scale map that it will be within the mile I need to operate. Here's what I need from them.

"A room to lie up unseen for a week or more, listening in to my bomb, and with no disturbance, no cause to move out. It has to be a room big enough for two of us, so that I have someone there ready to take messages and run errands, as the case may be. A thousand and one things can go wrong through no fault of mine, and we must have instant communication.

"That man has to be Liam, I reckon, unless you've any objections. He and I get on together, which is more than I can say for the rest of you."

Kelly forced a grin on his face to take some of the sting out of his words.

"Now, once the bomb is made and positioned and Liam and I are holed up in the hamlet, the farther the rest of you stay away the better I'll like it.

"The whole place will be crawling with security men before and during the conference, and if they get so much as a smell the Fenians are in the vicinity, it will double the risk of our getting caught.

"As long as we have communication, that's enough.

"Finally, I want an escape route planned for Liam and me. We might have to lie low for a few days after the bomb has exploded. It depends on how safe the hideout is. Maybe we can pull out as soon as the bomb explodes. Either way, it needs to be organized *now*."

Eamonn answered him point by point. In the light from the

156

spluttering oil lamps his scarred faced looked grotesque, Liam thought, even sad.

"Raymond will go back tonight over the Border and make contact with Mrs. McCabe to get the answers you need on the vases. He can also bring us up-to-date on preconference jobs inside the building. He will check everything out with me before we give you the go-ahead.

"As far as your room in the hamlet goes, Mr. Kelly, you're home and dry. The pub is 'safe' and has been for three years.

"But there are problems. The RUC use it all year round, drinking away half the night." He did not try to hide the disgust in his voice. "Whenever troops set up a roadblock in that area they use the pub too. The landlord is a former member of the British services and to them is above suspicion. You'd be astonished, Mr. Kelly, to know how many members of the IRA have served in the British forces. MacStiofain himself, once chief of staff of the Provos, was in the Royal Air Force for a time, did you know that? But the troops today either don't know or don't care."

They talked until a late hour. Finally, after Liam had served tea in pint mugs, Eamonn and the council drove off. It was a meeting that had been noticeably friendly.

Liam waxed optimistic after they had gone.

"You did well tonight," he said. "Had them eating out of your hand, did you know that?"

Kelly poured himself a huge drink and sat crouched over the fire, laughing.

"You know what pleased me most?" he chuckled. "Hearing that miserable bastard say 'magnificent'!"

Liam could only manage a mechanical snort at that remark. He'd forgotten how much Kelly hated the leader of the Martyrs. He changed the subject.

"Are you definitely going to pull out after this job?" Liam asked him. "Our American friends have bottomless resources, all from oil. You could be a millionaire in a year if you stayed around."

"No money in the world would keep me here after this job," said Kelly. "I'm not working for Eamonn one day longer than I need to. Anyway, it's too goddamn risky working in Ireland.

"And you're not even the Provos or the Official IRA, you're just a tiny little group playing at liberators. You can rob banks, you can bump people off in one or twos, but that's all. You've got all the money in the world behind you because of some link with a rich American—but nothing else.

"That rich bastard behind you knows you're not very much!

That's why he sent two of his top executives out recruiting! To smarten you up!

"Now don't look all pained and upset, Liam, I'm giving you the facts of life." Kelly was enjoying this. He was getting back for all those earnest lectures the little man had been giving him on Irish history the last few days.

"You're lucky you got me. I'm an explosives expert. With this woman's inside knowledge and my expertise your mob is going to be getting some attention. Eamonn's going to be a big man in Ireland.

"I just puke at the thought of helping him get that famous. That's why after this job you can all take a flying leap in the ocean."

Liam thought that over in silence.

"So who will you work for after us?"

"I've had a thought or two on that," said Kelly. "The answer is—Black September."

Liam looked shocked. "Black September?" He shook his head in disbelief. "You'd not join that murdering bunch of heathens, now, just for money?"

Kelly hooted with mirth. "Only an Irishman could say that and mean it. What are you doing if it's not murdering people?"

"You can't see the difference between your attitude and mine, can you?" said Liam angrily. "I can take a true belief, a national Cause, with me to confession. All you could take would be bloody hands."

It was now Kelly who changed the subject. It was bitterly cold in the farm, and he had a blanket over his shoulders and was crouching right over the embers. He held up the bottle.

"I really need this tonight," he said, "on account of this weather. If I fall sick, you don't get your bomb. See I have plenty, Mr. bloody caretaker."

Liam felt his anger ebb. Kelly's drinking was almost a joke between them by now. But he was still curious.

"There's something I don't think you know about this Black September."

"What?"

"They don't hire mercenaries. They don't need to. Take those Japs at Lydda airport. They sure as hell weren't in it for the money. They were part of a group in Japan who had connections with Arab groups. None of them got out of it in one piece, either. They were in it for something else, same reason I'm in it."

"Yeah? Well, you hired me, didn't you?"

"We hired you because we had to. We don't have enough experience in modern fighting to beat the British Army. But Black September, they know everything. They don't *need* you, Kelly. After us, you're going to have a lot of trouble finding work. If I were you I'd stick with us as long as you can."

Kelly felt a chill again, listening to Liam in that cold farmhouse. It was like the fear before the ambush, but different.

"How about some food?" he said. "I'm starving!"

For once Kelly let Liam cook, and the little man scrambled up some eggs. "Let's work while we're eating," Liam suggested.

"Concentrate all the time on talking like an Irishman, even thinking like one. In a few days' time you're going to be working in a building under the eye of a number of pretty shrewd Ulster constabularymen."

"I still think the best way to cut my losses is to pose as a former local who's spent all his time in America," said Kelly.

"They're not mugs," Liam warned him. "You'll need a lot more than that. Relatives. Home address. You'll have to know about people, and pubs, and Irish football. You've got to know the difference between the Shankill and the Falls. You have to know who Bill Craig is and Tommy Herron and men like Faulkner and Paisley, too. Take in what I tell you, listen to me well if you want to collect that hundred thousand dollars."

Neither of them mentioned Black September again. They talked until Kelly fell asleep. It was three in the morning and a witch's night.

Liam got a pile of blankets and drew them over the mercenary as he lay snoring by the smoky fire.

•24•

It proved to be easy to remove, measure, and duplicate the Delft urn's pedestal in lightweight plastic material.

As soon as Raymond was back from the North, Eamonn telephoned its precise measurement to his organization headquarters in Cork. The duplicate that Kelly needed came from a department store and was standing on the table in the farmhouse within forty-eight hours. While the entire revolutionary council stood around and watched, Kelly checked the measurements against Raymond's notes. It stood ten inches high, measured ten inches in diameter, reducing to seven at the base.

"Beautiful," pronounced Raymond. "Exact in every detail."

Kelly glared at him.

"*Everything* you get me for this job," he snarled, "has to be exact down to the last detail."

Eamonn broke in.

"Now," he said, "more good news. At least I think it is. The two Delft urns are kept all year round in the armory, together with a number of valuable paintings left by the first bishop. They only come out on high days and holidays. All the rest of the time they stand under armed police guard.

"The paintings are all in America, on loan to some exhibition in Boston, and they won't be back for months. The urns are in the armory awaiting cleaning.

"That's good news insofar as they're sure to be reckoned 'safe' at all times. On the other hand, Mr. Kelly, it may make it harder to change pedestals when you're in the building. Which brings us to the problem of getting you in there.

"Mrs. McCabe has already started to travel to the hotel each day, with a few other staff, under Army escort. I've asked her to contact us each night to keep us up-to-date with security arrangements.

160

"I'll see you get everything she tells me, right down to the last dot and comma, in case it helps in any way. She says that at this stage it's about what you'd expect, an unreasoning mixture of official fussiness and lunatic carelessness. She says they're really cracking the whip over this conference with the attitude that nothing but the best is good enough for our guests. What if the British prime minister himself comes? Think about *that*, Mr. Kelly!

"Of course, everything will change once the Army sends in that explosives expert. But at this time security is in the hands of a small number of Irish policemen, and they're getting a bit rattled with all the pressure. That makes it easier for us.

"Mrs. McCabe says the first of the workmen start arriving tomorrow. They're painters and decorators, and we don't have a cat-in-hell's chance of putting you among them, Kelly. These are old-school loyalists, they all know each other. They take two days to complete their work.

"Then come electricians and finally cleaners. All has to be complete by Tuesday, presumably one full week before the conference begins. I say 'presumably' because there's something else in the wind, something very secret that Mrs. McCabe can't get hold of yet.

"But a delay of a few days won't affect your device, will it, Kelly?"

"No," said Kelly. "The batteries will last—I don't know exactly how long but a month, maybe. So as long as they don't cancel the conference, we're all right."

"Right," said Eamonn. "Now back to our problem of getting you in. Here is the exact order of workmen as listed by Mrs. McCabe. Painters and plasterers first (and ruled out by us, anyway). Next, general workmen to see to carpets, fittings, curtains, rough-and-ready plumbing, that kind of thing, then polishers, and last of all, cleaners.

"I appreciate we must find you a job that necessitates carrying cans, big cans. Whatever we find for you, there's one snag. Most firms they use are known already to the police. In every case they must submit a typewritten list of names and addresses, together with work permits and accompanying photographs, not less than twenty-four hours before the man clocks in. This enables the police to ring each firm direct and even make snap calls on addresses picked at random."

"I've got an idea," said Kelly. "*Invent* a job that needs doing. Tell Mrs. McCabe about it and supply her with the phone number and address of the 'firm' to ring. When the 'boss' delivers the identity

161

photograph and work permit to the police, naturally my face and name will be on them. I'd be very surprised if there's any check on the firm other than a phone call. They'll be too busy. Anyway, let's hope so. In this business you have to take a number of calculated risks."

"You've still got to get the bomb inside the building," Eamonn reminded him, "and it has to be done on one day only—the day they take the urns out for their spring cleaning."

"And that one small point," Liam said, "would have canceled out any chance of Kelly getting in as a painter anyhow, purely on timing."

"Yes," Eamonn agreed.

The twins rarely said much. Neither was noted for his brainpower, but they were both wracking their brains trying to be helpful. This time they had a flash of genius, and Kevin turned to Eamonn.

"Make him a French polisher, Eamonn. They have to carry cans galore."

"What's that?" said Liam.

"He polishes wood, antiques, that sort of thing," said Sean. "I know one firm in Belfast that owes us a favor. They'd let us put a man in for a few days to answer the telephone. That's all we need. If the police check out the business, we could still get away with it."

"Which firm is that?" Eamonn asked. Sean told him. "I'll take a look at it myself," said the leader, "and make certain they know the score. We can't afford to have anyone talking."

"In that case," said Kelly, "I'm in business. You work out the details in your own way. I don't know French polishing from cleaning windows, so somebody will have to teach me."

"One more thing, Kelly," said Eamonn, "I want you to tell us how you made the bomb. We want our money's worth."

"If something happens to me?" finished Kelly with a grin. "Okay, I see your point. I'll play teacher. Let's begin with acid bombs. Make up the wrong mixture and a single delay at the traffic light can cost you your life. In unskilled hands all bombs are a bloody sight more dangerous to the manufacturer than the client, as revolutionaries have found out ever since the Chinese invented gunpowder. The last person you want in my line of business is a patriot—always send for a specialist. That way you will live to fight another day.

"I daresay some of you disapprove of my choice of a flower vase as the bomb holder. It sounds so obvious, the sort of thing they always choose in books and TV plays. Well, that's true enough until you consider the unique circumstances we have handed to us on a plate in this case.

"We've got two urns which are showpieces and so valuable they have to be guarded all year round. Who would think of looking for a bomb in something a policeman sits next to all day and every day?

"They're stored in a place no explosives expert would be expected to search. Furthermore, with any luck he won't even see these, before or after he's broken those seals.

"You've got a minister who's a collector himself and will take real pride in seeing these two rare pieces on his table.

"And lastly, they're so heavy in themselves that it would be entirely natural for the girl to ask a man to carry them for her. In this case the only men around will be policemen."

"Perfect!"

Kelly looked around. "All with me, so far?"

They nodded assent.

"Liam's told me you're a pretty new lot—all ex-IRA I suppose —not that I care. But let me tell you what I do care about. Execution, perfect execution. The thing you have to bear in mind is you have very little knowledge of sophisticated bombs. So, when I give you my shopping list, make certain you bring me *exactly* what I asked for.

"When you know how, a bomb like mine can be made in less than a day! Let's start with the urn. According to Mrs. McCabe, these urns weigh fractionally over ten pounds apiece empty, most of the weight lying in the pedestal. Fine. I take this pedestal out and replace it with a plastic mock-up, light as a feather.

"I mold my explosives around this plastic pedestal. At the foot I put the transmitter, receiver, detonator, and the separate transistor batteries I need to activate the bomb, plus an automatic timing device. All these are in a waterproof cover. The aerials are simply wrapped around the explosive and wired into the component parts. Look, you can see the finished article in my drawing."

Kelly passed a crude drawing around the table.

"You will see at once why the shopping list is so important. We have no space or weight to play with. I have everything worked out to the ounce in the exact space available inside that urn.

"We come next to choice of explosive.

"There are four types of choose from in this war—Quarrex, Togel, Polar Gelignite, and Gelemax.

"They can each do certain jobs best.

"The one we're going to use is Gelemax.

"It's very stable. A man can mold it like putty without risk, no matter how warm or cold his hands. It doesn't matter if he drops it or if it gets rolled around in the back of a car, for instance. And when you come to handle it for any type of bomb, it's easy to work out how much you will need.

"Gelemax comes in eight-ounce or four-ounce paper-wrapped cartridges. For a ten-pound bomb, then, you need twenty of the eight-ounce size or forty of the smaller size. A word of warning when you make your own bombs—*always* make sure you burn those wrapping papers! It's one of the first things a cop will look for when he searches a suspect building, and one paper overlooked will earn you a long stretch, my friends.

"Now, the detonator. For this bomb I will need a small, instantaneous detonator. It will measure one and a half inches long by one-quarter inch in diameter. Do you all know what a detonator consists of?"

"No!" said the twins in unison.

"It's made from an explosive acid called fulminate, which is crammed in a metal tube. Tubes come in various sizes, so keep a note of what I want. If you're picked up in a spot search, there's always room up your ass. Like burning the wrapping paper, it could save you a few years in jail.

"I've mentioned an automatic timing device. This is how we will make it.

"I must have a timepiece that will meet all these requirements—it has to be small, lightweight, completely reliable, long-running, and above all, silent. We daren't risk any kind of 'tick' problem, just in case there should be a last-minute check in the room by experts using a stethoscope.

"In the first bombs of this type, men used those big, noisy, hand-wound, twenty-four-hour alarm clocks. Christ, you could hear the tick a mile away! Then they progressed to the quieter, longer-lasting, seven-day travel alarm clock, which had the added advantage of being smaller and more compact, but still had a faint tick. A lot of these are still used.

"But I use a wristwatch that fits the bill exactly. It's a Bulova Accutron and will run for a year on a single tiny transistor battery that fits into the back of the watch. It has no conventional movement and therefore no tick. Being a wristwatch it is small, really small, and it weighs bugger-all. It costs, I don't know, maybe forty pounds or more, but you can buy one in any good jeweler's shop. All we have to do to convert it for our use is insert a simple switch through the face and connect it up to the rest of the bomb mechanism.

164

"Thus we have an automatic timing device that cannot be heard and is guaranteed to outlast the 'life' of the bomb, which of course depends on the lasting power of the main transistor batteries. I'll come to those in a minute, but take it from me, they last a month rationed by the timing device.

"These ministers from England will be busy people. I am convinced some of their talking will be done in the hours I have preselected. Postponement is something else, and we have to be prepared for it. With this bomb, if we have to sit back and miss a day, or even a week, okay, we can still hit the next time around.

"Now back to the shopping list. I want a roll of black masking or insulating tape and a roll of insulator wire like you use at home for electrical jobs.

"Have you ever seen radio-controlled model aircraft? I want one of those radio-control sets. I want two transmitters and two receivers, one set for the bomb and one set for my control panel. Buy a model plane as well. If you're searched coming back, you're just one more family man giving the kids a treat.

"This radio-control system is ideal for us. The transmitter on the ground and the receiver on the plane are tuned in to a special frequency. The man on the ground can use his transmitter to 'pilot' the plane over open country, which is what we're going to do with our bomb.

"These receivers are no bigger than a matchbox. The transmitter is bigger, say seven inches in diameter by two inches deep, but still something that can be hidden in the urn without difficulty. There is a tiny acoustic microphone, the size of a pinhead, which is very efficient.

"As soon as the alarm switches on the bomb, this microphone picks up and relays every sound. We'll know the general routine program for the day from Mrs. McCabe. Now do you see the value of this kind of explosive device? It's got a brain of its own. It says to me, 'They're silent now, they're studying documents,' or '*Flick! Flick!* the minister's still talking, after twenty minutes,' and it tells me this loud and clear from a mile away while it's surrounded by security people.

"I need two yards of wire for the bomb aerial. The aerial lays inside the top of the pedestal and runs down the Gelemax into the transmitter-receiver system. My alarm switch sets the bomb 'live' every day between 9:30 and 1:30, but no watch can tell night from day, which means eight hours burn in every 24. That's a big percentage. I will therefore put in two transistor batteries, a main and an auxiliary, to compensate.

"I also need a separate PP(9) or pen battery to fire the detonator—you can get it from any hardware store. The pinhead acoustic microphone is on sale in all HIFI shops. The on-off switch is two inches long and comes with your model aircraft set.

"Lastly I'll need a soldering iron to connect up the bomb circuit, but we don't have electricity in this farm. One simple way round that: I'll run it from one of the car batteries.

"When that's done, we're in business.

"Take another look at these two drawings I've made. One shows what the urn will look like with the bomb sitting inside. The other shows you a simple way to take it in and past the guards inside a five-gallon can—of polish, for instance. It will be sealed in a water-proof cover. The cops will open the lid, pour polish out to test it, smell it, but I'll lay odds they don't find the bomb. We can have more than one can, of course. We'll be afloat in polish."

The drawings were passed around the table. When they came back to Kelly, he said:

"Eamonn will tell you who buys which part. Don't forget my scales. I want everything here as soon as possible. After the last part arrives, I still have a day's work putting the pieces together. Then, when you get me my overalls, and the van, and the okay to move, I'll turn up at the hotel as a French polisher."

Eamonn had a question.

"What about the smell? The security people will put dogs in the room, won't they? Dogs specially trained to sniff out explosives?"

"They will," Kelly agreed. "Immediately after the seal had been broken, I would think—before the urns are taken in.

"In any case, dogs would smell around the floor and the fireplace. They won't get up on the table. Once again, it's a chance we have to take. My own guess is those dogs will have so much area to cover that morning they will be put in the conference chamber first and won't get near the urns at all."

Now Raymond asked a question.

"The urn you put the bomb in, Kelly. It's going to be solid inside from halfway down with Gelemax, below the pedestal cover. How is Mrs. McCabe going to put flowers in that lot without breaking the stems?"

"Good point," said Kelly. "But I've already thought of that. The pedestals have holes in the top to receive and support flowers. All she has to do is poke a knitting needle down first. It can't harm the Gelemax, which will give, and it won't activate the bomb. All she has to do if someone watches is make a joke, like 'Hey, I thought someone had cleaned these damned things?' something like that."

166

"Why won't water affect the bomb?" asked Kevin.

"Because water doesn't have any effect on Gelemax," said Kelly, patiently. "That's one of the reasons why I chose it, remember? The working parts are in a waterproofed cover. Think about it, man, you've got to water fresh-cut flowers or they die on you. I'm a great believer in the simple psychology of such things.

"The RUC men there are dog-handlers, not bomb experts—they get the Army sent in to deal with explosives—and the very sight of water being poured into those urns would be reassuring to any layman.

"I *want* those flowers watered. It looks good. It looks right. I'm all for the little touches."

Eamonn spoke again.

"Supposing," he said slowly, "that for some last-minute reason we wanted the bombing canceled. I can't think of one"—and the ghost of a smile flickered on his lips, the first Kelly had ever seen—"but assume the situation arose. We could send you a message ordering you to call it off. You might not trust that message, you might think the security men had got hold of me and were forcing me to give you the order, and for a variety of reasons no one can foresee you might start to hedge.

"How could we be sure the bomb was rendered harmless?"

"You forgot to mention the money I'd be losing," said Kelly, "but I take the point. Simple. Get me away from the control panel, or just remove the transmitter—or get Liam, or whoever is with me, to remove it. Then I can't send, and the bomb can't explode."

Eamonn was satisfied.

"Good," he said briskly. "I don't think there's anything else. You'll get delivery of every component part you asked for within thirty-six hours. Leave it to me."

· 25 ·

Major Welbourne ran up the steps leading into Land Forces HQ near Belfast, waited briefly while his papers were checked by an ultrasmart sergeant of military police, and then marched in to report to a staff colonel who, like himself, had formerly been decorated for gallantry in Aden.

"Hello, Welbourne," said the colonel as he shook hands. "Nice to have you with us."

"Sir." Welbourne saluted and remained at attention.

"Relax, man. Let's clear one thing up right away, shall we? I have been speaking to the GOC and know all about your local difficulties back in Tyrone. An official inquiry has absolved you of blame. And what's past is buried and forgotten inside this building. Enough said?"

"Thank you, sir."

The colonel waved him to a seat.

"No doubt the prospect of a desk job has been worrying you, eh? Well, we intend to keep you busy. The general has personally suggested you for a special task, starting immediately. Want to hear about it?"

"Of course, sir. And thank you again."

"Don't thank me, Welbourne, it's the Old Man's idea. I think his intention is to underline his confidence in you. Either that"—the colonel smiled briefly to take the sting out of his next words—"or you must have some powerful friends lobbying for you! The job is top secret and carries a lot of responsibility. Calls for initiative too."

Welbourne made no reply but felt a distinct glow of warmth for Sydenham.

The two officers spent the next hour discussing problems arising from the forthcoming conference at the Old Covenanter Hotel.

"Overall security will be our general responsibility until the

168

Special Branch arrive to take over. It will break down this way. Roadblocks on the approach road, manned by a company of Guards. Air surveillance, two choppers available at all times. The top brass will be lifted in from Aldergrove by chopper, other personnel attending will travel by road under Saladin escort.

"It's not the first time we have handled this sort of thing. Details are all set out there, and that document stays top secret. You will see my own notes about the Royal Ulster Constabulary standing guard inside the hotel and the grounds, as well as the orders concerning Felix.

"I have made the arrangements personally. Senior responsibility rests with me.

"But the general wants a man down there from this headquarters tying all the loose ends together. I think it is an excellent idea. It will take some of the load off my shoulders, and I believe it right you should be given an immediate chance to show the general his trust in you is not misplaced.

"I want you to keep an eye on all the day-to-day developments however small they may seem at first sight. Have a damn good look around, make yourself a confounded nuisance to the infantry, armor, and police, keep everyone right on their toes. If any of them try to pull rank on you, come straight on the line to me.

"In this context I am referring to our military police, of course. Don't go treading on any RUC corns. Try to make it appear strictly team effort, while always getting your own way.

"If you come up against any problems with the civil police, simply refer them to me, and I will speak quietly to the commissioner. All right?"

"I think so, sir. What about clerical staff?"

"They come under a different category. They're a handpicked few and they all have A1 security clearance, of course."

"Right," said the major. "Sounds absolutely watertight to me."

"Well," the colonel answered cautiously, "I don't know about that. This is Ireland, remember. I've been here eighteen months now and I'm beginning to believe in leprechauns. Make sure you don't let any get into that hotel."

He allotted Welbourne a room, introduced him to a handful of officers, and took him down to the mess. Here, they sat apart from the others, raising points about the conference as they came to mind.

"What's it in aid of, or shouldn't I ask?" said Welbourne.

"Can't say, officially," the colonel replied, "but it's easy enough to work out for yourself. There's already been a Border referendum and another White Paper on Ulster. The first resulted in bombs at the Old Bailey and elsewhere in London, the second was rejected by the Provisional IRA and other splinter groups.

"In my view, the business of this conference must be to define areas of responsibility for Ulster security once this new Assembly gets going."

"You said earlier it might be delayed," said Welbourne. "What could hold up a conference on that? Sounds logical and urgent to my way of thinking."

"Ah," said the colonel carefully, "I don't know how far I should go into that." He decided to take the plunge. "Look, for God's sake, keep this right under your hat.

"The government desperately wants the new Assembly to have a peaceful trial run. So there's going to be an offer to the terrorists to meet us—separately or together—under flag of truce to talk turkey. There'll be a time limit for acceptance, of course, for we don't want to chase rainbows. Where we meet them, and when, and what happens at such talks might affect the date and scope of our own conference. It's very hush, Dickie, not a word. The press must not get wind of this."

"Understood," said Welbourne. "I'll just carry on regardless."

Over coffee, the colonel asked him: "Will you go to the conference site today?"

"Might as well make my number with the RUC," Welbourne replied. "I want to have a good look around, anyway."

"There's an Inspector James Renton in local charge," said the colonel. "A good man. You'll like him, I think. There are also four or five civilian staff. The senior woman is a Mrs. McCabe. Consult her on any confidential matter—quite a remarkable person."

"What's she like?"

"Physically, you mean? I've no idea. Never met her. We've spoken on the phone often enough, and she sounds really clued up. Her own bosses think the world of her. I gather she's practically running the show!"

"Good. Anything else I should know?"

"Yes," said the colonel. "Something that was decided only this morning. We've decided to give our conference a code name to cut out any obvious risk.

"It's rather apt in the circumstances," he went on. "We're calling it 'Kipling.' "

Welbourne was baffled. "Kipling?"

170

The colonel laughed. "Yes. After his poem, 'If'—you know, if you can keep your head when all about you are losing theirs. . . . Rather good, eh? It was the Old Man's own idea."

"Yes," said Welbourne dryly. "Very apt."

Two hours later, Welbourne was heading down the road leading to the Old Covenanter. With him in the Land-Rover were his new driver, two riflemen, and a sergeant, all heavily armed.

First they had gone to Aldergrove and timed their run along the Crumlin Road and out of the city toward the hotel. From time to time Welbourne halted the vehicle, looked around, and made various notes. Now they were approaching the hotel itself.

Iron gates at the entrance to the estate were sandbagged and manned by armed police. It was an Ulster afternoon, gray and drizzling. Welbourne dismounted and walked slowly up to the guard. Two eyes watched him carefully every step of the way.

"Major Welbourne, HQ staff from Lisburn," said the major. "I telephoned ahead to Inspector Renton to say I was on the way."

He held out his pass for scrutiny.

"Hold on while I ring the inspector," said a voice. "And stay right where I can see you, sir."

Welbourne stood very still. After a while, the voice said: "That's all in order, sir. In you go. Collect your papers on the way out."

The major beckoned to his Land-Rover and climbed in. A notice inside the gates said: SPEED LIMIT IN THESE GROUNDS 10 MPH. IF YOU GO ANY FASTER YOU ARE LIABLE TO BE SHOT.

It was a magnificent choice for the conference, thought Welbourne, as his vehicle growled along in bottom gear. Crushed gravel covered the winding road, showing white against each grass verge. A high stone wall swept back from the gates as far as the eye could follow, two feet thick and reaching twenty feet up to a foliage of glass slivers and iron spikes. Here, inside the grounds, the first hundred yards of ground were cleared of every scrap of cover. Away to his left the major saw two policemen leading two German shepherds.

Behind them he could make out a small timbered lean-to with walls slotted for riflemen. Welbourne raised a hand and waved to the RUC men. One raised a hand in watchful salute.

A line of rhododendrons screened the top of the rise. Then he saw the hotel. In the two hundred yards from the rise to the roof of the hotel building, there was no point that could not be kept under watch every minute of daylight.

All around the building were the gardens. At this time of year it

171

was if they were ringed by a moat of gold, so thick were the daffodils nodding in the breeze. Stone steps led through rose arbors and past ornamental ponds to wide lawns directly in front of the hotel. Welbourne counted three stooping figures at work and wrote on his pad two words: "check gardeners."

A graveled path led to a final flight of steps and a huge raised patio. Pigeons sat still on the stone balustrade, and a fountain splashed away despite the rain. Welbourne thought of the lines of wretched terraced houses he had driven past that afternoon, whose postage-stamp gardens were lined, not with daffodils but barbed wire, and he sighed.

The walls of the Old Covenanter were dressed in ivy. Its windows were leaded and they glowered down from its flat stone face. The roof was ringed by a parapet and slender chimneys like sentries.

It was a building that exuded strength.

An iron-studded oak door fitted with a spyhole barred the way in. The major pushed it open and saw, across the hall, a uniformed police sergeant sitting behind the reception desk. There was a bell push by his elbow with a notice reading: ALL ROOMS. ALARM.

"Good afternoon. I'm Major Welbourne, here to see Inspector Renton."

"Yes, sir. Just a moment."

The sergeant picked up a telephone and spoke into it. Before it was back in its cradle, a door behind him had opened and the inspector came through. A line of medal ribbons gleamed on his breast. Welbourne picked out the Burma Star at once.

"Hello, Major. Nice to meet you. And what can we do for you?" Welbourne caught a faint chill of interservice rivalry behind the formal greeting.

"I've been given the job of coordinating security for Kipling," he said. "It was wished on me this morning. I've driven over at once to introduce myself and ask how we can best help each other."

"Right, Major," said the inspector. "Where would you like to tart?"

"As a matter of fact," Welbourne answered, "I was hoping to leave that to you. You live here. You know the ropes better than I can ever hope to do. If I know what you've prepared and what strength you have available, perhaps I can offer one or two suggestions from the Army point of view."

The inspector looked mollified. "Fancy a cup of tea?" he asked.

"Love one," said Welbourne, and followed him into the inner room.

It smelled of wet dogs and uniforms. Four men lay on camp beds, dozing. Capes and Wellington boots were scattered over chairs and along a wooden floor. Each man had a revolver in button-down holster alongside his bed. A fifth policeman sat facing a radio set. Two German shepherds lay in the corner of the room, eyes watchful, bodies immobile yet full of menace. To the inspector's right was a blue-painted door.

On it was pinned a handwritten notice that said: THIS DOOR MUST BE KEPT LOCKED AT ALL TIMES.

"Office and bedroom," said the inspector with a wave of his hand. "The relief radioman is out back there, making tea. I sleep in. The dog teams are relieved every seventy-two hours."

"And that room?" asked Welbourne, curious about the blue-painted door.

"Armory," said the inspector. "And a kind of glorified storeroom for all the valuables. Paintings, silverware, pottery, and deeds that go back to the original owner. Here, I'll show you."

He went to the desk and selected a key, which he signed for in the sergeant's book.

He unlocked the door, switched on the lights, and motioned Welbourne inside.

"No windows," he explained. "Everything under lock and key all year round, with my men right outside the door. Safe as the Bank of England."

Welbourne saw a line of rifles racked against the wall, each one chained and padlocked, boxes of ammunition, a row of gas masks and teargas canisters and four Stirling guns. In the center of the armory were open boxes of silver plate, two paintings ("The rest are in America, on exhibition," said the inspector), and two huge vases.

"What are they?" Welbourne asked him.

"Ugly bloody things, aren't they?" said the inspector. "Known as the Delft urns, or the bishop's pots. Worth over a thousand pounds apiece and the only two like them in the world, they tell me. We're afraid to go near them in case we break one. They take them out maybe twice a year when we have a do, clean 'em up and put 'em on show. They weight a bloody ton, too. Then back they come in here for the rest of the year, and each officer of the guard has to sign for them when he comes on duty."

"Hideous things," said Welbourne and dismissed them from his mind.

The inspector locked the door, put the key back in the desk, and signed again. Then he and the major sat back with their cups of tea.

"You're the fourth Army officer to call here in the past few days," grumbled the inspector. "Sorry if I was a bit short with you, but

173

we're up to here with it." He held a hand the size of a dinner plate to his throat.

"That's all right," Welbourne told him. "But look at it from my point of view. I only arrived in Belfast this morning. I didn't know the building existed till lunchtime. So don't hold it against *me*, please."

"You've seen the place from the outside," said the inspector. "Like a fortress in the middle of a desert, isn't it? We can cover every inch of the grounds with rifle fire. I've got four men and two hungry dogs walking around all the time, and two cubbyholes covering the drive and manned by police marksmen every moment of daylight. The day the IRA get in here, I'll give you a year's money on a silver platter, so I will. Every time we get a VIP coming over, the Army drive us mad. In two hundred and forty years there's never been so much as a window broken, did you know that?"

"I did not," admitted Welbourne.

"And now you come along, begging your pardon, Major, but still wet behind the ears as far as Ireland is concerned, to try to teach us about security. How do you intend to go about it? I ask the Army that one every time we have visitors."

"I haven't got a clue," said Welbourne, still trying to be diplomatic, "but I'll try damned hard. Don't begrudge me one soft job in eleven years' service, Inspector. I just have to look at that Burma Star on your chest to realize you appreciate the position I'm in right now."

"Sorry," said the inspector. "Subject closed."

He got out plans of the building and went through them step by step with Welbourne. Then the inspector showed him around room by room, the cellars, kitchens, bedrooms, bathrooms, and the reception and dining rooms. It took them more than two hours.

"Have you got closed-circuit TV?" Welbourne asked him.

"They offered it," said Renton, "but I fought against it—successfully, so far.

"This way we have to go around each room personally, and we do it in pairs, usually with the dogs, and we don't miss a crumb on the carpet as a result. If we relied on TV, we'd get fat and lazy and never look into the dark corners."

Welbourne wrote TV on his pad and put a query against it.

"I noticed a few gardeners as I drove in," he said. "All checked out, securitywise?"

"I'll say," said Renton. "We had an IRA gardener once. Now they're all former RUC men, and there's a gun for everyone in the event of trouble."

"What about the civilian workmen who are coming in to clean up the place?"

"I admit there has to be a risk there," said the inspector unhappily. "But the firms have to submit names and photographs of the workmen, with addresses, and we carry out spot checks on several homes. We poke our noses into every can of paint, we go through their vehicles and their pockets, and we keep an eye on the work done. We have a standing rule everything must be shipshape one full week before visitors arrive. I don't see what else we can do."

"I can get the Army in to do the cleaning and painting and plumbing, things like that," offered Welbourne. "We'd cut out all risk that way."

"Go right ahead," said the inspector equably. "You might upset the unions, but to hell with that."

"I'll mention it to the colonel," said Welbourne hastily. "Perhaps we have left it a little late this time."

"There's more to it than that," said the inspector.

"Think about it for a minute. We have these workmen in two, perhaps three, times each year. Sometimes they're needed and sometimes not. They haven't got a clue who is coming, if anyone. It's just easy money for them. But if you started driving in lorryloads of troops carrying paint and polish, you'd be asking for the IRA to sit up and take notice."

"Point taken," Welbourne agreed. "Forget it."

He offered his cigarettes and changed the subject.

"One last question, Inspector. What about the civilians working inside the building already, the clerks and typists?"

"You've just got time," declared Renton, "to meet the boss lady herself before their escort comes to take them back to Belfast. Hold on and I'll get her."

He rang an extension. "Inspector Renton here," he said. "Can you spare me a moment down here? Someone to see you." He listened for a moment and smiled.

"All right, m'dear," he said, "we'll come up to you."

He turned to the major. "No flies on that one," he observed. "Says she's got confidential papers lying around. My guess is she wants to make a good impression. Let's go up."

On the landing above the bedrooms Welbourne heard the clatter of a typewriter. They were in a rabbit warren of ill-lit corners and small rooms. The inspector tapped on one door.

He led the way. "Mrs. McCabe," he said breezily, "I want you to meet the new security officer, Major Welbourne."

Moira McCabe was an impressive woman. She was tall, almost

175

as tall as the major. Welbourne put her age at about forty. She had the deep red hair, green eyes, and whey complexion that mark so many Irish as descendants of the ancient Norsemen.

She smiled in greeting to the two men to show small, even white teeth. There was just a hint of perfume in the tiny office. Mrs. McCabe was dressed in a snow-white blouse and severe clerical-gray suit. The stockings were sheer and showed off two splendid legs. Her only jewelry consisted of two pearl earrings.

She looked clean, efficient—and cold. The major groped for a single word to describe her and in the end came up with a curious choice for so handsome a woman—"educated."

"How do you do, sir," she said. He could feel her assesssing him. She impressed him as the type of person who would weigh everyone, and everything, that crossed her path with the same deliberate care, a person not to be rushed.

In the context of his new job he entirely approved.

"Mrs. McCabe," he answered, and shook hands. "The inspector here has told me a lot about you."

The green eyes appraised his remark. "It doesn't do," she said, "to take anything for granted these days, Major. But I'll do my best to see that you don't miss anything."

He nodded. "Fine. Where do you suggest I set up an office?"

"These rooms won't be convenient," she said firmly. "There will be at least six more staff during the conference. The RUC quarters downstairs will be quite impossible. When I heard you were coming I presumed you would want privacy for a number of telephone calls.

"In the end I marked you down for this room—here." She pointed to a plan of the building that hung on the wall by her desk.

"The floor below, where the painters are working?"

"Yes, sir. It's a small room at the end of that corridor, right above the conference chamber and adjoining the bedrooms. Plenty of space for a desk and a camp bed. You'll be right in the thick of things there," she said, and for a moment her eyes gleamed.

"How soon can you get it fitted out for me?"

Mrs. McCabe made a note on her pad before she answered. "By midday tomorrow," she told him, "if you don't mind an unpainted room."

"That will be fine." The major looked at his own sheaf of notes. "However, I'll be here much earlier than that. I want you to let me have a copy of the file on all civilian workers first thing, and I'll go through it with the inspector while my office is being prepared. Who's been drawing up the list, you?"

"Well, Major," she said, "strictly speaking, I know it's not my job

176

to point out the jobs that need doing, or select the firms to do them. It is the responsibility of the Ministry of Works. But, on security grounds, they're not even in the picture yet apart from bulk issue of work permits on our say-so. So I do the picking and frankly I cannot see any other way, since security instructions are so rigid. Is there something you don't like in the arrangement? I've followed general procedure laid down by Colonel Evans for the visit last year of the home secretary."

"No, no, it's all right, Mrs. McCabe," he assured her. "I just want to know who is doing what. Let me have the list first thing tomorrow, please. Thanks a lot. 'Bye."

Her eyes followed him all the way to the door.

"Good-bye, sir," she said, and went back to her typewriter.

"Handsome woman that," said Welbourne to the inspector as they went downstairs, "but tough as they come. I bet nothing gets past her."

"She knows it all," the inspector agreed happily.

They looked at the room she had chosen for the major.

"It'll do," he said. "I'll be back first thing tomorrow. If anything turns up, call me at Lisburn. Thanks for all your help."

"Anything we can do," Renton promised. "Just say the word. And try to forget what I said when we first met. You can bank on my lads for one hundred percent cooperation."

Welbourne reported to the staff colonel as soon as he got back. "Looks to be an efficient setup," he commented, "and largely due to the beautiful and efficient Mrs. McCabe. She's getting a bed-sitter ready for me tomorrow."

The colonel laughed. "Like that, is she?"

"Good God, no," said Welbourne hastily. "In her youth I should think she was a corker—but! Very reserved, very capable, but definitely with her mind on her job."

"This came for you," the colonel said, handing over a package. "From Ministry of Defense, London. Came with the top-security bag. Is it something I ought to know about?"

Welbourne opened the seal. Inside was an improved Identikit drawing of the man who had stayed in the Donegal hotel. With it there was an old photograph of a man named Liam O'Connor. Clipped to the pictures was a note from Mr. Sydenham.

It read:

Following our most interesting meeting here in London, I am now authorized to forward these for restricted Army use. They are not,

177

repeat not, for general issue in view of current inquiries. In the event of any development, obtain permission to communicate directly with this department. Good luck, S.

Welbourne passed the package hastily to the colonel.

"I was questioned in London," he explained, "at some length over the ambush. There seems to be a line of thought that this man (indicating Kelly) was either imported by the IRA as an agent on Communist-manufactured weapons or is a Russian agent himself. The other man is a known terrorist. I was told they were seen together in Donegal just before the ambush and near the spot where arms were landed by a Russian submarine.

"Naturally you know all about that. I can only assume the pictures have been sent to me in view of my briefing. Of course, sir, my instructions have to come from you."

The colonel gave a wry smile.

"I know Mr. Sydenham," he said. "And deep isn't the word for that man. We've also got a copy of these pictures. What he omitted to tell us was that you would be asked to double up for him! Still, no harm done now that you and I have had a private chat. It explains a lot of things—why the Old Man sent for me yesterday and told me to find a job for you in security, without saying why. However, your first priority is this conference. Carry on as ordered. I'll handle the circulation of these pictures and see that they reach the right people with suitable warnings. You can take over the inquiry once this conference is out of the way. That suit you?"

"Down to the ground, sir." Welbourne thought for a moment and asked: "What about the conference? Do you want these checked against the ID pictures of every workman applying for a permit to work on the conference building?"

"Of course," said the colonel tersely. "Mind how you flash them about, though. Not that I think these men will turn up if they're agents. The Russians wouldn't touch an assassination attempt with a barge pole, however much other mischief they might stir up."

Not for the first time, he wondered about the major. It was painfully clear he was no "spook," as the colonel had first imagined. He was here only because Sydenham intended to use him and had pulled strings accordingly in Whitehall. He might be a good regimental officer and was indisputably brave, but as the colonel knew too well neither quality was necessarily calculated to help a man in intelligence.

The colonel regretted the choice of Welbourne as man in charge of conference security—even nominal charge—but knew it was too late to change now. The general would demand to know why, for nothing had happened, yet, that could be construed as any threat to security. He himself would have to keep a close eye on Welbourne and guide him, if only to make certain he stayed out of trouble.

"Keep in touch with all developments," he warned and dismissed the major.

The next morning Welbourne returned to the Covenanter. True to her word, Mrs. McCabe had him sitting at his own desk, in a comfortable bed-sitter, by noon.

"Is everything satisfactory, Major?"

"Absolutely fine, thanks."

"I have six more permits for signature. Will you want to deal with them yourself?"

"Not really. As soon as Renton and I have checked them out we'll pass them back to you for action."

During the afternoon his telephone rang. The staff colonel came on the line.

"How are things going, Dickie?"

"Well enough, sir. Spending most of the time checking these civilian work permits with Renton. A hell of a job."

"Excellent, excellent." Now the colonel prodded him ever so gently. "Try not to get bogged down with just one aspect of the security task, though. Sometimes one becomes unable to see the wood for the trees, what? I've just had a signal from Lyneham about the troops coming over for Kipling. If I may make a suggestion, you ought to be running maximum security checks on the village where they'll be billeted. Renton must know most of the inhabitants, dammit, it's only a mile or so from the hotel. Ask him to go with you. And keep hard at it, old lad. I'm relying on you for an awful lot."

Welbourne recognized the common sense behind his colonel's advice and rang down for the inspector.

"Jim," he said. "Can you spare a moment? Something I'd like to talk over with you."

The RUC officer came at once. "Anything up?"

Welbourne put the Indentikit pictures and photograph flat on the desk. "See those? I've been asked to run a check on them. No reason to suppose they will try to come here, you understand, this is purely a precaution. Let your chaps have a copy and bring them back to me. And, for reasons I can't go into, mum's the word all round, okay?"

"Don't worry about that," said Renton with a hint of stiffness. "My men are handpicked. They're not chatterboxes."

Welbourne read the signals and changed his tack.

"I know that," he said. "You misunderstood me. I'm merely passing on instructions. What I wanted to see you about is a check of the hamlet. The colonel wants us to do it together, since you're the expert. It will take a day or two, that's why I've shown the pictures now. Can you be spared from here?"

"No trouble," Renton answered. "My sergeant can hold the fort. We'll not be more than a mile away at any time."

"I'd like to ask you something else," Welbourne went on. "Strictly personal, me to you."

"Shoot."

"Mrs. McCabe. How well do you know her?"

"Only through the job, but well enough. Why?"

"I intend to show her these pictures, too, since she's doing half the work in sifting these permits."

"Ah," said Renton. "I see what you're driving at." He lit his pipe and reflected. "If you mean do I trust her, the answer of course is yes. If you're asking me if *I* would show her those pictures, the answer is still yes. Christ, man, she's probably handling more state secrets than you and me put together."

"That's not what I meant. Trust doesn't come into this. That goes without saying. It's a question of sticking to the rules. I'm not even supposed to show them to *you*, strictly speaking."

"All rules have to be bent sometimes," Renton reminded him. "Just when, is a matter of common responsibility. As far as I'm concerned, these are just two more men to watch out for. She'll look on it in exactly the same way."

He went on: "I certainly think it's a bit hard on her if we sit on photographs of wanted men and at the same time ask her to issue permits to every Tom, Dick, and Harry who is sent to work here."

"That was my own feeling. I just wanted your views. Stick around and I'll call her in."

He sent for Mrs. McCabe.

"This is off the record, Mrs. McCabe. Take a look at these two faces and memorize them. If you think you spot any likeness in any photograph of the workmen, I want you to tell me or the inspector here, right away."

She looked at the drawing and the photograph and read the descriptions. Her voice was steady, her face expressionless.

"These men, Major. Are these their real names?"

180

"We don't know. They may be."

"But you think they are going to try to get in here disguised as workmen?"

"I didn't say that. It's very unlikely, as a matter of fact. We just want you to remember their faces, in case they do."

"Any reason to think they might be in this area, sir?"

"That's the trouble, Mrs. McCabe. No one knows where they are. But with so much at stake here, we have to be on our toes."

"Very good, sir. I shan't forget them. If you don't mind, though, I won't say anything to my staff. The girls are pretty nervous as it is."

"Quite right. No point in alarming anyone unduly. Not a word to your staff."

"But Mr. Renton's men will have to know, won't they?"

"Yes. They will all see those pictures. We just want as few people as possible to know of their existence, that's all."

"I understand, Major." She looked at him thoughtfully. "Since you've brought the subject up, there are still quite a number of permits to be issued. Two carpets need replacing. All the windows have to be cleaned, a huge job. Then the big conference table, the bishop's table, that ought to be French-polished. There are scratches left from the last visit. Will you deal with all this or shall I go ahead and make the necessary arrangements?"

"You do it, Mrs. McCabe. Process all permits in the normal way. Then hand them to us for final check and signature."

"Very good."

She saw that he was impatient but went on relentlessly.

"Then there's the question of the kitchen staff."

The major groaned. "How many this time?"

"At least a dozen, maybe more," she told him. "They're Stormont staff, but you still have to clear them individually, sir."

"Hell. All right, I'll see to that when I get back. Meantime, keep those pictures in mind."

"I'll do that, sir. Anything else?"

"I don't think so, Mrs. McCabe, thank you."

You had to hand it to the woman, thought Renton when she had gone, *nothing* seemed to ruffle her, did it?

·26·

At the farmhouse in Monaghan, Kelly had finished making the bomb that could lip-read. The parts had been delivered within the time limit set by Eamonn, and this had included a flight to London by Raymond to buy the radio control system.

" 'Twas as easy as stealing candy from a baby," Raymond told Kelly. "Bombmakers never had it so good—no passport, no identity papers of any kind needed, and a plane available every hour in and out of Dublin. The Customs stopped me when I got back and said, 'What have you in there, sir?' and I showed him the lot, saying, 'A surprise present for my kid,' and all he said was, 'Isn't it marvelous what they make these days?' and waved me through."

Kelly had worked all night assembling the bomb, molding the Gelemax around the pedestal, squeezing it lovingly into shape. He attended to the wiring with infinite care; packaged the water-proofed control units with all the tenderness a mother shows for a difficult child. He checked and double-checked, he weighed each component separately and then together. Last of all he went around the room to collect and burn each section of wrapping paper.

Liam kept Kelly supplied with coffee all through the night and not for the first time marveled at the change that came over the man as he toyed with his jigsaws of death. The harsh lines left his face, his features relaxed, he smiled and whistled as the hours ticked by. Even the cold and damp seemed forgotten.

Liam timed him. It took eight hours and thirteen minutes from the moment that Raymond drove away. At last the mercenary stood back, like an artist admiring a finished painting.

"You looked bushed, Kelly," Liam said quietly.

"Well, there's a bit more to it than making homemade jam. That's some bomb and no mistake."

"I don't mind telling you," Liam said, "the sheer closeness of it turns my blood to water. Jesus!"

"It's as safe as a nun in a roomful of eunuchs," said Kelly. "Watch." He rapped the side with a wooden spoon.

Liam was sweating.

"Leave it be," he said. "Every minute you worked on it all through the night seemed like forever. I've known too many go wrong in my time. Where are you going to keep it?"

"Right here," said Kelly, "by the side of my bed. And you just watch me, I'll sleep like a baby. Relax, Liam, this bomb's like a good dog, house-trained."

He opened a bottle and took a long drink, his first for nearly twenty-four hours.

The Irishman continued to stare, hypnotized by the bomb.

Kelly jeered at him.

"You're too old for this game, Liam! Me now, I look at that bomb and feel *good*. There's eight pounds of murder unlimited there. Think of it. There's not a living thing it can't kill, I don't care how rich or powerful, and all it needs from me is one signal on the transmitter.

"Do you think Eamonn will sweat? I hope so. He should. When he left here, it was just a collection of wires and a clock. Right now it's worth one hundred thousand dollars to him!"

Liam prepared some food but was unable to eat anything himself. Kelly ate alone and went to bed upstairs. Liam could hear his snores from the kitchen.

At four in the afternoon of the same day Eamonn drove up with Raymond in a wind of gale force. The door of the farmhouse banged as they came in, coats flapping, hair tumbling over their eyes.

"Get Kelly," said Eamonn to Liam, who was smoking his pipe by the fire. "Quick."

The mercenary took a few minutes to rouse. Since he'd been in the farmhouse he'd never been tired enough to sleep before last night. Finally he came heavily downstairs to find Eamonn pacing. Kelly stared at him. "What's up?"

"They're on to us, that's what's up!" said Eamonn. "Moira got a message to me this morning. The Army have put out pictures and descriptions of you and Liam. They've already warned the

183

police at the hotel to watch out for you. They'll grab you the moment you drive up with your bomb."

"How's that?" Liam asked him. "We haven't shown our faces since we left Cork."

"It has to come from Donegal," said Eamonn. "That damned bird-watcher! Someone must have gone around asking questions. They've issued a photograph of you, Liam, and a sketch of Kelly here. You'll not get past the front door of the building, never mind blow the place up."

Kelly looked at him coolly.

"Stop squealing," he said. "We haven't even tried to get in yet. I've got a lot of money riding on this. You think I'm going to quit before I have a go? You and Raymond, come with me for a moment. I've got something to show you."

He led them upstairs and threw his bedroom door open.

"Look at that," he told them. "Isn't that something?"

Eamonn drew back fast like a fox sighting a snare.

"My God," he said. "So that's it. The Kelly bomb." He remained exactly where he was.

Kelly lit a cigarette and moved carefully between Eamonn and the bedroom door. "Yes," he said. "That's it. And just think, Eamonn, if it went off now there'd be nothing left of the farmhouse or us but a puff of smoke in the wind."

He blew a mouthful of cigarette smoke at the ceiling. "Just like that!" and he chuckled, not looking at the man with the scar. "Mind you, I made it too well for accidents to happen. A hundred thousand bucks, I keep saying to myself."

Raymond swung toward him.

"Ah, stop your damn teasin', Kelly, and try to think what the man is telling you. The police are on to you! Your cover's blown, man. How can you walk up there with a bomb inside a can of polish and them waiting for you with your picture in their hands?"

Liam spoke from the top of the staircase.

"Nothing to stop us sending someone else in. We could bring in a man from Cork, maybe."

"Not on your goddamned life!" Kelly was shouting. "That bomb is *my* baby, my golden handshake from the IRA. You think I'm going to hand it over to some dumb bastard from Cork after all the sweat I've put in? Never. I'll blow the farm sky-high first."

Eamonn kept his voice down and took charge.

"Cut it out, all of you," he said. "That will get us nowhere. Let's go down and talk it over quietly."

184

Following the tall, spare man down the stairs, Kelly chuckled at the thought that they all looked a little more relaxed now that they were away from the immediate vicinity of his creation.

Eamonn spoke first.

"Kelly's right. This is his pigeon." He touched the scar on his face and looked long and hard at the mercenary.

"This is why I can't go," he said. "And now they've got a good description of you, I gather. It's up to you if you want to take a chance. I just can't see you getting away with it."

"There's always Errol," said Liam.

"I told you a long time ago we'd never use that loudmouth again," Eamonn told him.

"Who's Errol?" asked Kelly.

"An actor we know in Dublin. 'Errol' is for 'Errol Flynn,' a joke name for the man. He's good with makeup and disguise. We used him once for a bank raid. He did us up so well our own mothers wouldn't have known us."

"So why didn't you suggest him in the first place?" Kelly demanded.

"Because the man is utterly unreliable," Eamonn said. "He's tight half the time and he's got a loose tongue. If he finds out what we're up to, it'll be all around Dublin within an hour of his return."

Liam stayed silent.

"And," said Raymond, "it won't be easy to hold him here very long. He's in a play right now, Kelly. There would be a hell of a rumpus if he just disappeared. His connections are pretty well known."

Kelly recalled a warning Liam had given him when they first met—trust the Irish to cut their own throats if no one else will do it for them.

"Can't the man fall sick?" he asked.

"We could persuade him," Eamonn said, "but that still leaves the problem of a loose mouth afterward."

Kelly laughed. "Let me have a word with him," he said. "I could tell him what to expect if he steps out of line."

Eamonn looked at him.

"He already knows," he said. "I doubt if he's learned his lesson. However, we've not much choice but to get him here. Like you, Mr. Kelly, I want this bomb to succeed, irrespective of all other consideration or risk."

He turned to Raymond. "Take Kevin with you," he ordered.

"Use any method you like, but persuade Errol to join us for a few days. Make sure a message saying he's sick gets to the theater. Let them know he's gone away.

"And Liam, you'll have to have a job done on you, too. I still want you to go with Kelly as his foreman. He doesn't know French polish from boot polish and he wouldn't fool a police dog with that accent of his. I have to rely on you to steer him out of trouble. *This has got to succeed, Liam.*"

"Okay," Liam answered. "We can't turn back now. They must have had my picture for years anyway—ever since I first joined the old IRA. Yours too, Eamonn, and Raymond's, for that matter. One more publication won't make very much difference."

"When do we move?" Kelly asked Eamonn.

"Depends on Errol, but tomorrow night, I think. I'll take you and Liam over the Border. We'll be met just outside the city. Our Belfast section will have a van waiting, complete with work permits, overalls, and all the cans you'll need as cover. The name of your firm has been painted on the side of your van just in case it slips your memory. We'll photograph you both here, after you've been made up, and do the prints. We'll put yours into the work permits and see that Moira gets a duplicate set.

"You'll be working inside the hotel for at least two days. That means you've got to have a 'home' address in Belfast. Liam will have all the details, all you need to remember is street and number. You will both be required to sleep there for at least one night after the job's done, in case of any police check. When you get a message to leave, you head for a pub that Liam knows and wait for transport."

"Right," said Kelly.

"Incidentally, we've got an ordinance map and gone into a little detail for you. Your control room in the hamlet lies exactly fourteen hundred eighty yards from the hotel as the crow flies—well within the range you laid down. Stay put there until after the explosion. I'll call for you personally to take you to Dublin, understand?"

"Understood."

"What about his cover story, Eamonn?" It was Liam again. "That accent worries me a lot more than it seems to worry you."

"He's likely to be questioned," admitted Eamonn, "if only out of curiosity. So the closer he sticks to near truth, the better. Born of Irish parents, went to America as a child. That settles the accent. Now he's come home and laboring for a crust, like a lot of other Belfast men. You're not only his foreman, you're his uncle, and you've given him a

186

home and a job. The same address will be on both ID permits. You've even got a wife for your stay in Belfast, Liam, how about that?"

"As long as she's not too demanding," said Liam with a grin. "What about neighbors?"

"We've had a word with some," Eamonn said. "You won't find any difficulties there."

"What about Mrs. McCabe?" Kelly asked him. "How do we contact her?"

"You don't," said Eamonn. "You don't go near her or even know her name. All you do is report to the police with your permit, Liam the same, and drive home at night. Moira will find you in the hotel in her own way at her own time. The rest is up to you. She's too valuable to be implicated in any way. You don't even *look* at her, hear me?"

Kelly yawned.

"I hear you. Relax, Eamonn, you ain't talking to some rube. I'm going back to bed. I was up all last night making bombs and I'm dead beat. If you've anything else to say, say it to Liam."

He clumped across the kitchen and up the stairs. Eamonn's eyes stayed on his back.

"I didn't think it possible to loathe a man like I loathe him," he told Liam. "That's the last mercenary we take, no matter what our bankers say."

"Yet he's the only man for this job, Eamonn."

"I don't doubt his ability. But I don't trust him as far as I can spit. He's not forgotten that beating in Kerry. He'll get even if he can."

"He's a professional," said Liam. "I know him better than you do. For a hundred thousand dollars he'll take the beating and like it. You *are* going to pay him, Eamonn? I swore you would."

They were speaking in whispers. Each man kept one eye on the stairs.

"If he lives," Eamonn said softly, "Kelly collects."

He reached over and patted Liam on the shoulder. "You just take care of yourself, old friend. We need men like you to win this war, a hell of a lot more than Kelly."

"Eamonn, I have to know for sure," said Liam. "Does he get that money?"

"I told you," said the leader. "If the bomb attack is successful and Kelly doesn't get himself killed or arrested, then he collects."

Liam suddenly felt afraid. Afraid to press Eamonn further, afraid

187

to tell Kelly of the doubt that now plagued him. He felt old and cold. Dispirited. For the first time in his long life as a revolutionary, he began to wonder if he wanted to keep on.

He changed the subject.

"Sorry I had to bring Errol into this. I know how you feel about him."

"Don't you worry about him," said Eamonn. "He won't get a chance to talk.

"You can't mean to harm him. He can't help being what he is."

Long ago, when they were ragged barefoot boys in Cork, Liam and the actor had run errands for the old IRA. They had shared hunger and fear, they had been beaten together, they had slept in rough beds and dreamed the same dreams. Errol was godfather to Liam's oldest son.

"I will not permit *anyone* to jeopardize the success of this operation, Liam. Errol will stay here while the conference is taking place whether he likes it or not. He can go home afterward—with a suitable word of warning. God help him if he opens his mouth."

"Whatever you say, Eamonn."

The leader drove off at two in the morning. Liam went slowly upstairs to his camp bed. From time to time he rubbed a hand across his stubbled face. He was filthy and close to despair. He thought longingly of his wife and children and for the thousandth time wondered how they were. He thought of the actor who trusted him and of what lay in store for Kelly. He thought of the trials and danger that awaited his own tired old body and he could have wept.

He tiptoed into Kelly's room.

The mercenary lay on his back, snoring. A bright moon shone through the window, and Liam could make out the shape of the bomb by Kelly's bed. A bottle of whiskey stood on the floor. Liam stared at it. It was a long, long time since he had allowed himself any. Suddenly, timid as a poor swimmer stepping into the sea, he reached down and took it. He brought the bottle to his mouth and gulped. The fiery liquor choked him.

In a second Kelly was sitting up in bed, revolver in hand, with the barrel pointing straight at the little man's belly.

He blinked his eyes in disbelief, looked from Liam to the bottle and back again at Liam. He smiled his contempt, a member of a congregation finding its vicar in sin.

"You crafty old bastard," he said. "Drinking on the sly all the time you were preaching, eh?"

Liam put the bottle down, shaking his head.

"No," he replied. "That was the first time I touched alcohol since I joined up with Eamonn. Maybe I'm afraid of your bomb and what it is doing to us all."

There were tears in his eyes. Kelly saw them quite clearly, glistening in the moonlight, and watched them roll down the old man's cheeks.

"Take the bottle," he said. "Get as pissed as you like. But don't you ever creep up on me like that again or I'll blow your head off."

He turned on his side and was asleep in a moment.

Liam was still wide awake when daylight came as Raymond hammered on the farmhouse door and burst in with Kevin, pushing the terrified actor ahead of them.

·27·

Inspector Renton watched the van pull up outside the main entrance of the hotel and saw an old man step out of the passenger's seat. The inspector was furious.

"Hey! You! What the bloody hell do you think you're doing, dripping oil right outside the front door?"

The old man looked confused.

"Is it leaking? Sorry, sir, I didn't know. We've been sent here to work for you. My instructions are to report to the authorities on arrival, which is what I was about to do."

"Get around the back," ordered Renton. "You'll see a police van in the yard. Report to the sergeant and show him your work permits. Get mobile!"

At Welbourne's suggestion, the RUC had brought in a trailer for searching workers and examining equipment on arrival. Renton picked up the phone on his desk and rang the sergeant on duty.

"Ley and Company," he barked. "French polishers. Vehicle number UL0984F. Name's printed on the van. Check it out, they're first-timers here. Usual drill with the men inside. I'm going into Belfast in a few minutes for conference with Major Welbourne and his colonel. You know what to do in any emergency."

The sergeant looked at the two men who walked into his caravan. They were both in their sixties, he guessed, and he silently named them Mutt and Jeff. One stood well over six feet in spite of his stoop, while the other barely reached to his mate's armpits.

"Permits," said the sergeant, holding out his hand. The smaller of the two had snow-white hair and spectacles.

"I'm the foreman, Sergeant," he said. "Here's mine." He turned to the big man behind him. "Come on, let's have your papers, Bob, we haven't got all day to stand around."

190

In the arrivals book the RUC sergeant wrote down each item, beginning with the foreman's card.

Name: Cyril Aynsley.
Employers: John Ley & Co., wood finishers, Albertbridge Road, East Belfast.
Status: Foreman.
Years employed: 38.
Age: 63.
Home address: Bryson Street, Newtownards Road, East Belfast.

"All right, Dad," said the sergeant, "take the weight off your feet while I put it all down. I'm afraid we'll have to search you both, and the contents of the van. Regulations."

"Suits me, Sergeant," Aynsley said, lighting his pipe. "We get paid by the hour whether we're stripping woodwork or you're stripping us, ha ha."

The sergeant looked at Aynsley and his photograph, and nodded, and handed the permit back. He had no need to refer to his "wanted" file. He had glanced at it for the hundredth time the moment the inspector had called. That Renton! He was driving them mad over this conference. Thank God he was going out for the day.

Next he copied the date from the big man's permit.

Name: Robert Aloysius Brady.
Employers: John Ley & Co., wood finishers, Albertbridge Road, East Belfast.
Status: General hand, a French polisher.
Years employed: 4.
Age: 56.
Home address: Bryson Street, Newtownards Road, East Belfast.

"That right?" the sergeant asked him, "same address as the foreman?"

"That's right," said the workman. "He's my uncle." He spoke in a curious flat accent the RUC man could not place.

"You're no Ulsterman, Mr. Brady," he said. "Where are you from?" The tone was friendly, but no one was fooled.

"I was born here, right enough," the old bent man told him, "but my parents went to America when I was a kid. I've been back ten years, working mostly in England. When my wife died, my uncle here offered me a home and a job."

191

The sergeant took a long, good look at the French polisher who spoke in a curious accent. The Welbourne Identikit picture came to mind.

Brady was very gray, with a suggestion of the original black showing faintly at the temples. He had a boozer's red nose, a great ugly beacon shining above a gray mustache burned brown amidships by nicotine stains. His eyes were brown, the skin around them wrinkled. There was a tattoo on his right forearm for all to see, blue heart and red flowers with the name MARTHA below. Once he must have been very tall. Now he stood badly, like a man with arthritis.

The sergeant saw his hands, They were stained with the varnish of many years, as were the foreman's. His overalls were washed clean. His boots were shining. The sergeant guessed he had gone to some pains to smarten up for a government contract.

"Now let's see your bits and pieces," he told them. They turned out their pockets, and he looked with practiced eye on the contents. The sergeant took up Brady's driving license and compared name and address to the work permit.

The sergeant came out from behind his desk and searched the two men without fuss or offense. He patted their empty pockets, ran a hand over each man's legs and under his arms.

"Good," he said, and grinned at the old foreman. "No guns so far, Dad. Now let's have a look in your van."

Brady opened up the rear of the vehicle. It was filled with drums, cans, bottles, wadding, rags, stools, wood supports, tools, a spare tire, luncheon boxes, newspapers, slippers, buckets, and a folding ladder.

It began to rain, but the sergeant was blessed with unlimited patience. First he pointed at the two five-gallon drums.

"What's in there?"

"Believe it or not," the foreman replied, "it's polish. We're French polishers, remember? You sent for us to work here."

"Men can carry a lot of things in drums that size," said the sergeant easily, "so don't be funny, Dad, just open them up for me to have look."

He watched Brady climb in to get the drums. "You fellers mix your own?" he asked.

Mr. Aynsley took his time in answering and emptied his pipe. "You can buy all the polish you need from any shop," he told the sergeant. "Why, you thinking of working at home?"

"That's right," said the sergeant.

"Well, I prefer to mix my own, always have. You might think it's old-fashioned, and I wouldn't argue, and of course there's nothing in

192

it as far as money's concerned. It's a matter of opinion as to quality. I maintain it's what you add in the way of gums and one or two other ingredients that makes a man's polish special."

Mr. Brady dragged a can to the end of the van, cursing as he cleared all else out of the way. Finally it was done. He pried off the lid, put his nose down and smelled, nodded approval, and offered the sergeant a dipstick.

The drum was three-quarters full. "That's the 'garnet,'" said the foreman. "The best for dark, warm stains. As you'll know, being a do-it-yourself man."

The sergeant said nothing but poked the stick down until he touched bottom.

"All right," he said. "Now the other one."

It was raining much harder. It took Brady longer than ever to get at the second drum and clear a way for it to the door of the van, while the sergeant and foreman got wetter and wetter.

"This," explained Aynsley, who was not minding the rain one bit, "is the 'button.' For golden walnut and similar tones, you know?"

The sergeant waited until the lid was off and advanced with the dipstick.

"For God's sake, Sergeant!" shouted the foreman. "Take that stick away! Look at it, still dripping with garnet. You're not putting that in my button, and I don't care if you put me in the cells for stopping you. What are you trying to do, lose me my job? Get him another stick, Bob, and be quick about it, the man's getting soaked out here."

Brady went down on hands and knees and searched. Rain drummed down on the van, sergeant, and foreman. Finally a new and clean dipstick was found. The sergeant, thoroughly wet and ashamed of his ignorance, barely went below the surface before handing it back.

"That's all right," he said. "Now come out while I have a look around."

Brady made sure the lid was tight back on before he complied with the sergeant's order. Then, with a wink, he joined his foreman in the rain. The sergeant pottered about, opening bottles, sniffing, opening cans of shellac, sniffing, using a clean dipstick here and there as the fancy took him. He pried into the bismarck and red sanders, he smelled the methylated spirits. Then he found the sulfuric acid.

"What's this for?"

The foreman knew then he had a tyro.

"There are three ways, well, three main ways of 'finishing,' " he said. "Did you know that, now? They're called stiffing, spiriting, and the acid method. You can glaze, too, but we don't." He sniffed contemptuously. "That's for cheap work.

"Imagine," he explained as the rain beat down, "you've completed the staining, the filling, fadding, coloring, and bodying. To finish by the acid method, you have to mix seven parts of clean, cold, distilled water to one measure of sulfuric. Are you with me?

"Shake it up, mix it thoroughly, and spread it on either with butter muslin or the palm of your hand. I use the palm, personally, always have. Then you take your pounce bag. . ."

He'll get washed away before he's finished, thought the sergeant. Or die of pneumonia. He climbed out of the van with no shadow of doubt in his mind. French polishers they claimed to be, French polishers they certainly sounded, and he had work to do.

"All right, all right," he said. "I haven't got time for a wood-finishing lesson today, nor have you. Sign the book, the pair of you. Sign it when you leave tonight and every time you come in and go out. And thank you for your cooperation. You know how careful we have to be these days."

He rang a buzzer on his desk. At the back door of the building, a head poked out—another policeman in uniform.

"Okay, Jim," the sergeant shouted. "Searched and cleared. Let 'em in." He watched for a while as the men unloaded and started to carry their wares inside. I might as well make a double check, he thought, and looked at the notepaper that accompanied their permits. He rang the number. A woman's voice answered: "Ley and Company, good morning."

He explained the nature of his call.

"Just a moment," she said, "and I'll put you through. Hold on." The sound of hammering and banging came over for a moment, and then a man announcing himself as Mr. Ley came to the phone.

He confirmed the number of the van, the age and description of foreman and worker. "I sent you the best," he said anxiously. "Is anything wrong?"

"Nothing at all. Merely making a check call. Thanks."

Against the two names he wrote in his register: "checked with employers." He put the permits aside and went back to the latest to come down from Mrs. McCabe.

Inside the main building Kelly and Liam began stacking their paint and polish and rags against the wall inside the guardroom. The

194

man on the desk sighed and said nothing—it was just one more inconvenience. The two workmen removed raincoats, hats, and jackets, and at a nod from the duty man, hung them on pegs alongside a line of damp blue uniforms. They took off their boots and donned zip-up slippers.

"So we don't carry any muck into the rooms," they explained.

Their overalls were tied in the back like baker's aprons, each with two deep pockets in front. Liam shuffled to the desk and waited to be noticed.

"Yes, Dad?"

"Is there someone who will tell us, please, what needs doing? The only orders we had was to report to the RUC, and it's taken us two hours already just to get through the door yonder."

"Hold on a moment." A call went through to Mrs. McCabe.

"It's like the Labor Exchange down here, ma'am. Now I've got two French polishers asking me what they can do! Can you send someone down who can give instructions, please, ma'am?"

Her voice crackled on the phone. The policeman answered politely: "I know you've got a lot to do, ma'am, but so have we. I'm due out now to change dogs and handlers. The inspector's at Army headquarters. The sergeant's taken over trailer search. I've only got two men to keep an eye on twelve workmen, and *that's* in their rest period."

He listened again and said: "Thank you very much, ma'am. I'll wait for you."

He looked at the old foreman and the stooped figure of his mate. "You're lucky, Dad, you're only here for a day or two. We've got to live here! You see how it is, we're so busy getting the place clean there's no one left to guard it."

The foreman gave a bitter laugh and looked about him.

"Those bastard left-footers have better targets in mind than an empty hotel," he said.

A door swung open, and Mrs. McCabe walked in.

"This is the third time this morning I've had to act as clerk of works!" she said. "I just type the instructions, I don't make up the jobs that need doing, you know. You ought to see the work we've got piling up in my office."

The policeman said nothing. Mrs. McCabe flicked through a sheaf of papers in her hand without a glance at the two workmen.

"Ah. Here it is. French polishing—I remember now, the big table, scratches and so on. Are these the workmen?"

"That's us, ma'am," said Liam. "I'm the foreman. If you just show me what needs to be done, I'll get right on with it, and you can go back to your own job."

"Follow me," she told him. "And bring your assistant with you." She led them into the hall and turned right. She halted at the second door in the corridor, selected a key from the ring at her belt, and went into the conference chamber. She was careful to leave the door wide open.

·28·

"Well done," Moira McCabe said to the two "workmen." "I thought you'd never get through that search. The sergeant took his time. I watched from the window."

Kelly looked about the conference room with professional interest. He noted with approval the sturdiness of the walls, the solidity of the woodwork, the profusion of mirrors. The bomb should do what it was supposed to do.

Liam whistled his own surprise. He found the room beautiful.

It was known as the bishop's study, a somber and secretive place where in days long ago men who shared the cleric's harsh beliefs had gathered to plot the persecution of Roman Catholics. It was a room from which no whisper, no hint of what was in store for the opposition, was meant to escape.

On its south face, two superb leaded windows set high in a bay looked down on gardens twenty feet below. From leaded pane to inner wall measured three feet, the thickness of the outer walls of the building. Shelf upon shelf of leather-bound volumes rose from the floor to the slope below the windows.

The study was perhaps thirty feet long, and all of it shone darkly, like water before a storm. Oak-paneled walls, rafters, floorboards, door, the soft leather binding of each book, the beaten-brass bedwarmers set in the fireplace, each arm and straight back of twenty-four chairs set around a table of gleaming Philippine mahogany—all of it shone in the light that filtered through the ivy-clad windows.

Above the fireplace hung a single painting, a portrait of the first bishop by Reynolds, circa 1760, showing a face of prodigious strength and harshness.

Behind each chair an oval mirror, the width of a man's back, was set in each oak panel, picking up the light and sending it back to the opposite wall and rival mirror to crisscross the length and breadth of the room.

No carpet sullied the oaken floor. It was so clean, so polished, one might have been walking on glass. The combined effect of dark woods and reflected light was mesmeric.

Mrs. McCabe spoke again.

"That's how you got in," she said, pointing to a long, thin scratch that scarred the deep surface of the table.

Kelly pictured her opening the big door, moving stealthily into the room, and disfiguring the priceless piece with a pair of scissors.

Mrs. McCabe looked at the open door and kept her voice low. "You have to be finished by tomorrow night," she told them. "As long as you don't ruin the damned table, it doesn't matter too much what you do in here. There won't be any expert supervision. The police have instructions to look in from time to time without warning. My guess is they'll bring you the odd cup of tea. Only one other workman will be allowed in here, apart from you two—the cleaner who comes on Saturday. As soon as he's finished, the Army will send an explosives expert to search the place, then he'll put a seal on the door which can't be broken until the morning of the conference itself."

"Where are the urns?" Kelly asked her.

"Locked up in that room behind the sergeant's desk," she said. "They're being cleaned this morning. I'll see you get told. If you're lucky, you'll have two hours at most to do what needs to be done."

Kelly nodded.

"Just one thing," he told her. "There's no need to worry when you put the flowers in next week. I'm the man who made this device and believe me it *can't* go off prematurely. But one look at you, and I know I don't have to worry."

Calm green eyes looked him over.

"I'll hold you to that," she said. "But thank you for the thought. Good luck, both of you," and she was gone.

Kelly turned to Liam.

"You did well with that sergeant," he said. "During the search, I mean. Where the hell did you learn all that bull about French polishing?"

"I did a bit of reading," said Liam, "to take my mind off the thing you'd done. Thank God the sergeant knew even less than I did!"

He went over and looked at the table.

198

"I don't know what the hell we're going to do about that scratch. It's a shallow one, we can remove it easy enough with meths. But the book says you have to let it dry afterward for forty-eight hours before rubbing it smooth—and we haven't got forty-eight hours. So what I'm going to do is dab it with iodine. She hasn't penetrated the finish, thank the Lord. After that we'll just have to pray, Kelly. That's a beautiful table, any mark is bound to be noticed."

Liam thought things over and went on:

"I'm thinking the cops will keep a closer eye on us than anyone else, since this is the conference room. That means we've got to look as if we know what we're doing. We'll use water stain and what they call a one-pound cut when it's dry. We just keep sanding and polishing and then add a few drops of oil to the shellac mixture. Leave it to me. I know enough to fool these policemen. I'll tell you what to do and when to do it. God, it's sacrilege to fool around with furniture as beautiful as this!"

"Keep your hair on, Liam," said Kelly. "It will all be matchwood in a week's time."

They both walked back down the corridor and into the guardroom. The sergeant was back at his desk.

"Going to get more stuff from the van," said Liam.

"Okay," the sergeant told him. "Come and go all you want. Just try to keep the place clean."

Kelly took in the locked blue door with a glance.

"We've got to fetch a couple of drums of polish and some bottles of stain," said Liam. "I daren't take them in that study. Can I leave them here somewhere?"

"Sure," said the sergeant. "Got a cloth? Give it here," and he covered an open space to the right of the blue door. "That do you? Keep the doorway clear. We've got to get some stuff out for cleaning later on."

For the next half hour Liam and Kelly made several journeys to and from the van. The guard changed. The weather was so bad now that the dogs were left in an outbuilding. The handlers came in, threw off their wet clothes, and sat around the fireplace, where they dried out over an electric fire. They ignored the two workmen.

"I'll make the cut," Liam told the room in general. Kelly looked blank. "Thin down to a one-pound cut," Liam repeated. He moved without hurry to Kelly's side, handing him shellac and methylated spirit, making it look as if they were working as a team.

He made the mixture, two quarts to one of shellac. Then he led the way back to the study. He showed Kelly what to do, and they began working on the big table.

They had the luck of the devil, Liam had to admit it himself, with the bomb. As permanent guard the RUC had to provide their own meals before the conference. Not unnaturally—having checked and searched each workman individually—they were concentrating more now on the meal than the men in overalls who moved among them.

The door banged open and shut, the rain was cursed, the telephone answered, potatoes peeled, and meat cut and water boiled at one and the same time. In the middle of it all, the art expert arrived to clean the Delft urns.

He was a precise and fussy man, an employer in his own right and an authority on rare pieces. The sergeant knew him and wasted none of his time. He took the key from his desk, signed for it, and unlocked the blue door. He carried the two vases gently to a point inside the door.

"If you'll be good enough to examine them for damage, sir," he said.

The sergeant went over to his radio operator and left him to it. The blue door stayed wide open. The man fussed around the vases, removed each pedestal and wiped it clean. He took a cloth and gently wiped down each blue outer shell. Liam thought it a crime to waste twenty guineas on so simple a task. Kelly knelt by his drums behind the door.

It took only a few minutes.

"Sergeant," said the art expert, "here is my certificate. There are the urns, both clean and undamaged. Sign here, please."

The sergeant handed him a slip of paper and booked the man out in his register. He locked the blue door, put the key back in his desk, and rejoined the radio operator.

"Good-bye, sir. Thank you."

One of the constables came up to him. "Dinner's on the table, Sarge."

"Right," he said. "I'm bloody well starving."

He joined the other policemen at the table in the far corner of the L-shaped room. The blue door was out of their line of vision, but all the sergeant had to do to see his desk was to turn around. He switched the radio on—loud—and sat down to eat. There had been a kidnapping that morning in Belfast, and everyone listened carefully to the bulletin.

200

Kelly seized his chance at once. He nudged Liam. "Start eating your food."

Liam walked down to the sergeant's table. "Do you mind, Sarge," he said, "if we eat in here and listen to your radio?"

"Sure," came the answer. "Make yourself at home. We'll have a cup of tea for you directly."

Liam sat near the desk and opened his package of sandwiches. Kelly stayed by the door, pulled on rubber gloves that reached to his elbows, and groped down in the big drum of shellac, feeling for the bundle below. It seemed to Liam that he was taking all the time in the world. Slowly, gently, Kelly lifted it out and set the dripping mass on a dust sheet by the wall. Liam tried to swallow his food but began to choke. He could not imagine how the police failed to hear his heart pounding.

Kelly cut the waterproofed wrapping away, laid the pedestal to one side, and stuffed the greasy plastic cover into a carrier bag. He stripped off his gloves, placed them in the bag, too, and wiped his hands dry and clean with maddening slowness. Now he crossed the room and bent down by Liam, as though to take some food. Instead he lifted the lid of the desk and took out the whole bunch of keys. He walked back to the blue door.

Liam could not bring himself to look at Kelly. He sat there chewing the same mouthful of bread over and over again. Suddenly he felt sick and began to retch.

The sergeant looked around. "Everything all right, Dad?" he asked.

"Piece of cheese went down the wrong way," quavered Liam. He prayed no one would get up. Suddenly the sergeant's chair scraped, and Liam's heart all but stopped with fright, but without looking around again the sergeant reached over to the radio and turned it down a fraction.

"So bloody noisy in here we wouldn't hear the inspector drive up," he said and laughed at his joke. They all resumed eating.

Kelly knelt by his bomb. He checked the wiring, made sure the aerial was firmly in place, examined the terminals, looked closely at the sealed watertight section that held transmitter, receiver, and timing device. When he was satisfied nothing had been disturbed, he took the keys from his pocket and looked for one to open the blue door.

He tried. Wrong key. Tried again. This time it worked. He took the false pedestal, opened the door, and stepped into the armory with the bomb. Kelly put the pedestal down and closed the door

201

behind him. He removed the original pedestal, placed it on the floor, and lowered the bomb carefully into one of the urns. He took a cloth and wiped carefully around until he was certain there was no mark, no smudge, on the costly china surface.

He looked inside the urn. It was impossible to tell one from the other. His watch told him he had been four minutes twenty-three seconds inside the armory. Time to get out!

He picked up the pedestal and opened the door just far enough to see Liam's face. The old man nodded. Kelly came out fast, closed the door behind him, and locked it again. He put the heavy pedestal into the drum of shellac.

Finally, he replaced the lid on the drum. Then he sat down on the floor and began to eat. He looked across the room at Liam and raised one thumb.

Almost at once, a policeman got up and walked toward them carrying two cups of tea. Kelly got up slowly, thanked him, and handed one of the cups to Liam. The policeman by this time was returning to his place at the other end of the room. Staying near to Liam Kelly managed to raise the lid of the desk and put the keys back on their ring while sipping tea from the other cup.

It was all over. Seventeen minutes exactly, from the moment Liam had asked permission to eat inside the kitchen. The policemen were sipping their tea and still listening to the World at One roundup.

"Back to work," said Liam. He took the cups and rinsed them before handing them back. In the study he held on to a chair and mopped his face.

"Look at me," he confessed. "I'm as wet as if I'd stepped into a bath with all my clothes on. Christ, I couldn't go through that again for a million pounds."

"I know," said Kelly. "And these contact lenses didn't help. I feel as if I've got a brick in each eye."

"Let's get on with it," Liam told him, "and get out of here. No sense in pushing our luck."

"We've got to come back tomorrow," said Kelly. "No point in panicking now. It's all downhill from here on. So let's concentrate on making this table look as good as new."

Liam showed him how to roll his lintless cloth into a ball, dip it into the shellac, and rub it on the surface in quick, straight strokes. Once it was dry he sanded the wood and began again.

On and on they worked, right through the afternoon. There was little to say to each other, and the thought of what lay hidden in the armory made Liam's blood run cold. The sergeant looked in twice and left without comment. At last they could see a definite sheen developing on the table.

"I don't know about you," laughed Kelly, "but I reckon we're bloody good French polishers!"

The door opened again without warning. Without turning his head, Liam cried, "Shut the bloody door, will ya, now? We mustn't have any change of temperature or it'll bloom on us!"

There was no answer. Liam and Kelly swung around. An Army major and a police inspector came into the study.

"Watch your tongue," said the inspector curtly. "The major here is in charge of security of this building. He comes and goes as he pleases."

Liam stood his ground.

"And I'm the foreman responsible for restoration of this table," he argued. "And I'm telling you if that door over there keeps opening and closing every five mintues, we'll get a drop in temperature in this room that will put a bloom on the polish and ruin all the hard work we've done this day."

Renton's face darkened at the impertinence, but Welbourne laughed.

"My apologies," he said. "It's certainly a beautiful table. What wood is it?"

Kelly went on rubbing. His stoop was very noticeable. Liam did the talking for both of them, which was right and proper. "Philippine mahogany, sir," he said. "A gorgeous coloring."

Renton peered over Kelly's shoulder.

"Looks pretty good to me," he commented. "Will you be finished tonight? I'd like you out as soon as possible."

"One more day, sir," Liam told him, "and we'll give you a polish that will last a hundred years."

"Fair enough," said Renton. "Carry on."

In the corridor Renton turned to Welbourne. "Everything going like clockwork," he said. "Another forty-eight hours and we can have the building sealed. It's never gone better."

"There's the kitchen staff," Welbourne reminded him. "Everyone takes them for granted because they work at Stormont. Let's check on a couple of homes tonight, eh?"

"We'll need an escort," said the inspector. "Will you arrange it?"
They walked upstairs to the major's office to settle the details.

Liam and Kelly gathered their things and took them into the guardroom.

"Finished for tonight, Sergeant," Liam reported. "We've got to come back tomorrow for a few hours. Through by midday if we can make an early start."

"Early as you like," said the sergeant. He was tired. "We work right around the clock, Dad. We'll be here. What about eight o'clock?"

"Eight o'clock it is, on the dot. Good night, all."

"Good night, Dad."

They took their time carrying everything into the van. At last Liam was satisfied. "Let's go home," he said with a sigh of relief, "nephew."

He warned Kelly to drive carefully through the city.

"The troops," he explained, "throw up roadblocks without any warning and carry out snap inspections of every vehicle. They particularly don't like vans. Let me do the talking if we get stopped tonight."

Their luck held, and they reached their destination without incident. Eamonn was waiting for them as they drew up outside a small terraced house. It was quite dark now. He told Kelly where to garage the van.

"Get straight back here," he ordered. "Don't let the neighbors see any more of you than they have to."

Kelly knocked on the door of the house ten minutes later. Inside, the house was poorly furnished but neat and clean. Eamonn told him, "I want you both to stay indoors all night, in case the police carry out a house search. Moira says they might. How did it go today?"

"Bombs away," said Kelly jauntily. "All locked up by a nice kind policeman."

"Good." Eamonn's eyes shone with anticipation. "Errol did a fine job with that makeup. Your own mother wouldn't know you."

"These bloody lenses are murder. They're coming out now."

"Remember to put them back if there's a search—and when you go back tomorrow," Eamonn told him. "We can't afford to take the slightest chance now we've come this far."

204

"How is Errol?" asked Liam tentatively.

"None too happy in Monaghan, I'm afraid," said Eamonn. "But Kevin's looking after him. There'll be no trouble."

"I hope not, Eamonn. It was his work that saved us today. No two ways about it."

Kelly looked around him and licked his lips.

"I need a drink after what we've been through today," he declared, "and I'm not kidding. Let's send out for something."

"There's drink here," said Eamonn. "We're beginning to know your tastes by now, Mr. Kelly. You'd better say hello to your aunt while you're about it."

The woman who came in was tiny, like Liam. She was neatly dressed and apple-cheeked and she smiled at the mercenary. She had already met Liam. Only Eamonn knew she had a shotgun in the kitchen.

"So you're my nephew," she said. "Big, aren't you?"

Kelly stood nonplussed—he had no communication with women. "You've got to call me Bob," he grunted.

"And I'm your Aunt Mary, your mother's sister, if the Army comes knocking on the door," she retorted. "I know my lines, don't you fret, you're not the first man I've adopted in a hurry."

She looked at Liam.

"There's a bottle in the cupboard behind you," she said. "Our nephew is going to have one, and so am I."

Eamonn gave a final reminder of the next day's orders—"Stay here tomorrow night, too, in case of a check"—and slipped out of the house. He faced another long journey through the paratroop patrols and across the Border into Monaghan and dared not leave it too late.

The woman called Mary went into the kitchen and prepared a meal.

"She's a tough old bird," Kelly remarked. "Mind she doesn't throw her weight around—Uncle."

"We're in her hands," Liam whispered, "just as long as we stay under this roof. Don't go baiting her, Kelly, for the love of God. She's not the dear little creature she looks."

A few minutes later "Aunt Mary" came in and put fish and chips on the table.

"Now," she said, "if you find you want to leave in a hurry, straight out of the kitchen door you go, and over the wall. Turn right in the alley and run like hell until you reach the pub on the corner. They'll take you in, no questions asked. Probably suit you, locked in the cellar." She laughed. "Get all that? Good, I'm going to bed.

Nephew, you're in the room on the left of the landing. And you're sleeping with me."

This was to Liam.

"Lay a finger on me and I'll tear your eyes out. I'm a respectable woman."

The door slammed shut behind her.

The two men looked at each other and began to eat their fish and chips. Kelly waited until he heard her reach the top of the stairs but even then he kept his voice down.

"I don't know about you, Liam," he said with a grin, "but I'd rather sleep with the bomb any day!"

Liam carefully refrained from comment.

·29·

As always in Ulster, Felix was under maximum pressure, and when the time came for an EOD officer to search and seal the hotel one week ahead of the conference, the duty fell to the same captain who had aided Welbourne on the night of the ambush in Tyrone.

The two officers recognized each other at once and shook hands.

"Good morning, sir," said the captain and added tactfully, "They don't give you any easy ones, do they?"

Welbourne smiled easily.

"I'm not sure how to answer that," he admitted. "I've got the paper responsibility for security here, but in point of fact the RUC do all the work. All I've done so far is supervise painting and polishing."

"All of which has been carried out by civilian firms?" Felix asked. "I see."

They sat in canvas chairs in Welbourne's office as the major sketched the security arrangements.

"The workmen finished yesterday," said Welbourne. "We spent all last night going over the building from toilet rolls to pillows and bedding. The inspector and I believe it's as clean as the proverbial whistle. We're doubly delighted to see you here, just the same."

Renton came in and joined them. He listed everything that had been done and he underlined his year-round responsibility for general security.

"We get this flap," he said, "with every conference. I can't see how we could have missed a trick this time."

The captain told him, "Trouble is, Inspector, there is always an element of risk in staging a conference of this kind. And when you import civilian workmen to prepare the site, then clearly you increase the theoretical dangers."

"Agreed," said Renton. "But we've seen the last of them now.

There is a full week to run, at least, before the VIPs arrive. That cuts down most of the risk."

Felix looked at the plans of the hotel.

"There are thirty-one rooms in this building," he pointed out. "Once I search a room and pronounce it safe, it has to be sealed. On no account whatever can that seal be broken afterward by any person but me, which will be on the morning the conference starts. Those rooms which you have to keep open and in daily use are your pigeon. I can only guarantee those that are actually sealed."

Welbourne answered him.

"There are quite a number of rooms," he said, "which have not been entered by these or any other workmen for months. We can rule out this room, those offices upstairs used by secretaries and ministerial staff, the police guardroom, and the armory. They have to be safe. I'll vouch for those and put it in writing for you. I want you to concentrate on the bishop's study—that's the actual conference chamber—the reception and dining rooms, the VIP bedrooms and bathrooms, and all toilets outside the guardroom. Seal all those off until you are satisfied we can use them without risk. That leaves us with the responsibility for the kitchens. Mr. Renton and I will take damned good care of them, don't worry."

Inspector Renton approved. "Sure."

"Very well," said the captain. "If I can have that in writing, Major, I will get cracking. There's still a hell of a lot to do."

He went out to his Land-Rover and spoke to his driver. The two of them began to carry in the tools of his trade. Welbourne and the inspector looked at them, fascinated.

The main items appeared to be stethoscopes. Some were acoustic, others electronic, used to sound walls and furniture.

They brought in their portable X-ray machine and developer.

"I'll have to clear everyone out of the immediate vicinity when we develop our prints," the captain said apologetically. "Bombs can be set off in a number of ways. And there is a danger of firing one hidden in a room by the radiation scatter from the X-ray apparatus."

He smiled at the two officers.

"Just routine," he explained. "I'll make sure you have plenty of warning."

"What about you?" Welbourne asked him.

Felix shrugged his shoulders.

"Yes," he said. "Good question." He lit a cigarette and began checking through the equipment.

His driver carried in an odd-looking instrument, something like an electric drill.

"What's that?" asked Renton.

"The sniffer, sir," the driver told him. "It's a vapor detector. Everyone and everything gives off a vapor. This is built to react to vapor given off by explosives."

Everyone left, and Felix got down to work.

In the rooms assigned to him by Welbourne, he pried and peered in drawers and crannies, he dismantled water cisterns and fireplaces with ruthless efficiency.

To the beds, mattresses, pillows, and old-fashioned bolsters still used in the hotel, he devoted more time and energy than any floor manager at sales time.

He opened doors and windows, he closed them gently, and slammed them shut. He flicked every switch and changed each light bulb. He searched the great boiler system and riddled the dead ashes one by one.

The stairs were next in line for his careful scrutiny. Each nail and screw were examined.

He went down into the sewer, he lifted each filthy cover as carefully as a miner searching for gold.

He took telephones apart and fitted them together again. Cupboards drew him like a magnet. He opened every one, looked inside them, tapped around them, cocked his head on one side to listen for the giveaway echo of a hollow boardframe. His patience was monumental.

Ceilings intrigued him, and floors entranced him. He paid minute attention to every inch of wiring. He took up carpets and put them back reluctantly. He looked up chimneys and down into waste pipes. He took off the backs from radio and television sets to peer inside.

He found nothing that caused him a moment's disquiet.

Sometime that afternoon he pronounced the bedrooms and bathrooms safe and sealed them off.

"That's about all I can do in the sleeping quarters," he said. "When the VIPs arrive, it will be up to the Special Branch to take over. I want those manholes leading to the sewers cemented down. Can your men do that before I leave tonight, Mr. Renton? Fine. And I suggest you see to the firing of the boilers yourself. But quite honestly, it looks pretty good elsewhere. The main target, if there's going to be one, has to be the conference chamber. I'll do that next."

He closed the door of the bishop's study behind him, and like Kelly before him, spent some time looking around with strictly professional interest. The severe beauty of the room escaped him.

The fireplace seemed to fascinate him, as though it were a work of art and he a collector. When open fires had been made redundant in the hotel two years earlier, the study chimney had been sealed off at head height. Now he climbed inside to poke and tap and scrape and rub until he felt satisfied it still contained nothing but dust and grime. He went out and checked it from the roof and made a note to make a second examination from the roof on conference day. Today he was certain it was clear.

He paid particular attention to the fireplace and spent some time actually removing and then resitting a number of firebricks. A sergeant knocked on the door and offered him a cup of tea.

It was the captain's only break during the entire search.

After tea he turned to the table. He smelled the polish used by the workmen, examined their work with a critical eye, but could find no fault. The table held no drawers or cavities where an explosive device could be hidden. Even so, he searched diligently for cracks and telltale hairline joins but could discover none.

He tested its enormous legs, as fat as the trunk of a telegraph pole. Every inch of the table gleamed innocently at him, and he turned to the chairs. They passed his scrutiny equally well.

The captain took off his shoes and stood on the table to peer at the ceiling. He spent forty minutes with the chandelier. Then he came down to earth and crawled over every inch of the brilliant oak floor, probing each crack and crevice.

He put the lights on and went to the bookshelves below the leaded windows. He took out each volume, weighed it in his hand, shook it, listened to it, flicked through its pages, and gently replaced it. He tapped the shelves this way and that as his mind gnawed and worried at the endless range of possibilities the study presented to an assassin.

He called in his driver to help him. They X-rayed the table legs, the Reynolds in its gilt frame, and the beaten-brass bedwarmers that were crossed like two golden spoons in the fireplace.

The mirrors followed his every move. He examined them, in turn, with great care. For one moment he could picture them in his mind's eye shattering into glass scythes and hurtling through the packed room. Now he unscrewed each one from its seat in the paneled wall, sniffed and smelled and rapped and tapped the wooden surfaces below before clamping them back, whistling tunelessly as he toiled.

He dismantled the light switches and looked at the wiring. He knocked on every inch of wall. He went out into the gardens and before the light failed lifted every leaf of ivy that clung below the window frames.

Only then was he sure the study was "safe."

He reported to Major Welbourne and waved a hand around the room.

"It's clean, sir," he said. "I can find no explosive device whatsoever. I'd like you to witness the seal, please, and ensure it remains unbroken until I come back to open the study for business in one week's time."

Welbourne thanked him and took him upstairs.

"Like a drink?" he asked.

"Thank you, sir. It's been quite a day."

Welbourne poured out two whiskies.

"Cheers," said Welbourne. "I don't envy you the job, I must say."

"At least I won't be out of work when I get back to civvy street," the captain replied. "Just think how many security men in government buildings right around the world must be doing an identical job at this very moment. It's the age of the assassin. Every terrorist, every dropout with a grudge against his government, they all try to play Guy Fawkes these days."

"What beats me," said Welbourne, "is how they go about it. The average man or woman can't have a clue how to construct a bomb, surely to God? How do they learn what to do?"

"Not as difficult as you might think," Felix told him. "There is a textbook on the art of bombmaking actually on sale in America, can you imagine? The fascination lies in the knowledge that there is no end to the list of targets a bomber can select. You name it, and technically they can blow it up. The terrifying thing is that there aren't enough experts in any society to protect that society fully, once the madness takes hold."

Inspector Renton had joined them.

"Look at Ulster," he said. "It's a field day for bombers."

"You can say that again," Felix agreed.

"What's the answer?" Welbourne asked.

"Make the punishment fit the crime," said the inspector. "If our young friend here took an IRA man chained to his waist every time he went out to defuse a terrorist bomb—standard practice!—I bet

211

there would be an immediate sharp reduction in the amount of explosives used in Northern Ireland."

"Christ, you can't do that," Welbourne argued. "It would be condemned as inhuman."

"Aye," said the inspector amiably, "it certainly would. But all of us in Ulster would sleep sounder at nights just the same!"

The telephone rang. Welbourne answered.

"Hello," he said and put a hand over the mouthpiece to say to the others, "My colonel." He listened for a while and then said:

"Of course, sir. Felix has just finished. We're all ready for the conference." He paused. "In that case I can hand over to Inspector Renton and head straight back to join you. Say half an hour? Right, sir. Good-bye."

"He wants me back at HQ right away," he told the police inspector. "Will you hold the fort until tomorrow, Jim? Good. Captain, if you're all through, I will escort you back into Belfast. I'd like to leave at once."

Guard dogs in the grounds barked furiously as the Army vehicle trundled through in the gathering dusk.

·30·

Neet's Hotel was a mess. Strictly speaking, it was a bar and no longer a hotel. It had a very limited clientele. No one could recall when it had last served cooked meals to casual travelers. Its timbered entry, designed for the long defunct Belfast–Dublin post chaise, was sorely in need of paint, and the whole front looked like a decaying tooth in the face of the High Street.

It owed its decline to progress. With the arrival of the steam train, and later the horseless carriage, the need for hotels like Neet's had disappeared. And it rotted slowly away, with brewers and a succession of poor tenants holding grimly onto the liquor license. Now it was seedy, shabby, run-down, a rheumy old hobo of a building designed for a different age.

Years before, a British Army officer and scholar had gazed on the stream that trickled behind it and christened it Lethe, after the river where the ancient Greek gods once drank to forget the past.

To the RUC stalwarts who stood guard patiently all year around at the Old Covenanter a mile away, it was an off-duty haven where licensing hours could be discreetly negotiated. Tony Pearce, the landlord, had served in the Royal Navy in World War II and was liked and respected as a man above suspicion in these difficult times. His pub had been attacked twice, presumably by the IRA, although damage had been negligible.

In recent years Neet's had become well known to a succession of bored British Army troops called in when a roadblock was needed nearby for some visiting VIP who had been put up at the isolated Old Covenanter.

In deference to the British caste system of drinking, Pearce kept an old flyblown notice handy to hang in the bar, marked OFFICERS ONLY.

His pub dominated the High Street, which in itself was a misnomer. It was the only street in the hamlet and equally in de-

213

cay. It contained—apart from the pub—a general store, a gas pump, and a dozen drab cottages.

In the days of horse-drawn traffic Neet's had catered mainly to travelers held up by rain or breakdown and impassable roads. Some must have been obliged to stay for days. The hotel still boasted six bedrooms, three of them in disrepair, a big kitchen, and extensive toilets in the yard. It was therefore a natural as temporary headquarters for each roadblock company.

The Army had also gotten to know Pearce on these fleeting terms and like the RUC regarded him and his ramshackle pub as both safe and friendly.

On both counts it was mistaken.

Pearce had relatives galore living south of the Border. Left to his own devices, free from pressure, he would undoubtedly have preferred to steer a straight course, abiding by the laws of the Six Counties he lived in. But Neet's was lonely as public houses go, and he was human and open to persuasion. Long ago the IRA had pointed out to him that many advantages lay in taking guests for the night with no questions asked, and he had accepted the reasoning.

He knew Eamonn well. On this damp, dark spring evening the man with the scar had warned him to expect two visitors.

Eamonn had not told him how long they'd be staying. The last thing he wanted to know was their business. At the appointed hour he slipped out of his bar and waited in the cobbled entryway. He stood there silently, unhappy and afraid, as two figures tiptoed through the yard. He forced himself to reach out a hand and touch the smaller man on the shoulder.

"Quiet," he hissed. "The police are inside. Follow me, quick, the pair of you." He led them through his back door, into the kitchen, across the hall, and up a flight of creaking stairs.

Liam and Kelly followed him like blind men, each man clutching the shoulder of the one in front—the landlord, then Liam, then Kelly—for all downstairs was in total darkness. Both of them carried haversacks on their backs. Kelly also had a big suitcase in one hand which contained the transmitter-receiver for the bomb that could lip-read.

There was a light of sorts on the landing. Five bedrooms led off to the right, with a bathroom halfway along. The sixth bedroom was on the left, far end, over the yard they had just left.

A notice was tacked to the door of the bathroom stating: FAMILY USE ONLY. THANK YOU. Beyond it Pearce had placed a chair on the landing carrying another handwritten legend, much bigger this time. It warned: CAREFUL BEYOND THIS POINT. FLOORING UNSAFE.

He led his visitors straight past, ignoring the warning. The floorboards squealed, and dipped, but held well enough. Pearce halted outside the last door on the right, unlocked it quietly, and led the two men inside.

Heavy curtains that let in no chink of light from the High Street's street lamp were already drawn.

Pearce moved like a cat in the dark and found his way to a small table lamp that stood on a crate in an alcove. He switched it on and warned them:

"No more light at any time."

Kelly looked around him without comment. A dust sheet covered the linoleum floor, perhaps to convince an unwanted caller that repairs were about to begin. A table of varnished pine stood against the wall to his left, with three chairs placed nearby. Two canvas sleeping bags were unrolled on the floor behind the lamp and out of the line of sight of the door. Cigarette ends and an old, yellowing newspaper lay in the empty grate.

Pearce was afraid to stay a moment longer.

"I'll come back when they've gone downstairs," he whispered. "Stay quiet till then." They heard the boards squeak on the landing, the noisy flush of a toilet chain—Pearce's excuse for leaving the bar—and steps on the stairs, then silence.

Kelly and Liam slipped off their haversacks. The mercenary placed his suitcase at the wall by his side, lowering it gently. Then after locking the door from the inside they both lay down on the sleeping bags to await the landlord's return. Kelly took out a Colt .38, checked that the chamber was loaded, and placed it on the dust cover beside him. He switched off the light with a word to Liam and lay still.

"This won't do," he said softly. "Not for a week, with the transmitter set up. Too bloody exposed."

Liam grunted noncommittally, "At least we're inside."

They heard the clatter of a motor starting, then the revving of an engine in the yard below and the slamming of doors as the police drove off. It was close to midnight. More doors slammed downstairs, bolts crashed home, footsteps sounded faintly on the stairs.

Kelly pressed Liam's shoulder, warning him not to move. He took his revolver and floated on stockinged feet to a point behind the door. From the landing the man's voice hummed a bar from

"When Irish Eyes are Smiling," the signal Pearce always gave to Eamonn's visitors to say he was alone.

Kelly let him in. He saw Pearce had a canvas bag in his hand.

"Food," said the landlord. "Here." He placed a loaf of bread, a hunk of cheese, and two bottles of stout on the table. His eyes never left the gun in Kelly's hand. He reached into the bag again, slowly, and drew out a bottle opener. Kelly put the gun away.

"Don't be alarmed, Tony," said Liam. "No one's going to hurt you. My friend is just taking elementary precautions."

Pearce was small and plump. He was sweating freely in spite of the cold. "We don't want any trouble," he answered. "Please."

Kelly ignored him and sat down at the table to eat. He broke off a crust of bread and wolfed it down with some cheese. As he chewed he opened one of the bottles and swallowed a mouthful of the dark, foaming beer.

"That's good," he said, surprised. "Bloody good."

Liam offered the landlord a cigarette and waved him into the third chair. "Sit down, Tony," he said, "while we have a little chat."

"I don't know how long you intend to stay and I don't care—it's none of my business, and there's the clinch. But the sergeant said tonight we would have soldiers here in a few days' time." Pearce looked nervously from Kelly to Liam and back again.

Liam told him, "We've got a special job to do. May have to stay a week, even longer. The room won't do, it's too exposed here. What else is there?"

Pearce puffed away at his cigarette and thought for a moment.

"Well," he explained, "there are only three rooms in use. Bedrooms, I mean. My wife and myself, we have that one at the top of the stairs. My daughters have a room each, coming down the landing. The rest are empty. This one goes to the Army when they want to sleep in, which isn't very often. The other two really are falling to bits. I was only expecting you for the one night. That's the usual drill."

"Let's take a look," Kelly suggested.

The three men walked along the landing. Pearce opened doors and showed them inside each room.

Kelly stopped outside the third bedroom, next to the bathroom. It had a double bed, a small armchair, and a long wall mirror and table below, with the girl's makeup scattered untidily across its surface. A padded stool fitted neatly underneath the table. It was tailor-made for Kelly and his control panel.

216

Like every room on the landing it was spacious enough, built to take six or more stranded travelers in an emergency a century back, each rolled in his cloak on the floor.

Liam intercepted the landlord's protest.

"Be a good feller," he said pleasantly, "and ask your daughters if they will double up for a few days. Apologies from me for the inconvenience, it'll not be for long."

Pearce looked distinctly unhappy.

Liam added, "No need to bother the girls tonight, Mr. Pearce, my friend and I will be quite happy in the room you set aside. Ask her to move her things out first thing tomorrow, how about that?"

It was an order. Tony Pearce nodded glumly.

"Sure," he said. "I'll bring you some hot breakfast in the morning and have arrangements made by then. Anything else?"

His visitors said no and thanked him. Kelly and Liam went back to the end of the landing and their room for the night.

"That's great," said Kelly. "That makeup table, it will do fine for my control set. The window must be overlooking the main street, which is another help. The bed's big enough for two, or we can take turns keeping watch."

"We'll think about it," Liam answered, already in his sleeping bag. He had the feeling things were going too smoothly. The bomb in position, the monitoring about to begin. There had been no hitch in getting out of Belfast, no search of their "digs," no awkward moments on their final day working inside the bishop's study. But what the hell, maybe it would be that way right through. He fell asleep in an instant.

Kelly found it harder to relax. Pearce, the landlord, looked scared out of his wits. Would he be capable of standing the strain of hiding two gunmen for a week right under the noses of the police and Army? There was even a chance the soldiers would take over this room, in which case the chances were they would first search the hotel top to bottom. There were a thousand things that could go wrong, with Pearce the weak link. Kelly was still wide awake and worrying when daylight came.

217

·31·

In spite of the urgency of his summons, Major Welbourne spent more than four hours kicking his heels after escorting the Felix crew to its quarters. It was close to midnight when the colonel sent for him.

"Sorry to have kept you so long," he began, "but requests and reminders are flying fast tonight between Whitehall and the Army. How are things at your end?"

"Fine. Ready when you are."

"In that case doors open on the fifteenth. Six days from now."

"Right, sir. I'll let Felix know." There was clearly more to come.

"There's just one thing." The colonel gave him an odd look. "Your first customers may not be quite the ones you expected."

Welbourne was baffled and not a little weary. "I don't quite get the drift, sir."

"That's what tonight's flap has been all about. The main topic for the Kipling conference will be planning for long-distance security. To examine, in particular, the role of the Army."

"That can't come up for auction," said Welbourne. "We come under Whitehall. Now and always."

"Quite so," the colonel agreed. "But now that a blueprint has been established for a new-style local government, it may be considered advisable to push the Army more into the background and leave ground security more and more in the hands of the police. There is considerable pressure from the Dublin cabinet on these lines. But if such a course is going to stand any chance of success, it will need guarantees of much greater civilian cooperation. Are you beginning to get the drift now, Dickie?"

"I think I am," said Welbourne reluctantly. "A deal with the terrorists?"

"No deal," the colonel replied. "Exploratory talks, rather. I told you sometime ago feelers had been put out. Tonight we learn that first results have been distinctly promising."

Welbourne chewed that one over. "Where?"

"I gather," said the colonel, "the plan now is to hold them immediately before Kipling—in the Covenanter."

"Waste of time," Welbourne told him. "Those sods want surrender, not peace."

"That may well be," said the colonel. "I am afraid the matter is out of our hands. Two gentlemen are on their way here at this moment to iron out a few details. We just do what we're told."

Welbourne felt the anger spill over inside him.

"Colonel," he said, "some of my friends were murdered by these men only a few weeks back. I lost a regiment and a career in the process. Do you really intend I wet-nurse them, in a place I have personally made safe, while they sit on their arses and debate if they'll agree to a cease-fire provided the Army pulls out first?"

"I didn't hear that, Dickie," said the colonel gently enough. "Try me again."

Welbourne drew a deep breath.

"I will rephrase it, sir. I am very strongly opposed to the idea on personal, moral, and security grounds."

"Then you and I think alike," the colonel told him, "along with the general and the rest of the Army. But this is a political decision. The Army can voice objections to some part of the plan perhaps on pure security grounds but nothing more. Personal feelings don't come into it. We simply carry out orders. You know that as well as I do."

His telephone rang.

"Duty officer, Aldergrove military," said a wide-awake RAF voice. "Good morning, sir. We have an aircraft due to land shortly with two passengers heading your way. There's a little activity in the Crumlin Road, and we've asked for a bigger escort to bring them down. There may be delays."

The colonel logged the call. He turned to the major.

"They'll be here soon," he told him. "A bit of a holdup at this end, thanks to our friends from the IRA. I imagine we'll have at least an hour to kill. Let's got through that Felix report while we're waiting."

There was no mistaking the human jelly who came wobbling into the office at 1:30 that morning. Welbourne smiled as he rose to shake hands.

"You look well, Major," Sydenham observed. "Do I take it that desk work agrees with you after all?"

"I'm coping," Welbourne said, "or rather I thought I was until tonight. But it's good to see you, sir."

Sydenham nodded affably at the colonel, shook hands, and introduced his companion, Commander Tom Finney, a senior officer from the Special Branch. All four sat around the colonel's desk.

"Any trouble getting through?" the colonel asked.

"The Royal Marines said it was routine," said Sydenham, "although there were moments when it seemed a little lively to me. Now, gentlemen, I won't waste your time—you know my brief. I want to hear any Army problems in the security sphere arising from these proposed unofficial talks, find a satisfactory way to overcome them—a mutually satisfactory way—and reach firm agreement with you then on a date. Would you like to start the ball rolling, colonel?"

"Certainly," said the colonel. He studied his hands for a moment. "As you are fully aware, the general has raised a number of matters concerning these talks with the minister. Not on the decision itself to hold talks, which is and remains a political responsibility. But on the place and the timing. Militarily speaking, the staff believes the Army is gaining the upper hand in this campaign. A cease-fire gives the IRA a golden opportunity to regroup and reinforce. If the talks break down, as they have in the past, we lose lives in restoring the situation."

Sydenham brushed that aside.

"I see no point in my commenting on that, Colonel. The subject has been raised and overruled at highest level on the grounds that any risk is worth the ultimate prize, which is peace in the province."

"Agreed," said the colonel, "but it has a direct bearing on one subject which is our concern, namely, security. The Army staff would vastly prefer to have these men flown secretly to London for their talks. We are against holding them in Ulster for a variety of reasons. We feel they may provoke strong UDA extremist reaction, for one thing. We also hold very strongly that to invite them into the Covenanter on the eve of our own Kipling conference imposes an almost intolerable strain on all responsible for general security."

Sydenham handed around his fat Turkish cigarettes.

"I sympathize with you," he replied. "But the IRA men have refused to go to London for these talks. They insist on meeting here in Ulster—which they consider to be still a part of Ireland. That's one of their arguments. They also maintain that to be invited here at all, even secretly, still implies recognition.

220

"Recognition is a matter of paramount importance to the IRA. At present it is even outlawed by the Irish government in Dublin. In both North and South its men are pariahs who stand to be jailed in the South and shot in the North for serving in an underground army that officially does not exist. They feel that if they make peace possible by laying down their arms they will earn recognition and the right to a seat at the talks that must follow between the two governments.

"Their agreement to talk at all is conditional on the conference site being in Ulster. On this they refuse to budge."

He caught sight of Welbourne's face.

"Something is clearly worrying you, Major. Out with it."

"I'm completely baffled," said Welbourne, "by the need to consider their feelings and wishes at all. Why should we give an inch to these thugs?"

"Because," Sydenham replied patiently, "they are responding to our initiative. We have asked *them* to stop shooting and start talking."

"You couldn't choose a better place," maintained Welbourne stubbornly, "to insult the Prots. What you are doing is tempting two sides to blow the hotel up instead of one."

The fat man struggled to keep his temper.

"Your colonel has just spent considerable time reminding us how heavy a guard will be needed whoever comes. The Covenanter is like a fortress—I know, Major, I have stayed there myself! Recently you yourself, I understand, have spent a great deal of time and energy in making it safer still. What could be a better, safer place for talking to anyone, if it has to be in Ulster?

"Let us not be naive, sir. Protestant ghosts in that building cannot harm us, numerous though they may be. And you surely do not see the IRA delegates secreting a bomb in the cellar to blow the Kipling representatives sky-high a few days later, do you?"

"Both sides are capable of laying on a terrifying demonstration of force," said Welbourne doggedly. "With respect, you underestimate them, Mr. Sydenham."

Sydenham wanted no lectures. He had been sent to smooth badly ruffled Army feathers and get a date firmly fixed for the talks, no more, and now the charade bored him. He turned to the colonel.

"The greatest strategist of our time, no mean soldier himself, once declared, 'Jaw-jaw is better than war-jaw.' We have been fighting these people since 1969, and I am referring only to this campaign! And we have paid dearly in property, lives, and money. Surely any peaceful approach is worth a try?"

"Those are the minister's views, almost verbatim," the colonel agreed.

"And I, sir, am asking your views as a staff officer."

"The answer has to be yes. It is sometimes difficult to give an unbiased reply when one is an Army officer—and a target for the IRA—living here in Ulster. But if there's a real chance of peace, of course it's worth a try."

"Good. Excellent. Now we can proceed to the next step and fix a starting date." The fat man rubbed his hands with pleasure. "Now then, Major. Has the building been pronounced safe to your own satisfaction?"

"Yes, sir."

"And sealed by Felix?"

"Apart from rooms in daily use by staff and police guard."

"No sign of terrorist intrusion? No local activity?"

"None whatever."

"Then we can get down to business. I want a date set as early as humanly possible."

"Hold your horses," said the Special Branch officer, who had remained silent while Welbourne made his protest. He was a senior man and had no fear of Sydenham. "There are one or two things I have to know first. I'll be responsible for the safety of some highly unpopualr men. Tell me, how do you propose to fetch them in and out of Ulster? They stand a fair chance of being lynched if word gets around."

Sydenham turned to the colonel. "Well, sir?"

"Armed escort for local delegates," said the colonel after a pause, "and choppers for those arriving from south of the Border. Always assuming you can get clearance from Dublin."

"I imagine we will," Sydenham told him, "in view of the stakes. And the shorter the notice, the better, from a security point of view. Not so much time for tongues to wag."

"Objection," said Welbourne. At least two pairs of eyes regarded him with growing exasperation, but he plowed on. "You will be asking for trouble, real trouble, if you let anyone know *in advance* the location of this conference."

"It's a point," admitted the colonel at length.

"Surely you could take the delegates in blindfolded," said the fat man crossly, "and have everyone searched for weapons first?"

The Special Branch commander took Welbourne's side.

"I don't give a hoot," he began, "about the ethics of any political conference. Invite who you like. My job and Welbourne's job is to

222

make sure whoever comes stays in one piece. And I think the major has made a very valid point. So I'd like to put down a few ground rules for the benefit of everyone present in this room.

"Point one, IRA delegates must agree to come blindfolded to the conference.

"Point two, they must agree to physical search by my own men on entering and leaving the province.

"Point three, to be strictly observed, no indication of any kind where the talks are to take place other than a promise it will be somewhere in Ulster.

"I think the situation warrants a tough line, especially since the Army feels it has the upper hand. Either they accept our conditions—with guarantees of safe conduct—or they don't come at all."

He lit his pipe and puffed away defiantly. Welbourne could have sworn he saw the slightest wink across the table. "If all these points are agreed to," said the policeman, "I have no objection to two, three, or even four consecutive conferences taking place in the same building."

Sydenham took the vote.

"Colonel?"

"I agree fully with the commander."

Next, out of politeness, he asked Welbourne.

"Major?"

Welbourne's answer was one of grudging consent.

"I'll do whatever has to be done, sir."

"Then we are, ahem, agreed." Sydenham painted a smile on his face. "Two separate conferences to be held, one unofficial, one official, but both complementary in their bearing on future security in the province.

"The first will take place on the fifteenth of this month. The security forces will remain in site thereafter, until the results of those talks have been analyzed and Kipling has been called.

"Present security arrangements at the hotel to remain in force under Major Welbourne until the arrival of the Special Branch.

"That concludes our business, gentlemen. The commander and I have to return to London and draft a joint report. Thank you for your help."

He mopped his brow. It was 4:00 A.M., and he was a man who liked the simple creature comforts, such as bed.

The colonel produced a bottle of whiskey and handed drinks around.

"Ah." The deep-set eyes gleamed appreciatively. "Most acceptable, colonel. Your health."

Welbourne was talking to the commander. The colonel seized the opportunity to speak privately to Sydenham.

"I was delighted to see that you knew Welbourne. Of course, I realized someone in Whitehall had pulled strings to get him posted here."

"Not at all, Colonel. I had to question him in connection with the delivery of those RPG-7 rocket launchers. The description of the two main characters involved and the search for them was a quite natural follow-up. It is no concern of mine where Major Welbourne actually serves. How can it be? We serve different masters."

"Precisely." The colonel had made his point. "I have come to the conclusion he is not suitable for this kind of job. He is a soldier, a front-line type, very solid and straightforward—not one of us, Sydenham. Too naive by half. I intend to have a quiet word with the general when this is over and see if we cannot get him shipped back to regimental duties somewhere."

"It takes time to train a man for intelligence work."

"And some longer than others."

"That is so."

Sydenham poured the whiskey down his ample throat and shamelessly held out his glass for more.

"Could one be more straightforward than that, my dear Colonel?"

"Have your little joke, Sydenham. But I mean what I say."

"Of course."

He rolled over to stand beside Welbourne and drew him aside.

"Forgive me if I appeared harsh tonight," he said. "Truth to tell, I admired your stand immensely. But there are times when one must learn to bend with the wind. Do you follow me?"

"Not really. To me the question is simple. I hate the IRA's guts."

"Insofar as the conference is concerned, let us turn that hatred and distrust to our advantage. When the IRA delegates arrive have a good look at these men, for we may not be finished with them yet. Memorize their faces. Check them against your wanted file. Talk to as many as you can. Listen to what they have to say. Use your time well."

"You can be sure I will," said Welbourne.

"Your colonel thinks I was wrong to seek your help. I do not share his views. But be discreet. Do nothing to harm your career. Call on me whenever you are in London—socially, of course. Au revoir, my dear Major."

•32•

Life in one room cooped up with a human tiger had tested Liam's nerves severely. There had been scenes from the beginning, when they turned the Pearce girl out to make room for them.

Pearce had called on the two men on the first morning, pale and frightened, to say that his daughter refused to move.

"'She's locked herself in," he said. "I can't do a thing with her, by God. She just says to leave her alone."

Liam took a reasonable attitude.

"Look," he said, "we don't want to upset anyone. But we have our orders and we cannot leave yet awhile. You can see how exposed we are in this room. If the troops check your 'empty' rooms as a security measure at any time, we've had it.

"But if a pretty young girl locks her door when there are soldiers billeted in her father's hotel, no one is going to suspect anything. Don't you see? It is that much safer for us. Let me talk to her. It's only for a day or two, after all."

Pearce shook his head.

"Trouble is," he replied, "she is scared stiff. She says if they find you in her room she will be sent to prison. Her mother and I can't persuade her otherwise."

Kelly took the gun from his pocket and began to clean it. Pearce's eyes followed every move.

"Tell your daughter," said Kelly ominously, "she has five minutes to move. And don't you argue with me. Ever."

Pearce scuttled out. They heard his daughter shouting and weeping through her bedroom door.

"There was no need for that," Liam told him. "I don't think you realize, Kelly, how much we need the help of these people."

"Show the slightest weakness and people will walk all over you. No family man ever argues with a gun. Shut up and grow up, Liam. Sometimes you act like you think we are playing Monopoly. This is the war game, remember?"

They could hear Pearce shouting at his stubborn daughter. Then Mrs. Pearce came upstairs and started screaming. Kelly thought everyone in the High Street must hear every word and marched along the landing to shut them all up.

"Get your daughter out," he said to Mrs. Pearce. "*Now.*"

Tony Pearce cried out, "Did you hear him, Molly? For the love of God, girl, open that door."

A key rattled in the lock, and the bedroom door crashed open. Molly Pearce was nineteen, and she had an Irish temper. She came out like a wildcat and tried to claw Kelly's face.

He slapped her face. Just once. She stopped and stared, terrified by the mercenary's calculated brutality.

"Listen," Kelly said, turning again to Pearce, "once and for all. Do as you are told, and no one gets hurt. Do anything else, and you get dead, very, very quickly. Get the girl's clothes out of that room and keep her mouth shut. Move!"

The girl's father looked at Kelly and back to the sobbing girl.

"You're twice as big as me," he said slowly, "and you have a gun. But don't ever lay a hand on one of my family again."

"Just make sure they do what they are told." Kelly turned his back on the Pearces and walked back down the landing.

He spent the rest of the morning wiring up his control panel. Liam watched from the window without a word, admiring despite himself Kelly's absolute command of his materials, his artistlike dedication.

Finally it was done.

Kelly said, "You have a gun, Liam? Okay, let's keep them both loaded and lying handy from now on. Just in case our friends downstairs get any ideas about using the telephone. One of us awake at all times from now on. Always one of us, at least, in this room. We'll work in shifts, six on, six off, off-duty man has the bed. That suit you? I will sleep first. I want to be awake and on watch when Pearce has those cops in for a drink tonight."

The afternoon dragged by.

Behind the locked door tension was in the air, as real as the faint perfume left behind by the girl. Kelly dozed, as wary as a cat—gun under the pillow, one eye flickering open at the slightest sound, even the rustle of Liam's clothes, or his cough, or the pad of his stockinged feet on the floor, or the scrape of a match.

Liam was spring-taut with fear and tension. The minutes

dragged by. He was out of his depth and knew it. He discovered, and not for the first time, that terrorists can get desperately homesick like anyone else, and he envied Kelly's total independence, even hated him because of it. He caught sight of his face in the mirror and was shocked.

The makeup had long been removed but he was silver-gray still. He had lost a great deal of weight in the past weeks. On some men that looks good; on Liam the flesh sagged, to make him look ill. His eyes were puffy with strain, his fingers brown with nicotine. He needed a shave. He stank of sweat. His feet hurt him, so his shoes were off and one big toe poked through a torn sock. He looked about as dangerous as a down-and-outer in a bread line. The eyes were still watchful, but even they mirrored his fatigue.

In his bones he felt trouble ahead, yet knew himself to be helpless as a passenger on a runaway train with every signal showing red! It was the longest afternoon he had ever known.

Kelly woke exactly on time.

Each man took turns padding down to the toilet, carefully avoiding flushing it in case the sound carried below.

No police came that night after all.

At half-past ten Pearce came to the door, gave them a tray of stew and potatoes, and left without a word. The terrorists ate in silence. Kelly heard it strike midnight. At two in the morning a rain shower beat a tattoo on the windowpanes. Passing headlights lit up the room as an Army patrol headed back to Belfast from the Border. Kelly shook Liam awake when it was time to change shifts.

So it went on, with little to say to each other. The silence suited Kelly. It made Liam even sicker with fear and dread.

Eamonn arrived at noon on the third day. There was no warning, no telephone call, no sound of a vehicle in the yard, no footstep heard on the stairs. He just materialized with a tap on the door, a turn of the key.

If he knew of the trouble with the Pearces, he gave no indication.

"Routine call," he explained, "to make sure everything is okay. The council want me back in Cork urgently. I'll not see you again before the conference. Mrs. McCabe confirms the starting date is the fifteenth of this month. Not long to wait now."

"Thank God for that," said Liam fervently.

Eamonn turned to Kelly. "You all right?"

"Couldn't be better."

"Good. Wait three more days, then go ahead whenever you like."

"Not when I like, Eamonn, when the bomb tells me."

"Have it your own way! Bear in mind, Mrs. McCabe says these conferences have a habit of starting early. She has to be at the hotel before 6 A.M. on the fifteenth."

"But we have a timing mechanism that begins to work only at 9:30 A.M. We will just have to wait. They'll still be talking, never fear! You want to see how it works, Eamonn?"

"Sure. What time is it now?"

"Close to 1 P.M. The conference should be going strong at this time of day. Right now there will only be police activity. Let's see how it goes."

Kelly switched on. There was only a faint click, but it was clearly heard in the bedroom, and Liam jumped nervously. He and Eamonn watched the dial closely. Kelly reached out a leg-of-mutton hand and slowly, gently, tuned in to the bomb's transmitter signal. A whine came through, but the needle stayed still. Kelly tried again and tuned more finely. Still no movement.

"What's wrong?" Eamonn spoke in a whisper, as though afraid to waken the apparatus too suddenly.

"Wait," said Kelly. "Give us a chance."

Then the needle jumped. *Flick!* It leaped across the face of the dial and fell back. And again *flick! flick!* dancing in exultation as it betrayed the sound of human voices. It whipped from side to side. Its custodians watched closely like customers at a strip joint.

"By Christ," said Eamonn, licking his lips. "Just look at that thing."

Liam looked at his watch.

"See the time?" he said. "One o'clock exactly! Do you know what that bomb is telling us, Eamonn? That the police guard is switching on the news as they have their dinner. You remember, Kelly, how loud they had it turned on the first morning we worked there?"

"Right," said Kelly. He watched the dial. "The sergeant and the others, they'll be sitting around the table at this very moment. But they're not saying a word. See how regular the needle is? That's the BBC announcer all the time, with the radio going full blast."

Eamonn was impressed.

"Mr. Kelly, that is some broadcast."

The three men stared at each other in jubilation. It was as if they knew they had reached journey's end. The tension had gone out of the room. Liam's face was alight. Kelly was grinning. Even Eamonn looked pleased. For the first and only time in their association, all experienced a momentary share of the warmth that binds all comrades-in-arms.

Eamonn was the first to shrug it off.

"Good," he said. "It works! Go ahead and fire it, Mr. Kelly, at your discretion after three days have passed. No further contact required. Just sit tight here until we get you out after the explosion. Is that understood?"

"Sure," said Liam, still exulting in the bomb's display.

"Don't leave getting us out too long," Kelly warned him. "The Brits will go mad when the smoke from that bomb blows away! There ain't going to be anything left of the men who walked into that study. Not a wall left standing. Not a stick of furniture. Not even a coat button, let alone people. And there is going to be one god-awful search for the man who pulls the pin. They'll want revenge. Don't you doubt that for a moment."

Eamonn looked at him. "The closer you are to the hotel, the safer you will be."

"Not for long," Kelly replied. "Once they discover it was a radio bomb, they will take this hamlet apart brick by brick."

"I'll have it all under control on the day," Eamonn promised. "Trust me." He shook hands briefly and was gone. His last words to Liam were, "Never fear, old friend, I will have you safely out."

Kelly poured himself a drink. He offered the bottle to Liam, who was tempted but refused.

"That was some demo," said Liam. "I never realized any bomb could be made so sensitive."

"Yeah." Kelly was cynical again, now that Eamonn had gone. "Say, Liam, that bastard really better get his skates on in getting us out of here, I kid you not. We'll never see the Border alive if he pussyfoots around."

"He gave us his word." Liam shut his mind to the bad night he and Eamonn had shared back in Monaghan. Today he had sworn to get them out safely, had he not?

"You'll live to collect. Never fear."

"I aim to," vowed Kelly. "One way or the other."

He left the little man to ponder just what he meant by that.

·33·

Because of fears of extremist Protestant reaction, the negotiations to bring the IRA leaders to the conference table were conducted with great stealth.

But—for all the secrecy—there has to be an official record ready to be produced later, like a rabbit out of a hat. Such an inventory makes no mention of secret flights of men like Sydenham to Belfast in the early hours, nor does it include any hint of collusion in high places. Only the bare bones are presented.

It is left to the probing histories, or an insider's memoir, to put on the flesh much, much later, when the political repercussions have melted away. For this meeting—on which in some quarters such high hopes were placed—the official record was given in the form of a confidential exchange between the minister for Northern Ireland, who was then in Belfast, and his prime minister.

It ran as follows.

Following your proposals last month, I am able to report some success in efforts to arrange personal talks with representatives of the various factions of the so-called IRA movement.

I have made it clear that such discussions must be looked upon as exploratory and that they can have no official standing nor in any way be considered binding upon HM government.

On the other hand, I have undertaken to convey to you fully all points raised by these leaders at this conference, in the hope that they will contribute to the cause of peace in the province.

Accordingly, a total of sixteen so-called staff officers from four groups based in Eire, plus six more self-styled brigade commanders from Belfast and Londonderry, have agreed to meet me under flag of truce on the fifteenth day of this month, that is, tomorrow.

I have given them all guarantees of safe conduct.

The sixteen from Eire will make their own way to Newry where they

230

will be met by officers of the security forces. From there they have agreed to be flown by helicopter to a meeting place of our choosing, under conditions laid down by us and at a time to be determined on the day. Arrangements have been made for the other six to be driven under Army escort and under conditions laid down by the security forces to the conference site.

I have agreed that such unofficial talks will be held in Northern Ireland, without prejudice.

Together with the GOC I have guaranteed their safe return when the unofficial talks have ended, so that these men can debate certain proposals and counterproposals in council and frame a joint reply.

I have given them an assurance that a bilateral cease-fire will be observed in Ulster, if such an agreement is reached at these unofficial talks, until their replies have been received.

It is our earnest hope that such talks may help pave the way for the new Assembly to take office in normal and peaceful conditions. We will, of course, inform the members of the Assembly fully of what is discussed at such talks and invite their views.

Lastly may I say that while I personally feel, on all the advice available to me, that the climate is ripe for such unorthodox approaches, I accept your own view that any premature disclosure of the nature of such approaches could prove damaging.

I have therefore impressed on all parties concerned the need, at this critical stage of negotiation, for total secrecy.

No leak of this report found its way to the outside world. Although the fifteenth of the month was mentioned as "tomorrow," the message was in fact drafted seventy-two hours ahead.

This was to allow time for the Guards and armored cars to be flown in from England without publicity and take up roadblock duty around the Covenanter long before the delegates set out.

The troops set up tented headquarters in the fields behind Neet's, avoided the bars as they would the plague, and caused a minimum of inconvenience to the public in general and Pearce in particular. They had strict orders not to draw attention to their presence other than by normal roadblock stop-and-search routine.

No attempt was made to search any room in the hamlet, far less the pub. Kelly and Liam remained undisturbed. Each day at 1:00 P.M. Kelly made a radio check on his bomb. For the rest, they simply waited. Kelly found it a long three days.

Early on the morning of the fifteenth four helicopters chuttered over Neet's at rooftop level, and the earsplitting noise brought both men to the window.

"What the hell was that all about?" asked a sleepy Liam.

"Heading for the conference," said Kelly. "Jesus, they're early." He looked at his watch. "It's only seven." He lit a cigarette and paced the bedroom.

"Could be anything." He was speaking to himself. "Troops, maybe, extra guards for the site."

"What do you think we should do, Kelly?" Liam asked.

"Nothing. Whoever it was, they'll still be inside at half-past nine. We'll just wait, just as we planned. Go downstairs and organize some coffee."

·34·

The sixteen IRA men flown in by helicopter from Newry were not their highest-ranking commanders. Fearing a trap, the two main groups had sent middle-rank executives from their separate councils, with the power only to report back. Of the small splinter groups, only the Fenian Martyrs—sensing a chance to grasp temporary leadership in the negotiations—arrived in strength. The entire council of Eamonn, Raymond, and the twins decided to attend the conference.

Whatever their rank, the sixteen were an impressive sight.

A British Army officer at the helicopter park at Newry worked it out.

"Set seven hundred murders," he said, "and five thousand odd woundings down to their joint account. They make the Mafia look like a ballet school."

All were blindfolded as they stepped into the choppers at Newry. They had no idea where they might be going. Most of them thought the conference would be held inside Stormont itself.

The brigade commanders from 'Derry and Belfast were met separately at points outside the two cities, blindfolded and searched like the others, and taken under heavy guard by road to the conference site.

The timetable was so carefully worked out that they drove up to the gates as the last helicopter was disembarking its passengers.

The British themselves, while happy to talk, also had some reservations about the company they were to keep and had planned accordingly. Some significant changes had been made in security arrangements at the Covenanter, for instance. Inspector Renton's RUC guard had swollen in size and now included a dozen Special Branch sharpshooters from London. They wore RUC uniforms for the conference.

Four more men dressed in Army uniforms had Minox cameras

cleverly concealed in what appeared to be walkie-talkie sets. Front and side views of each of their charges were discreetly obtained as they stood guard on the incoming helicopters.

"It ain't sporting," Renton admitted happily, "but it's bloody necessary just the same. If these talks break down, which is highly likely, the pictures may save a lot of lives later on."

Even the catering staff was not all that it seemed. There were more Special Branch men in the kitchens than cooks, drawn from Belfast and Londonderry as well as from London.

Conference day at the Covenanter began at 5:00 A.M. when the young captain from Felix drove into the grounds. He checked the seals, made certain that none had been tampered with, opened the rooms personally, and then handed over the keys to Special Branch Commander Tom Finney, who had been placed in overall charge of the conference, over Welbourne and Renton.

"Your pigeon now, sir," he said. "Conference room as clean as a whistle, as of this moment. Likewise the bedrooms, though I gather you won't be needing them just yet, and both reception rooms on this floor. Don't let any of them get dirty before the talking starts, will you?"

"I won't," the commander told him. "Not staying to see the show yourself?"

"No, sir. Duty calls."

"Pity. You might get a few tips from the gentlemen coming in. On second thought, though, you know them all anyway."

"One can always learn, sir. Particularly in this game. I must say I am delighted to see the IRA arriving as guests. I hope I haven't overlooked anything that might *disrupt* the conference. . ."

The wise young face cracked into a wide grin.

"What a tempting target they make, to be sure," responded the Special Branch chief.

Commander Tom Finney was not a vindictive man. He'd been in the Special Branch for close to fifteen years and in the day-to-day pursuit of all kinds of criminals had learned to suspend any moral outrage when dealing with them. He felt much the same about political criminals, which he considered the IRA to be. He'd do anything he could to stop them achieving what they were trying to achieve but he didn't hate each man jack of them personally, far from it. To both Felix and himself, the IRA were just a nuisance, a

234

dangerous, bloody nuisance, but just that. They had the true professional's outlook.

When he'd been given this job, he was glad. It would give him a chance to study them, learn the way they thought and spoke, which might help him to keep track of them after the conference when they were out blowing up post offices, or whatever they might get up to. He might recognize a few as well, overhear something—there were a lot of possibilities. As for security, he had had years of experience and had no fears on that score.

After Felix had left, Commander Finney sent for Welbourne and Renton. The three of them made a final round of the building, posting sentries outside each room that had been unsealed. It was 6:30 A.M.

"You chaps satisfied?" asked the commander.

"Absolutely," said Renton.

"Completely," Welbourne agreed.

"Right you are. I am going to post my men on the roof and in the grounds. Major, I'd be obliged if you would come with me and check out our rooftop radio communications. There's a signals sergeant up there with three of my men. Inspector Renton, you take over on this ground floor. The delegates should be here within a half hour, depending on how things go in Newry. Warn your men to be absolutely poker-faced when the guests arrive, no chitchat, no abuse, no sign of recognition—just silence, you hear? Oh, by the way, you can move the pencils and papers, et cetera, into the study. Let your men do it. No one else, not even secretarial staff, allowed in from now on to the conference room."

Mrs. McCabe and her own staff had been at the hotel since before Felix had arrived. She had organized them a meal on arrival. They had been typing nonstop since. Now she timed her moves to perfection.

She saw Felix drive off under escort and personally brought in a sheaf of fresh-cut flowers from the gardens. The substitution of the IRA delegates for the prime minister and his party had been carefully withheld from her as it had from all but security staff.

"I don't think we'll be needing the urns today, Mrs. McCabe," Renton told her.

The inspector had seen Mrs. McCabe earlier and notcied that she looked strained. He put it down to the early start. Even so, he was surprised now at the look which passed over her face as he spoke—it was one almost of pain.

"I haven't got time to mess around, Mr. Renton," she said harshly. "The minister *always* has fresh-cut flowers. And he particularly likes to see those urns we've just had cleaned. Come on, now, I really am busy."

Renton wondered what to do. Clearly she had no notion of the change in plans. He himself was forbidden to mention them under the Official Secrets Act. Nonetheless, she was right in one particular—if the Northern Ireland minister was coming, he would normally have flowers on the table whoever else was present.

So he decided to give the IRA delegates flowers too.

"What was I saying?" he asked her. "Of course. Let's have them."

"Here," she said, and handed over some magnificent red and gold tulips. "You'd better search them for bombs."

"Oh, I will," he told her, "even though I know full well you picked them yourself. We can take no chances today, Mrs. McCabe."

The telephone jangled on his desk. Renton listened briefly and then slammed it back in the cradle. He raised his voice.

"All Special Branch men," he said, "wanted upstairs in the major's room. Final briefing by your commander starting now."

He was left with his own policemen and gave his sergeant the key to the armory.

"Let's have the urns out," he told them, "and careful you don't drop the buggers. Put 'em over here."

"Thank you," said Mrs. McCabe. Her voice was very husky.

The Delft urns were carefully set down by the inspector's desk. He shuffled the flowers halfheartedly.

Mrs. McCabe looked pointedly at her wristwatch. "Get on with you," she said. "It's a woman's job. I can spare you five minutes. Now, mind, out of the way."

Jim Renton had plenty to do. He walked away to brief his men for the day. No one paid the slightest attention to red-haired Moira McCabe. The Special Branch detectives, who would certainly have been curious, were all upstairs for their own careful briefing.

She had no idea which urn held the bomb. At the last moment her nerve almost failed—her legs shook, her hands trembled, her cheeks paled. She tried to put one tulip stalk through the pedestal cover but found the hole blocked below. She had discovered the bomb, first time. Summoning every ounce of strength, she walked across the room to her handbag and took out a knitting needle.

"I thought these were clean?" she said to no one in particular. "Filthy!" She poked the needle down into the Gelemax, gingerly

236

enough, but just as Kelly had told her. She dealt with each separate hole in this way, taking her time, fighting panic. At last she was through. She fitted the tulips into position, then filled the next urn as well.

When Renton next looked across to her, the vases were ablaze with red and gold and blue.

"Let's have some water," she said. He filled a jug from the tap and carried it to her. He watched as she poured half into each vase.

"Don't drown them," he said cheerfully.

"Here, give them to me," he went on. "Go and put your feet up. You look tired."

"Thank you," she said. "I did have a wretched night. My mother isn't at all well. But I'd better finish here."

Renton called two of his burliest policemen across. "Take hold of these monstrosities," he said, "and carry them into the study. For Christ's sake, don't drop them, lads, we'd be paying damages for the rest of our days."

Mrs. McCabe stood outside in the corridor and watched as the urns were set down gently on the gleaming, dark-red table. She handed over a basket filled with ashtrays, notepaper, pencils. Another policeman appeared beside her, wheeling a trolley of glasses and water jugs. She ticked off each item on a pad as the men set them out in the study, forcing herself to look busy. The inspector himself went around the room arranging everything. It was all done in a matter of minutes.

Renton checked his watch. It was 6:47 A.M.

"There you are," he announced to Mrs. McCabe, "all done! And I can swear on the Holy Bible the only person to enter this room since the seal was broken is myself. Security, Mrs. McCabe! It pays to do things by the book!"

She went upstairs and sat at her desk, feeling sick.

The Special Branch officers came back downstairs from their last briefing and took their appointed stations.

The dog teams were doubled.

Saladins began their roadblock patrols, each observing radio silence as ordered.

Major Welbourne put in last-minute telephone calls to his colonel and received situation reports from the Newry, Belfast, and Londonderry areas. It was 6:54 A.M.

Suddenly all the dogs began barking. A group of four helicopters, buzzing like huge wasps, showed up as blurred dark shapes on the skyline. The sound of their engines increased until they passed over Neet's and the hamlet with only feet to spare.

It was exactly seven in the morning.

Mrs. McCabe got up from her desk and ran to the window as she heard the roar of the engines. The other women secretaries joined her and for once she did not rebuke them or order them back to work.

She watched wide-eyed as the choppers settled on the lawns, with every blade of grass flattened by the sweep of their whirling blades. She could not imagine what was happening. Her hand went to her mouth as she saw separate groups of blindfolded men being led from the machines.

One of them she recognized in spite of the bandage around his eyes. The purple scar, shock of hair, jerky walk—it was unmistakably Eamonn. Then she made out the twins, and one more figure—surely it was Raymond?

She went to the door and opened it, to find herself face-to-face with a strange man in RUC uniform.

"Sorry," he said with a smile. "No one goes downstairs without the commander's permission for a while, ma'am. Don't worry about me. I'm here to protect you."

"Protect me from what?" she asked.

"The IRA," said the man, puzzled. He had no idea that government staff inside the building might not know what was happening. "They've just landed a bunch of them by helicopter."

"What on earth for?" She was dreading the answer.

"Peace talks," the detective explained. "They're hoping to arrange a cease-fire. I don't know any details. All I know is they're going to meet HM minister for Northern Ireland for talks today."

"All day?" Her eyes were enormous.

"I imagine so. Maybe longer."

She shut the door and forced her legs to walk back to her desk.

Down below, in the guardroom, Major Welbourne looked on as police removed each blindfold and led the men into the first reception room. Special Branch "waiters" handed around coffee and biscuits, and the men stared about them. Welbourne wondered grimly how many deaths these men might have caused, and if any of those drinking coffee had been in action against his men during the ambush in Tyrone.

It took exactly thirty-eight minutes for the Special Branch men

238

to search them. At 7:38 A.M. the guardroom was finally cleared.

Commander Finney addressed the IRA brigadiers when everyone had gathered in the reception lounge.

"Her Majesty's minister for Northern Ireland," he said formally, "will be here to join you as soon as possible. Copies of a précis of his intended speech will be passed among you to give you a chance to read some of the points he intends to raise with you and to discuss them among yourselves before he gets here. Don't mind us. We have orders to stay with you—for your protection. If you want anything, ask for me or the major here. We will do our best to help you."

It was not long before everyone recognized where they were. One or two of the diehards, old hands steeped in bigotry, were incensed at what they took to be a subtle insult, considering the history of the rendezvous. The majority saw the Irishness of the situation and grinned their delight.

The Fenian Martyrs were appalled.

They stood in a shaken group apart from the others. Eamonn was breathing hard. He felt trapped and numb with terror. His mind twisted and turned as he forced himself to think of a way out.

Raymond thought of the bomb standing on the table just one room away, the unspeakable device garlanded with spring flowers and ticking away the hours until ordered to destroy them all. He felt physically ill. He had planted many a crude bomb in pubs, hotels, and by parked cars in crowded streets filled with shoppers, and now, in his mind's eye, he could already visualize himself sans brains, sans limbs, sans teeth. His legs began to tremble.

The twins clenched their ham fists and stared helplessly at their leader, silently calling on him for inspiration. Both felt consumed with an illogical, burning hatred of Kelly, the bombmaker, who was safe, a mile away. The sweat gathered in beads on their foreheads.

All around them the room grew smokier and noisier. The draft copies of the minister's speech excited a lot of comment among the delegates.

Welbourne. standing next to the Special Branch commander, listened to their every word, sick at heart, hating his position. He heard one delegate growl, "We'll tell the bloody man straight, we're not having this!" The major remembered his own defeat and his dead comrades, and to his surprise felt a great and growing urge to shoot them all.

Instead he rammed his hands firmly into his pockets and forced himself to speak casually to Commander Finney.

"Got plenty to say, haven't they?"

"Not to worry, Major. That's what a conference is all about. I find it far better to see them here, talking, than think of them out in the field shooting at the lads."

Eamonn by this time had regained some of his usual composure and gathered his group about him, pretending to study the draft speech. Raymond spoke first.

"By the sweet Jesus," he whispered, "let's get out of here, quick!"

"Keep your voice down," Eamonn warned. He was resolved to stamp out panic. "It's not eight o'clock yet. The timing device won't start operating for another one and a half hours yet. If we can get a message to Liam, we can put the whole thing off for twenty-four hours or even more. Keep your heads while I work something out."

Raymond still had difficulty getting control of himself.

"Make it good, Eamonn," he pleaded. "And for God's sake, make it soon. I just can't sit here and pretend I don't know there's a bloody great bomb ticking away right next door to us!"

"Now listen to me," said Eamonn, who was no coward, "it *can't* go off until 9:30 at the very earliest.

"I've watched Kelly give it a trial run. I know how it works. Christ, Raymond, you've planted bombs before now and with only minutes to spare! Now calm down. Moira is upstairs in her office. She'll have seen us arrive, she'll know the score. She has a telephone call coming in any time now, with an excuse to get her out of the building. As soon as she is away, she'll get a message through to Liam. She will stop it, for certain."

Raymond was not so sure.

"What if she doesn't, what if they stop her?"

"All right," said Eamonn. "We'll give it till 9:15. If she has not found a way to let us know—somehow—by that time that Liam has been informed of our position, I will personally go to the police here and tell them about the bomb. I swear it! But not till 9:15. Everyone agreed? We wait till then?"

"It's cutting things awful fine," Raymond whispered.

"9:15," Eamonn insisted. "If there is the slightest chance of keeping the bomb on ice, I intend to take it. If Moira gets out and Kelly and Liam keep their heads, we can contact them ourselves tonight and plan for another day."

The twins plucked up enough courage to back his decision.

"Okay, Eamonn," they said unhappily. "Either you go to the police at 9:15—or we will. And no one's going to stop us."

240

Raymond nodded, white-faced and miserable.

"Right," said Eamonn once again, "we sweat it out until then. Now will you look at this bloody piece of paper and try to appear intelligent, or you'll have the whole room wondering what is up." Four heads stared wretchedly down at the paper. Try as he might, Eamonn could not stop his hand from shaking.

At 8:12 the door of the reception room swung open and a guard beckoned Major Welbourne. Everyone looked up. The two men spoke briefly, and Welbourne hurried out after a quick word with the commander.

"That will be Mrs. McCabe," Eamonn whispered triumphantly. "Her call has come through."

He guessed correctly. Welbourne was already talking to her from the telephone on Inspector Renton's desk.

"Mrs. McCabe," he told her, "the inspector has just taken a call from your office in Belfast. They have had a message saying your mother is seriously ill. The inspector says you were up half the night with her. Why didn't you tell *me* earlier she was ill?"

"I thought you had enough to worry about as it was," she said apologetically. "There was a neighbor with her. I felt sure she would be all right."

"It seems to be serious," he said. "You'd better go on home at once. As you must be aware, the big conference has been put back for a day or two because of these other visitors. We can manage without you for the time being. Get down right away, and I'll order a car to take you home."

She was down very quickly.

"Thank you, Major." He thought she looked very distressed. "I won't forget this."

"There's just one thing," he reminded her. "I am obliged to warn you officially, however unnecessary it may be, not a word to any-one—your colleagues, or family or anyone else—about what is hap-pening here this morning."

"I won't say a word," she promised. "If you want, I'll just go and see how she is and come back later if I can."

"No need," he told her gently. "I am only carrying out my duty, Mrs. McCabe. Off you go, and good luck."

Inspector Renton logged the time of the police car's departure in the book on his desk. It was 8:32.

As Mrs. McCabe was taken through the gates, the minister for

Northern Ireland drove in. The guard waved him through, and the escort, and telephoned Renton from his spyhole behind the sand-bags.

Everyone forgot Mrs. McCabe in the bustle of activity that followed the call. Everyone, that is, except the four delegates repre-senting the Fenian Martyrs. They thought about her constantly, and at least two of them prayed fervently nothing might delay her journey.

·35·

Tony Pearce had grown visibly older in the past week. His uninvited guests had stretched family harmony near to breaking point. His daughters set off to work in Belfast each day pale and weeping at what might happen—would certainly happen—if the security forces found out their secret. Mrs. Pearce, who was no coward, daily grew more belligerent with the provision of free meals and strain of hiding two armed terrorists under her roof.

Pearce was a careful man, but even the worm will turn. Liam and Kelly had lived for days just ten feet or so over his head, and still he had not the slightest clue what they were up to. He lived on the razor's edge of sheer panic every time the police dropped in for a drink, and his nerves were in shreds. He was fearful of Kelly and even more afraid of the sinister, scarred man named Eamonn who from time to time suddenly materialized from the shadows to confer with his cronies in that bedroom so close to his own.

He could not imagine what was afoot but knew it spelled trouble—for the authorities and through them for his own family. He had reached a point where he had to know or go out of his mind.

This morning he had heard the helicopters roaring low overhead and had listened to the two men moving about restlessly afterward, and he felt certain there was a connection between the aircraft and their presence. He could not say why but felt in his bones this was the day of decision.

His chance to find out something of the truth came when his telephone rang. It was 8:43 A.M. He was in the bar cleaning glasses when the call came.

"I have to speak to Liam," said a woman's voice. "It's urgent."

He ran up the stairs, warning signal forgotten, calling Liam's name. The door of the bedroom opened, and the little man poked his head into the corridor, answering at once.

"What's up, Tony?"

"Woman on the line for you. Says it's very urgent."

"I'll be right down. Tell her to hold on a moment."

Liam padded into the bar in his stockinged feet. He stared at Pearce until the landlord withdrew into the kitchen.

"Who's calling?" he asked. Behind the kitchen door Pearce was straining to catch every word. "Ah, hello, Moira. What is it you want?"

Liam listened very carefully to whatever the caller had to say. Pearce heard him reply, "We can stop it all right. That's no problem. The thing is, how do we let Eamonn know?"

There was another pause, and Liam told her, "Christ, that gives us less than an hour If they don't hear soon they'll really panic.

"Sure, I understand, Moira, of course you can't go back. You couldn't contact Eamonn in any case. It has to be one of us. Look. I'll have a word with Kelly now and decide what we have to do. Sure. Leave it to me. God bless you for calling."

Liam slammed the phone down and ran back upstairs. Pearce gave him enough time to reach Kelly and came through the kitchen door. He tiptoed up the stairs, stealthy as any cat burglar, and pressed his ear to the bedroom door.

"That was Moira," he heard Liam say. "Jesus, the whole bloody thing has gone wrong for us! There isn't any British conference, Kelly, they've got all the top IRA leaders there discussing cease-fire terms instead! You remember those helicopters this morning? That was our boys being flown in. Moira says she saw Eamonn and Raymond and the twins, all there."

"You've got to be joking." There was flat disbelief in Kelly's voice.

"This is no joke, Kelly. No one's going to play a fool trick like that to stop you firing the bomb! No, she told me everything went according to plan. The police carried it in, the study was all ready, her own getaway phone call was arranged—and then she saw Eamonn stepping out of one of the helicopters! One of the guards told her the rest. She didn't have a clue, no one did, except the police and the Army."

"So what does she want? We can hold off for a day, two days, another week or more if need be. What's the panic?"

"Don't you see, Kelly? Eamonn and the others were all blind-folded, she said. They wouldn't know where they were until the blindfold came off and they found themselves inside the Coven-

244

anter. She can't get a message to Eamonn herself. She daren't go back now. And she reckons if Eamonn doesn't get a message from us soon, his nerve will crack, he'll have to tell the Army where to find us and the bomb. Jesus, what a bloody mess! Look at the time, Kelly, it's a quarter to nine already. It might be too late now. What are we going to do?"

"Do you fancy giving yourself up?" It was Kelly's voice again.

"I think the two of us ought to go to that roadblock and say we have an urgent message for Eamonn."

"You're out of your mind, Liam. They wouldn't take us to him! All we would be doing is sticking our own heads into a noose."

"Whatever you say, I'm going, Kelly. And you'd be mad to stay here. Eamonn doesn't trust you an inch. You think he would let you sit here, with your finger on the trigger, with him and the others stuck inside? You've told him often enough you intend to get even for that beating. Even if he sees me, he won't believe it. He'll still go to the police and blow the gaff."

"Don't tempt me, Liam. I could hold you here and try my luck with the bomb. There's a chance I'd still shake Mr. bloody Eamonn and the twins."

"And lose the chance of making your fortune? Don't be a fool. Come with me. Let Eamonn see us. Every IRA man there today is under a flag of truce, they'll not harm us. And they'll not know about the bomb. We can always come back and fire it later."

"We can't just leave the control panel. What if Pearce finds it?"

"Kelly, if we stay here, we get caught red-handed. Eamonn can't sit there and see himself and the council and all the IRA leaders blown to kingdom come. He's going to talk."

So that was it, Pearce thought to himself. A bomb. I've got them now. He knew exactly what he intended to do when the two men left his hotel. He drew back from the door and inched his way down the landing and stairs, silent as a snowflake settled on the ground. He therefore failed to hear Kelly say:

"All right, Liam. I'll go. I'll surrender in my own name to the roadblock troops and tell them it's their responsibility if they don't tell Eamonn a man called Kelly wants to reach him with a message. If they hold me but just send on the name, it will be enough to let him know he's okay. You stay here. I don't want that bastard Pearce sniffing around this control panel, I don't trust him."

"Ah, bless you, Kelly! I swear you won't regret it. I swear by all that's holy to tell the council you gave up everything to save their lives. I'll see you get paid, sweet Jesus, so I will!"

245

"Yeah." Kelly was already dressed. "Like I believe in Father Christmas. Understand me, Liam, I'm going because it still gives us a chance to use that bomb, not to save Eamonn's skin."

"One last thing, Kelly. Mrs. McCabe thinks if the soldiers won't take us to Eamonn, they might listen if you ask for their security officer. His name is Welbourne. For God's sake, hurry now."

Pearce was carefully polishing the counter when Kelly came hurtling through the bar.

"What's up, Mr. Kelly?"

"Shut your mouth. I need a car. You got one?"

"It's not much good. An old Ford, at the filling station."

"Get it. Bring it around to the front door. I'll give you two minutes, Pearce. Or I'll burn your bloody hotel to the ground, so help me."

Pearce ran out through the yard.

Kelly climbed into the car at seven minutes to nine.

"I've left Liam in the room. Stay away from him, Pearce, or you'll end up a dead man. I'll be back tonight or tomorrow with Eamonn. Now get out of my way."

The tires squealed as Kelly drove off like a bat out of hell.

A Guards sergeant waved him down before he had covered four hundred yards. He had no idea where the car or the driver had come from and he took no chances.

"Hold it right there, mister."

The sergeant was covered by three immaculate Guardsmen, each with his finger on the trigger of an FN automatic rifle.

"I'd like you to step out here while we search your car. And I want to see your driving license. While we are looking at your vehicle, you can tell me all about yourself—where you're from and where you are going. Out you get!"

Back at the hotel Tony Pearce had come to a decision. He looked about the bar and he peered up the stairs. His family was out. The hotel was empty. Liam was locked away in the bedroom. It was the perfect opportunity for him to get even with Kelly, with no one to know who had betrayed him.

The Confidential Line is unique.

Whoever first thought of it as a weapon to fight terrorism in Ulster showed a rare touch of genius, a compassionate and wholly

246

Irish understanding of the divided loyalties that lie in so many hearts.

In America the Mafia would render it unworkable within a week. In England it would fail principally because of the unwritten but accepted code that to inform is to break the rules of the game. But in the Six Counties it is a way out for the uneasy conscience and it pays rich dividends.

No tip, no scrap of information, no hint, no nod or wink is ignored in a province where fear of reprisal has made eyewitnesses to crime as rare as the coelacanth. Everything is followed up, although the police appreciate that many false calls are planted by the terrorists to blur the trail.

Pearce had to be quick, in case Liam should come down or a customer walk in.

He called the confidential police line and said:

"There's a man known as Kelly, big feller more than six feet tall, on his way to give himself up to the Army, near the Old Covenanter Hotel. Where the helicopters landed. Twist his arm and you'll find he has a bomb hidden inside the building."

It took only fourteen seconds to betray Kelly once he was through to the confidential line. He rang off, slamming the phone down as though it burned his fingers, and scuttled back to his bar and his shining beer glasses. He was astonished to feel beads of sweat running down his back and his hands shaking. Pearce poured himself a large Bushmills and began to feel braver.

"That'll teach you," he whispered, "not to push my family around, you bloody, stinking great ape."

·36·

HM minister for Northern Ireland was on his feet inside the bishop's study, using every parliamentary ruse acquired in a lifetime of public speaking trying to win over the toughest audience he had ever faced.

It was four minutes past nine.

He had been lecturing, entreating, warning, and cajoling ever since he first stood up, using every trick he knew in verbal infighting to try to dent the bigotry worn by his listeners like a suit of medieval chain mail. The air about him was blue with tobacco haze. The flowers were beginning to wilt a little in the graceful Delft urns on the table before him. A small section of his audience was openly and continually looking at watches, as if to remind him to cut things short. He had given strict orders to his security guards that on no account whatever was his opening speech to be interrupted before he gave the word.

"Not even," he told Commander Finney jokingly, "if you find a bomb under my chair that the estimable Felix has overlooked."

As the minister spoke, the Special Branch chief was sitting in his office off the kitchens puzzling over the anonymous telephone call to the confidential line.

While it could not be ignored, the allegation that a bomb was hidden in the building did not tie in with the report that the man who had planted it was on his way into the danger zone.

If true, there was only one possible explanation as the commander saw it—that the bomb had been hidden sometime earlier, designed to wreck the original Kipling conference.

The IRA bomber had discovered, or he had been tipped off, that his own comrades were inside the Covenanter instead of the British VIPs he had expected. He could not get word to them directly, so he was showing them by his personal appearance that they were in no immediate danger.

248

It still left too many questions unanswered. For how long were they safe? If there was a bomb, where was it hidden? And why would this warmhearted man risk his own neck rather than let his friends tell their guards where the bomb was hidden?

The only answer could be that he wanted to keep his secret and use the bomb another day—when Kipling started, for instance. That must be it. If so, then it was Finney's job to try to frighten the guilty delegates who knew about the bomb that they were still in danger. He called in the duty sergeant.

"Sergeant Jones. *One,* get Felix back here.

"*Two,* prepare to escort the minister out of the Covenanter right away. I will ask him to go back either to Stormont or London.

"*Three,* keep every one of those IRA delegates in that study as long as you can. Lock 'em in if you have to. The longer they sweat, the better our chance of someone's nerve giving way.

"*Four,* get this man Kelly in front of me as fast as you can, so I can lean on him till he sings like a canary.

"That's all! *Move!*"

The commander then sent for Major Welbourne, who had been on the phone to his HQ ever since the report had come in about Kelly.

"Felix on his way, Major?"

"Yes, sir. Should be here very soon."

"What's the word from the roadblock company? Is Kelly on his way here?"

"Don't know, sir. They have radio silence."

"Then break it. I want their CO—sharp."

Before Welbourne could comply with that order, a motorcycle roared up to the guardroom door. Seconds later the desk sergeant knocked at the commander's door and was admitted. He was accompanied by Inspector Renton.

"Don-R arrived from Bravo company, sir. Your man's on his way in."

The dispatch rider handed over a written message, hurriedly put down on an official form. The commander sighed at the Army's rigid insistence on obeying regulations.

FROM OC BRAVO company roadblock

TO MAJOR WELBOURNE Covenanter security

INFORMATION suspect Kelly height six three fair age forty plus claiming to be Fenian delegate demands meeting with chief delegate EAMONN

repeat EAMONN or see you personally stop en route with escort ends
TIME   0859
ACK

"Excellent," said the commander and rubbed his hands in anticipation. "Look after him when he arrives, Major. Search him yourself, right down to his socks. See what you can get out of him but
don't lay a finger on him. He might be genuine, he just might be a
delegate, this might have been a malicious call to the confidential
line, and we don't want to screw up the conference if we're wrong.
I'm going down to the study to watch the reaction of the delegates as
the clock ticks away—after the Old Man has gone. I'll be up as soon
as I can to have a word with chummy."

He rubbed his chin and spoke to Renton.

"Jim, get those dogs of yours sniffing around to see if they can
find anything to help Felix. Don't let the delegates see you."

Kelly entered the grounds of the Covenanter under strong escort,
company sergeant major and six Guardsmen, each one as big as
Kelly himself. Their Land-Rover roared through the hotel grounds,
ignoring the speed limit. All he had said so far was, "tell Eamonn or
Major Welbourne I'm here. I don't intend to talk to you dumb
bastards."

The sergeant major loved him.

Once they entered the guardroom, he left Kelly with his men,
marched up to Welbourne, and saluted. Welbourne murmured
something in a low voice. The sergeant major turned on Kelly.

"You! That's right, mister—you! Get up against that wall. Rest
your great big ugly bloody nose on the brickwork, hands above your
head. LEAN FORWARD! Guardsman Kerr, you're big enough,
help the gentleman get into position, the major here is going to
search him."

Kelly's neck went scarlet with rage.

Despite the emotion aroused by the sight of the man in the
Identikit picture Welbourne managed to search him expertly. There
was nothing on Kelly, no gun of any kind, no knife or ammunition,
just a handkerchief, car keys, cigarettes, and matches.

The major raised his voice: "Where are your papers?"

"I don't have any. I got drunk last night, Major, and I missed the
rendezvous in Newry. That's why I have to see Eamonn and tell him
what happened."

"Who are you? What's your full name?"

"Brian Kelly. Fenian delegate. I don't have to tell you any more."

250

"A delegate? I don't think you're even an Irishman!"

"Get Eamonn here. He'll identify me."

Welbourne felt slightly drunk himself. From the moment he first read the name "Kelly" and the brief description contained in the dispatch rider's message, he had prayed it would be the same Kelly who had ambushed him and killed so many of his men in Tyrone. Now he was certain. The only question left was, was he a Russian or not. It would make a big difference in the way they handled him.

"We may call him later," Welbourne said. "Tell me, Mr. Kelly, how did you know where to find him?"

Kelly hesitated.

"I heard back in Newry. It's all over town, now."

"Where did you hear my name?"

"Same place. We have a good intelligence service, Major."

But not that good, said Welbourne to himself.

"Sergeant Major, take this man upstairs to my office to await further inquiries. One of these policemen will show you the way. Keep a sharp eye on Mr. Kelly until I get back."

"I will, sir."

Inside the bishop's study, the commander himself had interrupted the minister. No one heard what was said. The minister nodded and at once swung around to face the delegates.

"Gentlemen," he said, "something quite unforeseen has come up, and I regret to tell you that I have to return to Stormont for a while." He held up his hand for silence.

"A helicopter is on its way, and I shall be back with you very shortly.

"I therefore suggest we adjourn for an hour or two to give you an opportunity to talk over the proposals I have outlined. Sandwiches and coffee, or something stronger for those who prefer, will be served to you here. You will have complete privacy and my assurance that you will not be disturbed. I will be back as soon as I can to listen —and, I stress, to listen in good faith—to your views and counterproposals. It is my earnest wish that enough common ground can be found to draw up a blueprint for a lasting cease-fire, the first essential step to peace. Thank you all for your attention."

As he turned to leave, a scar-faced delegate pushed and hurried around the table as though he had the devil at his heels, while a great buzz of conversation arose as the other delegates started to discuss the minister's words.

It was exactly fourteen minutes past nine.

The scar-faced man was within five feet of the commander when Major Welbourne burst into the study.

"Commander," said Welbourne urgently, "that man Kelly we're holding upstairs—he's the same man that Sydenham—"

Welbourne's tone was low, but Eamonn heard the major quite clearly. Kelly was in the building! Mrs. McCabe had managed to warn him in time. Liam hadn't been mentioned, so they could assume he was still at the control panel in Neet's, undiscovered. They were safe! Thirty seconds more, and he would have blurted out their secret to the British police, and all would have been lost. Relief and delight gleamed from the scarred, cruel face. Finney watched him poker-faced, as he made his way back to his friends, and he saw the instant relief on their faces, too. Welbourne was tugging at his sleeve, ignorant of the damage he had done.

"Not in here, Major." The commander tried in vain to keep the disappointment and anger out of his voice. Outside in the corridor he glared at the Army officer.

"Do you know what you've done?" He was spluttering with wrath. "One minute more, and that man was going to cough—the lot! Then you walk up and let him know Kelly is here and the bomb is safe! Christ almighty, man, don't you know when to keep your mouth shut?"

Welbourne gaped at him.

"I had no idea. Absolutely none. I felt you should know at once the man we are holding upstairs is the same man Sydenham is looking for, the one he believes is a Russian agent."

"Let me get the minister away. You wait here."

The minister was clearly unhappy with the situation.

"If it's safe to leave those men in there, it's equally safe for me to be with them," he argued. "If there is any danger, then in common humanity we have to bring them out. Which is it going to be?"

The commander explained what had happened.

"I have to insist that you leave, sir," he repeated. "It need not be for long. I shall question the man Kelly to see what I can find out, although I fear the opportunity has gone. As soon as Felix arrives I will clear the building, and it will remain cleared until he has finished. If need be we can arrange an alternative site for your talks with these men."

"I'll give you till midday," said the minister. "If you are still in doubt, I shall have the men brought to Stormont if need be. If the two sides can reach a compromise, we are halfway to peace in Ulster.

252

I'm damned if I am going to be thwarted by every half-baked anonymous call that comes in."

"Till midday, sir," echoed the commander. He could cheerfully have shot Welbourne there and then.

Commander Finney spoke to Renton when he got back to the guardroom and hid nothing from him.

"The IRA men can stay where they are until Felix arrives," he said finally, "then you can shift them out into the grounds. When you do, tell them the truth, we've had an anonymous tip there's a bomb hidden in the building. Meantime, get your own chaps out of it, all your kitchen staff, and not forgetting those women in the offices above. Send the women back to Belfast but don't let on why. Now I'll go and have a word with chummy and pray that Welbourne doesn't screw it up again."

The major was waiting for him in the corridor. Finney spoke sharply. "I just want you in the room with me as witness. Don't say a word unless I ask you to. Is that clear?"

"Yes. Quite clear," Welbourne choked out.

"Come on then."

When they reached the Major's office where Kelly was being held, they dismissed the Army escort and went to work on the mercenary. Kelly was ordered to sit opposite the commander. Welbourne sat on a chair by the door, right behind Kelly. The commander steepled his fingers and gazed at the scowling terrorist for a full minute.

"I have just spoken to the delegate called Eamonn. He says you are *not* one of his men."

"I don't believe you. Bring him in here."

"Not much point in that. He didn't say he didn't know you. Simply that you are not a Fenian delegate."

"You get him here, and I'll show you different."

"He doesn't like you very much, Mr. Kelly, did you know that?" A light flickered briefly in the pale-blue eyes.

"And how would you know that?"

"The way he shopped you."

"You're wasting your time, copper."

But there was just a hint, a whisper, of doubt in his voice. No one in the Special Branch has the gift of second sight. The commander's question was a guess, based on his reading of the IRA's fundamental aversion to mercenaries. Now he was on surer ground.

"He hates your guts, Mr. Kelly. Did you know?"

There was no answer.

"Not only did he disown you, Mr. Kelly, he talked about you. Quite freely, as a matter of fact. I think the general idea is for you to carry the can."

The light flickered in those blue eyes again, just for a fraction of a second.

"Horseshit."

"You're wrong, Mr. Kelly. It was very interesting. It is amazing what a man will say to save his own skin."

"What's that supposed to mean?"

"You know very well what it means, Kelly. Would you like to tell me your side of it?"

Kelly spat on the floor. He sensed Welbourne stir behind him.

"Let me tell you some of the things he said about you. Let's start with the ambush in Tyrone, shall we? When you used those rocket launchers on the major here?"

Kelly swung around in real alarm. "You?"

"That's right," Welbourne told him. "Me."

"You were responsible for twelve deaths," said the commander. "That guarantees you a lifetime in an English prison. For a start."

"I came here under a flag of truce. I'm a delegate. You can't arrest me!"

"Then there is the disappearance of a man called James to account for."

"I'm not answering any more questions."

"An old man, a bird-watcher, Kelly. He vanished the day you booked into your hotel in Donegal. Don't worry about identification. We've got witnesses who saw you arrive. You were met by a man who called himself Liam O'Connor, remember, about forty-five, a small, mild-looking fellow. Not the terrorist type at all. Not like you, Mr. Kelly."

Kelly felt his palms beginning to sweat. It looked like it didn't matter whether Eamonn had shopped him or not. They had too much on him already.

"I don't know anything about this bird-watcher."

"Eamonn says otherwise. I am inclined to believe him. I think a court will, too."

"Why should Eamonn tell you anything? He's a delegate, he—"

"Not like you, huh, Kelly? So you admit you're not a delegate."

"I admit nothing."

"Getting back to why your friend Eamonn would tell us anything, he was afraid, I think, that a bomb planted in this building might go off if he didn't do something about it."

254

There was no hiding the fear and anger in Kelly's eyes now.

"Did you hear me, Kelly?"

Kelly didn't answer.

"A man will says lots and lots of things when he's trying to save his own skin. You sound as if you've spent a lot of time in America. Do you know what a 'fall guy' is?"

Kelly could picture the scene. Eamonn and the others panicking when they realized where they were, then hoping against hope that Mrs. McCabe would call off the bomb in time, the minutes passing, until finally they could stand it no longer. If these people knew about the bomb, it had to be Eamonn. The slimy coward! That's why they'd been on to him from the start, from the moment he'd been picked up. He'd put his head in a noose, cool as you please.

Commander Finney, reading Kelly's face, decided to gamble.

"Liam, you know, got clean away. That leaves you, Kelly, holding the bag."

"Are you offering me a deal?" asked Kelly slowly, studying Finney's face in turn. "I tell you everything I know about the Fenian Martyrs, and you make it easy for me?"

"Let's say I'll tell the judge what a help you've been. I'll put it to you this way, Mr. Kelly. If you don't tell us your story, we'll have to go along with Eamonn's—not that I believe it all, but it's the only one we have, Kelly. You want to put the record straight?"

Kelly took a deep breath. "You bet I do," he said.

Commander Finney remained in perfect control of his elation. "First," he said, "I have to caution you that anything you say will be taken down and may be used in evidence. Do you understand me?"

"I do. Where do you want me to start?"

· 37 ·

Once Kelly decided to talk and had helped himself to a bottle of whiskey produced by the commander, he found it easy going. Something had gone out of him, whatever it was that made him keep going, made him want to survive, to avenge his father, make a lot of money, even retire to someplace where no one knew his name.

It was easy to talk about his life with the Martyrs. The problem for the commander was not in getting him to talk, but in getting him to stop. Kelly, more and more, began to resemble the garrulous drunk, the type who grabs your elbow in a bar and won't let go until he has told you every crackpot dream he ever had about his wasted life.

At least that was the thought which occurred to Welbourne as he listened to Kelly's recital. Katanga, the Martyrs, sometimes got confused, but Welbourne with mounting excitement was able to pick out the details he was interested in.

The more Kelly drank, the wilder he became. And the belief that Eamonn had double-crossed him angered him more than anything else.

"That bastard!" he roared, over and over again. "That smug, sour-faced bastard! He hated my guts from the beginning!" He turned to Welbourne. "You know something, he never realized how much I hate you British scum for what you did to my father? There wasn't one in the whole bunch who knew I would sit down and make bombs for *nothing* just to even the score! You know that? I *enjoyed* killing those British soldiers in their armored cars. I was happy making a bomb to kill a lot more. And that Eamonn was too dumb to see it!"

Kelly did better than answer any question fired at him—he volunteered information that hadn't been sought, acting most of the time as if neither Welbourne nor Finney was in the room with him.

256

"Sure. I know about that bird watcher. Not that *I* killed him, one of Eamonn's boys did that, Ryan, his name was."

Another huge drink. "But I had a hell of a time rigging the old geezer as a booby trap. Even got one of your boys with it, didn't I?" (This to Welbourne, with a drunken, triumphant smile).

"That submarine? Yeah, it was a Russki all right. Not me, though. Oh, no. British born—so help me—but Irish raised and American trained. In the Army, the United States Army! First they couldn't wait to ship me to Korea, and then they decided they couldn't let me go, the dumb bastards. So what if I didn't have the right papers? I was big enough—and by Christ, I sure was good enough."

Finney kept trying to lead the big man back to the bomb. "You must have had a devil of a time getting the bomb into this building. . ."

"Shit. It was easy. You, major, you made it real easy. Why, we even had a little talk right here in this building, the day I planted it, and right friendly you were, too. You looked at me polishing the table and you said 'Jolly good show,' you silly dumb prick, while I was planting a bomb right under your nose," he said, mimicking the major's accent.

Welbourne sat there like a man carrying an unbearable weight on his shoulders, but said nothing.

Kelly wouldn't leave him alone. As the time wore on, he seemed to focus only on Welbourne, ignoring the commander entirely, as if making the major break down was the most important thing he had left to do.

"You call yourself a professional soldier? My Katangese were better trained than your lot! You walked into that ambush like a bunch of bloody schoolboys!"

Welbourne turned white, then red, then said very quietly, "Shut your big mouth, Kelly, or I'll shut it for you once and for all."

Kelly kept taunting him: "Jesus, the Baluba showed more brains than your lot."

Finney turned Kelly around with his next question.

"And how much did you get for that night's work, Mr. Kelly?"

"Four thousand pounds! Not much though, is it, Major? Dead British soldiers don't rate very high. The pay was just for blowing up those armored cars."

Finney belted Kelly across the face with the back of his hand, knocking him onto the floor.

Kelly lay on the floor, holding his face and grinning like a madman.

Both Welbourne and Finney were standing now, glaring down at the mercenary. A guard had poked his head in when he heard Kelly hit the floor.

"Anything I can do, sir?"

"No thanks, Sergeant," said Finney. "Mr. Kelly just fell down."

"While I have you, sir," continued the sergeant, poker-faced, addressing himself to Welbourne, "telephone call."

Welbourne left the room and was back almost immediately.

"Commander, that was HQ. They want a report on the disruption in the conference fast. The minister is most anxious to continue the conference if at all possible."

Welbourne spoke very quickly—in a soft, strained voice. But Finney didn't have time to consider it unusual. He looked at his watch. Twelve o'clock. He had told the minister he'd have something for him by noon. "All right, Welbourne, keep an eye on him. I'll be back in five minutes."

As soon as Finney was out of the room Welbourne placed himself near Kelly, who had managed to get to his chair again where he sat with his head in his hands.

"Now tell me, Mr. Kelly, how does this bomb of yours work?" Welbourne's voice was cool, professional. Only his hands shook a little as he poured Kelly a huge drink.

"Any Fenians still left in the building?" asked Kelly, raising his head and looking around with a grin.

"There might be," said Welbourne, in that odd, strained tone.

"Then why not do us both a favor, major, and blow the whole goddamned lot sky high? They don't intend to agree on any ceasefire, you know that as well as I do. Why not use the bomb on *them?*"

Major and mercenary looked at each other, each relishing the prospect. Kelly slammed the bottle down on the desk. "All you got to do, major, is transmit on the good old twenty-seven megahertz band, push the key down, and that's their lot. Zap!"

Kelly crashed to the floor, stunned, his head bleeding from the blow dealt by Welbourne with the butt of his heavy army revolver.

"You murdering bastard," said Welbourne thoughtfully. He leaned down and hit Kelly again with the gun to make certain he was unconscious. He hoped he might have cracked his skull.

Then he reached for the telephone, which had a direct line to the

258

GPO in Belfast. Although strict radio silence was observed throughout the roadblock zone, a standby GPO unit was on duty twenty-four hours a day ready to relay any emergency radio message to roadblock headquarters. They acknowledged the call at once.

"This is Major Welbourne, Covenanter security. Relay the following message via HQ to Roadblock Squadron 1:

BRAVO ONE HATCHES DOWN REPEAT HATCHES DOWN PATROL MOTOR ROAD ZERO MILES PER HOUR SEND ON 27 MEGAHERTZ BAND.

He set the receiver back on its rest. Now it was done, and sweat beaded through his blond hair and down his neck. He knew his voice had sounded weak and distant over the phone, and he nerved himself. He picked up the instrument and repeated the order in a louder, more confident tone.

The giant Kelly struggled to his feet and leapt at him. "You gone crazy?" he shouted. "You trying to kill *us* too?" He grappled with the British major and fought desperately to wrench the telephone away.

Radio silence was broken immediately. Roadblock HQ monitored the order. Welbourne's instructions were relayed to Troop Sergeant Robson, Saladin commander on patrol nearest the Covenanter gates. He gave the order on intercom, "Hatches down," and said to his driver, "Drive straight into the hotel grounds. Then proceed, minimum speed, while I transmit."

His Saladin, code-named Bravo One, had to travel half a mile to reach the grounds of the Old Covenanter.

It took Commander Finney less than a minute to reach the minister at Stormont Castle from the radio room in the hotel. But before briefing him on Kelly's confession, he ordered the radio operator out of the room.

"This is for the old man's ears only," he told the man. "Won't take long. Go out in the grounds and have a smoke till I call you back." Then he spoke rapidly for ten minutes to the Secretary of State, outlining the whole story.

He looked at his watch. 12:10.

"I can't do much about the bomb till Felix gets back here," he said finally. "Of course, sir. I'll keep the building cleared of all IRA delegates and duty personnel until after the device has been dismantled. I will report back as soon as that is done. Right."

He went into the corridor, intending to head for the bishop's study. But he heard scuffling at the top of the stairway. He looked up and saw Kelly dragging a limp Welbourne onto the landing.

"What the hell," shouted Finney and started to charge up the stairs. Kelly's voice sounded spent, empty.

"We've had it, buddy," he said and put a foot into the major's back, kicking him down the stairs to land on top of Finney.

Sergeant Robson's Saladin was inside the grounds.

He had not received Kelly's countermanding order. Sergeant Robson turned the frequency knob of his radio to the twenty-seven megahertz band and whistled tunelessly into the microphone, a bored, tubby, nice, decent family man doing a military chore and wondering what the hell was going on.

At 12:13 P.M. the Bomb that could Lip-Read exploded.

Inside the Old Covenanter were the IRA delegates, the Special Branch commander, Major Welbourne and the man called Kelly.

The leaded windows of the bishop's study blew outwards in a violent red gust. Inside Hell had been unleashed.

The blast of the explosion rolled along the top of the mahogany table and cut all the delegates in half. Heads and trunks disintegrated. For a half second the remainder of the bodies below table level pumped blood until the severed arteries were congealed by heat.

The mirrors fractured and imploded, singing through the clouded air like scythes in a hayfield. Oak splinters, some a foot long, with rims jagged as a saw's edge, whizzed and howled like tomahawks. The electrical system came apart, firing the escaping gas which exploded in a second and even louder bang. The walls collapsed and like everything else, bodies and bones, mirrors and paintings, table and chairs, were soon devoured in the flames. Across the lawns hurtled fragments of white hot metal. Smoke, and dust, and the delegates' dreams of independence shot a hundred feet into the rainy Irish sky.

260

Epilogue

The press in Britain, Northern Ireland, and the Republic broke the story wide open in the next few days. Wild accusations were traded back and forth across the choppy seas between Dublin and White-hall. Special Branch Commander Finney was the massacre's only survivor and bore the brunt of the Irish papers' outrage. One columnist even hinted that it had all been a plot to trap and kill the IRA leaders, then make out that it had been a terrible miscalculation on the part of a splinter group.

The British press, on the other hand, concentrated on Major Welbourne and the mercenary Kelly. Several reporters who arrived at the scene of the explosion while the fire was still raging heard from a dazed and injured Commander Finney that he and Welbourne had been interrogating Kelly just before the bomb went off.

There was a great deal of speculation about Kelly and whether or not he had been, in fact, a Russian agent. One popular weekly declared they had found out Kelly had never spent five years at sea in the British Merchant Marine but instead had trained at the old Soviet School for Urban Warfare near Sverdlovsk, in the Urals. Part of the evidence for this theory was Kelly's skill in handling the Russian-made weapons in the ambush of Welbourne's troops.

Questions were raised in Parliament, in both Westminster and Dublin, about Welbourne's stability and the choice of this already disgraced officer to be in charge of preconference security.

Commander Finney was quoted as saying Major Welbourne was a "babe-in-arms" as far as security was concerned. The commander, interviewed in the Army nursing home where he was recovering from the effects of the blast, also accused Welbourne of telling Felix his job, telling him which room to search and which ones to leave alone.

"Welbourne had no nose for security," chaffed the commander, whose own career had been cut short by the scandal. "All I can say

261

is, whoever assigned him to that post ought to be shot for negligence."

The commander was still suffering from his wounds and under medication when he delivered his diatribe. The more responsible newspapers played down his remarks, but not the big-circulation dailies, which saw a chance for a good swipe at the government and what they considered its "kid-gloves" Irish policies. They called for a full-scale investigation.

An official Army inquiry was set up. One of the first things it did was curb Finney's tongue. In his official testimony the commander gave a calm and factual account of what had happened during the interrogation of Kelly, which served to condemn Welbourne more completely than his earlier statements. "My real mistake," said Commander Finney before the board of Army generals, "was to think of Major Welbourne as a fellow professional."

Major Welbourne's wife, on the other hand, publicly defended her husband, recounting his promise that he would never kill Kelly even if he had the chance and—which was paid more attention to—that his assignment to the post at the Old Covenanter was no coincidence.

"He would never volunteer for a job like that. He hated 'desk work.' He said he couldn't explain it, but that someone important had assigned him to that place on some kind of special mission."

Her remarks were made to a journalist researching a story on the wives of British servicemen serving in Ireland and received wide circulation.

Responding to increased criticism from the prime minister and his cabinet, Sydenham was more determined than ever to suppress the sighting of the Russian submarine. He put out a story that the major was *not* on a special mission, but *had* been seeing a psychiatrist. In the "leaked" account of Welbourne's psychiatric care, mention was made (in suitable psychiatric jargon), of his obsession with his defeat at the hands of an Irish terrorist, and his determination to get revenge, on the whole Irish nation, if necessary. Kelly's name was not mentioned, and the IRA cooperated (for their own reasons) in letting the speculation around his connection with Russia die down.

The press dropped most of the political aspects of the "Covenanter Outrage," as it had come to be called, and concentrated on Welbourne the man, letting the Army, the government, and the British secret service off the hook.

In Moscow, determined to capitalize on the renewed wave of anti-British feeling sweeping Ireland, Russian Intelligence began planning a new campaign of infiltration.

As for Kelly and the Fenian Martyrs, they were mourned all over Ireland, both North and South, and their names added to the long, long list of martyrs for the Cause.